The Wizard Charter

By
Guy Antibes

STRINGS OF EMPIRE

BOOK THREE

THE WIZARD CHARTER

BY
GUY ANTIBES

CASIE PRESS

SALT LAKE CITY, UT

The Wizard Charter

The Wizard Charter Copyright ©2025 Guy Antibes. All Rights Reserved. No part of this book may be reproduced without the permission of the author.

~

This is a work of fiction. There are no real locations used in the book; the people, settings, and specific places are a product of the author's imagination. Any resemblances to actual persons, locations, or places are purely coincidental.

Published by CasiePress LLC in Salt Lake City, UT, February 2025
www.casiepress.com

ISBN: 979-8309931408

Cover Design: Kenneth Cassell (modified illustration utilized Adobe Photoshop AI)
Book Design: Kenneth Cassell
Reader: Bev Cassell

Author's Note

We are immersed in a pseudo-Asian setting in this novel. Mostly in a pseudo-pseudo-Asian setting. So, my standard cautions. I made up primarily Japanese names. I have no idea if these are real or not, so my apologies in advance for any inadvertent meanings. The names have no meanings for purposes of the book other than names for people and places. For anyone who noticed, I changed the map after writing the novel to be more consistent with the characters' movements.

— Guy Antibes

The Wizard Charter
Map of Kippun & Slinnon

Strings of Empire
Book Three

The Wizard Charter

Chapter One

THE KIPPUN BORDER WAS HALF A MILE AHEAD, and Quint Tirolo and his friends were at the end of a long journey to cross into the fief of Gazima.

"There seems to be more people leaving the fief than entering," Vintez Dugo said, eyeing a frowning family headed in the other direction.

"Every fief is different," Dakuz, the oldest and likely wisest wizard in the group, said. "Uniformity is not a strong point in the country of Kippun. Perhaps there is an exorbitant fee."

Quint thought of the fat purse each of them was given by King Boviz of Narukun as a reward for saving his kingdom from a Green rebellion. "We can afford whatever they are charging," Quint said.

Two hours later, Quint was walking around, exercising his tender skin after the grievous burns he had suffered fighting a Green master when rescuing the king of Narukun. His notebook of spells was changing more than it was increasing. He still was a very young master, but Quint was still emerging from his extended rehabilitation.

The line had ended when the group ahead of them entered the border into Gazima.

"How many in your group?" the guard asked. Quint was taken aback at the different style of uniform. The guard wore a long tunic with pointed shoulders over a skirt with white pantaloons tucked into his boots. He had a scaled leather cuirass strapped to his chest and wore an odd hat.

"Four travelers," Dakuz said.

"All of you are from Narukun?"

"We are standing on Narukun soil, so the answer is obviously yes. Three of us are natives, and one comes from South Fenola."

The guard's eyebrows rose. He walked into the guard shack and returned. "South Fenola? One of you is Quinto Tirolo?"

Quint sighed. "That's me," Quint said.

"You aren't allowed into Gazima since you are on the list."

"What list is that?"

The guard snorted. "Those who aren't allowed into Gazima. What of it?"

"How long is your list?" Dugo asked.

"You don't want to know. Pages long."

"Do we need to pay some kind of entry fee?" Dugo asked.

"A bribe? Not acceptable for Tirolo," the guard said, glaring at Quint. "I could manage to let you and your other two friends in."

Quint looked at the other three. "We are traveling as a group?"

"Of course we are," Thera, a female former wizard in the Narukun Royal military.

Dakuz pulled out a map of Kippun. "The nearest Kippunese border post on this map is to the west,"

"Then it's west, we go," Quint said. He mounted and led them back down the road to the crossroads a few miles back where they had come.

Once they were alone, Dugo asked, "Can't we sneak in? There isn't a wall around the fief."

"And once we are stopped for something, anything, the charge of trespassing in the fief will be made. Fief guards arrest people all the time," Dakuz said.

"Looking for bribes?" Thera asked.

"Of course," Dugo said. "It is the way of the world."

"Not so much outside of Pinzleport," Dakuz said. "We weren't bothered in the capital if you recall."

"What challenges do we face in Shimato fief?" Quint asked Dakuz.

Dakuz shrugged. "That kind of thing isn't recorded on the maps. Maybe that will be an opportunity for surprise," he grimaced as he said it.

They were almost at the crossroads when Thera glanced behind them. "Riders traveling fast."

"After us?" Dakuz asked.

"Probably," Dugo said, pulling his sword from the sheath tied to his saddle.

"Not yet," Quint said. "Let's talk first. We are all magicians, so let's get our shields up."

They continued to ride for a few more minutes before turning their horses around. Quint and Thera already had a string gyrating in their palms, barely glowing in the afternoon sun.

Quint tossed his string between his group and the riders. A flash of flame rose into the air.

"You are after us?" Dakuz said to the guards.

Quint noticed the guard denying them entry into Gazima fief among the seven uniformed men.

"We are. You are to be detained. Extinguish your strings and follow us, or there will be bloodshed," an officer said. Quint could tell he was an officer because his odd hat was trimmed with a band of silver threads.

"It won't be ours," Dugo said. He was the weakest magician in the group, but his string glowed the brightest.

The officer blinked and moved his head back. He seemed ready to throw his arm across his face, but Quint may have been hoping for the best.

"We are in Narukun," Thera said. "You are the ones who are trespassing. Perhaps it is you who must lay down your arms and follow us all the way to Baxel."

The officer grunted, his eyes wide. "Preposterous! There is no Narukunian presence for miles."

"We don't need them," Quint said while casually tossing another ball of flame within a pace of the officer.

Quint had made sure that string made a sound.

The horses in the front backed up a few steps forcing the guards to struggle with handling their mounts.

The officer glared at them. "You can give up all hope of entering Gazima," the officer said.

"We already have," Dakuz said. "Be on your way."

Quint could almost taste the compulsion string that Dakuz had used. The officer wheeled around, and the seven guards were quickly lost in sight.

"What was that string?" Dugo said. "I almost joined them in retreat."

Dakuz's smile was almost a grimace. "I thought I should learn a few new strings if we encounter new adventures. Quint thought I might survive longer if I knew a persuasion string."

"The situation was right," Quint said, "and it cuts off the tension. None of the guards had shields, so…" he shrugged and turned around, "we need to get out of here. They may return with more of their brothers and sisters. That string lasts less than an hour."

"Half hour for me," Dakuz said. "I tested it. It will be enough to get us on our way."

They turned east at the crossroads and proceeded to the next village some miles away to spend the night.

"I didn't expect to spend another night in Narukun," Dugo said as they entered the village

Quint looked at the lane filled with quaint architecture on both sides. It reminded him of the village at Tova's Falls. "Get your fill of Narukun. I suppose we will be wearing Kippunese-style clothes before evening tomorrow."

§

The line moved faster at the border post leading to Shimato fief. There were lines on both sides of the road. Guards collected exorbitant fees and checked the amounts given more than those who paid. The guard, dressed similarly to the Gazima guard with a different hat, didn't even ask their names.

Quint was almost tempted to sneak into the fief going overland, but that thought was stopped when each of them received a wooden token.

"Write your name on the other side and make sure it gets a red stamp. If you don't have one of those, you'll be spending your nights in the local lockup," the guard said.

They stopped at a table on the other side of the border and used a wax crayon to write their names. The guard at the table applied the red stamp, a circle with a bird halfway into the circle. Quint guessed it was a bird flying past the moon, but he could be wrong.

Armed with their new tokens, it was clear that many travelers used tokens to verify who they were as they crossed the border.

Everything seemed different in Shimato fief. Once across the border, some travelers stopped at a roadside stop and changed into Kippunese-style dress. Those leaving the fief did just the opposite.

They stopped for a light meal and to water their horses with the border still in sight.

"I'm surprised King Boviz doesn't have a presence at the border crossings," Dugo said.

"That is a good sign," Dakuz said. "If trouble kept popping up at the crossings, Boviz would have to station guards. No Narukun guards, no trouble."

"I hope you're right," Quint said. His eyes drifted to two men standing by a cart laden with produce, changing into Kippunese costumes.

With his minutes inside Kippun, including the encounter at the Gazima border, Kippun was as strange as everyone had warned. But people were people and would gravitate to human norms in many things. He still hoped that would apply to the Kippunese, but he was gathering some doubts so far.

The food seller at the stop put bowls of noodles on the table. Quint stared at the food. The thick fat was already congealing on the surface of the broth. He was given eating sticks. He had used them in the international quarter of Bocarre, Racellia's capital, and pursed his lips before eating.

He raised his eyebrows when he realized the taste wasn't so bad once he stirred the hot broth. The Kippunese food he had at Seensist Cloister wasn't seasoned like this, not that the broth tasted that good. His only complaint was the bowl wasn't served hot enough. Quint looked at his companions' faces. They didn't tolerate the taste like Quint. Each of them pulled out their seasoning bags and ruined the flavors he had tasted.

As they stood, Quint noticed his bowl was the only empty one.

"You should give the food a chance," Quint said. "You have to stir the noodles first. The flavors are delicate, but they are better than what is normally served as Kippunese food cooked by a Narukun chef. Perhaps a little string of heat might make it more palatable."

Thera, Dakuz, and Dugo stared at Quint as if seeing him for the first time.

"Racellian," was all the Dakuz muttered as he mounted.

Dugo nodded and Thera looked at Quint and pursed her lips before narrowing her eyes. She sighed. "I'll have to try that."

The others grunted, and then they were riding toward their new adventure.

CHAPTER TWO
∼

ALTHOUGH MORIMANU, THE CAPITAL OF SHIMATO, was a modest-sized city, the castle sat on a man-made hill above the city. The rooflines were exotic, with the corners curved up. He had seen the style in the villages and two towns they had ridden past, but Morimanu had added elevation to its skyline. The castle dominated the city, and the rooflines were a mix of high and low buildings.

A five-story building may sit next to a single-story restaurant or a two-story house. There was no rhyme or reason to Quint, anyway. He absorbed the view and reserved judgment other than to admit everything was exotic to his senses.

People wore Kippunese costumes, and the four attracted stares as they rode through the cobbled streets.

"Suitable inns should be at the foot of the castle hill," Dakuz said. "It is a common characteristic of fiefdom capitals."

They found an inn that looked a bit more conventional to Narukun sensibilities and rode through the stable gate into a large courtyard. The inn consisted of single-story buildings with a four-story tower. Each story above the main floor had a walkway around that level that acted as an awning for the floor below. A stairway was protected from the elements with slats and a roof as the only protection from the weather.

The lobby looked similar in layout to most inns Quint had entered. A small lobby with a counter led to a common room on one side and a corridor leading to the stairway on the other.

"We'd like rooms," Dakuz said.

"Narukunese?" the girl at the counter asked with a barely noticeable frown.

Dakuz blinked. Quint hadn't heard anyone called Narukunese in Narukun. "Three men and one woman. I don't know what is cheapest for that in Morimanu."

"I have rooms for three or four. One single for propriety and a shared room for the rest." She offered a price, and Dakuz gave her coins that should have worked.

"Another one of these," the girl said, pointing to a large silver coin.

Dakuz looked at Quint and shrugged.

"Go ahead," Quint said.

"The boy leads?" the girl said, looking suspiciously at Quint.

"He does. He is a master wizard, and the rest of us are not," Dakuz said.

The girl shrugged and frowned, but besides that she gave two keys to Dakuz. Quint noted the numbers on the tags attached to the keys. It appeared that Thera was going to be on a different floor.

"When is the common room open?" Dugo said, looking into the empty room.

"It is open an hour after sunrise for breakfast, an hour before and after noon for lunch, and an hour before and four hours after for dinner. It is what all the eating establishments in Morimanu do." She looked at her guests with pursed lips. "You might find it easier to fit in if you purchase Kippunese clothes. There is a market three blocks directly to the west."

They took their bags to their rooms. Thera was on the other side of the tower, one floor up. The shared room was on the bottom floor, facing the stable. Quint grimaced when he smelled the stable in the room.

"Maybe one night here," Dugo said, making a face as he sniffed.

"Then let's get some new clothes so the next inn won't put us in a room like this," Dakuz said.

"We could go back and ask," Quint said.

Dakuz frowned. "We might get something worse."

"Is there anything worse?" Dugo asked.

"Probably," Quint said, slipping more coins in his purse.

They locked the door with the key and with magic. The windows were made of decorative slats and papered. They wouldn't keep anyone out who was determined to get in, but Quint also locked the window frames.

Thera was waiting for them in the lobby, chatting with the girl at the counter. The girl seemed friendly to Thera, but the faint frown returned when the three approached.

"Shall we go?" Dakuz said to Thera, nodding to the girl and giving her a smile.

"We shall," Thera said.

She led them onto a street and toward the market.

"Our hostess wasn't happy about renting rooms to foreigners and was adamant about fitting in with the Kippunese," Thera said.

Quint took a deep breath and smiled. "Then let's not disappoint her."

The market was like any other, except some of the stalls had eaves with curved eaves, mimicking the buildings that surrounded them.

"Let's walk around and see what would work for us," Dakuz said.

Quint had done much the same thing when he bought clothes in Pinzleport after his first escape from Seensist Cloister. He noticed better off Kippunese followed by servants carrying their purchases.

"Perhaps something in between," Quint said after having his friends observe on their own.

They found a few stalls and decided on one that seemed to split the difference.

"We are new to Kippun," Quint said.

"Goes without saying," the stallkeeper sighed, noting that Quint stated the obvious.

"A few outfits for today," Dakuz said. "We are wizards. Do they wear anything different in Morimanu?"

The stallkeeper shrugged. "There is nothing special about wizards in the capital. Anything you choose will do." He tried to sell them servant clothes, but in the end, they bought outfits closer to the better off rather than servants.

Wearing their new purchases, the four returned to the inn and received an approving nod from the girl at the counter.

"The common room is open now," the girl said.

Quint anticipated eating exotic street food. It seemed he was the only one who appreciated Kippunese cuisine, so the others hoped the common room food would be better.

They ordered drinks. Quint and Thera ordered watered wine, and Dakuz and Dugo ordered beer.

"Now that we are here, what is our next step?" Dugo said, taking a sip of his drink and wincing.

"Get in touch with wizards," Quint said. "It might not be easy since wizardry is so disorganized in Kippun."

"At least in Shimato," Thera said. "We can make inquiries tomorrow to see if there is some kind of registry."

Quint nodded. "Any other ideas?" Quint asked.

"Show off our magic and have magicians contact us," Dugo said.

"Our magic?" Dakuz asked.

Dugo cleared his throat. "Quint's magic. We can be there to bolster his presence."

"You can at least do that," Dakuz said drily.

"Then let's try to get used to this food," Thera said. "I'm not going to be able to avoid it while we are in Kippun."

"Don't season it," Quint said. "The flavors are subtle. I think the cooks at Seensist and throughout Narukun ruin the cuisine."

"But they use too much fat," Dakuz grumbled.

"Mix it around, like the noodles we had yesterday on the way here, or remove the food from the fat. It tastes different, but it's okay if you don't eat it drenched in fat. I didn't have any trouble."

"But you are a Racellian," Dugo said.

"I'm a human who can taste. So are you."

Thera smiled. "I'm willing to give it a try. I will follow your example."

"Then let each of us order something different and have a tasting test. At least you can find some less objectionable dish," Quint said.

"Good idea!" Dakuz said. He raised his arm and beckoned a serving girl.

"What is good here?" Dakuz said as the serving girl approached.

"Everything. What do you expect me to say?" the girl said before pursing her lips.

"Then give each of us a different dish. We are from Narukun and will probably like lighter dishes."

"I'll serve it to you, and then you'll gunk it up like every other Narukun I've served."

Quint's ears perked up. "You serve a lot of customers from Narukun?"

"I've been here four years, and your kind visiting was a novelty, but not so this year. Most of them do their business and are gone in a day or two," she said.

"Anything similar about them?"

"Similar to you?" the server asked. She shook her head. "They never wore Kippunese clothing and were mostly wizards or warriors, or knights."

"How did you know they were wizards?" Dakuz asked.

"Your kind has a different kind of swagger than a fighting man," the server looked at Thera, "or woman."

"I'm not a fighting man?" Quint asked.

"Too young, too skinny, and not grizzled enough."

"Are you implying that I am grizzled?" Thera said with the hint of a grin.

"Of course not. I must get your order in." The server gave them some ideas and left them, shaking her head.

"You have some kind of swagger," Dugo said to Thera.

Thera chuckled along with him. "That's because I can out-duel any of you with a blade."

"I don't deny that," Quint said. "How can I get some swagger?"

"Get older, put on some weight, and don't shave your face," Thera said. "She told you."

"And practice more?"

"It isn't practicing that produces swagger; it's winning," she said.

Quint counted eleven men with swagger entering the common room as a group. They wore Kippunese-style uniforms with more boiled leather protection than the border guards. They laughed and joked as they pushed some tables together and sat down, calling for the server. Quint noted that they were older, thicker, and definitely grizzled.

Some of the men had metal scales attached to their armor, and others had armor with more leather protection. They certainly looked like fighting men, and Quint doubted they were city guards but attached to an active fighting unit.

The same server who took their order went over to the ruffians. She smiled more and flirted with the fighters. She laughed at a question and pointed to Quint and the group. Two soldiers rose and walked to Quint's table.

"You are Narukun magicians?" the tallest of the two soldiers asked.

"We are," Dakuz said.

"You aren't Green?"

"I'm not until I taste some Kippunese food," Dugo said. He smirked rather than smiled. Quint thought that was a mistake.

"On your own, eh?" the soldier said. He nodded to his companion, who left the common room.

"What do you mean?" Quint asked.

"You don't have any friends about?"

That was a warning that something terrible was going to happen.

"No," Thera said.

No one had worn weapons into the common room, and that was a mistake since the soldiers were bristling with them. Quint shook his head. There was no reason for these men to fight. Were they waiting for Green magicians? Was that what they meant by asking if Quint's group was Green?

The soldier returned to the table and leaned over to speak to his fellows in low tones. The looks on their faces when Quint would glance at them from time to time weren't encouraging. The server arrived with the food and turned to look at the soldiers.

"I'm sorry, but you should be prepared for something. What, I don't know, but I don't think they will let you go." She scurried away.

"Eat away," Quint said. He chose a noodle dish with meat and vegetables. Quint scooped the goopy fat off the top of the bowl and stirred. His first bite wasn't so bad. The others tried the same technique and shrugged.

"Are you sick enough?" the tall soldier said from his seat.

Dugo shook his head. "Not at all. I take back what I said."

The soldier jumped to his feet. "That's not easy to do in Shimato." He looked at the entry to the common room. Quint turned to see more soldiers staring at them. They couldn't fight so many people in a common room filled with customers.

The soldiers advanced on them. Quint grabbed another bite of noodles and stood. The first soldier reached him, and Quint put him to sleep. Seeing their compatriot sink to the floor, the soldiers attacked. Quint was able to put a few more soldiers away before being put to sleep the conventional way, a blow to the head.

§

Quint woke, looking into Dugo's eyes, who had both hands on Quint's head.

"Ah, you are awake. I don't think you have any injuries," Dugo said.

"You're a healer?"

"Of sorts," Dugo said. "You had others surrounding you in Seensist and Feltoff. I can do most things, but Dakuz and Thera's capabilities aren't quite up to mine," Dugo said.

"You wait until now to tell us?"

Dugo shrugged as he stood up. "I was thinking of being a healer and trained for a few years, but the good ones were much better. I'm better than a sharp stick in the eye."

"I'll remember that," Quint said. He put his hand to his head. "Not even a headache." He looked around in the musty bedroom lit only by a magician's light. "I take it we aren't in the inn?"

"No. When you were struck down, we surrendered."

Quint shook his head. "I didn't intend to fight back. I know when the circumstances aren't right, but they were attacking."

"The tall soldier, their senior person, stopped any bloodshed. We are in an unoccupied mansion in another part of Morimanu, the capital," Dakuz said. "They don't know what to do with us and had no stomach for killing us if we weren't going to put up a fight. They knew the soldiers you put to sleep would be dead otherwise."

"I wasn't about to put all those in the common room at risk," Quint said.

"We felt the same," Thera said.

"What about our things?"

"Outside the room. The room is locked and sealed with a joining string," Dakuz said. "They will find out who we are before we are released."

Quint ran a hand through his hair. "How are they going to find that out? No one in Shimato knows us!"

Dakuz frowned. "Don't get mad at me. I don't know either. I told them you are known to King Boviz of Narukun, which made them laugh."

Quint looked around their cell. He stepped to the window and looked down to the ground. They were on the second floor of the mansion. "We can even climb down from here. Do they expect us to escape?"

"There aren't any floors above us," Thera said. "We could even break through the roof."

"Or the floor," Quint said. "Let's give them some time to come back to us. If we aren't in a crowd and they don't have a hostage, I won't be so reluctant to use some force."

"As a last resort," Dakuz said.

"Any fighting is a last resort in the middle of a hostile country," Quint said.

"Fief," Thera corrected.

"In a fief, too," Quint said. "Did they say when they would return?"

Dugo shook his head. "You know as much as we do."

"Or less," Quint said.

They decided to go back to sleep now that Quint had recovered, and Quint woke to the rattling of a key in the lock. The door slid aside. Most doors in Kippun slid on a track. He thought hinges were better, but maybe they didn't use them in Slinnon or Pogokon, being a polens thing. He looked back at the window. It had hinges. He shrugged and woke Dakuz, Thera, and Dugo.

"You are intact?" a bearded man dressed in black said.

"Yes," Quint said. "You don't look like the soldiers who abducted us."

"We aren't. We are wizards like you. There is a safer place to stay than here. Soldiers follow orders and are not to be trusted to keep you safe."

"And you are?" Dakuz asked.

"That is for you to determine. I can offer you safe passage to a manor outside of Shimato, and there, you can determine what to do." The man chuckled. "Perhaps you will tell us who you are."

"If you have food and a better bed than the dusty mat on the floor, I'm willing to follow," Dugo said.

"We don't know who to follow, but if my colleagues agree, we will let you lead us," Thera said. She looked at Quint, who nodded back to her.

They left a few sleeping soldiers in their wake as they walked out of the moldering mansion and into the sparsely populated streets of Shimato. Four wizards walked behind them but didn't talk as they continued through the city.

"It is still a few hours before sunrise," their rescuer said as they walked.

Quint asked them to stop and let them re-pack their belongings. "At least they brought these when they took us from the inn."

"They aren't bad people, but we don't like strangers, as a rule. I think the circumstances got away from them. It's their superiors I worry about. We don't know who commanded them, and that's why we extracted you," the wizard said. "Some officers are good people, and others aren't good at all."

They settled into a quick pace and soon left the city. The small gate was unguarded, and the wizard unlocked it to let them out and locked it again when they were on the other side.

"Is this a crime?" Dakuz asked. "Doesn't Morimanu demand an entry fee?"

The wizard chuckled. "And an exit fee, but what they don't know won't hurt them. This gate isn't used often."

Quint was faintly relieved that some defied the minor laws of the city and likely the fief. He hoped there was some flexibility in this society, but not too much.

They walked until sunrise and stopped at a gate with the curved ends in a gabled archway. "We have arrived," the wizard said.

The manor was a quarter-mile from the gate. It was expansive, comprising six or seven smaller houses with interconnecting walkways. A few houses were taller, one-level structures, and two were two stories high. The grounds weren't in the best shape, but the pathways were weeded between the raised walkways, and the place hadn't been left to decay like the mansion they had left in the city.

The roofs had overhangs that covered porches that surrounded each building.

"Is this similar to how polens live?" Dakuz asked.

"This manor is an exact copy of a manor in Slinnon. Even the builders were brought from Slinnon. The less accurate the style, the less value in the eyes of Kippunese buyers."

"Is this your manor?"

"No!" the wizard said. "It belongs to our benefactress, and she owns other manors."

"In different fiefs?" Thera asked.

The wizard nodded. "She is a very popular singer. You won't meet her since she is touring in Slinnon."

"My fellow wizards will return to Morimanu, and I will stay with you."

"You will be our guard?" Dugo asked.

"Your host," the wizard said. "Let me show you to your rooms."

Rooms included a study area, a sitting area, and a sleeping area. There were only partitions separating the areas. Each story of one of the two-story buildings had four rooms. Quint was the last left.

"You get a room in your building," the wizard said as he led Quint across a courtyard to a single-story building.

When the wizard opened the door, Quint could tell the same organization was duplicated in his quarters, but the rooms were much bigger.

"We could fit all four of us in here," Quint said.

"But they aren't as important as you," the wizard said.

Quint sighed. The Kippunese wizards knew predictor strings.

"I'm not that important," Quint said.

"You are already their leader," the wizard's head nodded toward the building where his friends were, "and you are a fascinating case, Quinto Tirolo."

"I go by Quint. And you?"

"Hari Bitto-sensei"

"And that means?" Quinto asked

"My given name is Hari Bitto. The sensei at the end means 'master.' You should be Quinto Tirolo-sensei."

"Too long. Quint still works best."

"Whatever you desire," Hari said with what appeared to be a genuine smile. "Get some sleep, and we will talk in the morning. There are some snacks for you on that table."

Quint looked at the table laden with too much food, especially after a night with little sleep.

CHAPTER THREE
~

HARI TAPPED QUINT'S SHOULDER. "IT IS TIME TO RISE." Quint blinked the sleep out of his eyes and took in his surroundings. "What time is that?"

"An hour after noon," Hari said.

Quint looked at the four young women dressed identically behind the master. "And they are here to do what?"

"Get you ready to meet with Shimato's warlord. I have arranged a meeting."

Quint frowned. "Wasn't that what was to happen when the soldiers caught us?" He spoke to Hari, but his gaze lingered on the four maids.

"No," Hari said.

"And the maids? I assume that is what they are."

"Your servants while you stay here. They are totally at your disposal." Hari smiled and raised his eyebrows and then dropped them. "If you know what I mean."

"I think I do, but being at my disposal means I don't have to…to…" Quint sighed, and the girls giggled, making Quint blush and then blush some more.

"No, you don't, but they will clean and tidy your rooms and fetch whatever you need."

Quint was about the object until Hari said, "At no expense to you."

"Really?" Quint asked. "My friends are guests, too?"

Hari smiled and bowed. "Of course. I have my own servants," he said.

"You benefactress is covering the cost?"

"She is. The money is being spent, anyway," Hari said.

"Then I suppose I need a bath drawn."

"We leave for the capital in an hour, so don't take too long."

Quint frowned. "Are my friends invited, too?"

Hari grinned. "They are getting ready now."

Quint took a cold bath by himself and let the maids help him arrange his clothes properly. Dressing properly was not as easy as it looked. Polens dressed differently than the hubites in Narukun, and he was told the Kippunese wore a hubite variation of the Slinnon style.

He walked out to the courtyard and stood before his friends' building. Dugo and Dakuz were the first to exit, and Thera arrived accompanied by two maids. Thera's transformation was remarkable. The flowing lines of her outfit accentuated her femininity. Even Hari sighed when he saw her.

"Your friends make a fine retinue. I will join you, of course."

Quint nodded. "Of course." He felt out of control, but Quint's group wasn't treated like captives. If they were, it was a luxurious captivity.

A carriage drew up to the front of the manor just as they stood at the gate to the front courtyard. The carriage was unlike anything Quint had seen. Two horses drew it, but the carriage had only two wheels rather than four.

"In Kippun, Slinnon, and Pogokon, four-wheeled carriages are taxed, but if it has two wheels, there is no tax. T here are few four-wheeled carriages in Kippun. The only common four-wheeled vehicles are open wagons that carry goods from place to place," Hari said.

"I'm sure there are unique traditions everywhere you go," Quint said, trying to hide his feelings about the stupid tax.

"There are," Dakuz said with pursed lips as he helped Thera into the carriage, and soon, they were trotting down the lanes at a decent speed.

They reached the capital, headed northeast toward the castle, and entered the road that wound around the built-up hill. Steep stone walls overlooked the road.

"The road is a defense," Dakuz said. "Wizards can cast all kinds of things down at an invading force."

Hari chuckled. "He is right. All the warlords have castles based on this defensive model. Once inside, the castle itself is five stories tall. Narrow and tall rather than sprawling."

Every so often, Quint had a view of the castle tower as they continued around the hill until the ascent ended, and they stopped on the flat ground of the castle's courtyard. They emerged from the carriage and looked above the castle rise above them.

An entourage of eight uniformed soldiers emerged from the castle's steps, followed by four in more ornate costumes. Quint had a hard time thinking of what they wore as uniforms. The hats had large plumes of various colors. The scaled armor was enameled to match the plumes, or perhaps it was vice versa. Medallions were plastered on the left upper chest of the men. There were a few medallions sparsely sprinkled among the honor guard.

Hari rushed forward and descended to one knee. "Honorable Lord," he said to one of the plumed men. "I have brought special people from Narukun to speak with you."

The plumed man raised a finger and pointed to Dakuz, who looked to be a similar age.

"You must be Tirolo."

Dakuz bowed but did not descend to a knee. "That would be this young man. I am one of his followers." He withdrew until he was behind Quint.

"You are the master?" the warlord asked.

"I am," Quint said. "Do you need a demonstration?"

The warlord put his hands out in front of his as if to push Quint away. "No, no! I don't generally trust magic or wizards."

"Maybe you should," Quint said. "You can trust me to tell you the truth. Why did you summon me and my followers?"

"The truth? What is the truth?" the warlord said. "I suppose you can enlighten me about your version. Come inside."

The entourage turned around and headed up the steps back into the castle.

"We follow?" Quint asked.

Hari smiled. "That was as good an invitation that you will get. Let's go."

Quint and his group followed Hari behind the warlord's people and stepped into a small foyer with stone walls. It was smaller than Quint expected. He noticed arrow slits in the walls. This was a defensive castle, after all. A wizard could cast a fire string through the slit and do a lot of damage to invaders.

The warlord led them through the foyer and along a corridor full of short turns, opening into another foyer with stairs leading up and down. They walked up to another level and through another twisting corridor before it opened onto a straight hallway.

One of the plumed men spread apart two sliding doors that led to a large room with low seats perpendicular to the gilded throne that faced the door. The warlord walked confidently to the throne and sat while the plumed men took the first three low seats near him. Hari had them proceed no further than the seats closest to the door.

"We stay standing," Hari said quietly to Quint, and then the wizard master glared at Dugo, who was about to sit.

Dugo turned red under the stern visage of Hari Bitto, but Quint couldn't resist a smile while they waited for the plumed men to mutter amongst themselves.

"You may approach," one of the plumed men said. "This is Lord Bunto Bumoto, Warlord of Shimato."

Hari stepped forward and re-introduced Quint, followed by Dakuz, Dugo, and Thera last. "Tirolo-sensei is the wizard I told you about last night," Hari said.

"You seem a bit young for a world changer," Bumoto said.

"I'm not a world changer yet," Quint said. "I'm not sure if I'll ever be. I have a mission that will take me to a different continent."

"And the mission is to take over the world and create your own empire?" Bumoto asked. "That is implied via the predictor strings Hari and his people have cast."

"I don't believe that is what was predicted," Quint said. "My future is murky other than achieving unique notoriety."

Bumoto chuckled. "You have a way with words, Tirolo," the warlord said. "What are your intentions while you attempt to wander around Kippun?"

"I'm not sure I have any intentions," Quint said. "I am touring the continent. I want to spend some time in Kippun and do the same in Slinnon. After that, my mission will take me away from North Fenola."

"You aren't going to take over the warlords?"

Quint smiled. "With an army of three? I don't think so. I'm not sure I'll be welcome in all the fiefs, but I'll visit those where my presence is tolerated."

"You think you are tolerated here?" Bumoto said while his subordinates nodded and muttered to each other. The warlord joined them in their whispering.

"I don't know. I would hope so. Is there anything we can do for you while we are here?" Quint asked.

"You are supposedly a great wizard. Do something about Shimato's pesky wizards," Bumoto said. The warlord nodded to Hari. "Hari Bitto, no exception."

"My army consists of three wizards, but we aren't assassins."

Bumoto gave Quint a twisted smile. "I said nothing about assassination. Be creative. I'll give you Hari Bitto to bolster your army. Now it's a third larger."

"Lord!" Hari said.

"It needn't be permanent, Hari," The warlord said. "You may go. Return with a concept in three weeks."

§

"That didn't turn out like I expected," Hari said once they were in the carriage, returning to the manor outside the city.

"I thought he liked you," Dugo said to Hari.

"It ebbs and flows like the tide," Hari said. "I've never had it turn around so fast."

"I have," Thera said. "We saw the same kind of thing in Narukun."

"Wizardry?" Hari asked.

Quint nodded. "Exactly, although from what I could see, Bumoto's three friends had more to do with his change in demeanor than any string I've seen. Now you are in my tiny army."

Hari sighed. "It isn't as tiny as you might think. Do you have any ideas?"

"About what?" Dakuz said. "As far as I can see, the warlord thinks that wizards are 'pesky,' but is that the problem? How the wizards are irritating the warlord is the first question to ask before we can devise a plan." He looked at Hari. "Any ideas?"

"It is a complex situation," Hari said.

"You might as well tell us now," Quint said. "We have only three weeks to come up with a solution."

"You have heard the expression about herding cats?" Hari said.

Thera giggled. "I have literally and figuratively. Are the wizards of Shimato acting like cats?"

"In a way. We have factions like everywhere else, but no one wants to do the same thing. Warlord Bumoto has tried to integrate wizards into his army, but the result has never been as effective as not having wizards at all. A good group of archers can take care of wizards in short order," Hari said.

"And how have you achieved some level of Bumoto's confidence?' Quint asked.

"I've always been loyal. Lord Bumoto's father took a liking to me, and that relationship persisted. However, I'm a wizard, not a leader."

"Maybe you are more of a leader than you think," Dakuz said. "Didn't you convince other wizards to free us from the soldiers?"

"My associates," Hari said.

"Are they as loyal as you?" Thera asked.

"To me, but not to Bumoto."

"Is there a wizard organization that registers all wizards?" Quint asked. "There is a wizard registry in Narukun, although not much is done with it, as far as I know."

"Not much is done with it other than to use it as a recruiting tool for the Narukun wizard corps," Thera said.

"I'm not sure that would work in Shimato," Hari said.

"You won't know unless you try," Dugo said. "Has anyone tried?"

"Not in my lifetime." Hari frowned and looked at Quint. "Do you really think you can tame Shimato's wizards?"

"We won't do it in three weeks, but we can devise a plan," Quint said. "First, we need to talk to lots of wizards."

"Why?" Hari asked. "You can ask me anything."

"And will you answer the exact same way as any wizard we find walking on the streets?" Dakuz asked.

"No. We all have our own…" Hari frowned. "I see what you mean."

"Today, we come up with initial questions and tomorrow we start asking," Quint said.

∽

Chapter Four

The group assembled in Quint's house, the biggest used by the group. Hari didn't seem as animated before meeting the warlord, and Quint was uncertain what to do.

"Perhaps we should propose two wizard organizations," Dugo said, being asked by Quint for an idea. "One is a wizard corps since Thera and Quint have experience with that, and the other is a duplication of the cloister environment."

"Won't work," Hari said. "Wizards aren't integrated into Lord Bumoto's forces. They wouldn't survive. In a battle, they work on their own. You know how the soldiers felt when they abducted you."

"What if we changed that as part of the plan? We could devise a plan to integrate the wizards," Quint said. He looked at Thera. "We could do that, couldn't we?"

Thera smiled. "We could, indeed."

"I'll not be bottled up in some keep like wizards are in Narukun," Hari said.

"Cloisters aren't mandatory in Narukun," Dakuz said. "There are wizards who don't want to fight and don't want to join a cloister. Perhaps you can think of another arrangement to unify wizards."

"You could have guilds rather than cloisters," Dugo said.

"Like a stonemason guild? Wouldn't that be a step down for wizards?" Hari asked.

"No," Quint said, "but we can come up with a set of services that a guild would do and then call it something else? You need classifications, registration, perhaps even a clearinghouse for wizard work."

Dakuz's eyes flashed. "Like lawyers and solicitors. In Narukun, you'd rather hire a chartered lawyer if you were to go to court. You could throw fighting wizards in the same boat. What would be a good name?"

"Members of a Charter?" Hari said. "Wizards could be chartered then. If one was a chartered wizard, they could ask for more money if the classifications were honest."

Quint shrugged. "We could call the organization who administered the rules after the governing document, the Wizard Charter."

Hari grunted. "It's nice to talk about it, but talking isn't doing," he said.

"Then let's use the charter concept as a framework. With a better organization, perhaps wizards can be less 'pesky,'" Quint said. "All wizards can't be docile creatures, kneeling at the warlord's feet, but if we can get enough wizards to abide by a charter, the problem will get better."

"Perfect is the enemy of good," Dakuz said.

Hari took a deep breath. "Will everyone have to accept what you say?" the wizard master looked at Quint.

"No. We create a charter that we know will be changed, but we allow wizards to give their opinion," Quint said. "Don't ask me what gives me the authority to do that. I don't know, but I do know if the charter brings more money to a working wizard, others will follow."

"I can see that," Hari said. "I was there when the warlord gave you the task. You are in charge, for good or ill."

"Then let's start putting down ideas," Thera said. "Are there writing materials in here?"

Hari brightened. "The lady of the manor would never let us down." He retrieved a modest stack of blank paper and pencils. "There is ink when we are ready to make our ideas more permanent."

"Let's start with the organization," Dakuz said. "A central administration that registers and rates wizards, finds them jobs, and does training?"

"That is an opportunity for jobs," Quint said. "Perhaps creates some standards for training that enterprising wizards can follow as they teach wizards throughout the fief."

They didn't get into much detail but wrote down the goals of the Charter organization. It had to be kept small and independent. It took until lunchtime to write and rewrite until they agreed they had done enough.

At lunch, Hari showed himself to be a gourmet of sorts. Quint thought the master wizard was more of a Slinnon cuisine acolyte, agreeing with Quint that one had to clear away some of the "binding" elements of Kippunese cuisine (fat, mostly) to reach the nuanced flavors of the core cooking.

Their session resumed, hammering out the principles of the wizard corps element of the warlord's army since there weren't any. Hari was mostly at a loss, listening to Quint and Thera discuss and sometimes argue as they defined how everything might work.

"You know we will need to talk to actual military leaders," Quint told Thera. "They need to become open to trying this out."

"We succeeded in doing that at that inn," Dakuz said sarcastically.

"Perhaps a little more success is in order," Quint said.

By the time, the framework for a wizard corps was in place, Thera left to walk around the grounds, claiming she was tired. "Arguing with all of you would give anyone a headache, and I am no exception," she said as she walked out of Quint's quarters.

"And that means the rest of us, as well," Dakuz said, rising, taking Dugo and Hari with him.

Quint was left shuffling through the papers they had scribbled on. There were only a few blank sheets left, and he decided to sort their work. In a few minutes, he had done enough and retreated to his bed to rest his eyes.

The next time he opened them, the sun was setting, and maids were setting the low table with dinner for them all.

Quint inspected the dishes and sampled a few before the group drifted in. He yawned, trying to generate some energy after sleeping so long in the afternoon.

"These dishes are good," Hari said, "but they are more Slinnon-style than Kippunese."

"You don't need to apologize," Dugo said with his mouth full.

"Enough talk about food. Where are we?" Dakuz asked.

Quint showed Dakuz the notes he had rewritten. "I think we've taken this as far as we should. It's time to get wizard feedback," Quint said. "Why don't each of you review what we've come up with? I'm going to take a walk to wake up a little more. I've already eaten enough."

The twilight was cool, but Quint found that refreshing after such a long nap. The manor was busier than before. Servants were scurrying around, and the gardeners were cleaning up the grounds.

"Do you generally do all your work in the evenings?" Quint asked a couple of groundskeepers raking the gravel. Quint noticed a pile of weeds at the side of the area.

"The lady is arriving in the morning. It's unexpected, but at least we were notified a few hours ago. We'll have it looking right by the time she shows up."

"Can I help? I wouldn't mind a little exercise," Quint said, thinking that a bit of work would properly clear his head.

"Just remember you volunteered," the gardener said. "You can start in that section." The man pointed to a gravel plot across the courtyard and handed Quint his rake. "Pull the weeds first and then rake the gravel in a design like this."

Quint looked at the arcs in the gravel. He could duplicate that pattern without any trouble. He stood in front of the plot and wondered if he could use a string or two to help. The weeds weren't that bad throughout the manor, so Quint decided it wasn't worth the trouble.

One thing he could do was spell a light string to help him as the sky darkened. It would be a better light than the torches and lanterns lit throughout the manor. Quint became one with the task, and his work was invigorating.

"You are a busy little bee," A female voice spoke from the darkness.

"I'm just helping prepare things for the lady," Quint said.

"You are new around here? You haven't been issued work clothes yet." Her voice was smooth with a hint of amusement. Quint didn't think she was a servant. Perhaps she was a senior housekeeper from the confidence in her voice.

"You know a little magic, too?" the woman said.

"I'm not without some talent," Quint said.

"Perhaps I can put you to better use around the manor," the woman said, turning around and disappearing around a corner.

Quint continued his work and finished his plot. Lights were still burning, but he had done enough. He found a hot tea pot in his rooms and had a few cups before turning in.

§

"The lady of the manor has arrived, and we will join her for breakfast," Hari said, waking Quint, who was still a little stiff from his evening work.

Dressing for breakfast solved Quint's stiffness problem, and Dakuz walked with him to the owner's dining room in the main building.

Thera was talking to an attractive woman not much older than herself. Thera was pretty, but the lady of the manor was stunningly beautiful. She was polennese. No wonder she was a successful entertainer. Quint thought she was a feast for male eyes, remembering the saying. Thera seemed to enjoy talking to her, which played in their hostess's favor.

"Sit," the woman said. Her eyes lit up when she noticed Quint at the back of the room. "You make a marvelous gardener," the lady said.

Quint quickly remembered the well-modulated voice. It was the woman he had a conversation with the previous evening.

"I hope my work was acceptable, madam," Quint said, smiling.

"Oh! Don't call me madam. I sound like an old woman. I am Shira Tommato." She giggled. "That's my real name. My father was polennese and lived in Pokogon. Tommato, tomato." She smiled wryly. Every expression on her face was enjoyable to see. "I use a stage name, mostly anyway. I'm known throughout North Fenola as Shira Yomolo, and many just call me 'Shira.'"

"I've heard of you," Dugo said. "You toured through Narukun a few years ago."

"I never did make it to Pinzleport. It's too dangerous for me," Shira said with a smile. "Sit down and let's eat. I've talked enough for a morning."

Hari made formal introductions.

"Your background is why you tend to serve polennese food?" Dakuz asked.

"It is. Kippunese cuisine takes a bit of getting used to, but it is delicious when prepared the right way."

"That's not how a typical family cooks," Hari said.

"Sadly, that is so, but taste is so subjective, so don't take offense at what I like or don't like," Shira said. "You eat what you like."

"Or what you are served," Dugo said. "At Seensist Cloister, we had a cook who styled herself as an expert in Kippunese food." He shook his head. "She was wrong, but we had to eat it or starve."

"Dugo is right," Quint said.

"And my kitchen's labor is satisfactory?" Shira asked.

"Yes," Dakuz said, "and I'm particular."

They ate and talked about her singing. She didn't seem to mind. Breakfast was about over when Shira turned to Quint.

"You've been silent enough."

Quint shrugged. "I'm not too familiar with North Fenolan music," he said. "I'm from South Fenola."

"He is the master I told you about," Hari said.

Shira raised her eyebrows. "You are? I thought Dakuz…"

Quint laughed. "Everyone thinks that. Perhaps I should turn my hair white," he said. "I'm often underestimated because I'm so young."

"And young you are. In your case, youth makes you more interesting," Shira said. "We can talk later. I have things to do today, including a trip to Morimanu. Let's meet again for dinner. You can stay here as my guests for as long as you like."

She smiled at them all and swept from the room.

"Did she not know who I was last night when she arrived earlier than expected?" Quint asked Hari.

"I'm not sure," Hari said. "She asked me if I had hired any new people while she'd been gone. I presume she was talking about you. I think she was impressed."

"I don't think so," Quint said. "We only exchanged a few remarks."

"Watch yourself," Thera said. "You might be caught in her web."

"I can think of worse situations than that," Dugo grinned.

"I do mean to change the subject," Thera said. "What do we do today?"

"Seek out wizards," Quint said. "We only have three weeks to come up with a concrete solution. A few pages of our ideas won't be enough."

"I can confirm that," Hari said. "I know the people to see."

Quint was putting the draft charter into his bag when Shira Yomolo walked into his quarters. He couldn't get the image of a tomato out of his mind to think of her real name.

"Lady Shira," Quint said. "I thought you were on your way to the city?"

"When Hari said you were going into the city, too, I thought there might be room for your group in my carriage. We might as well travel together."

"But we don't have the same destination," Quint said, frantically thinking of a way to decline. She made him uncomfortable.

"I am making one stop and can find my way around Morimanu from there. Hari knows when I shall be done. He said you'd have enough time."

"How can I say no?" Quint asked.

"Just say 'no,'" Shira said. "But don't. Sit for a bit, and let's chat. The carriage won't leave without me."

Quint sat at a low table, and Shira gracefully sat across from him. Quint looked at her and tried to look elsewhere.

"What do you wish to talk about?"

"Hari said that you are something special. I could see that last night. No wizard would be a groundskeeper plucking weeds for me."

"The magic light? That is one of the easiest strings for a wizard to master."

"But you could have used strings to do the work," Shira said.

Quint frowned. Her lack of magical knowledge made talking and looking into her beautiful eyes easier.

"Not really. Sometimes, it's faster to do the task yourself without magic than to figure out how to manipulate strings to do a mundane task."

Shira laughed softly. "Surely, you jest."

"Have you had any magical training?"

"No one has ever offered. My appearance has a power of its own," Shira said as a tease.

"I can't disagree with that. Can I use a few strings on you to see if you have any potential?"

Shira frowned. "You aren't going to turn me into a rabbit or something, are you?"

"No, but wouldn't you like to know if you have magic?"

Shira blinked and patted her chest. "This is quite unexpected."

"Yes or no. If you don't feel up to it, just say 'no,' like you advised me."

After closing her eyes and taking a deep breath, she opened them again and said, "Yes. Will it hurt?"

Quint laughed. "Not at all. Sit there and close your eyes if you wish."

She gave Quint a weak smile and then closed her eyes, balling her hands into fists.

Quint first removed any shield or mask that she might be wearing. It was best to get the worst string over. She took a breath and wavered as Quint cast the string. She had been manipulated, but her face remained as beautiful as ever. A mask was the worst thing, but he didn't know what the shield had been doing.

"Do you feel any different?"

"I was lightheaded for a moment. Do you know why?"

Quint sighed. He had to tell her the truth. "Someone had placed a psychic string on you. I can't tell what it was, but I removed it." He didn't tell her he had eliminated any possible mask.

"I need to hold your hand for the next string," Quint said.

Shira didn't hesitate to extend her hand. Quint took it and used a magic detection string. He had little use for it, preferring to see someone use strings for evaluation. Since Shira said she knew no magic, the detection string was the best approach.

Quint blinked as he invoked the string. Shira's power was unexpectedly strong.

"I feel different. What did you do to me?"

Quint let go of her hand. "The psychic string must have masked your magic potential. Have you ever exhibited magic before?"

"Not that I can remember," Shira said.

"Even as a child?"

Shira laughed. "Children fabricate memories. How can you believe your own?"

"Do you remember having power as a child, made up or not?"

The woman furrowed her brows. "Of course I do. I was able to make a magic light like you did once. I don't know how I did it. My parents had a few wizard friends, and I imitated their gestures. I thought I was imagining things. I told my mother. She confirmed it was my imagination. I didn't have any wizardly indications after that."

"Perhaps one of your wizard friends invoked the spell. Were they powerful wizards?"

"They all wore robes," Shira said. "My parents could make simple strings."

"Or not so simple," Quint said. "They used your beauty and voice rather than your arcane abilities," Quint said. "Do you want some lessons?"

"You will teach me?"

"It's better that I don't. Dakuz had lots of experience with beginners as a librarian/instructor at Seensist Cloister. Dugo has enough knowledge to teach you enough to know what you don't. Dakuz is a little gruff, but you will learn much faster."

Shira smiled mischievously. "I know how to overcome gruff, Quint." She looked away for a moment. "Let me think about it. I don't have to go to a Narukun cloister or anything else?"

Quint shook his head. "We'll talk about the charter and what we intend to do with it in Shimato on the way into the capital. Even if you decide not to learn, you can always change your mind. I can probably figure out the shield that was placed on you all those years ago."

Shira pouted. "Not that many years ago," she said.

Quint was aware of Shira's innate non-magic effect on him. "We should go."

After looking at the clock, Shira stood. "We have spent enough time together, for now. Are you ready?"

Quint nodded, and they sought the others.

∽

CHAPTER FIVE

SHIRA REMAINED SILENT ABOUT LEARNING MAGIC while they traveled to the capital, but she was interested in the discussions about the charter. Too interested in Quint's estimation. It was clear she was thinking in terms of wizards. Hari shot Quint a glance but said nothing.

When they dropped Shira off at the lawyer's office in the city center, Hari spoke as soon as she was gone. "What did you tell her?"

"You know Shira's parents?"

"Knew, they have both passed on. I was a close friend of her father."

"When Shira was little?" Quint asked.

Hari grunted. "Perhaps we should continue this discussion between the two of us."

The others looked clueless, and Quint agreed.

Where do we go first?" Dakuz asked, pointedly changing the subject.

"We will visit three friends who lead wizard factions. None of the factions are large. Wizards are disorganized in Shimato."

"Tommato, Shimato," Dugo said, grinning. "It rhymes."

"Among other things," Hari said, his good temper gone. "Your goal is to get others' opinions."

"And that includes those who aren't leaders of factions," Thera said.

Hari narrowed his eyes. "Of course, but leaders, first."

"Aren't you a faction leader?" Thera asked.

Hari nodded. "I am at that level, but I advise the warlord."

"Then let's talk to some of your fellow wizards, too," Dakuz said. "We have the time."

Hari gave an address to the driver and returned to the cab before they proceeded through the capital.

"Since you are a leader, what do you think? It would be useful for us to know how the others will react," Thera said.

"I agree with most of it. My concerns don't change the major points," Hari said. "I would do things different administratively."

"Like?" Dakuz asked.

"There should be a stronger entity. The wizard corps will work better if they can operate independently from the warlord," Hari said.

"That might not be acceptable to the military," Thera said. "In a military operation, a single command at the top is vital to executing a battle plan."

"You speak from experience?" Hari said.

"I do," Thera said.

"In military operations, when the wizard corps is attached to an army, I agree," Quint said. "However, if the general or whoever runs the operation doesn't like wizards, they won't be used to the fief's advantage. That shouldn't mean the wizard corps leader of the chartered wizards can't report past the general leading an operation."

Hari sat back and nodded. "I see. The operational decisions are the military's, but they don't run the wizard corps."

"That was never the intent," Quint said. "Pesky wizards are those who complain. With a clear chain of command administratively and a different one administratively, we can reduce the complaints."

"We can talk about that. It may come up in our discussions."

Quint gave Hari a faint smile and looked out the window at the passing city. Morimanu still seemed very exotic to Quint, and he wondered what other issues could come up that he would never anticipate.

The carriage stopped in front of a modest mansion. The courtyard was too small for the carriage, so they alighted and followed Hari to the gate.

Hari spoke to someone behind the gate who opened it. Quint could feel a faint pulse of magic. The wizard used magic in his own house, which comforted him for some reason.

Hari walked past the man who had opened the gate, pointedly ignoring him. Quint nodded to the gate opener. The man, who seemed to be in his early thirties, smiled and nodded back to Quint.

An older woman walked out of the main building. There were three small buildings facing the gate. It was a smaller version of Shira's mansion. There might have been another building behind the main one, but Quint didn't have time to find out.

They followed the woman back into the main building and sat where Hari placed them. There was a main seat. It wasn't a throne, but it was set up for the master or mistress of the house, and there were two lines of five chairs facing each other between the host's chair and the door.

Hari took one of the closer seats to the female wizard, and Quint was shown to a seat closest to the door with Dakuz, Dugo, and Thera between Quint and Hari. A man was sitting at the front facing Hari. The servant who opened the gate stood by the door after he closed it with his hands folded in front.

Hari made introductions at the woman's request. The woman was Miro Gorima, the supreme wizard of the Three Forks faction. Quint didn't ask what kind of forks they meant.

"Our friends from Narukun have devised a proposal for a new organization within Shimato. I have helped them with what they call a charter."

"And this charter is between wizards and…?"

"The warlord," Hari said.

"What about the factions?"

Quint knew the answer, but Hari wanted to answer and told Gazima they must pledge their loyalty to the charter. That wasn't how Quint would have phrased it.

Hari presented the concept of a wizard corps but neglected to mention the difference between administration and operations allegiances and made it seem that the wizards were under the thumb of the military commanders.

Quint was disappointed in their host. Quint wouldn't agree to the organization as Hari presented it.

"The charter is more flexible than Hari described," Quint said.

"Are you accusing me of lying?" Hari asked.

"No. We are here to present a draft document. There is room for change. I'd be happy to discuss aspects of the charter," Quint said.

Gorima glared at Quint. "You have no right to speak here. Look where you sit. Everyone must speak before you can."

Quint hadn't heard of that rule before, but he suspected Shimato wizards had many rules he didn't know, and Hari had purposely placed him in the seat with the lowest status. Quint suddenly knew he had been naive in trusting Hari, and Miro Gorima was plainly not interested in implementing a new way for wizards.

"I think we have talked enough," Quint said. He rose from his seat. "Dakuz, Thera, and Dugo come with me. We won't get a fair hearing with these people. The Three Forks are against us, as is Hari Bitto." Quint bowed to Hari. "Thank you for rescuing us from the military, but I think they are the next group we will contact."

Hari sat, looking shocked, as they entered the small courtyard. The servant stopped Quint. "If you would come this way, there is a better way to exit the manor."

"But that's the way we came in," Dugo said.

"Come this way, please," the servant said.

"Let's follow him," Quint said.

Thera frowned, but Dakuz grabbed her arm. "Let's go along, shall we?"

The servant walked around the side of the main building and into a smaller building behind. Quint had guessed there was more to the manor.

"If you would give me a few minutes to get some refreshments, sit at the table." The youngish man smiled. "Anywhere will do," he said as he closed the doors.

Quint sat facing the door with his friends on either side. It took more than a "few" minutes, but finally, the servant opened the doors and let in Miro Gorima and the man who faced Hari. They represented the Three Forks faction. The servant closed the doors and sat next to Miro.

"I'm sorry about the act," the servant said. "I'm not who you might think. My name is Rimo Gorima, Miro's son. We couldn't talk freely with Hari Bitto in the room. He is heading back to Lady Shira's manor."

"Is the lady not to be trusted?" Dakuz asked.

"Oh, she is, but Hari makes use of an old friendship with her parents. It has served him well for the past four or five years as Lady Shira's fame has grown," Rimo said. "He takes advantage of the relationship. Everyone knows that."

"And your comments in the other building?"

"For Hari's benefit. An organization like you described would harm Hari's influence on the warlord unless he is the head."

"Then why did he save us from the military?" Thera asked.

"So he could manipulate you without interference," Miro said.

"Have we just been abducted again?" Dugo asked.

Rimo laughed. "Not at all. We have arranged for you to meet two other faction leaders on neutral territory. You can use a different carriage and driver to return to Shira's mansion."

"And you are the master of the Three Forks, not your mother?" Quint asked.

"Not quite yet. When you arrived, our plans were delayed, especially when Hari took an interest. You are the predictor string disruptor?" Rimo said.

"I am," Quint said. "I used to think predictor strings useful, but I can't use one on myself, and as I found out in Narukun, it's the same with everyone else connected with my actions. Everyone else thinks I will be important in the future."

"There is no other person whose predictor string performs the same, and it's true, those around you are similarly disrupted, but that is because of you," Miro said. "We don't want Hari manipulating our future, hence the performance in the main hall."

"Is there a rule that the person furthest away from you can't speak?" Quint asked.

"There is, but there are exceptions. Don't worry about it. The rule played well with Hari," Rimo said. "He is very upset with you for getting in his way."

"Does Hari know who you are?"

"He does," Rimo said. He cast a string on himself and removed the mask he wore. "A person of Hari Bitto's stature wouldn't notice a gatekeeper."

"But as a master, he should have been able to see through a magical mask," Quint said.

"Not if he doesn't look," Rimo said with a grin.

"I was fooled by a mask worn by a woman until I learned how to look." Quint waved his hand to change the subject. "Do you mind if we talk to some of your faction's wizards to see how they feel about the charter?" he asked.

"I think it's a grand idea," Miro Gorima said.

The lack of resistance to Quint's suggestion showed him who to trust more, but trust was a relative thing in Shimato. He didn't want to interact with Hari, especially suspecting the wizard was likely the one who throttled

Shira and her magic, regardless of Hari's intentions.

"Is Hari Bitto a real master?" Dakuz asked.

"Barely," Miro Gorima said. "He loves to use the sensei title, but the rest of us don't. It's for very formal introductions. Any master is equal in Lord Bumoto's mind. Hari has an outsized influence in the warlord's court."

"You have other masters?" Quint asked.

"There are eleven in Shimato. Two are retired. Nine are active. A master should lead factions, but that isn't the case now," Miro said.

"And you are a master?" Quint asked Rimo.

"Mother has spared no expense to make me one."

"It takes talent and money unless someone is bribed," Quint said.

"Not an unlikely event in the other fiefs, but Bunto Bumoto only recognizes true talent no matter how you think of him. You are the twelfth master currently in Shimato," Rimo said.

"Now that we've gone through all the gossip, what do you really think about the charter?" Quint asked.

"I'd rather read the thing than listen to Hari manipulate the contents. I listened to his words and read your faces," Miro said. "Do you agree, Rimo? We haven't had the chance to talk about it."

"I agree. Do you have copies?"

"Hari's got a few copies, but I have the original," Quint said.

"I can produce copies," Rimo said. "One of my unique strings. I was doing the administrative work for the faction and modified a string for duplicating artwork, which works for written documents."

"I haven't heard of an artwork string or a copy string. I could have used that in my former life," Quint said.

"It is not master-level. There is paper in that desk," Rimo said to the male wizard who had sat across from Hari.

"Here is the original," Quint said, removing it from his bag. "Can you make a few more?"

Rimo shuffled through the charter. "This is short enough that I can do that in a few minutes."

Quint carefully followed Rimo's strings, from threads to strings to the way he invoked the string. He saw enough that he could learn it. It didn't seem like a high-level string to him, either.

"Some others in your organization know how this string works?" Quint asked.

"Do you know how I made the string?" Rimo said, nodding.

"I think I can duplicate it."

Rimo slid a small stack of blank paper and the original charter toward Quint. Who needed a few attempts before he was making copies himself.

"That can save a lot of time," Dakuz said. "Printing can be so tedious."

Dakuz used to work in a library," Thera said.

"I ran the library if you don't mind the correction."

"Excuse me. Ran the library in Seensist Cloister in Narukun."

Rimo glanced at the pages he had made. "We can meet again tomorrow afternoon?"

"Can we visit the other faction members tomorrow if you can get these copies to them today?" Quint asked.

Miro nodded and smiled. "We would be happy to arrange meetings after ours. You said you wanted to speak to common wizards?"

"I did," Quint said. "I want independent-minded wizards, not someone who will automatically say what they want you to say."

"I have a few in mind. We can include them in our meeting. Return one hour after noon tomorrow."

"That would be wonderful. Can we get a carriage to return to Shira Yomolo's manor? I hope we will still be welcome," Quint said.

"If you aren't welcome, we can give you proper lodgings. We'll have our driver wait for your word before he leaves you there."

§

Quint had expected their bags to be waiting outside the front gate, but they were let into the large courtyard. Quint returned to his quarters and found his possessions hadn't been tampered with. He stepped outside and spotted a servant.

"Has Hari Bitto returned from Morimanu?" Quint asked.

"Returned with the lady, but he left soon after. The lady would like a word with you as soon as you returned. Shall I go with you so you can be announced?"

"Certainly," Quint said.

Shira Yomolo entered the front area of her quarters and grinned at Quint. "Would you sit? I'll pour some tea."

Quint settled himself into a low chair and waited while the beautiful woman showed that her graceful actions were as lovely as her face.

She waited for Quint to sip from the small teacup before taking some tea and sighing. "I've known the man since I was young. I showed him a magic light, thinking he would be delighted. Hari was not. He admitted nullifying my power when I was barely shown my magic. My parents wanted me to concentrate on my singing. I had no say in the matter. Hari couldn't believe I was cured of his curse, but after I proved him wrong, it was time to show him to the front gate. Only the years he spent helping me did I relent and lend him the carriage." She grinned. "I have decided I want to learn magic and what I can do with magical potential. Wizard performers are looked down upon in Shimato fief but not in other areas of Kippun and the rest of North Fenola."

"Do you risk your popularity if you are exposed?" Quint asked.

"Not if I can tastefully wind magic in and out of my performances. That will be my goal, although it may take years to realize," Shira said.

"Will there be repercussions about separating from Hari?" Quint asked. "He seemed to be running things in your absence."

"Don't worry about that. Hari wasn't as involved as he might have presented himself."

Quint grunted. "We found out about his true self today."

"I could discern how he boasted about besting you in front of the Three Forks mistress," Shira said. "I don't know anything about Shimato's wizard factions."

"You will," Quint said. "Thank you for receiving me. I trust we can rely on your graciousness for a while longer?"

"You'll rely on me for more than that, Quint Tirolo."

Quint left the lady and gathered his three team members in his quarters after he told the Three Forks driver to leave. He gave his friends reassurances about their staying in the manor.

"What about Hari's revenge?" Thera said. "I can't see him getting fooled by you and not doing something about it."

"That is why we are going to visit the military tomorrow morning before we meet with the Three Forks wizards in the afternoon," Quint said.

"Now, I will teach you how to make copies. I think it's something Dugo can do, too."

By the end of the day, all four of them had made more copies of the charter. Quint was armed with his proposal to present to the military. He didn't know who in the military he'd visit, but even if Quint would have to embarrass himself by asking some random people, he would find who he'd have to meet.

CHAPTER SIX

~

PERHAPS QUINT WAS TOO HASTY IN FORCING HARI to leave their group. Shira Yomolo didn't know where Hari had gone, so even Quint had reconsidered since he could not find the military office. Dakuz was his partner, but he didn't have any good ideas.

They ended up at the inn where they were abducted when they first entered the capital, sitting in the common room drinking a light white wine and munching on a few snacks.

"We need some inspiration," Dakuz said, looking around at the almost-empty common room, "but I think we made a mistake choosing this place."

They were about finished when the tall soldier who had kidnapped them a few days ago entered the common room with three other soldiers. Dakuz and Quint could handle four soldiers in a common room not filled with bystanders.

The four of them didn't notice Quint and Dakuz until they sat a few tables away.

"I hope we have found our entry pass into the military," Quint said with a smile. He walked over to the soldiers' table.

"You must live here," Quint said. "We found nicer accommodations." Quint pulled a chair from another table and sat next to the officer.

"You've grown braver since we saw you last," the officer said. "Aren't you afraid of us?"

"Not just four of you," Quint said. "In Kippun, my name changes. I could be known as Quinto Tirolo-sensei, but I think the 'sensei' tag is presumptuous."

The soldier's eyebrows shot up. "You are a wizard master?"

"I am," Quint said. "I didn't fight back before because some innocent people would have been inconvenienced, but that's not the case now." He reached over and put one of the soldiers to sleep. His head thumped against the table. "I can do the same to the three of you with one string."

"What do you want with me? We know a squad of wizards rescued you."

"We were, but I'm not seeking revenge. I'd like a little help," Quint said before giving the soldier a quick description of the wizard charter.

"We'd be even then?" the soldier asked.

"More than even, I'd say." Dakuz joined them, sitting on the other side of the table.

"He is a powerful wizard," Quint said.

The three soldiers, still conscious, looked at each other.

"You need to speak to an officer," the tall soldier said.

"Do you know an officer that would give us a listen?" Quint asked.

"Someone who would support your charter?" The soldier shook his head. "Wizards aren't held in high regard by the military. Surely, you know that."

Dakuz dropped another soldier, but he grabbed the soldier's head before it bounced on the table.

The tall soldier's eyes grew, and he swallowed hard. "I know just the person but don't tell them I told you," the soldier said.

"How could I do that when I don't even know your name?" Quint said.

"A name and an address," Quint said. "Don't play me for a fool unless you intend to move in the next few hours."

Dakuz dropped the last of the three soldiers. "Think of what I can do to these slumbering men," Dakuz grunted.

"All right," the tall soldier said. "There is a military building on the south end of the big square a block over. Seek out War Leader Chibo Hobona. He leads the army. If you are from Narukun, you would call him a General."

"That's good enough for me," Quint said.

He reached over and pinched the tall soldier's shoulder and laughed when he didn't invoke a string, but then he woke two of the soldiers while Dakuz deactivated the sleeping string on the third soldier.

One of the waking soldiers rubbed his forehead and was about to pull his sword.

"The young one is a master wizard," the tall soldier said. "He is playing us fairly."

The soldier grunted and sheathed his sword.

"Enjoy your morning," Quint said, tossing a gold coin on the table. "That should take care of your bill."

Quint and Dakuz exited the inn.

"That was a generous payment for a name. We didn't even get an introduction," Dakuz said.

"I didn't think it wise to push it. I'll bet more soldiers are staying at that inn," Quint said. "We now know where a military building is without asking a bystander and a name that might or might not be someone we can meet."

They had walked far enough to enter the vast square and headed south.

"Wait up!"

They looked back to see the tall soldier with one of the soldiers, whose forehead had turned red from an encounter with the tabletop.

"You paid for far more than a breakfast at the inn. I thought you might want an introduction," the soldier said.

"First, you can introduce yourself and your friend," Quint said.

"I'm Force Leader Tipo, and this is Narisu, one of my squad."

Dakuz shot Quint a quizzical glance, but Quint ignored it. "Lead the way. I assume we are headed in the right direction?"

"We are," Tipo said with a grin. "You will be recognized as Narukuns."

"We can't grow long hair in a week," Dakuz grumbled. "I'm old enough to be lucky to grow any hair at all."

"Your costumes are good enough," Tipo said.

"We'll see how good they are when we meet more soldiers," Quint said. "I spent years in the military in South Fenola."

"You are too young to have spent very much."

"I was pressed into service as soon as I came into my magic," Quint said.

"Did you fight as a wizard?"

"I know how to use strings."

"You really are a master?" Narisu asked, narrowing his eyes.

"He is. Do you want him to prove it to you?" Dakuz said.

"No. Just wondering."

"You are serious about this charter thing?" Tipo asked.

"I am. I wasn't when I arrived in Shimato, but I am now," Quint said. "Wizards don't get much respect, but the way things are structured in Shimato, they might not deserve any. Magic is a resource that shouldn't be left to chance. It needs some organization, and that's what the charter gives. The military has its specific needs, and that's why we propose planning the charter to recognize that."

"Let's see if Chibo is in Morimanu," Tipo said. "If he isn't, we can find someone else to listen. I'm not a supporter of the idea, but I'm not a detractor."

"Better than nothing, I suppose," Dakuz said.

They reached the military building. A small courtyard in the front was wide enough for a carriage or horses to park, but an iron picket fence surrounded the property. It stood next to a building of similar proportions; the Revenue Committee said the stone title above the wide doors.

Quint thought one side might be where the fief collected funds, and the other side was the vehicle for collecting them, or the military building was the source of lots of guards to protect the hoard of money within. Who knows what the truth was?

Tipo walked up to the gate leading into the courtyard. "I'm here to introduce a distinguished guest of Shimato to see War Leader Hobona." Tipo puffed out his chest.

"All you have to say is let me in," the guard said, laughing. "Don't make any trouble this time."

"I won't," Tipo said, as they walked across the courtyard to the three-story building with its' curving edges.

Quint was surprised they weren't escorted, but perhaps Tipo was the escort. Tipo walked through the foyer to the smiles of some walking past. Tipo was well-known, and it looked like he might be a character.

On the third floor, Tipo led them around the building that surrounded an inner courtyard and knocked and then opened a door to an office.

"I'll have a word with Chibo before you come in."

They waited five or more minutes, with people looking at Narisu curiously. Surely, a uniformed soldier was common, but perhaps not on the third floor.

"Come in," a voice said from behind the door.

Narisu opened it and offered Quint and Dakuz to enter ahead of him. Chibo Hobona sat facing out an open window, looking at shorter buildings below.

"Sit," the War Leader said.

When Dakuz and Quint were seated at the first seats in the facing parallel row of four seats on a side, Chibo turned around. The uniform was like the ones Quint had seen in his audience with the warlord, but the face was that of Tipo, his escort.

"Surprised?" Tipo said with a grin.

"It's a trite joke," Dakuz said, "like something you would read in a novel."

"Where do you think I got the idea?" Tipo/Chibo said, laughing. "I like being around my men. My living quarters are in that inn when I'm in the capital. No one is comfortable when I'm wearing my real uniform."

"And surrounded by your friends?" Quint asked. Evidently, Rimo Gorima had read the same novel and played the servant.

"By my comrades in arms. I like to know what the common soldier is thinking," Chibo said. "It is more useful than carousing with my peers."

"It seems I've already given you my idea about the wizards' charter."

Chibo chuckled. "Do you have it written down?"

Dakuz carried the bag with the copies and presented one to Chibo.

"Give my aide, Narisu, one too if you have an extra."

Both men read the charter while Quint and Dakuz waited.

"And what do you expect from the military?" Chibo asked.

"A chance to participate in making wizards less 'pesky,' as Warlord Bumoto said," Quint said.

"What's in it for you?" Chibo tapped on the copy of the charter.

Quint pursed his lips. It was an unanticipated question. "I have something to do, and I'm waiting for the proper place and time to do it. Until then, I need experience in working with people and organizations. I have certain talents to keep me moving in the right direction, but I'm not yet twenty years old and require some seasoning. This is a worthwhile project since it allows me to stay in the fief for a while."

"Can you leave this with me for a few days? Where are you staying?"

"We are the guests of Shira Yomolo," Quint said.

"Ah," Chibo closed his eyes and smiled. "That means Hari Bitto rescued you from my clutches. I wondered who it was. I never had time to find out before you showed up at the inn this morning."

"They have had a falling out, I'm afraid," Quint said.

"That's good. I've never trusted Bitto. With him not in the midst of things, your case is made stronger. I will visit Shira Yomolo at her manor at noon, two days from now."

"Are we dismissed?" Quint asked.

"Of course. Two days," Chibo held up two fingers on one hand and pointed to them with the other.

§

It was still mid-morning when Dakuz and Quint stepped onto the square and sat on a bench. "What do we do now?" Dakuz asked.

"I suppose we try to find the Three Forks manor and wait there," Quint said.

"I remember where it was," Dakuz said.

Half an hour later, they stood at the open gate of the Three Fork headquarters or the Gorima mansion. Quint didn't really know which it was. A servant, not Rimo Gorima, sat on a stool and rose to his feet when Quint and Dakuz stepped in.

"Your business?"

"We have a meeting in an hour with Rimo and Miro Gorima," Dakuz said. "More of our group will arrive on time, but we finished our morning tasks early."

"I will inquire about finding a room to wait."

Quint looked at the man with narrowed eyes. "Are you in the Three Forks faction?"

"Of course. All of us are Three Forks wizards."

"Can we speak to you while you mind the gates?"

The man shrugged his shoulders. "I don't see why not. You might give me an inkling about what went on yesterday. The young master gave me the day off, and I know something happened, but the Gorimas can be stingy with their information. Not that there is anything bad with that."

"Can you join wood to lock the gate?"

"I wouldn't be sitting here if I couldn't."

"So Rimo didn't have to man the gate," Dakuz said.

The man nodded. "That's right."

"Would you read a few pages for us? We have an idea about unifying Shimato's wizards," Quint said.

The man shrugged and held out a hand. Quint gave the gatekeeper a copy of the draft chart. Dakuz and Quint waited while the charter was read. The man sat back and thought for a minute.

"Are you serious about this?" the wizard asked.

"We are. That is why we are here to talk to the Gorimas today. Can you give us your opinion?"

"There is a saying among all the factions, 'in unity there is strength.' I see a whole lot of strength here, but the problem is if someone is accumulating too much strength, that leads back to fragmentation."

"You've seen that in Shimato?" Dakuz asked.

"And elsewhere. I'm not from here but from a fief close to Pokogon. The power accumulates to masters everywhere I've gone, and average wizards like me become more like slaves."

"Magical manipulation?" Quint asked.

The man shrugged. "Maybe in some places, but not much of that kind of thing is tolerated in Shimato." The man tapped the draft charter. "To make this work, you've got to allow wizards to move up and down if you want an organization that will protect everyone."

"Based on merit?" Dakuz asked.

"Exactly. Not just how many strings a wizard has or how long they've been around, but what they contribute to the guild or the charter, whatever you call it." The gatekeeper looked at the rolled-up charter in his hands. "Can I keep this? I'd like to show it to some friends. Not all are Three Forks members. Is that all right?"

"We'd like that," Quint said.

Thera and Dugo walked through the gate.

"We must go. Thanks for your time," Quint said.

The man nodded to them. "Those are your friends?"

"They are. I didn't ask for your names."

Dakuz let the gatekeeper know who had entered the mansion grounds.

"Oh. I was told you could go to the back courtyard for your meeting when all of you arrived."

Quint nodded to the gatekeeper, and they headed toward the place where they met with Rimo and Miro without Hari Bitto.

"You found an objective wizard?" Rimo asked.

"I don't know how objective he is, but his perspective was valuable," Quint said.

"What is it?" Rimo asked.

Quint didn't like his pushiness, but he half-expected some touchiness about talking to one of his Three Forks wizards without permission. He had a response ready.

"I'll tell you what he said after meeting with the others. Where are they?" Quint asked.

"They will be here at half past the hour. Mother and I wanted a word with you first."

"That's fine. What is on your mind?" Quint asked, consciously trying to make his comment innocuous.

"Are you intending to run the charter organization?" Rimo said. "Are any of you of that frame of mind?"

"I thought we answered that yesterday. I have other things to do."

Rimo seemed mollified by the answer. "I wanted to make sure. I don't want to bring a viper into a meeting with associates."

Quint laughed. "I'm no viper, literally or figuratively."

"If you show fangs unexpectedly, Three Forks will immediately withdraw our support," Miro Gorima said.

"Is that what you think Hari Bitto had in mind?" Thera asked.

"Of course," Rimo said. "He did a poor job hiding it, regardless of his description of the charter."

The other wizards walked into the hall followed by a train of servants bringing refreshments. They sat in facing double rows and drank light wine while Rimo made the introductions. Five factions had shown up, including the Three Forks.

"I approached the Shouting Hawks and the Shining Strings," Rimo said. "Our larger brothers deemed it a waste of their time."

One of the wizards scoffed. "One is considering aligning with the Greens of Narukun, and the other is in Bunto Bumoto's pocket."

"One is 'pesky,' and one isn't as far as the warlord is concerned?" Quint asked.

Some of the wizards chuckled. "You have truly met Lord Bumoto," one said.

"You are all pesky?"

"And proud of it!" another wizard said.

Rimo let some bantering take place. Some of it was boasts, and some comments troubled Quint's confidence in reaching an agreement.

"Shall we focus our minds on this charter proposal?" Rimo asked the group. "A quick summary, Quint?"

Quint nodded and stood and gave a quick summary. "This is a draft," he said, holding up a copy. "Drafts are meant to be modified. I'm bound to present a version to Warlord Bumoto in a few weeks. I'd like it to be the product of the wizards of Shimato."

One of the wizards pulled a folded copy from his robes. "It isn't the words that are important, but how they are implemented. This sounds good and noble, but I can see some enterprising wizard or faction dominating the charter organization and putting us all under their thumb."

Quint knew that to be the biggest weakness, and he suspected that the gatekeeper had told him the same thing from a different perspective. "Is there a way to prevent that from happening that you could see?"

"Time limits on those in charge. We don't want a leader with an indefinite term," another wizard said. "That can be corrupted, too, but at least there is a plan to escape a domineering leader who has secretly aligned himself with a political faction or is doing the warlord's bidding. The Shouting Hawks follow the warlord's lead in everything. The Shining Strings have recently shown undue coziness with the wizards of Gamiza who are open about a pending alliance with the Greens of Narukun."

"I know the Greens well," Quint said. "I wouldn't wish an evil organization like them on any fief."

Wizards nodded their heads in agreement.

"What kinds of limits do you have in mind?" Quint asked.

The discussion began now that objections had been voiced. In an hour and a half, all the factions had suggestions discussed and some of them had been incorporated into changes that all agreed could be incorporated in the next draft. The other wizards exited, leaving Quint's group and the representatives from the Three Forks in the meeting hall.

"What is your next step?" Rimo said. "The charter is better, in my eyes, but you've only talked to factions representing less than half of the wizards in Shimato."

"I have met with a member of the warlord's military. He is currently reviewing the first draft, and I'll send him a copy of what we have decided today."

"Who did you contact?" Miro asked. "You can't expect a common guard to speak for anyone."

"I spoke with the only military leader I know, Chibo Hobona."

Miro blinked, speechless for a moment. "He is called the People's War Leader."

"He wanted a few days to think about it, but I think some of our changes might interest him. We have to address the linkage to the military before I can present something to the warlord."

"I agree. I would have suggested someone less independent, however," Miro said. "But let's see what Hobona thinks."

"He's led his men to capture us on our first night in the capital. Knowing his rank, I would guess Hari Bitto had something up his sleeve when he rescued us later in the evening," Quint said.

Rimo nodded. "The less Hari knows, the better, in my estimation. He is loosely aligned with the Shining Strings but has always kept himself aloof with his master status."

"He doesn't have to worry about rivals in court that way," Rimo's mother said. She made a sour face before uttering, "A scurrilous villain."

"We will deliver copies to you in the morning," Quint said. "All of us know how to make copies, thanks to you." Quint bowed to Rimo.

"Let us look at the changes before you send any out," Rimo asked.

"We can do that. It isn't our intent to hold back any secrets. It defeats the purpose of our project," Dakuz said.

"Until tomorrow. I will be in all morning," Rimo said.

CHAPTER SEVEN

~

"There is a Todo Yinsu to see you. He is with a few others. They say they are wizards," a maid said from the door to Quint's quarters.

"I should know him?" Quint asked.

"He says he keeps a gate. Does that make sense to you?" the young woman asked.

"It does!" Quint said. "Show them in, and then notify Dakuz and the others that the gatekeeper has come to us."

Todo was accompanied by two men and a woman, all about Dakuz's age.

"Sit," Quint said, pointing to one side of a line of chairs. Dakuz and Thera showed up a few moments later. Dugo was occupied making the charter copies they would show to Rimo and Mori later in the morning. "You've looked at the draft charter?"

"We have." Todo introduced his friends. Each one was from a different wizard faction.

"You have some comments?"

Todo grinned. "We do. What happens to the factions if Lord Bumoto accepts the charter?"

The woman raised her hand shoulder-high. "I came up with that one." She smiled shyly but was anxious to hear Quint's answer.

"We didn't address that," Quint said, "but wizards won't have to belong to factions to be registered or members of the wizard corps. No relationship with an outside group is required and the charter workers get their positions because they deserve it, not because of their affiliations. Is that a realistic assumption? The Three Forks leaders didn't mention it."

"Then they are waiting to see which way the wind blows," another wizard said. He quickly glanced at Todo and then back to Quint. "Don't think they haven't thought about it."

"Should we dismember the wizard factions?" Quint asked. "Do they provide benefits other than camaraderie?"

"They do, but nothing the charter couldn't provide," Todo said. He gave Quint a note. "I anticipated your answer and wrote down what we get from our factions."

The factions provided employment services, sick compensation, magic education, wizard testing, and an opportunity to rise in the faction hierarchy, which came with connections, seniority, and merit.

"Where do the factions get the money to provide these services?" Dakuz asked after Quint handed him the note.

"There are secular sponsors who contract with the factions for wizardry services. We contribute a percentage of what we make on our own as wizards," Todo said. "Members of the military keep all their pay except for a fixed fee."

The woman piped up. "Every faction does things a little differently, but Todo is mostly right."

The other two nodded.

"Should the charter organization do the same?"

"Yes!" all four said simultaneously.

"But with a lower percentage and fee," one of the men said. "I served in the warlord's force and had to pay my faction a huge fee, but I didn't mind it at the time because I liked the military lifestyle when I was younger. Now, I'd be very reluctant to return."

"If the charter takes the factions' places, then wizard life won't be the same," the woman said.

"Is that a bad thing?"

Todo worked his mouth before speaking. "It might. We all have long relationships with wizards in our factions. I don't want to lose them," Todo said.

"Do you have a solution in mind?" Quint asked.

"No. That's why we came to you. Rimo Gorima isn't objective. I'm sure he'd rather not lose any power. It's the same with all the leaders," Todo said.

"I'm not disparaging the leader of my faction. If you ask him about the Three Forks' relationship to the charter, he will clearly tell you that the factions remain."

Quint sat back. Todo described what Quint understood to be human nature. What would the factions want if the charter was to succeed without being ignored as soon as everyone's back was turned? Quint's group would have to ask Rimo in less than an hour.

"Do you have any specific requests?" Quint asked.

Todo presented four papers with comments on them. "I know you have to meet with Three Forks soon. We wrote down our own impressions."

"I'll let you know what happens," Quint said.

The visitors followed Todo out the door and out of the mansion.

"The mountain seems to have gained some altitude," Dakuz said.

Quint glanced at the notes. "I'm not so sure. Their comments match the tone of the faction leaders we talked to yesterday. I'll represent their viewpoint during our time with Rimo."

"We didn't get any input on kickback fees from the faction leaders," Thera said.

"That's why I wanted to talk to ordinary wizards, and they came to us. That's better than the factions selecting people who would parrot their thoughts," Quint said.

"Let's find out," Dakuz said.

§

Rimo let them wait for an hour before he showed up. Quint could feel a chill in Rimo's demeanor.

"You talked to others," Rimo said.

"I did. I said I wanted to speak to common wizards, which happened earlier today," Quint said.

"I didn't say you could talk to one of my employees."

Quint took a slow breath. Todo was right about his employer.

"Is Todo your slave? Can he not converse with someone other than a Three Fork member?"

"Of course, he can. He can talk to you all he wants because I released him when he told me of his visit."

"Did you ask him about the ideas he presented?"

Rimo looked at Quint with blank eyes. "Why would I do that? He's just a servant."

"He is a wizard," Quint said, trying to keep his temper composed. "He has ideas about what the charter should do?"

"Did he say he wanted to run the organization? Is that secretly what servants do, think about revolt?"

"Those pesky servants," Quint said sarcastically. He nodded to Dakuz, who left the revised charter behind. "We can talk later, but not now. I think I'll wait to hear from the military."

Quint's group walked out of the compound. He noticed the mansion was missing its gatekeeper.

"I misread Rimo Gorima," Dakuz said.

"The social gap is stronger than the wizard faction," Thera said. "I suppose Todo told us in his own way that what we saw was the reality in Shimato."

Their carriage drove up, and they piled in. The ride back to the mansion was glum and mostly silent.

Todo and another one of the visiting wizards sat outside the gate when Quint's group arrived at Shira's mansion. Quint had the carriage let him off.

"We had a brief visit with Rimo," Quint said before Todo could say anything. "You know, your former master."

"He never was my master. I was an employee. I used to run the mansion for Miro, but when Rimo achieved his master rating, Miro gave him the mansion, and I was demoted to the gate."

"Would Rimo have fired anyone else?"

Todo shrugged. "Yes. Asako was in a similar situation as the First Master's valet. Rimo knew Asako and I were friends and ensured we were fired and banished from the faction."

"Do you expect me to find you a job?" Quint asked.

"Not exactly. I don't lack funds, and neither does Asako. We wanted to know if we could help you with your charter. We thought about the meeting this morning and decided with the warlord's support, there could be some change."

Quint chuckled. "You had less faith in your master than I did, and I'm afraid I have less faith in the warlord than you do. Let's talk about it some more. There might be an opening for a steward at this manor. I can talk to the owner."

"Shira Yomolo?" Asako asked. "You've met her? She is beautiful in every way."

"I can't deny that," Quint said. "Let's see if she's in."

Shira was in the main building, starting lunch with Dugo, Dakuz, and Thera.

"I brought two guests," Quint said.

"The pair who were loitering at my gate?" Shira said. "What are their names?"

Quint made introductions.

"If you are friends of my friends, then join us," Shira said, giving the pair a dazzling smile.

Quint explained the plight of the two wizards.

"With Hari gone, I could use someone to manage the manor. I would expect more than what Hari Bitto did."

While they ate, Todo explained his background to Shira. Quint was surprised at how far Todo had fallen. Only his loyalty to the Three Forks had kept him from walking out on Rimo Gorima. Todo was also closer to achieving master rank than Quint thought.

"We can get you to master status between Dakuz and me if you wish."

Dakuz nodded. "You are never too old if your memory holds."

"Memory has not been my problem."

Shira clapped her hands. "Then let's do this. I will sponsor Todo to achieve master, and he will manage this manor. Quint and his friends can stay here until the charter is approved."

Quint thought that was optimistic, but he wouldn't argue otherwise. Todo seemed to be an honorable sort, but then he had felt the same about Rimo Gorima.

Shira took the two Shimato wizards with her while Quint went to his quarters to contemplate what to tell Chibo Hobona tomorrow at noon. He decided he would be honest with Chibo, although it appeared that honesty was a flexible concept in Shimato.

Although the clock was ticking toward the three-week goal, everyone decided to do nothing about the charter until the military had given them a chance to talk about the charter. Quint still felt it was the right goal, but he was concerned they lacked a viable approach to the organization.

Todo was learning about the manor and the staff, and Asoka followed Todo around, acting like his assistant. Perhaps Todo had arranged for Asoka to fill that role. If so it was fortunate that Shira was the tolerant person that Quint believed her to be.

After dinner, Shira visited Quint in his quarters.

"I wanted to tell you that Todo should do an excellent job. I spent some time with both in the late afternoon, and Todo told me what I should do to improve the running of the manor."

"Good. He wasn't treated well at the Three Forks mansion in the capital."

"It happens," Shira said, sitting across from Quint at the tea table in one of the building's alcoves. She leaned toward him. "What is your goal?"

"Have the warlord approve the charter," Quint said.

"No, no, no. After Shimato. Your friends have told me there is more you must do after leaving Shimato. Hari said you blur predictor strings, and your life could affect the future of the world. Dakuz said you are looking for someone."

"Simo Tapmann. I don't know where he is, but he is a unique individual, and I'm too young to encounter him."

"Too young or too inexperienced?" Shira said.

"Both," Quint said. "My magic may not be sufficient since Simo is likely much more powerful than me. So much so that I might never defeat him in a duel."

"Might?" Shira asked.

Quint nodded. "He is a mysterious character who has gone by at least one other name. A woman asked me to find him. She knows him intimately, but Tapmann has withdrawn from his perch in society, at least in North and South Fenola."

Shira frowned. "She can't find him?"

"I don't know why she asked me rather than do it herself, but I'm honor-bound to find him."

"Honor," Shira said. "She has a hold on you? A woman you love?"

Quint laughed. "I have the greatest respect for her. She taught me a few strings that I didn't know before, and she propels me even now. I lost my magic before I started my journey to Shimato. Her teachings enabled me to replace my magic with something else."

Shira rubbed her arms. "It sounds mysterious and maybe even mystical. I've never heard of another magic."

"It's ancient. Dakuz knows, but he is one of the very few, and I intend to keep it that way until I've found Simo Tapmann."

The woman's lower lip extended into a pout, making Quint smile.

Shira raised her eyebrows and erased the pout from her face. "That won't work to get the information from you?"

"No, it won't," Quint said, almost laughing. The woman's pout was a cut above anything Quint had ever seen, but it was such a blatant act he couldn't keep a straight face. "That will have to do other than I was told Votann was the last place Simo lived."

"You have a long journey ahead of you."

Quint smiled. "I'm looking for adventures that will forge the experiences I need."

Shira sighed. "I wish you well. If you need a female companion to talk to and share your troubles, I will be happy to fulfill that role."

Quint's smile vanished more quickly than Shira's pout. "You aren't serious."

"I am," Shira said. "Your group are all wizards, and I wish to learn. It will take a few years to know my potential, right?"

"It might take that long, or it might take a few months," Quint said. "It all depends on you and your teachers."

"I have reason to believe you four are the best teachers in Shimato. That is why I want you to stay here while you are in Shimato. If you ask me to join you on your travels, I can know when you will leave easier. Todo will always know where I am."

"You are serious."

"I said I was. If you ever run out of funds, I can earn vast sums singing my way through the capitals of the world."

"Dakuz and Dugo can start your training for now."

"No. I want you to train me," Shira said.

"Dakuz for a week with the basics. He was my teacher and is better at the simple part. You can come to me at any time with questions. Fair enough?"

Shira narrowed her eyes with a slight smile on her face. "I can live with that. When can I get started?"

"Now. I'll find Dakuz. Where will you be?"

"Right here."

Quint left her and found Dakuz listening to one of Dugo's stories.

"Shira wants to learn magic. I convinced her that you teach her a week of the basics," Quint said.

"I'll do it," Dugo said enthusiastically.

"You want her well-grounded?" Dakuz asked.

Quint nodded. "You can assess her abilities better than I can. I've got some thinking to do before we meet with Chibo Hobona tomorrow. Could you start right now? She's in my quarters, and I can think there while you are working with her."

Dakuz shrugged. "I've had worse duties." He looked at Dugo. "I can hear the rest of your fascinating story tomorrow."

Dugo looked very disappointed, but it wasn't because of the story.

Shira was doodling something at Quint's desk when they walked in.

"Dakuz can get you started, but I'll be here, working out what to discuss with War Leader Hobona."

Dakuz took Shira to the sitting area, and Quint took Shira's place at his desk. The woman was an artist in drawing and singing he decided as he set aside her doodling.

Quint wrote down the names of the players he knew in the drama he found himself in. It seemed that Kippunese could put on a good front and let the teeth come out once they were ready to pursue their interests. Hari and Rimo were two excellent examples.

Chibo seemed to be more benign, at least the current manifestation of Chibo. Quint would have had a better idea of his true character if he had found out what the soldiers would have done to them in the morning after their abduction. Would they have tortured Quint's group or would they have released them as the climax to a joke?

Shira was a surprise. She cut Hari out of her life instantly, but then the wizard had spent years betraying her. Todo and his friend were untested, but they were Shira's responsibility now, not his.

The uncertainty almost overwhelmed Quint as he thought about it, but then, with perfect knowledge of all that happened, he knew at any given time, events could reduce certainly to uncertainty, and in his few conversations with the goddess Tova, uncertainty was part of her life as well. He suspected her glimpses into the future were much better than using a predictor string.

Quint concluded he had to deal with the present and assumed that everyone couldn't be trusted entirely. In other words, Kippun was no different than anywhere else he had been, even at home with his parents. The best solution was to be prepared for everything, knowing that he could be put in danger at a moment's notice.

He heard Shira raise her voice and then Dakuz followed that up with some grumbling comment. Quint left his desk and found the two on their feet, glaring at each other.

"What's going on?" Quint asked.

"He," Shira pointed her finger at Dakuz, "is asking personal questions. I refuse to answer."

Dakuz rolled his eyes.

"What personal questions?" Quint asked his friend.

"I asked her when she noticed her magic begin to blossom, and she became defensive."

Shira frowned. "It was during a sensitive time of my youth," she said.

"Moving from childhood to womanhood?" Quint asked.

Shira's eyes grew. "Yes, if you must know."

Quint sighed and Dakuz folded his arms, looking away. "That is the time for most wizards' magic to grow along with the rest of you."

"He didn't have to put it so personally," Shira said.

Dakuz sat down and Quint suggested that Shira do likewise.

"Magic is very personal," Quint said. "I was a developing adolescent when I first noticed my magic, and a few weeks later, I was impressed with Racellia's wizard corps. Dakuz is only personal," Quint sneaked a glimpse of Dakuz before turning back to Shira, "because everyone is different, and indicators of that difference are within you. If you want to learn magic and about yourself and magic, you need to open and accept that questioning is needed to understand where you've come from to assess your potential."

"It is necessary?" Shira said, her face slightly flush.

"Give him some leeway. As I said, he's better at this diagnostic stuff than I am," Quint said.

"All right," Shira said.

Dakuz nodded to Quint and shooed him out of the area. Quint was glad to leave. He didn't know if what he said was right, but knowing that Shira had a temperamental streak was useful.

When he returned to his desk, he put a discreet note by her name. He was relieved that she calmed down when he entered. Quint would have had no choice but to reject her offer to travel with them if she hadn't.

He laughed at the thought. Shira was impulsive and temperamental, and maybe her earnestness to travel with them would fade away as the days passed. In fact, he hoped it would. He wouldn't like Shira and Thera to fight over him.

Quint shook his head and reminded himself that the world didn't revolve around him.

CHAPTER EIGHT

CHIBO ARRIVED AS THE SUN PEAKED IN THE SKY with an entourage of five soldiers, all dressed like common guards. They looked like the ones he had met in the inn, including Narisu.

"I don't have much time," Chibo said as they sat in the main hall.

"Are you going to reject the charter concept?" Quint asked. "That won't take much time."

"No, no, no," Chibo said. "I like the concept more now that I've thought about it. So, count me as a supporter. How has your work gone with the wizard factions? Hari Bitto isn't a supporter any longer. I found him complaining about you to one of Bunto's ministers."

"There is a reason for that," Quint said.

"I already know a few, and those are enough."

"I met with the Three Forks and found that Rimo Gorima intended to take over the charter organization. When I rejected him, we were tossed out of the Three Forks mansion along with a couple of servants who had been nice to us," Quint said.

"Gorima has been under his mother's thumb for most of his life and is anxious to get out. It hasn't happened yet, you should know," Chibo said.

"Can you improve the integration of the wizard corps into your plans?" Quint asked.

Narisu scooted forward in his chair. "We liked your overall concepts, but mixing wizards and soldiers doesn't work so well."

Chibo nodded. "Wizards don't like following orders, so they do their own thing and…"

"And they become pesky," Quint said. "Is that the source of the warlord's dissatisfaction?"

"Most of it," Chibo said.

"Did you come up with any ideas?"

Chibo laughed. "Am I supposed to do your work?"

"If you want to," Quint said. "I don't have first-hand knowledge of your issues, and I intend to help, not hinder, your effectiveness." He explained how the wizard corps worked in Racellia again.

"We have reason to think there will be a border incursion by Chokuno fief in a week. Why don't you see Shimato's wizards in action? We can both observe and lend some leadership. Border squabbles typically consist of a few battles, and everyone goes back home to tend to the wounded and bury the dead."

"What about my three-week deadline?" Quint asked.

"I will put you in contact with the two major wizard factions. Most of the wizard corps members are from their ranks. You'll have a few days with the men on the road and then a few days in the field. Bumoto will be more interested in that than your talks with the factions, anyway."

Quint felt he had no choice, and when he was gone, Dakuz would be finished assessing Shira's potential.

"Have a wizard from each faction accompany us so I can talk to them about the charter, and I'll go. I will take one of my group with me."

"The female fighter?"

Quint nodded. "She has more battle experience than I do, and we are both strategists. When will you leave?"

"Tomorrow morning. I'll be here with some of my staff. We can discuss the charter on the trip, as well."

Quint saw Chibo out the gate. Todo came up to Quint after the war leader was gone.

"Do you know who he is?"

"War Leader Chibo Hobona," Quint said.

"You do know him," Todo said. "What makes you think you can trust him?"

"Nothing. How can I trust anyone, even you, Todo," Quint asked.

Todo smiled. "Good! Experience is the best way to evaluate trust. Words mean nothing."

"I wouldn't say nothing, but words carry no innate credibility, only actions," Quint said. "Right?"

Todo grinned and nodded.

"I'll accompany Chibo to the border to witness the warlord's forces in action. I'll be gone for a week. Make sure you give Shira Yomolo every reason to trust you."

"I will. Don't worry about that," Todo said.

Quint found Shira had moved her lesson to the main hall, continuing lessons with Dakuz. She sat with a writing board on her lap, taking notes.

"Am I doing well, Dakuz?" Shira said as Quint walked in.

"You are. We should get to some basic strings during the first week," Dakuz said.

"I'll be gone for a week starting tomorrow," Quint said. "Thera and I will travel to a battle site with Chibo Hobona to observe how Shimato's wizards perform."

"Shira and I can continue to work?"

"If you both agree. Dugo may help you since I don't have an assignment for him," Quint said. "Chibo will bring two members of the big factions so we can continue to talk about the charter. He liked what we have written so far."

"So he says," Dakuz said.

"At least he said something," Quint said. "He admitted that most of the warlord's frustration is on the battlefield. Wizards are like an army of cats."

Shira laughed. "Every member moving around at their whim?"

Quint nodded. "That will have to stop if we are to succeed."

§

Thera and Quint waited for Chibo, who didn't arrive until after lunch.

"My wizard friends sometimes disregard the importance of time," Chibo said to Quint.

Quint looked back at Chibo's entourage to see two men dressed as civilians. They had to be the wizards. Their arrogant faces irritated Quint even before he met them.

Chibo introduced Quint and Thera to the others. The soldiers were from the inn and had seen Quint before, but the wizards looked pained.

"This is Thera Vanitz, formerly of the Narukun Wizard Corps, and this is Quinto Tirolo," Chibo said. "He is a master from Racellia on South Fenola.

I have given Quint a temporary commission in the Shimato military to lead the wizard contingent if required."

"You are a braver man than me, War Leader Hobona," one of the wizards said. "How can you trust a teenager, even if he claims to be a wizard master." The wizard turned to Quint. "And how many strings do you think you know?"

"Over one hundred. I have mastery of over eighty. Knowing and mastering are two different things," Quint said.

"Is he trying to tell us something?" the wizard, Kimo, said from the Shouting Hawk faction

"Since you asked me, let me ask both of you. How many strings do you know?"

The two wizards looked like Quint had slapped them in the face.

"How rude. If you must know, I command more than thirty," Kimo said.

"Forty-three as of this month," the other, Roshan, said.

Quint nodded. This pair was far from what Quint considered master level, he suspected. "Do you want a demonstration?"

"I suppose so," Roshan said. "We have a master in the Shining String faction."

"When we are on the road," Quint said.

"Afraid to fail?" Kimo asked.

"No. I don't want to leave a mess."

Ten minutes later, Quint spotted a dying tree. Its branches dropped, and the leaves had turned light green and were falling off.

"We can stop here," Quint said. "Note that I am using one hand."

Roshan sneered. "Impossible. There are no such things as one-handed strings."

Quint pointed with his chin. "The sick tree." He used his left hand and created an explosive lightning string. Using Tova's magic, what would have been a lightning spear was now much more.

He cast the string, holding the reins with his right hand. The lightning bunched as it traveled through the air and obliterated the dying tree with a loud bang.

Kimo covered his face with an arm. "Gruesome! You shouldn't be able to do that."

"And yet, I did," Quint said. "One-handed. I have some special strings that I have learned that I doubt few can duplicate."

"You would kill whoever was struck by that bolt," Roshan said, his voice suddenly respectful.

"That should end the youth and inexperience comments," Quint said.

"It does for me," Chibo said.

Thera chuckled. "He has outdueled Green masters, who I had thought were more powerful." Quint almost winced since he knew a few Green wizards would have killed him if he hadn't removed them from the world. Thera continued, "The Green masters he had defeated disappeared, but Quint was almost killed in his last fight."

"But you mean to change Shimato's wizard contingent?" Timo said. His tone wasn't as humbled as his fellow wizard.

"I do. Have you heard about the wizard charter I have developed for the warlord?" Quint asked.

"I've heard you are doing something, or Lord Bunto will kick you out of the fief," Timo said.

Thera handed both wizards copies of the latest draft of the charter.

"Read those today, and we will talk about it tonight. You'll understand what Quint is trying to do," Chibo said.

They stopped at a roadside rest stop. Neither wizard had spoken much to Chibo and hadn't engaged Quint after the demonstration. However, they had been busy murmuring to each other and had been reading the charter when Chibo reiterated it would be a good idea for them to do so.

Before the sun set, they rode into a town. It wasn't a market day, so everything looked a little sleepy. Narisu said they would be staying in the best inn in the town and the surrounding area.

Quint believed him when they rode into the courtyard of a four-story inn that looked like a squat tower sitting on one side of the courtyard with a stable on the far side and a two-story building facing the gate. Narisu led them into the two-story part.

"War Leader Chibo Hobona and his entourage," Narisu said to the female attendant at the counter.

"The fourth level is taken," the woman said. "A contingent of visitors from Gamiza fief. There are good rooms on the second level facing away from the courtyard."

"We'll take those," Chibo said. "I'll restrain myself from kicking the foreigners out."

The woman looked relieved and handed keys to Narisu, showing him which was for the war leader.

"An hour's rest," Chibo said, "then we eat dinner in the restaurant behind the counter."

Narisu pulled Quint aside and gave him a key. "Take all your belongings and lock your door with magic. I'll be locking Chibo's door as well as my own."

"You're a magician?"

Narisu produced half a smile. "It's a poorly kept secret. Personally, I like your charter. Don't give up, no matter what happens."

Chibo's companion gave keys to the others and suggested locking their doors. The escorts were given rooms in dormitories on the second floor of the restaurant building.

After resting and washing up, Quint entered the restaurant. The escort had already taken a table for themselves, and Timo was talking to Narisu at a table for six. The others hadn't arrived, but Thera tapped Quint on the shoulder.

"Chibo is right behind me," she said.

"Where is Roshan?" Narisu asked when they arrived. Chibo walked quickly into the restaurant.

"The other wizard has left us to join the party from Gamiza. I wouldn't have known if I hadn't passed him talking to the Gamizans," Chibo said. "I'm not sure if he will join us tomorrow." The war leader grimaced and sat at the table. "Roshan is more Green than I suspected."

"Are there many Greens in Shimato fief?" Thera asked Chibo, shooting a quick glance at Quint.

"The warlord is suspicious of them, and for good reason. He doesn't encourage Green-influenced soldiers in his military," Narisu said.

Chibo ordered a family-style meal. "I always like sharing the table with everyone," the war leader said. "It builds camaraderie. Besides, you need to broaden your exposure to Kippunese food."

Quint knew camaraderie was essential to the war leader from his encounter when Chibo and his "family" abducted them. He heard loud voices from a party entering the restaurant and spotted Roshan pointing Quint out to his new hosts, saying something that made the Gamizans laugh. Perhaps Roshan wasn't as impressed by his background, Quint thought.

Chibo watched intently as the Gamiza group sat on the opposite side of the restaurant. Timo asked Chibo a question, but the war leader raised a finger to stop the conversation as he continued to glare from across the room.

"Narisu?" Chibo said.

"They don't want to believe Roshan, but two others in the group have heard about Quint's fighting their best wizards in Narukun."

Quint was surprised that Narisu was so adept at reading lips unless he employed a listening string that was new to Quint.

"Roshan has been told less than politely that he can't join the group, but they want to use him as an observer."

Chibo nodded. "That's enough. Let them talk."

Narisu created a tiny string and cast it. Quint guessed that Chibo's aide cast a string when he passed Roshan in the corridor. He would have to see if Narisu was willing to trade strings.

"Are you going to send Roshan home?" Thera asked.

Chibo chuckled. "No. If we know where our conversations are going, we can feed the Gamizans whatever we want." He glared at Timo. "That includes you."

"I'm no Green," Timo said.

Good!" Chibo snorted. "Now, let's enjoy our meal. It should be a treat for our guests."

Quint didn't classify the Kippunese food as a treat, but it was better than most, adhering more closely to Slinnon culinary practice.

After dinner, Quint took Thera outside for a walk around the inn. "What did you think of dinner?" Quint asked.

"You are a better judge of that than I am," Thera said with a smile. "I can't rid myself of the sludge served as Kippunese food in the capital."

Quint shook his head. "Not the food, Roshan and the Gamizans."

"I'm not sure I can believe that Roshan would go to the other side so easily."

"Right. I don't think there is a listening string after reviewing all the strings I know."

"Chibo is playing us?"

"He likes his games," Quint said. "Maybe the Gamizans aren't Gamizans."

"You mean this is an elaborate ruse for our benefit. Do you think Chibo would bother going to such lengths?"

Quint shrugged and smiled. "We must be ready for anything. I could be wrong, but Chibo's glare and the lip reading seemed off."

"It seemed off to me that we would be staying at an inn where Gamizans happened to be," Thera said. "Greens have too much influence. Is Chibo a Green?"

Quint sighed. "I don't know. I was hoping you would have a better idea than me. As I said, we should be ready for anything. It will be dangerous on the battlefield, but perhaps everything will reveal itself along the way."

Thera groaned. "As long as we can survive the truth."

§

Roshan had rejoined them and didn't seem fazed by his rejection by the Gamizans the night before. Chibo didn't speak to him while they prepared to leave the inn, but all this could be an act for Quint's benefit.

"Where are the Gamizans?" Thera asked Narisu as they left the town.

"Still at the inn," Narisu said. "I'm sure they wouldn't want to approach the battlefield with us or before us. Our forces might do something untoward."

"You openly fight the Gamizans?" she asked.

"Sometimes. Only a skirmish or a brawl in a pub."

"Like last night?" Quint asked.

"They were on good behavior, weren't they?" Narisu said.

Chibo turned around for a quick look at his aid. "With Quint in our midst, I'm sure they wouldn't dare be unruly."

It didn't stop Chibo from abducting him on his first night in Shimato's capital, but the situation was different, and Quint didn't quite know how different it was. Neither Narisu nor Chibo said anything revealing.

"I didn't get my conversation about the charter," Quint said.

Chibo nodded. "We can rectify that at our rest stop."

"I'll make sure you get your information," Narisu said, half-smiling. He turned to Roshan and Kimo riding in the rear. "Did you get that?"

The two wizards looked at each other and nodded. Quint fell out of the line and ended up at the back of their column before Chibo's escort. He didn't trust anyone to make sure the wizards commented on the charter, but Quint also couldn't trust what the two men said.

Roshan looked back at Quint and narrowed his eyes. Quint fell back and talked to the first two riders of the escort group.

"Please make sure the wizards don't run away," Quint said loudly enough for the wizards ahead to hear.

The officer in charge grinned. "The order has already been given." The soldier gave a reply that the wizards definitely heard.

Quint wouldn't get anything else from riding in the middle of the column other than a bigger helping of dust. He rode back into line beside Thera.

She smiled at him and said, "We all heard your request."

"Yes, we did," Narisu said. "Good move."

The exchange made Quint feel a little more secure about Chibo and Narisu, but his anxiety about the wizards, particularly Roshan, increased.

They reached the roadside stop. The food seemed to be prepared by a Narukun chef and was a big step backward as far as Quint thought. The Kippunese didn't seem to mind.

"Now, the charter," Quint said.

Roshan said he didn't like the idea of a unified wizardry in Shimato. His faction would lose power. Kimo was more circumspect. He admitted his faction wouldn't exercise its current privileges, but he could see his unaffiliated friends benefitting from an organization.

"What benefits do you get from being in a faction?" Quint asked Kimo. Roshan's comments weren't productive, and Quint ignored him except when Roshan left to go into the woods.

Kimo scratched his head. "Your charter makes it a social alliance."

"Is that bad? How does being in a faction make you a better wizard?" Thera asked.

"I have wizards who see me as their superior."

"Like a lieutenant in the military?" Quint asked.

"Similar."

"And what happens when a senior wizard asks you to do something?" Narisu asked.

Kimo raised his eyebrows. "You should already know," he said to Narisu.

"You fall into line like everyone else, but how does your faction improve your life?"

"It's a job," Kimo said.

"Can a faction hire wizards under the charter?" Narisu asked.

"I didn't read anything that said they couldn't," Kimo said.

Quint smiled. "So, if you want to take orders from your faction, you can still do that. With the charter, if you wish to leave your faction, you can without consequences. You'd probably have a hard time doing that now."

Kimo just nodded and looked at Narisu and then Quint.

"If you want to join the military, you can do so without a faction and without paying the faction a percentage of your wages," Quint said.

"How did you know about that?"

Quint smiled. "From the Three Forks. The only people who will be disadvantaged by the charter will be the top leaders of each faction, but even then, it depends on the wizard and the charter."

"I'll have to think some more while we travel."

"Then I'll give you that opportunity," Quint said. "You can talk it over with your friend, Roshan. I need to leave you for a few minutes."

"Going into the woods like Roshan?" Thera said, smiling through pursed lips.

"Very likely," Quint said.

Quint walked through a clearing and into the vegetation to relieve himself and was in an almost defenseless position when he heard rustling coming from behind nearby bushes.

Quint backed away as he hitched up his trousers, looking for cover. He created a string in each hand as he bumped into a tree and heard a voice behind him.

"You are surrounded. Raise your hands, fingers outstretched."

Quint dropped onto the forest floor as a spear of flame hit the tree where he was standing. Quint rolled away, turned his palm toward the sound, and cast a potent sleeping spell. He heard a few bodies drop. Quint crouched down as he stood up. Another lightning bolt brushed his back before he moved behind the tree, trying not to step on the inert bodies. Roshan was one of them.

He heard rustling in the direction of the attacks and cast his other sleep spell toward the bushes. The sounds stopped.

Quint carefully approached the bushes, but there were no attacks. There were the seven Gamizans at the restaurant's table, including Roshan as Quint recalled. He had the seven slumbering men dragged into the clearing.

Quint stood above the bodies. Three of them had held weapons, and four must have been wizards.

"We wondered if a wild beast had eaten you," Chibo said, entering the clearing and looking at the line of bodies along with three escorts and Narisu. "Are they dead?" Chibo asked.

Narisu shook his head, kneeling by Roshan. "Sleeping string." He looked at Quint. "We decided to follow Roshan after you left the roadside rest stop, and it looks like you found him before we did."

"Excuse me while I make sure they didn't start a fire," Quint said.

He left Chibo and his men inspecting the bodies as he returned to the woods and employed a water string to quench the smoldering bark on the tree. He bent over to pick up a weapon dropped by one of his assailants and felt some pain in his back. A one-handed water string quenched whatever was still hot on his back before returning to the clearing. The sleeping Gamizans and Roshan were being stripped to their underwear.

"You can kill them if you want," Chibo said. "Fortunes of war and all that."

"Waking up unclothed in the woods is punishment enough," Quint said, "but wrap their hands tightly. There are wizards among them."

Narisu nudged one of the bodies with his foot. "Why didn't you cast that sleeping string on us when we first met?"

"I would have put half the inn to sleep," Quint said. "That wouldn't have been the case when I woke up later, but Hari Bitto had rescued us, so I didn't need to do anything."

"I suppose the rescue was fortunate for the both of us," Chibo said. "Can you extend their slumber?"

Quint nodded and applied another sleeping string. One of Chibo's men had stood too close and fell to the ground.

Chibo grimaced. "Now we have to carry him out. I have my other men looking for their horses. We'll take those and make their lives a little more difficult."

"I suggest you leave them here," Quint said. "A little hardship getting back to the road will do them some good."

Chibo laughed. "You aren't as soft as I thought."

Soft enough not to kill sleeping men, Quint thought.

When they returned to the roadside stop, Chibo's party mounted and took the Gamizan horses. Narisu led them off the track and into a village of woodcutters a few hours later.

"I bring gifts," Chibo said, leaving the horses. He laughed as they galloped away toward the battlefield. "I know a few good veterans living in that village," the war leader said. "The horses will be welcome."

CHAPTER NINE

They spent another night in a less glorious inn at a market village. It wasn't originally on their route, but it was after their detour to drop off the Gamizan horses.

Three hours after breakfast, guards stopped them at a barricade across a road.

"Battleground ahead," one of the guards who wore a little braid on his uniform tunic said. "What is your business?"

One of the other guards put a hand to his forehead. "You don't recognize War Leader Hobona, do you?" the lead guard said to his companion.

The offending guard stood ramrod straight and saluted along with the others. "You may proceed. There was only a skirmish so far," the lead guard said. "Do you know the way?"

"We do," Narisu said, waiting for the barricade to be removed.

Narisu conferred with the officer of Chibo's escort before sending them off to lead them into the Shimato military camp.

Soldiers and support troops scurried around, erecting tents and fire rings. Food was being stationed at every fire and the ground was being pounded into dust with all the activity.

The skirmish was still underway a mile away, a commander said, reporting to Chibo.

"We are observers," the war leader said. "I'm not in the chain of command. Unless I am needed, you remain in charge. How many men in the field?"

"Three hundred before casualties," the commander said. "Most have been injuries. Not many are dead. I'll have men take your horses if you come with me into the command tent."

Kimo joined Chibo, Narisu, Thera, and Quint as they followed the commander through the activity to the command tent.

"My two best officers run the skirmish with a third of my contingent. We have just moved closer to the border."

"How close?" Kimo asked.

The commander almost sneered at the wizard as he pointed to the map unrolled on a table. Dressed rocks held the edges down.

"We are still unpacking," the commander said to Chibo.

"Whatever works in the field," Chibo said.

"Right, sir," the commander said. He pointed to the map. "The Chokunese plunged three miles into our territory. We think their objective was to loot the town of Nimogata."

Quint noticed that Chibo was initially headed to that town. "Does the town have anything of particular value?"

The commander shook his head. "It is an easy target. It's been hit before. I have almost a hundred men stationed in the town in case the Chokunese split their forces and come from a different direction."

"It has defenses?" Thera asked.

"Stone walls, but the townspeople aren't adept at defense. Our forces are stretched thin on the border, so we converge when the enemy attacks."

"Any wizards in your contingent?" Chibo said with a half-smile.

"Most of my wizards are at Nimogata. Wizards aren't of much use in the field. You know that."

Thera pursed her lips and grabbed the hilt of her sword.

"There are four wizards in front of you," Chibo said.

"Major Narisu, I know, but the others, sir?"

"Thera Vanitz has just been detached from the Narukun military, Kimo is a member of a capital faction, and Quinto Tirolo is a master wizard from South Fenola," Chibo said.

"A master?" The commander looked appraisingly at Quint. "So young. You must be good to have attracted the attention of Shimato's war leader."

"Attracted enough," Chibo said. "He defeated a small force of Gamizans who attacked him yesterday."

"With your escorts?" the commander asked.

"Alone while he was communing with nature if you know what I mean."

"Wizards and soldiers?" the commander asked again.

"Both. It was only seven," Quint said.

The commander sputtered. "Seven against one?"

Chibo nodded and responded to the commander. "I arrived on the scene while Quint was dragging the bodies into a clearing. He put them to sleep." The war leader laughed. "We stripped them and left them to wake up without clothes and possessions. That was Quint's idea. Kimo, Quint, and Thera are here to observe. They will instruct me how to better use wizards in the field."

"With respect, sir."

Chibo smiled. "Yes?"

"Wizards don't work on the battlefield. All they do is spout flame and wind and lightning for a few feet and expect the opposing forces to lay down their arms," the commander said.

Quint and Thera tell me otherwise," Chibo said.

"A squad isn't enough for a thousand men," Quint said. "Fifty to a few hundred could be employed effectively depending on the strategy employed. Do the Chokunese use wizards?"

The commander shrugged. Something Quint was sure he wouldn't do in response to anything Chibo said. "Why?"

"Can we go to the front line and see how the skirmish was fought?" Thera asked.

"Or is it being fought," Narisu said. "The troops are still in the field. Are you up to it?"

"I am," Thera said. "Is there an observation post overlooking the battlefield?"

The commander laughed. "You don't know the terrain at the border. Flat as a lake with trees all around. It might be dangerous."

"I would be casting a shield," Thera said. "That wouldn't stop everything, but I will try it."

Quint nodded. "We are here to give Chibo our perspective on using organized wizardry."

"They are," Chibo said. "Narisu and my escort troops are already wearing armor. We are willing."

The commander sighed. "Very well. It could be my life if anything happens to you."

"And it may be your life if you refuse me," Chibo said.

The commander straightened up. "Yes, sir," he said, saluting. "I will lead you."

Quint didn't believe that for a second. The commander would have someone else lead, but the man would accompany them to the battlefield.

When the commander returned after donning his armor, Kimo said he would prefer to help defend the camp. Chibo laughed when the wizard begged off a trip into harm's way. Chibo reacted differently when the commander said if Kimo stayed, he would also remain in the camp to protect the guest. He called his senior officer to take his place.

"Let's get going while there is still light to get there and back," Chibo said.

The detachment was twenty strong, including Chibo's escort, Quint, Thera, and a squad of cavalry to protect the commander's officer.

The fighting was supposed to be half an hour from the camp, but they could hear the sounds of battle before then. Quint was relieved that the Shimato troops weren't in retreat.

The commander's officer held up his hand. "Most of the skirmish is taking place in a large meadow not far away."

They picked their way through the forest. At least there wasn't much underbrush to impede their progress. Quint would ask Chibo if he wanted a shield, but Narisu had already performed that service for his superior and the escort troops during their current stop.

Quint drew his sword, and Thera followed Quint's example.

Soldiers fought on either side of a wide creek, splitting the meadow. Quite a few skirmishes had been fought at the site since there were rock walls on both sides of the large stream that looked like they had been there for years.

"Where are we regarding the border?" Quint asked.

The commander's officer spoke up. "We are a mile and a half inside our border."

They stayed inside the treeline on the Shimato side of the meadow. The Shimato fighters surprised Quint by two or three running to the edge of the creek and hurling verbal insults at the Chokunese soldiers.

A few arrows sped past the soldiers, and one of the soldiers was proficient enough to dodge arrows and waded across, striking the archers down with his sword.

"An enhancement string," Thera said. "That wizard can't hold that up for long."

As she said it, an arrow got through and struck the fighter in the calf. The game was over, and two Shimato soldiers dragged the wounded one back behind the rocks.

Quint turned to the commander's officer. "What is the strategy here?" Quint asked. "Do you fight for a week or so from behind your defenses and then return home?"

Chibo smiled. "Yes, what is the strategy?" he said to the officer, who looked nervous.

"That's what we generally do."

"A squad of good wizards could blast holes in the enemy's wall, and you could drive them back to the border," Quint said. "Unless you have another motive for engineering a stalemate. I would guess an uninterested party would surmise that someone is getting rich off resupplying after the stalemates. If the fighting stops, the income stops. Am I right?"

The officer's face turned red. "Of course not. You are accusing us of treason."

Quint sighed. "I'm presenting an alternative to a waste of time and soldiers."

Chibo looked at Narisu with an amused expression. "What would you suggest to budge the Chokunese out of the meadow and spank them hard enough to send them back to the border."

"Do you ever change how you fight the Chokunese?" Quint asked.

"Why would we? Border skirmishes are great for training purposes," the commander said. "If we don't fight, we lose the ability to wage war."

Chibo sputtered but remained quiet.

"I'd like to see a map of the area," Quint said. "Thera, help me sketch out an attack."

They dismounted, stepped away from the others, and devised a plan with a wizardry element and a conventional attack before returning and showing their strategy to Chibo, Narisu, the commander's officer.

Quint looked at Chibo. "Do you want to see some action?"

"I'm not averse to getting my hands a little bloody," Chibo said. "The commander said there can't be more than a wizard or two over there. I don't think any of our troops have sufficient magic to blow a hole in the way you envision."

"Nor do I," said a grinning Narisu.

"Then shall we execute the plan? Thera and I will do the sapping. We both know how to create explosions."

"We have a few wizards," the officer said.

"Are they trained? Can they break apart a rock wall?" Chibo asked.

"How am I supposed to know that, sir?" the officer said.

Chibo grimaced and turned to Quint. "You two do that on your own, but I can see how a squad can work from what you've planned."

Chibo and Narisu took over, leaving the commander's officer as a spectator. A junior officer gathered five wizards.

"Our contingent," the young officer said as he delivered the soldiers.

Quint took the four men and one woman aside and quizzed them on their abilities. He had each demonstrate their best shield. None were effective against anything more than a thrown dirt clod. It looked like Thera, and Quint would do all the wizardry.

"Useless for what we are going to do," Quint said when they returned. "We can attack when you are ready,"

"Fifteen minutes," Narisu said. Chibo's aide gathered the leaders of the Shimato military.

§

Quint looked at Thera. She would be his protection if his strings depleted too much of his magic. If the rock wall was cemented, he could use a string to weaken the bonds, but these were big, loose rocks. The officer claimed the wall on the Shimato side was built the same way. Quint wished he had a chance to test his string, but if he did, the enemy would be tipped off.

The sun was dipping, casting long shadows from the surrounding trees. Narisu tapped Quint on the shoulder. "We are as ready as can be."

Quint nodded, slipped around one end of the wall, headed across the meadow, crouched down, and snaked toward the enemy. He and Thera moved along the creek that bisected the meadow until they reached the center and moved toward the enemy wall one hundred paces toward Chokuno fief. Reaching his central position was the signal for the Shimato troops to begin their movements from either side of the wall.

Arrows began to reach them, bouncing off their magical shields. Quint didn't have to reach the walls to cast the strings, but he had to give the troops time to get into position. A lightning bolt lit up the field, missing Thera and hitting the creek with a hiss. Fire spears and more lightning continued but weakened and stopped. Whoever did the casting had used up their magic.

It wasn't time. Quint looked left and then right until he spotted troop movements at the edge of the meadow. Quint waited as Thera, and he were flat on the ground until Quint felt the troops were ready to attack. He rose on his knees and built his strings. The glow of the magic would soon be seen as the light began to fail.

He gathered his Tova-based magic and cast the multi-string spell at the wall. Quint had combined lightning and earthquake strings and watched the bright ball of lightning hit the wall. The rocks exploded as the earth shook. His shield protected him from rocks that had become projectiles.

"Are you uninjured?" Quint asked Thera.

"My mind is unsettled, but my shield held. I wasn't prepared for anything close to that strong."

Quint shook his head. "That makes two of us."

When the dust settled, Quint groaned. Ahead of him was a large gap, perhaps fifteen feet wide in the wall. Bodies were spread out on the other side and Chokuno troops were running in full retreat toward the forest on the other side. There would be no more fighting for the day.

Narisu stood in the gap with fists on his hips and beckoned Quint to join him.

"I've called for wagons to remove the wounded and the bodies," Chibo's aide said.

Quint viewed the back of the wall. He didn't want to count the damage, but not all the troops died. He did spot Roshan, the wizard, among the casualties.

"The Gamizans joined them," Thera said, nudging Roshan's body with her foot. "Perhaps they provided the magical attacks once they found clothes to wear."

"Does it matter?" Quint said.

"It sure does," Narisu said. "I'm sure Chibo is going to visit Nimogata next."

"A sieged town requires a different strategy," Quint said.

Narisu grinned. "Of course it does."

They rummaged around the battlefield and decided that at least three more Gamizans were killed when Quint blasted the wall.

Chibo expressed his gratitude as they rode back to the Shimato camp to spend the night, passing empty wagons heading into the meadow to be filled with the casualties and left on the other side of the meadow for the Chokuno troops to fetch.

"I can't say I'm sorry you were pressed into action," Chibo said. "If we had an army as courageous as you two, we would be invincible."

"It seems that no one is invincible," Quint said. "I'd be more worried about an alliance of the Chokuno troops and the Gamizans. The Gamizans aren't afraid of using wizards."

"And you think we are?" Chibo asked.

"I do, unfortunately," Quint said. "I think Thera would agree."

The young woman frowned. "I do, but that isn't the only problem. Narisu's attack would be as effective," she said. "I think the problem on both sides was that no one was eager for a victory. The warlord has a leadership problem as much as he does a wizard problem."

"Am I part of that problem?" Chibo asked.

"I don't know," Thera said, "Are you?"

Chibo tugged at his lower lip. "I suppose I am. I promoted that idiot who never left the camp."

Quint chuckled. "I think you are saved by the Chokunese being the same as you, but you noticed the Gamizans baring their teeth along with them. Unexpected alliances can destroy the status quo, and I would guess the fiefdoms have been stable for some time."

"Stable enough, and I was worrying about the Green influence among the Gamizans but not the Chokunese," Chibo said. "Why are you two so smart?"

"Almost as smart as me?" Narisu asked.

Chibo raised a finger. "Not quite, but they may be catching up."

They arrived in camp in darkness. Narisu rode in front with magic light, and Thera rode behind the detachment. Chibo, Quint, and the commander's officer rode close to Narisu. The soldiers at the meadow would spend the night ensuring the enemy didn't reclaim any land.

The commander was finishing up his dinner with Kimo and his staff when he saw the war leader and stood. "How was the skirmish?"

"Routed," Chibo said. "Congratulations to your troops."

The commander's eyes widened. "There was a decisive action?"

The commander's officer dismounted and gave an account of the skirmish.

"You made a hole in the enemy's rock wall?" the commander said to Quint.

"Roshan is dead?" Kimo stood, shocked.

"Yes, to both," Quint said. "The Gamizans managed to find clothes and mounts and joined with your enemy and fell to the shards of exploded rock."

"Gamizans." The commander looked shocked. "That could change things."

"It does," Chibo said. "You'll be getting more work if you are up to it."

Quint and Narisu answered more questions as they were served the kind of Kippunese cuisine offered in Narukun.

"What will you do, sir?" the commander asked Chibo.

"We will disinfect the local town," the war leader said. "I want you to set up patrols to make sure things don't get out of hand. I will lead a force to check on Nimogata, and then it will be time to head back to the capital."

∽

CHAPTER TEN

IN THE CENTER OF A LONG VALLEY FILLED WITH CROPS was the town of Nimogata. It wasn't large by any means, but large enough and central enough to serve as the local market. Stone walls surrounded the town, and Quint was glad mortar joined the stones. The town should have a strong defense, but he was concerned about the smoke tendrils twisting their way into the sky from the west side of town.

"Narisu, take men through the city gate but watch for an ambush. Quint, Thera, and I will head to the west gate. The entrance has seen a recent attack," Chibo said.

The war leader accurately described the state of the wall. The gate had been chiefly destroyed by lightning bolts and fire spears, as evidenced by the state of what was left of the wood. The enemy had run into the town, setting fires, but were quickly repulsed. The Chokunese then created a defensive barricade facing the smoking gate, but they had retreated out of arrow range before launching an attack.

"They want a defensive presence in case the townspeople counterattack through the gate," Narisu said.

"Are you thinking of blowing the barricade up, too?" Thera asked.

Quint stared at the defenses. "Why waste the magic? Let's burn it down."

Quint and Thera cast fresh shields and were close enough to set the barricade ablaze. There were no Chokunese magicians watching the barricade while the pair walked around setting the wood on fire until the enemy belatedly decided to protect their barricade.

"What should we do now?" Chibo asked with an amused look.

"Ask them to surrender?" Thera said.

"And if that doesn't work?"

"Then reinforce the entrance and march from the opposite ends of town while the enemy is collecting at this gate. Our forces can attack from three points: left, right, and ahead. We will let them surrender before we have a big battle," Narisu said.

"Simple," Quint said. "First a drenching." Quint climbed up a particularly rough side of the wall next to the gate and cast water spells to stop some of the burning in the west part of the city. Then, with his shield preventing him from getting skewered, he cast a downpour onto the enemy soldiers who had begun to gather behind the barricade.

Quint waved to Chibo, and a few riders took off for the eastern entrance. A lightning bolt emerged from the barricade and energized Quint's shield.

"You can surrender. We are currently reinforcing the city forces on the east and both units will converge on you. If you come out without weapons, holding your hands up, we will allow you to head for Chokuno," Quint said from his perch on the wall.

"If you have a short memory of the magic you have just observed, may I tickle your memories?"

Quint cast an explosive lightning string into the center of the barricade, exposing a six-foot gap just as the two Shimato columns arrived to flank the barricade.

An officer raised both his hands after removing a sword and a couple of knives. "We give up!"

Thera counted one hundred and sixty-seven fighters who exited from behind the barricade. The soldiers from the town and the detachment from the commander's troops quickly surrounded the Chokunese soldiers. Chibo had the enemy searched and would send them east toward Chokuno, a half-day walk from the town.

"We made a bit of money today," an officer said, looking at the loot removed from the enemy.

Chibo walked up. "This is the warlord's booty. I ran Shimato's forces today." The war leader winked at Quint.

Thera suggested a sweep of the town before the forces left, and surprisingly, twenty-five more Chokuno soldiers had infiltrated Nimogata during the invasion. The townspeople had found two more of the Gamizans, both wizards. Quint thought the pair looked familiar. Chibo wanted to interrogate them and as one of the pair began to cast a string, Quint put both men to sleep. They were stripped of their possessions. Their purses were especially fat, and a packet of letters indicated that Gamiza and Chokuno were about to enter an alliance.

"Two of the Gamizans?" Narisu asked.

Quint looked at the enemy soldiers kneeling in rows just outside the east gate. "The third Gamizan must be among them," he said.

"He could be dead," Chibo said.

Quint pursed his lips and walked over to the two kneeling Gamizans, still in their underwear. "Where is your third companion?"

The men looked defiant. "We are Chokunese."

'Where did you get these? If you are Chokunese, then three of the Gamizans are kneeling along with you."

Quint recognized the pair but couldn't remember what the last Gamizan looked like.

A solid spear of fire knocked Quint to the ground, but his shield held.

"It came from that person," one of the Shimato warriors told Chibo.

Quint approached the wizard and shot a weak lightning bolt at him. The lightning glittered as it hit the attacker's shield. Quint reached down and put the man to sleep.

"Search the wizard!" Narisu ordered as the body was dragged over to Chibo and stripped of all clothing. A soiled document was found in the man's underwear.

"You can read it, Narisu. You found it," Chibo said.

Quint couldn't help but smile.

"Contacts and addresses in the Chokuno fief and contacts in the little army that attacked Shimato," Narisu said. He gave it to Chibo's escort officer, who delicately handed the document to one of the Chibo's soldiers.

"Copy it," the officer said.

Chibo turned to the two Gamizans. "We found all three of you. I'm not certain we need you for anything else." Chibo turned away from the pair, still kneeling.

"The sleeping wizard is the most powerful," Thera said. She turned the wizard over and found a tattoo on the man's forearm. "A Green wizard from Narukun."

"That is an uglier alliance than Gamiza making nice with Chokuno," Quint said to Chibo. "Have you seen enough?"

"Enough is right. It's time to return to Morimanu," the war leader said. He turned to Kimo, who had remained silent and out of the way. "What do you think of the charter now?"

"My eyes have been opened," Kimo said. "I think my faction needs to discuss it and what you have discovered on the battlefield in the last two days."

Kimo's continued presence surprised Quint, and Kimo's comment was even more surprising. Quint hoped he was speaking the truth.

After visiting with the commander, who would stay another week to determine what kind of strengthening Nimogata needed, Chibo's party returned to the capital. Kimo spoke with Thera as much as Quint about wizards on the battlefield. The wizard clearly feared the budding alliances, and he had changed his mind about the usefulness of organized wizardry.

§

Chibo stopped at the track to Shira's manor.

"Do you have a better idea of how to present your solution to the warlord?" Chibo asked.

"I think I do, but I'd like to present my case to Narisu and you first."

"Three days," Chibo said, holding up three fingers. "I will visit Lady Shira in three days."

"Can I attend?" Kimo asked. "I'd like to bring the faction leader."

Quint nodded. "The more the merrier."

Dakuz and Dugo sat underneath a gazebo in the courtyard, sipping tea and watching Shira practice strings, when Quint and Thera walked in carrying their bags. Todo and his friend had taken their horses to the stables.

"How goes the instruction?" Quint asked.

Shira beamed at Quint and held out an outstretched hand. "Five strings!" she said. "I'm learning three more. Dakuz said I might get to fifteen."

Dakuz smiled and nodded to Shira. "She isn't the strongest, but probably the most enthusiastic student I've had. We will see how she fares at ten to determine her magic potential."

"Good for you!" Thera said. "I can't think of better tutors."

Shira smiled shyly. "He said you can teach me some spells more suited for a woman."

Dakuz blushed. "There are some strings that I'm not very good at."

"Or too embarrassed to teach?" Thera asked. "I can help, don't worry." She turned to Shira. "Get to your ten strings first."

"I will!" Shira said.

"We will clean up and then tell you about our two battles," Quint said.

Quint fell asleep in his bath but determined he had slept for ten minutes or less by the temperature of the water. He jumped out, changed into clothes he hadn't taken on the trip, and returned to the gazebo, which was empty. Unsurprised, he returned to his quarters and found Todo waiting in his meeting area.

"Is there something wrong?" Quint asked.

"I heard that the Three Forks faction and another will attack the manor. I don't know what to do."

"You are doing it. When will it occur, and how many attackers will there be?"

"More than three. My friend and I are wizards, but we don't know enough offensive strings to be useful."

"How many attackers do you think will show up?" Quint asked gently.

"Five to ten," Todo said.

"When?"

"The night you return from Nimogata."

"So, anytime."

Todo nodded, twisting a cap in his hands.

"I want you and Asoka, your friend, to fill every bucket you can find. There might be fires, and you two will be our firemen."

Todo brightened. "I can do that."

"You can get the servants to help. Locate Lady Shira and have her deploy her staff to defend her property. I'll find my friends."

Quint ran to the building where Dugo, Dakuz, and Thera were and told them what Todo said.

"This is serious," Dugo said. "I may miss my dinner."

Dakuz grunted, but Quint could tell Dugo's joke amused him.

"You've spent more time at the manor. Where is the weakest point?" Quint asked.

"The stables," Dugo said. "The wall dips down behind them. Even I could get over it."

"Dakuz and Dugo defend the stables. Hopefully, servants are willing to help."

"That's not assured," Thera said.

Quint sighed. "They are probably after me, so I'll be in the front courtyard facing the gate. Thera can be my backup."

"Can you shield the servants?" Dugo asked. "Your shields are better than mine."

Quint cast shield strings on his friends. "I'll do the same for as many I can find," Quint said.

He found Shira adjusting the men's clothes she had just put on.

"It is easier to fight when I don't have to worry about my clothes," Shira said.

Quint folded his arms. "I'd like to cast a magical shield. Your strings might not be strong enough to fight the Three Forks wizards."

"I'm willing to have every advantage I can," she said.

"Good. You are in charge of your servants. If there are fires, it's up to you and Todo to save your manor. Until then, try to stay safe. A wizard fight in an open area is one you aren't prepared to fight."

Finally, Quint looked across the grounds. Except for the few magic lights and lamps burning in the buildings, it was dark. Thera suggested that they extinguish any flames. He hoped Todo's warning was wrong, but it made sense to a warrior. Was Rimo Gorima a warrior? Could another faction be pushing the Three Forks to attack? Quint hadn't thought the Three Forks so vindictive, but Todo insisted the mother and son were focused on an agenda to keep Three Forks small and strong. It had worked until now, but Quint thought Rimo's arrogance was breaking down the faction's goal.

Quint sat on the edge of a building's porch. His body was tired. The last week was full of action and riding. At least he had taken a bath, and that had helped, but Quint needed rest. After the fight, he thought.

After another hour of waiting found the moon directly overhead. Quint looked across to the stable and spotted movement. He cast a light across the grounds and let it hover in front of the stables, revealing a group of black-clad intruders. They were too far to use a sleeping spell, Quint's preferred fighting technique. The bright light should have destroyed their night sight.

Two fire spears emerged from the darkness and took down one wizard, but the other's shield was too strong, and the fire splashed against the shield.

Could that be Rimo? Quint thought. He rose and ran toward another position behind a decorative rock garden.

Two servants ran across the stableyard, and fire spears slammed into them. The gauntlet was thrown as far as Quint was concerned. The invaders were crouched down, retreating toward the stable, when Quint shot two quick lightning bolts. Two more attacking wizards dropped to the ground.

Quint crept behind a different rock as a wizard cast a lightning string of his own and shattered the side of the rock where Quint had been seconds previously. That was all Quint needed, and he combined a fire spear and a lightning string from each hand. Quint's attack began to splash against the wizard in a blast of light, but Quint kept his attack going until it pierced the shield of his target. The wizard went down, and as the intruders began to retreat, two more were attacked, presumably by Dakuz and Thera.

By Quint's calculation, that left one remaining attacker. After reinforcing his shield, he stepped out from his protection and was hit by a blue fire spear, which knocked him to the ground but didn't otherwise harm him.

He rolled on the ground and ran toward the new wizard, which Quint bathed with a lightning string and a weaker fire spear. The wizard staggered, but his shield held until Quint threw a crossbow bolt and brought the person down.

The stableyard was clear. Magic lights began to appear, and Shira joined Quint as Todo organized the servants to extinguish a few fires that had started.

Dugo and Quint began dragging the bodies. Quint used his sleeping spell on the few wizards that still breathed. The wizard with the blue fire still breathed.

Shira pulled down the black mask of the last fighter to reveal the face of Miro Gorima, Rimo's mother. Her wounds revealed Quint's double attack had done damage once her shield was defeated.

Todo and Asoka dragged the last black-clad body into the courtyard. It was Rimo. "Eight fighters and both heads of the Three Forks are gone."

Asoka looked more triumphant than Todo. "She deserved it more than her son."

"All the attackers got what they deserved," Quint said. "She had an interesting string."

"The blue fire?" Dakuz asked. "I've seen it twice in my life by a senior master. I don't know the string, but it is a powerful attack."

"We will be dealing with a new leader," Thera said.

"No, you won't," Todo said. "With the Gorimas gone, the Three Forks won't continue. Everyone will seek different factions."

Quint grinned. "Can't we take over the faction?" He looked down at the bodies of the mother and son. "Maybe not, since we dispatched the leaders."

"No one will blame you for killing them," Todo said. "You know how I feel about the Three Forks, but plenty of wizards will find another faction."

"Is that what happens?" Dakuz asked.

Asoka nodded. "We left because we had to. They were despicable leaders."

"Won't that cause more disruption in the wizardry ranks?" Quint asked.

"More disruption than what? You are the disruption," Todo said. "Change is never easy."

Dakuz nodded. "He's right."

Shira weakly smiled. "I hate to interrupt your conversation about the charter, but what am I to do with all the carnage?"

"I'll go to the village and get a guard out here," Todo said. "No sense bothering the capital about a break-in."

"One that involves the leadership of a wizard faction?" Thera asked.

Todo barked a laugh. "The Three Forks weren't much of a faction compared to the others. The big fight will be over the Three Forks mansion."

"There aren't any heirs?" Quint asked.

"No, but I'll bet the succession will be brutal, and when the struggle is over, the faction will die, just like I said," Todo said. He looked at Shira. "Can I take a horse?"

"Any but the ones Thera and Quint used, and bring a healer back with you," she said. She made a face. "Let's at least get the bodies covered and get the ones left alive into the main building."

When Quint bent down to lift Miro Gazima, he found her throat had been cut. She had expired, and the secret of the blue fire might have gone with her. Quint sighed. No wonder Asoka and Todo were so sure Three Forks was no more. He didn't know who had done it, but he wouldn't be the one to find out.

Two intruders were alive when placed just inside the doors to the main building. Thera worked on them and declared that both could survive if the healer were competent.

Quint collapsed into one of the chairs in the main meeting hall. It was two hours after midnight. The actual fight had taken minutes. He closed his eyes and was shaken awake by a uniformed guard. Two healers were working on the surviving wizards.

"You killed the wizards?" the guard asked.

"There were a lot of magical bolts and spears flying back and forth," Quint said, blinking the sleep out of his eyes. "I'm sure some of my attacks hit their targets."

"I've heard of the mother and the son," the guard said. "Both masters. And you?"

"You would consider me a master," Quint said. "The person who fetched you received a tip that the Three Forks would attack."

"Why would they do that?"

"Professional jealousy," Shira said. She had changed into a dress. "I see it all the time in the entertainment arena. They weren't happy about Quint's efforts to improve the life of wizards in Shimato."

"I don't need to know anything about that," the guard said.

"Rimo Gorima wanted to run the wizard charter organization. I told him he was unfit, and that angered him," Quint said. "Rimo was a very arrogant man."

"I'll inquire about that. You aren't leaving Shimato, are you?" the guard asked.

"No. I just returned from a tour of the border conflict with Chibo Hobona. My business isn't done in your fief," Quint said.

The guard perked up. "I'll check on that too if you don't mind."

"He will be visiting us in two days, seeing as tomorrow is now today," Quint said with a weary smile.

"I'll take care of the intruders later in the morning. You will have to make arrangements for the folks you lost tonight." The guard left as soon as the healers had finished.

"Do you trust him?" Dakuz asked Quint.

"No reason not to unless something untoward happens before dawn. He seemed to ask the same questions I might. He has no reason not to trust us."

"But there were eight black-garbed intruders!" Shira said.

"We could have put different clothes on them, couldn't we?" Dakuz said.

"But we aren't so devious," Shira said.

Quint yawned. "I think it's time for bed. We should have the servants keep watch for the rest of the night."

"Rest of the morning," Dugo said with a grin.

"Until dawn," Quint said.

"Right!" Dugo grinned even wider.

CHAPTER ELEVEN

THEY WEREN'T BOTHERED UNTIL CHIBO SHOWED up two days later with a few more people than expected, including the warlord.

"Tirolo. I hear you've been busy," the warlord said as he dismounted and walked into the main meeting hall. He took the chair at the head of the rows of chairs. Chibo sat on the first row, facing Shira, and then Quint looked across at a man he'd never met. He noticed Hari Bitto standing in the back with the warlord's and Chibo's escorts.

"I have, Lord Bumoto. I'm sure War Leader Hobona told you of our adventures on the Chokuno border."

"He has. I'm very impressed with your help. I thought you were all talk, looking for a piece of my treasury, but I was wrong about that," the warlord said. "You fought two masters a few nights ago in this very manor. Tell me about it."

Quint gave the barest facts to the warlord and gave as much credit to the Gorimas' magical prowess as he could while minimizing his own.

"That's not what my people say," the warlord said.

Quint pursed his lips, trying to keep his composure. With Hari still in the warlord's retinue, anything could have been said.

"You used your prodigious strength to defeat the two masters of the Three Forks," Bunto Bumoto said. "A few people doubted you would be able to defeat them."

Quint noticed the warlord's gaze drifted to Hari in the back of the room, who blushed.

"I've seen and heard enough. I will allow you to continue to work on your charter, but only for six months," the warlord said. "Since the Three Forks mansion is available, with the Gorimas dying intestate, I will let you use it for now." The warlord rose, and all those seated rose to their feet. "I will return to the capital. I understand the war leader, and you have things to discuss."

The hall was silent while Lord Bumoto exited with his staff. Todo flashed a thumbs-up sign to Quint while his face was split with a wide grin.

The war leader escorted Shira to the seat vacated by the warlord and sat on the first row, looking directly at Quint.

"I'd like your version of what happened the night you were attacked," Chibo said.

"Why did the warlord give us the Three Forks mansion?" Quint asked.

Chibo stretched his arms wide. "Think about what you've done since you arrived in Morimanu. The three weeks were to verify if you had good or bad intentions. I think you put any questions to bed."

Quint gave Chibo a half-smile before launching into his perspective of the fight. He then had Shira talk. Because of her perspective, she had seen everything and verified Quint's version with minor differences.

"What stupid people!" Chibo said. "I've got commanders like the one you met in the field, and you've got faction leaders like Miro Gorima. We both have work to do. I need you closer to create a viable wizard corps for Shimato." The war leader leaned forward and spoke more quietly. "The warlord is very concerned about external alliances. That is the prime reason for moving his decision up."

That made sense to Quint. "Then we will move tomorrow if that suits Lady Shira."

"Of course. I can still have visitors, like Dakuz and Dugo?" the lady asked.

She was talking about magic lessons, Quint decided. "It's up to them. I would like Todo to return with us. Perhaps you can talk Asoka into being your steward."

"Already done," Shira said. "Todo expressed a desire to become a follower so he can follow you to the capital. Asoka can take his place." She giggled. "Everything will work out just right as long as I can be a follower when you leave Shimato."

"If it makes sense for both of us," Quint said. He glanced at Thera, who nodded without a smile.

"Can I be dismissed?" Chibo said with a smile. "I've talked to the guard who showed up at the manor. There will be no difficulties there, and with that, I'll send someone first thing tomorrow morning to escort you to your new home."

§

All the buildings in the Three Forks mansion were smaller than Shira's country manor but more than large enough for Quint and his people. Todo no longer manned the gate, but Quint assigned him to run the estate again.

After they arrived, Quint assembled his close staff, Dugo, Dakuz, Thera, and Todo.

"I feel a little adrift not having an immediate deadline to meet, so we will first establish a list of goals. First, we need to meet with all major factions at their headquarters and the minor ones, if they are willing to come here. We present the charter and solicit any changes that are sticking points. Second, Chibo wants the wizard corps defined and worked into the warlord's fighting strategies," Quint said.

"I'll lead that effort," Thera said. "I've got as much experience as you, and we can work together when needed."

"I can make the faction appointments as long as I don't have to mind the gate," Todo said with a smile. "I have contacts among all the lower-level wizard factions and can use those as starting points."

Quint nodded. "Time is still important. We have no strategy against the encroachment of the Greens into Kippun, and I will work on that." He looked at Dakuz and Dugo. "Can you two work up the administrative systems for the charter? I don't have any experience rating wizards and with the logistics of it all."

"I suppose that is a safe enough task before we have to rate anyone," Dakuz said. He shivered. "I hate to contemplate how that will change when everyone must be rated. You never gave me any trouble at Seensist Cloister, but it was a trial for everyone involved. At least all the wizards were already rated at Feltoff."

"I'm up for it," Dugo said.

Quint clasped his hands together. "Then, we need to start and finish our charter in less than two weeks to proceed."

Everyone agreed, although Quint was intent on finishing his planning part in a few days. Chibo showed up the next afternoon. The war leader met with Thera and Quint.

"I'd rather work with you," Chibo said to Quint after being informed of Quint's plans, "but we are close enough to keep each other informed of what the other is doing. The warlord expects me to ensure he is current in your efforts."

"Good. Thera is more experienced with military details."

"What are your intentions regarding the Gamizans?" Chibo asked.

"For the warlord?"

Chibo nodded. "For all of us."

"I need to do some investigating that might take weeks," Quint said.

"Including a surreptitious trip to Gamiza fief?" Chibo asked.

"Perhaps, but I might visit Chokuno first to determine how close the two fiefs have become."

"You can work with Narisu. I'm too well known among the bordering fiefs," Chibo said. "All you two have to do is change your wardrobe style and grow beards or something." Chibo leaned closer to Quint. "You can grow a beard, can't you?"

"Enough of one to make my face look dirty," Quint said.

Chibo chuckled. "That would be enough. I'll send him over. Talk to him over dinner. He knows good restaurants in the capital better than I do."

They discussed timing, and Thera volunteered to show up the following day to get started.

"I have a group of planners in the building that she can start with. The biggest challenge will be my commanders, but if they don't cooperate, I'll fire them," Chibo said. "You don't want to be a fired commander in Shimato fief."

Chibo left after an hour of his time, and Quint gathered all his staff and discussed the visit.

"You are leaving us alone to do the work?" Dugo asked.

Quint sighed. "Not alone. I'm leaving all of you with work to do. My work involves investigating the situations in Chokuno and Gamiza. Narisu will be with me. Todo needs to manage the manor, Thera works in Chibo's offices, and Dakuz and Dugo have a mountain of rules, regulations, and procedures to create."

"But what do we do with the appointments I set up?" Todo asked.

"You will take Dakuz or Thera, whoever will do the best job or who, quite frankly, has the time. I can be added to the list if I'm around," Quint said. "I expect to take about the same time to do my investigation as you to get started on your respective tasks."

"And we can't all do everything together," Dakuz said, looking a little cross. "I don't like working like that anyway."

Dakuz hadn't been pressed very much, and Quint was relieved Dakuz showed some irritation.

Narisu arrived about an hour before sunset and shepherded everyone a few blocks away to a Narukun-style restaurant. The meal was a decent mix of Narukun food seasoned more like Slinnon cuisine with some local foods mixed in. It was the kind of menu that depended on who cooked it. This time, the chef was very good at cooking without too much fat.

Narisu pulled Quint from the group and let them get ahead for a few moments.

"I'd like to leave tomorrow morning. The quicker we complete the task, the less chance we will be discovered," Narisu said. "It is easier to enter Gamiza from Chokuno so we can visit both fiefs in a single trip."

"What kind of clothing do we wear?"

"I'll take care of that. Wear your plainest clothes tomorrow morning. I'll bring horses and weapons. We don't want to take anything made in Shimato," Narisu said, "except for what we wear."

"You've done this before?" Quint asked.

"I have, and I know people who have done this more times than I have. Your accent isn't identifiable as from Shimato, but I may sound a little weird sometimes to cover how I speak," Narisu said. "We can do more planning once we have left the capital. Our route will take us farther north than our last trip to the border."

∽

CHAPTER TWELVE
~

NARISU AND QUINT ATE AT A TABLE FOR TWO next to a wall. Narisu told Quint to look at the other tables often. He said it made them seem more like outsiders. Quint didn't think looking nervous was a good defense, but he followed Narisu's suggestion.

"Eat up. It's your last meal in Shimato," Narisu said as their dinner was served.

Quint tasted the food, retrieved his seasoning pouch, and began to sprinkle herbs on his food.

"What are you doing?" Narisu asked.

"Making this more palatable," Quint said. "It's something I picked up in Narukun. Their cooking is bland, and everyone has a packet like this." He lifted the packet, folded the flap, and tied it shut. Quint shut his eyes as he put his first morsel in his mouth and nodded. "That helps."

"Can you season mine?" Narisu asked.

Quint grinned and put the same seasoning mix on his companion's food. "Everyone has different tastes."

Narisu shrugged. "I'll take the risk." He tried his food and raised his eyebrows. "You learn something new every day."

Quint laughed. "I learned I just surprised you."

"Once. The seasoning pouch is a giveaway that you are from Narukun. I've not seen the like used in Chokuno or Gamiza. Our counterparts in the other two fiefs might notice," Narisu said.

"I didn't realize," Quint said.

"You do, now. We are intruding into enemy territory tomorrow morning." Narisu looked at the seasoning packet on the table. "I may try that again in a safe place."

Quint nodded and put the seasoning packet away. "If someone sees it in my bag, I can say we use it when we are cooking on the road."

"That works."

Narisu asked about cloister life, and that filled up the rest of the evening.

When Quint took to his bed, he vowed to learn everything he could about being a spy in a hostile land. He wasn't as new to the game as Narisu thought, but perhaps he could play that to his advantage.

After a bland breakfast, Narisu and Quint rode off, and just before lunch, Narisu took Quint through a set of wooded hills. Chokuno's border was somewhere in the small mountains ahead of them, but Narisu didn't have a precise notion of where the border was. Two ranges of hills defined Chokuno. They were to proceed for another two hours until they came to a Chokunese town.

Quint could tell the difference in architecture, but he let Narisu point out the few differences, anyway. Quint patted the seasoning packet as they sat down for lunch. Narisu shook his head, and Quint replied with a nod. They had decided that Quint would utter monosyllabic responses for the first day.

Silence would be better than a single syllable, Quint thought, and lunch didn't reveal anything to anyone listening in. Narisu asked a few open-ended questions about the road ahead that led to some conversation about the state of Chokunese banditry and the Chokunese warlord's inability to stop it.

Once they were on the road, Narisu laughed. "The villagers don't know that some of the bandits are employees of their warlord. The local guard won't be bothered to offend the leader of their fief."

"Does Lord Bumoto do the same thing?" Quint asked.

"Not regularly, but if he does, it is for a bigger reason than to line his already full pockets," Narisu said. "Chibo has a trusted commander in charge of eliminating banditry. Keeping the peace in the fief is harder than one might think."

"If someone wants to rob another, it is difficult to stop unless there is a threat of being caught."

"Or death, in the case of the Gorimas and the Three Fork faction. However, there are exceptions as you guessed, where the local guard might not have done much if Chibo wasn't involved."

"Or the warlord," Quint said with a smile.

Narisu laughed. "Especially the warlord." He held up his hand and peered ahead. "Speaking of bandits. Is that a tree across the road?"

"Can we go around it?"

Narisu pursed his lips. "Do you want more information, or do you want to give the bandits doctored information?"

"We fight with our Chokunese weapons and leave something behind?"

Narisu shrugged. "We do if we are better fighters than they are."

Quint raised his hand, palm up. "Between you and I, there are other ways to win."

"No magic, yet. That's why we carry weapons. It's a cover."

Quint nodded. He still cast a strong shield to slow an arrow or an edged weapon. Narisu did the same. They stopped thirty paces from the obstruction.

"Can we go around?" Quint asked in a louder-than-normal voice.

"Or we can cut it in half and drag the shorter part out of the way enough to pass," Narisu said.

"I vote for going around," Quint said as he drew his sword. "But it has to be a trap."

Narisu drew his sword and nodded. "Follow me and be ready to fight."

Quint nearly smiled, knowing they were watched. The loud conversation wasn't much different from what they had discussed out of range, except for the magic.

"Stop right there," a voice commanded from the forest.

"If you noticed, we haven't moved for the last few moments," Narisu said.

"Then, don't move!" the voice said, sounding more flustered.

Four scruffy men and an even scruffier woman walked from behind trees on the other side of the obstruction.

"Five against two," the voice, a bald, paunchy ruffian said.

"It's easy to see you are at a distinct disadvantage, so let us pass, and you won't be injured," Narisu said.

"One of us is a wizard," the bald man said.

"Who is to say we both aren't wizards?" Narisu said.

One of the brigands took a step back. The woman stepped forward and tossed a weak fire spear in front of Narisu. "Perhaps you are at a disadvantage," the woman said haughtily, but clearly, she wasn't brilliant.

"You aren't politically connected to anyone or any faction?" Narisu asked.

"Why let someone take a cut for doing nothing?" the bald man said.

Narisu nodded to Quint. "My friend is a magician of middling talent. Why don't you show them what you can do with the tree?"

Quint had to conceal a look of surprise. What happened to keeping their abilities secret? He sheathed his sword and shot a lightning bolt using a two-handed string. The tree shattered, sending chips of wood in all directions. The bandits scurried out of the way.

"I suppose we can continue?" Narisu said, doffing his hat at the bald man and the woman.

After they passed the tree, Quint felt a little pressure on his back. The woman had tried to shoot a fire spear at Quint's back. Quint stopped and wheeled the horse around. The sad group of outlaws fled into the trees. A few tripped and moaned as they fell, bringing a smile to Narisu's face.

"I don't think they learned anything," Quit said.

Narisu laughed. "They shouldn't have stopped to talk," he said. "I thought it was safe to eliminate their extra advantage, the wizardess." Narisu chuckled. "What a beauty and her magical talent!"

"She shot me in the back when we left."

"I wondered what happened. When you turned around, the bandits took off like the rats they were. I almost feel sorry for them, but people like that are rarely trustworthy. Her attack proved it. I doubt the warlord funded this bunch."

The whole episode was pitiful, but he was sure the brigands would be ready to stop the next person on the road when they repositioned their tree.

§

Speech in Chokuno was a little different. There were regional differences in South Fenola, but Quint ignored the dialects before Narisu mentioned it. Quint now understood about Narisu sounding weird.

The concept of speech differences made Quint contemplate the uniqueness of people and groups. His troubles at Seensist were exacerbated by the little behavioral things he had brought with him from Racellia, his home country. Regional cuisines were the most recognizable to Quint, and now he would have to absorb the complete cultural changes when he tried to understand different kinds of people. His use of the seasoning pouch and Narisu's mild reproval were evidence of that.

Quint almost winced when he realized how different he truly was since he was pressed to serve in the Racellian wizard corps. It wasn't just a hubite in a sea of willots. Skin, hair, and eye color were only part of it, and now that he was in a land where he physically fit in, differences remained, and for some people, those subtle differences affected how others perceived him.

"You seem immersed in some profound thought," Narisu said.

Quint smiled. "I was. I think I was overcome by being a stranger in a strange land."

Narisu looked askance at Quint. "Haven't you always been a stranger wherever you've been?"

"Mostly," Quint said. "But I was thinking of the nature of being different and how that affects how I see others and how they see me."

Narisu grunted. "You have realized the essence of spycraft. It isn't easy to fit in if you don't make the effort; you can't be a good spy."

"Or you have to be so different that it covers up what others are looking for," Quint said.

"That, too. Don't think too deeply, or you'll step in that hole in front of you," Narisu said.

Quint pulled on the reins of his horse.

Narisu burst out in laughter. "You were in another realm!"

Quint felt embarrassed. "I was. There is no hole."

"Of course, there isn't. Horses have eyes, too." Narisu said. "We continue to be itinerant swordsmen when we stop for the night. It's more important not to practice wizardry."

"More people about?" Quint said.

"Right. We want to listen a lot more than talk this evening. Tomorrow, it's taking the main road through the center of Chokuno to Tiryo, the capital, and then we will plunge far to the south into Gazima. We will find more information along this route than any other in the two fiefs."

Quint agreed. Information traveled quickly along well-traveled roads. He had picked up that nugget of information when he worked for the late Colonel Julia Garocie of the Racellian Military Diplomatic Corps.

They stayed in a modest inn that Narisu knew about. Quint noticed a higher concentration of armed men and wondered if that was significant.

Narisu chose a table at the side of the fireplace. Quint realized that it put them in shadows with them facing each other. More spycraft, he thought.

A woman, who looked polennese, walked up to their table. She was shorter than usual, with long dark hair pulled back. Quint guessed she was about Thera's age and dressed just like the men in the common room.

"Do you have space for another itinerant?"

Narisu nodded. "As long as you don't bite," he said, "too hard."

Quint wasn't used to Narisu flirting with a woman that way, but his companion seemed to throw caution to the wind and let her sit between them. She faced directly toward the crowd. She was good-looking enough to distract anyone looking their way. Was this unintentional spycraft?

"You made good time," she said quietly. "I honestly thought I'd have to spend a few evenings in this place."

"Lucky you," Narisu said. "Have you learned anything new?"

"The border was uncomfortably active for Chokuno the last few weeks. The warlord thought to bite off a town for a season or two and seize some farmland, but some foreigners and the Shimato war leader stopped the plan. The foreigners were master wizards." She gazed at Quint. "How are your strings this evening, boy?" she asked.

Quint chuckled. "I'm too young to be a master wizard," he looked at Narisu. "I am, aren't I? I don't know much about wizardry."

She looked at Quint. "But you are a foreigner?"

"Caught me," Quint said. "I've never been to Chokuno fief before."

The woman looked at Narisu. "Not bad for an amateur."

"Yes," Narisu said. "I've got him on an accelerated course." Narisu leaned forward and put his hand on the woman's wrist. "Quint, I'd like you to meet Masumi. No last name. She knows me as Nomi." He picked up her wrist and traced the woman's palm print. "Right, Masumi?"

"Of course," Masumi said.

"Quint can know anything you have to tell me," Narisu said.

"Anything?"

Narisu grimaced. "Anything related to our current mission."

She nodded and smiled at Narisu seductively. "I can handle that." A serving maid arrived, and Masumi ordered for them all, making a point that Nomi/Narisu promised to pay.

"The local army was embarrassed, very embarrassed, and lost some face, while the fief lost a few officers. There were 'friends' helping, and those nasty Shimato wizards still prevailed. The Gamizans lost more than face; they lost people in the battle."

"A few, but a large percentage," Nomi/Narisu said. "Quint, give Masumi a neutral summary of the two incursions."

Quint did so, trying to be as vague as his companions. He thought he had succeeded until Masumi pursed her lips. "Now I have to ask you penetrating questions," she said. "I hope you won't get hurt by them."

"Go ahead."

Her questions were clarifications but kept to how the Chokunese forces fought.

"That's enough," Narisu said.

The maid laid out an array of bowls of snacks, cups, and a flagon of wine.

Masumi poured drinks. Quint was surprised at how little she filled everyone's cups. He would ask until he realized she didn't want them drunk. Masumi hadn't told them anything about current events other than the Chokunese side of the battle that Quint had fought.

"In case you are wondering, I work for myself, but I'm partial to helping Nomi out occasionally," she said. "I spend all of my time in Chokuno."

Narisu nodded to Quint. "You didn't hear that, right?"

Quint shook his head. "I'm so lightheaded that I can barely think straight, much less make much sense when Masumi is flirting with you," he said, playing along with covering for Masumi's activities.

"I'm flirting?" Masumi said. "It's Nomi who is flirting with me."

"Whatever," Quint said. "I think I've had enough and am going to my room."

Narisu flashed his eyes. "A wonderful idea. We'll eat breakfast here before we leave in the morning."

Quint left the pair. Masumi moved her chair closer to Narisu and whispered in his ear when he last glanced at them.

∽

CHAPTER THIRTEEN

WHEN QUINT ENTERED THE COMMON ROOM FOR BREAKFAST, Narisu and Masumi were chatting like the friends they must have been.

"I asked Nomi if I could join you," Masumi said. "I come at a high price, but I'll be worth it."

Narisu shrugged. "She has her ways of convincing people," Narisu said. "I was convinced."

They were seated next to other itinerant swordsmen, and Quint could tell Masumi was giving her excuse to join them to anyone who cared to know.

In half an hour, they slipped under the town's gate. The wall was a wooden palisade that snaked its way around the town. No one stopped them, but guards were checking incoming carts and carriages.

"Are you uncomfortable traveling with a woman fighter?" Masumi asked Quint.

"The other foreign wizard was a woman warrior," Narisu said. "She isn't a master, but she is strong enough."

"And good with weapons?"

"Good enough," Quint said. "Better than me."

"I'll test that out soon enough." She narrowed her eyes and looked at Quint appraisingly. "I think you are right; you are too young to be a master wizard."

"Are you a wizard?"

Masumi laughed. "Slinnon is gifted with many wizards."

"That doesn't answer my question, and if I'm not mistaken, you are part hubite and part polennese."

"She has a little power," Narisu said. "I've got more."

"I can believe that," Quint said.

Masumi's pouted. "That I have little power?"

"No, that Narisu has more power than he lets on."

"But Quint has the most. He can do one-handed strings. I've never seen anyone else succeed trying," Narisu said.

"Show me," Masumi said.

Quint could see people ahead and behind them. "Not now, but later."

"He has promise?" Masumi asked Narisu.

"At this point, I think promise is all he has as a spy, but that's not his mission in life," Narisu told her about Quint's charter.

"I am impressed. And Narisu said you are destined to lead the world," Masumi said.

"I'm not so sure about the leading part," Quint said. "I have an important task that may have an impact."

"He also said you were too modest."

"I did," Narisu said. "You are too modest, but that might be better than becoming too self-important."

"In Slinnon, predictor strings are scoffed at. In fact, most things are scoffed at. Wealth and ancestry mean more than anything else." Masumi stuck out her lower lip. "My family was poor, and after a couple of generations, no one knew who anyone was. That's why my father left Slinnon for Chokuno to make his fortune. The best thing for him was meeting my hubite mother, of course."

"Of course," Narisu said. "That story seems to change every time we meet."

"Destiny does that," Masumi said.

"I don't quite understand that," Narisu said.

"Neither do I," Masumi said. "I know a wonderful camping place. I brought some food with me that we could cook on the road. The camp is secluded enough to show each other their prowess." Masumi made a sound that sounded like a low growl.

After an awful Chokunese lunch at a roadside restaurant which Quint couldn't surreptitiously use his seasoning packs, they finally stopped for the night a few hundred yards down a forest track. A wide stream ran down one side, and rocks and logs had long ago been placed to provide seating and a firepit.

Masumi went right to work. She took whatever Narisu and Quint had. Narisu revealed that Quint had a seasoning packet, but Masumi didn't want to be disturbed while she cooked and asked him to close it.

As Quint walked past Masumi's bags, he saw the butt-end of a hand-held crossbow sticking out. "Do you have crossbow bolts?" he asked.

"Why would I have a crossbow if I didn't have any bolts?" Masumi said playfully.

"I can shoot the bolts," Quint said.

"Show me," Narisu asked.

"I might use up your bolts."

"That crossbow isn't that powerful," Masumi said. "Give me a minute, and I'll watch."

She put a few of Quint's herbs in the pot, too much in Quint's estimation, and left the pot boiling.

"Show me your stuff, big boy," Masumi said.

"I'm not that big," Quint said.

"I wasn't talking to you." She smiled mischievously and looked at Narisu, who quickly turned his gaze elsewhere.

Quint grabbed three bolts from the bag that carried the crossbow.

"Give me a target," he said.

"That sapling over there," Masumi said.

Quint sighed. He wouldn't play around this time. He cast the string and focused on the bolt, splitting the sapling in half, which he did.

"I wasn't joking. My shot would have hit the ground before it reached the little tree," Masumi said, the shock plainly in her voice. "You destroyed it."

"I forgot to bring any bolts," Quint said. "Perhaps you can buy some in the capital."

Masumi nodded. "I would be happy to. Any kind will do?"

"Handheld size is best. Perhaps a couple of dozen."

"Plus, one more, you owe me one." Masumi ran back to her pot, which was boiling over, and returned to work.

Not long after that, they sat around a small campfire, having the soup that Masumi had made. Slightly stale bread was given to Narisu and Quint to dip in the broth.

"This is a Slinnon recipe?" Narisu asked.

"Like me, it is the best of both cultures. The broth is light and flavorful, and the bread is thick and stale."

"I won't ask you which part of the recipe refers to what," Narisu said.

Quint kept his mouth shut unless he was eating the soaked bread which was the best way of consuming Masumi's effort.

"In Slinnon, instead of bread, there would be rice or noodles to fill your stomach," Masumi said.

Quint was happy to change the subject of crossbow bolts to Masumi's cooking, but in the morning, Masumi wanted to know if Narisu could learn the one-handed technique that added more power to the bolt.

"I can try to teach him, but so far, no one else has been able to learn. I had a little boost from a supreme master who could infuse my magic with more strength."

"You never told me about that before," Narisu said.

"I doubt if you would believe me," Quint said.

"Try me," Masumi said. "I'm open-minded."

"It happened in Feltoff Cloister," Quint began. He told them about the apparitions first. "I was close to the wall and brushed against it and was transported somewhere else."

"Where?" Narisu said.

"Tova's domain."

"The goddess? You met the goddess?" Masumi asked. She giggled. "Tell me more." She obviously didn't believe him.

Quint nodded. "She gave me some strings and said she had a task for me. I was transported to wherever the master lives a few times. Before I departed from Feltoff, I think she did something to me. I learned how to do one-handed spells from an ancient book in Pinzleport, but the power increased after she gave me some of hers. I fought a couple of Green master wizards. They were supreme masters. The second one almost killed me. The last string I cast killed him in a duel, but I was grievously injured.

"I woke up with my magic gone, and all I have is Tova's magic, I think. It is different from what I had before. I can put bolts deep into a tree trunk."

"When I retrieved the bolt from the tree, it was ruined," Masumi said. "You were right, the bolt didn't survive. All that was left was the bolt head I kept as a souvenir." She gave Quint a quick smile.

"There are more where that came if you wish," Quint said.

"We will buy you a crossbow in the capital," Narisu said, "to give you an excuse for carrying all those bolt heads."

"I won't refuse that offer," Quint said. "I should have remembered to do that before we came, but you said no weapons."

"I did, didn't I?" Narisu said. "Even I make mistakes."

Masumi laughed. "I don't know if I can believe you about Tova, but your power is undeniable. Tell us about Green wizards."

"They are supremely confident. I can fight them, but surviving is another thing. I sent two wizards someplace in Tova's domain with a string gave me. It was a last resort. The third died at my hand. I told you that I nearly didn't survive. If the Greens have more wizards like those three on North Fenola, all the fiefs are in trouble."

"Except Shimato while you are with us," Narisu said. "Let's hope you eliminated all of them."

§

Tiryo, Chokuno's capital, was smaller than the city where they met Masumi.

"The current warlord grew up in this place. The capital has switched a bunch of times between the two cities," Masumi said. "The warlord hires soldiers in the old capital, and that's why there are so many itinerant swordsmen there."

"Will we have trouble being swords-for-hire in the capital? Quint asked.

"No. The warlord refuses to hire in his capital so that we will be ignored by most," Masumi said, "if we don't do anything suspicious. No magic."

"Magic is forbidden?" Quint asked.

"No, but the warlord drafts wizards he finds in the capital."

"Oh, but that makes no sense," Quint said.

"Does it have to?" Narisu asked.

"I suppose not." Quint looked at Tiryo from a hill at the edge of a large plain, poking up from the fields. A castle five or six stories high, built in the same style as Lord Butto's castle, dominated the city's skyline. A lazy river lined with trees and vegetation wound through the fields, kissing the city on its way to the other side of the plain.

The first city was more impressive, Quint thought. More buildings were taller than the ubiquitous two-story dwellings. Morimanu, the Shimato capital put both cities to shame.

The line to get in through the gate was long, and it took almost two hours to finally pass under the thick-timbered entrance in the late afternoon.

"They didn't ask for any identification," Quint said.

"You are an itinerant. They care more about collecting taxes from vendors entering Tiryo to sell their wares," Masumi said.

So far, Quint was as used to Chokuno as Shimato. The differences in the fiefs were noticeable but not significant in his eyes. The high taxes charged vendors entering the city were unique to the capital, Tiryo.

Masumi led them to another modest inn. This one was two stories, but there were more merchants and fewer itinerants, as Masumi called swords for hire. She arranged a large room for the three of them. Thera's aggressive behavior concerning their relationship had diminished after Quint's recovery in Narukun, but Masumi's flirtatiousness hadn't toned down from the time they first met.

They reached their room after seeing to their horses. Quint sighed when he saw partitions separating the room into four sleeping areas. They were going to sleep on blankets above and below them on the woven mat that covered the entire floor, which was no different than other nighttime arrangements in the fiefs, Narisu claimed.

"I hope there are few listeners tonight. I think I'll be doing a lot of snoring," Narisu said.

Masumi giggled. "Then you take the far stall, and I'll sleep on the other end. Quint can sleep in between."

"I'm willing to do that," Quint said. He narrowed his eyes at Masumi. "Do you snore?"

She winked at him. "All the time."

Quint groaned. "How about dinner?"

"Changing the subject?" Masumi asked. "I don't usually snore at dinner unless I've had a lot to drink."

Quint sighed. "I'm also hungry."

They left their things and locked the door. Quint stood by the door, thinking about binding the wood, but Narisu put his hand on Quint's wrist. "Don't worry about anyone stealing our things."

Quint didn't believe Narisu's words, but he did get the intended message. No magic.

In the dining hall, Narisu said, "Pass that pouch of packets," as he looked down at the food that he had ordered.

"Oh, that's right, our trail spices," Masumi said louder than needed.

Quint had brought his pouch to brighten up his food surreptitiously, but he thought he was supposed to keep it a secret.

Narisu winked at Quint. "Those trail spices have come in handy. I must remember to bring mine the next time we eat."

The loudness of the pair's request for Quint's spice pack made him smile. He might have made a couple of converts to Seensist Cloister's practice.

When they were finished with dinner, they stepped outside. Lantern lights filled the street.

"What is going on?" Narisu asked a man passing by.

"Once a month, the city is full of merchants selling their wares at night. We call it the Light of Tova."

"I forgot that was this evening," Masumi said, looking up at the rows of lanterns hanging from frames. "We should walk around. I doubt we will be here next month."

Quint doubted along with her. "Perhaps we can buy a crossbow tonight," he said.

"There is a street of weapon makers not far from here if my memory is correct," Masumi said.

Quint didn't doubt Masumi's memory. She led them directly through the throngs out on the street. Quint marveled at how much light lanterns could make when stacked as they were in Tiryo. The weapons lane was as bright as the rest of the shopping district, but fewer people wandered around.

"This is a good shop," Masumi said.

The patrons and shopkeepers turned to them as if on cue when they walked in. That wasn't natural at all. Quint gripped the hilt of his sword.

"My friend would like to buy a hand crossbow and a few dozen bolts if you've got them," Masumi said.

"Which friend, the one I know or the young one I don't."

Narisu laughed as he hugged the shopkeeper. "Gomoru! It has been too long!"

"Only because I haven't worked closer to Shimato."

Quint looked around. No one in the shop seemed alarmed at the blatant talk of Narisu's relationship with the man.

Masumi laughed. "This is a spy den," she said with a mock whisper."

"Indeed, it is," Gomoru said. "Who is the young man? A protege? You've never had one before."

"I think I'm the protege, and Quint is the master."

A woman pretending to be a customer asked, "He isn't the young wizard who was responsible for the Chokunese defeat just days ago, is he?"

"The very same one," Masumi said. "This is a training mission. We intend to see what is going on in Gamiza."

"Don't spend too long in that fief. Something is stirring. It's affecting the capital, too," Gomoru said. "Gamizans are unsettled with their new Narukun allies."

"Greens?"

"Is that what you call them? Powerful wizards espousing a glorious future. Everyone will become rich, I heard. It's all a lie, of course."

"The wizards are after a future where they run everything with an iron hand," Quint said. "They are still trying in Pinzleport and almost assassinated the king of Narukun. There is no glorious future with them in charge."

"We are beginning to realize that. You have been to Narukun recently?" The woman customer asked.

"I have," Quint said. "I helped save the king…"

"At great risk to himself. Quint was nearly killed," Narisu said. "I was at the border skirmish where Quint and one of his followers broke an intentional stalemate and then defended the town of Nimogata. Quint is a master wizard."

"He must be blessed by Tova," Gomoru said.

Quint was about to respond, but Narisu put a hand on his wrist. "May Tova bless us all."

The others intoned the short prayer. Quint was too surprised to join in.

"You aren't a believer?" Gomoru asked.

"My relationship with Tova goes beyond belief," Quint said. "I'm not from Kippun, so I am unfamiliar with your practices."

"Chokuno believes in Tova and Tizurek more strongly than Shimato," one of the others said.

"The crossbow?" Masumi asked.

"Oh, business. I'll help Quint while the others give you more details on the roads to Gamiza."

The shopkeeper beckoned Quint to a counter where Gomoru placed four hand-held crossbows on the countertop.

"Which is best?"

Gomoru shrugged. "I'm not a big proponent of these weapons. They are underpowered compared to normal crossbows and are much less accurate than a bow and long arrow. Why would you bother with one of these?"

"The crossbow is decoration. I use my magic to transport the bolt to wherever I want. Anything within one hundred paces works for me. It is the bolts that I need."

"This one is the best of the lot," Gomoru said. "It isn't the most expensive, but the mechanism is superior since it is from Slinnon. They make better weapons than any of the fiefs. I have a box of three hundred bolts that will fit this, so you can take as many as you can carry."

"Can I try it somewhere?"

Gomoru nodded. "In the basement." He turned to the rest of the shop. "I'm taking Quint into the basement to try out a crossbow."

"Can I come?" Masumi asked.

Gomoru led them down a narrow stairway into the basement. The weapon shop wasn't very large, so the basement wasn't either.

"You realize that you can't divulge the real purpose of this shop," Gomoru said. "If you did, your life would be taken along with our own."

"He's right, Quint," Masumi said, "but you already know enough about us."

"Not really," Quint said. "I don't know what your organization is or what your rules are. What is the real purpose of your shop? I can tell you two, but no more."

"That didn't seem to scare him," Gomoru said.

Masumi laughed. "You are the one who should be scared."

Gomoru waved Masumi's comment off. "Do you need instructions on how to use this?"

Quint examined the weapon after casting a brighter magic light. "I think I can figure this out."

"Where do I shoot?"

Gomoru drew a curtain and revealed a tunnel into the side of the basement. At the far end, Quint spotted a crude mannikin. The distance was less than twenty-five paces, but that was enough for Quint. He asked a question about cocking the bow and found a lever that pivoted out that acted as a ratchet for pulling back the metal bow.

Quint aimed and released the bolt. It hit the mannikin in the wrist.

"I thought you would have better aim," Masumi said.

"Let me use my magic this time. I don't need to draw the bow," Quint said.

He laid the bolt on the channel and cast the string after concentrating on the head of the figure. Quint shot, and the top half of the head broke off from the impact.

"I thought you were boasting," Gomoru said, amazed at what he saw. "Why did you even try to use the crossbow."

"No magic like this in Chokuno, right?" Quint asked.

Gomoru shrugged. "Not at all! I suppose you have made the right choice. Let's go upstairs and make a deal."

If Quint thought the transaction would be free, he was wrong. The bow and bolts were more expensive than if he had purchased them in Narukun.

"We will deliver the bolts tomorrow in a suitable travel bag," Gomoru said. He looked at Narisu. "Have your inquiries been answered?"

"More than I had expected," Narisu said. "We will stroll around for a while before returning to our inn."

Quint strapped the crossbow on with the holster and belt that came with the purchase and continued to enjoy the light and the joyful attitude of the people. He had expected Chokunese to be dour and suspicious, but that wasn't the case with the commoners unless a noble and his or her retinue paraded through the streets. Everyone parted to let them pass.

"Shimato isn't as partial to the nobility," Narisu whispered to Quint.

Before returning to the inn, they ate some street food and watched a puppet show.

"Did you enjoy your evening?" Masumi asked on their way up the stairs to their room.

The room seemed undisturbed, but Masumi and Narisu showed Quint the telltales they had left. Most of their possessions had been disturbed.

"You knew this would happen?" Quint asked Narisu.

"Of course," Masumi said. "Itinerants might not be questioned at the gate, but they are followed and their belongings examined to see if they are a threat to the warlord."

Quint opened his seasoning pouch, and his orderly packets of herbs and spices had been opened and not closed very well. "My telltale, I guess," he said, showing the disturbed contents.

"A small price to pay," Narisu said. "If we were suspected, we would have been apprehended before we returned to the inn."

"Did we compromise the people in the weapons shop?" Quint asked.

Masumi shook her head. "If we did, the shop would have been raided."

They knew more than Quint did. It was time for bed, and Quint didn't know if he could get the weapons shop out of his mind enough to go to sleep. He removed his clothes behind the partition, leaving the empty spot between Masumi and himself.

CHAPTER FOURTEEN
∾

QUINT DIDN'T SEE ANY DIFFERENCE in his two companions in the morning.

"Are we leaving today?" he asked Narisu as they ate breakfast.

"No reason to stay," Narisu said. "No one is hiring. We'll try our luck elsewhere."

After breakfast, where it was a challenge to find the right seasonings, they rode out the west gate before finding a track that would take them south toward Gamiza as soon as Quint's crossbow bolts arrived.

"Did you learn enough?" Quint asked when they were alone on the road.

"Enough," Narisu said. "Nothing that would discourage us from concluding that Chokuno and Gamiza are entering an alliance. Chibo's spies aren't placed high enough to know more than that."

"Does anyone else's spies know?"

Masumi grinned. "Chibo's spies keep their information to themselves. That is why they felt safe enough joining us at the weapon shop."

"You aren't one of his spies?" Quint asked.

"As I told you when we met, I'm more of an associate or a freelancer. Narisu pays me, and I do some work. There aren't too many people like me."

I assume there are rivalries between spy factions?" Quint asked.

Narisu nodded. "There are, and no one is above exposing another's network even if it is detrimental to Shimato."

"That's not very efficient."

"It isn't meant to be efficient, but it is meant to keep everyone on their toes."

No wonder Kippun remained fragmented. There was no trust, and he had seen that within the wizard factions. Shimato was like that, and maybe every Kippunese fief was the same.

"What if someone unified Kippun?" Quint asked.

Narisu and Masumi laughed. "Alliances never last long."

Not until the culture is changed, Quint thought. There would have to be a dictator for a generation, at least. That person would have to be effective and know how far to go. The charter might help with that.

"You know the Greens better than we do. What would they do to unite our country?" Narisu asked.

Quint hadn't thought he'd have an opportunity to explore his idea so quickly. "They are brutally repressive. If they still have many master wizards, there will be war before long. Kippun needs a benevolent dictator. If there was a benevolent dictator who knew how to balance a firm hand with a permissive mind, the fiefs could be eliminated, and a stronger, unified country would arise."

"Is that something you think you can do?" Masumi asked.

Quint could tell she wasn't serious, but he was. "No. I'm too young and too untested. Recognizing the need and knowing how to fulfill it is something beyond me. My wizardly strength would not be enough to overcome my lack of wisdom."

"At least you're honest about it," Masumi said.

"The kind of person you need wouldn't be, unfortunately," Quint said. "Too many factions mean too many promises, and some of those promises can't possibly align with everyone's wants. I'm not good at lying."

"But everyone can lie," Masumi said. "Polite lies, impolite lies, misdirection, putting out misinformation. You've done some of that, I'm sure."

Quint raised his eyebrows. "Perhaps."

"It's the same thing, but on a bigger scale."

Quint frowned. "A much bigger scale."

"It just takes more practice, in your case," Masumi said with a smirk.

Quint hadn't considered himself totally naive, but he did now.

"Am I worthless at this?" Quint was becoming alarmed.

"She said you only need more practice," Narisu said. "Don't let her get you down."

"That's easy for you to say," Masumi said to Narisu.

Narisu groaned. "Lies always put you into peril. One never knows when a lie will turn on you. I'm glad you feel the way you do. As long as you modify the truth for something other than greed or raw power, I think you'll do all right."

"But with practice," Quint said. Narisu's words had calmed him down.

"We should reach our last stop before the border with Gamiza," Narisu said. "Neither of us has any friends in the town, but we will have to buy a few accessories to look more Gamizan when we enter the fief tomorrow."

Masumi talked a little about Slinnon, which interested Quint.

"Don't think that Slinnon is like Kippun, except with polennese rather than hubites. Kippun is a pale imitation of Slinnon without its depth of culture. You won't appreciate that until you've spent some time in my home country."

"Have you been to Slinnon?" Quint asked Narisu.

The Kippunese nodded his head. "She's right. I must admit I am intimidated when I've visited. There is that depth that Masumi mentioned that makes it unlike Kippun. If you strip the polennese style from our culture, we are much more hubite than we'd like to admit."

"That's what I like about Narisu, his insight. That's something rare for Kippunese." Masumi said. "Insight is something that is not always looked upon with admiration, I'm afraid."

Quint could see that. The motivators in Kippun, at least in Shimato fief, were mostly about power and money. Quint ran into the same thinking outside the Narukun cloisters and in South Fenola, but not with the universal intensity embraced by the Kippunese.

Narisu was no ordinary aide, it seemed. He thought independently, which Quint counted as a good thing.

The discussion made Quint more anxious to experience Slinnon, but he had more to do in Kippun. The cultural aspect might mean that what worked in Kippun might not be as successful in Masumi's home country.

§

Yomaha was a village masquerading as a town, Quint thought. The main street had town-sized buildings, but the rest of the town was modest in size with most shops and dwellings single-story affairs. It was big enough to have a permanent outdoor market, and that was where the three of them ended up after finding a modest inn with a stable.

"I hear there is a good cookware stall in the market," Masumi said.

"Oh, really?" Quint said.

Narisu chuckled. "Really. I think our camp pot needs replacing, don't you, Masumi?"

"Definitely." Masumi turned to Quint. "You'll tag along, won't you?"

"I will," Quint said, not feeling he had a choice.

Masumi didn't know her way around the market, but it wasn't a large area, and they found a few cookware stalls. The second stall they visited was their target.

"You are from Slinnon?" the stallkeeper asked. "I've heard of a woman buyer named Masumi who travels around Chokuno."

"What a coincidence!" Masumi said. "That's me." She slid closer. "What did you hear about me?" she said after giving the man a flirty smile.

The man looked around. "If you leave Chokuno, it will be dangerous, and Gamiza is getting harder to understand." He looked at Narisu and Quint and nodded.

"Can you give us some tips about how to look more Gamizan?" Masumi said.

"Hats. The kind that are knit with a couple of stripes. Walk around, and you'll see them. Your clothes are good enough." A couple walked up and began going through the merchandise. "Stay here, and I'll get the pot you wanted to see," he said, looking at the couple, who weren't noticing, but Quint could tell the stallkeeper assessed them.

"Something we can use on the road," Narisu said as the stallkeeper turned away.

The couple moved on, and the contact returned with a box. "Go around to the back. My assistant will exchange your weapons."

"I just bought crossbow bolts," Quint said.

"No worries. If you bought them in Tiryo, they were probably made in Gamiza, not Slinnon."

Quint showed the stallkeeper his crossbow.

"That was made in Slinnon."

Narisu pulled out his knife and cleaned a fingernail.

The stallkeeper shook his head. "Three knives and three swords. If you come back this way, I'll trade them back. I couldn't find the right pot," the man said as more shoppers showed up.

They nodded to each other, and Masumi led them through the crowd to the alley between stalls. They had to thread their way past carts, and animals hitched to stakes.

"This one," Masumi said. She flipped back the canvas door. "We bought some weapons your owner said we could exchange."

The teenage girl beckoned them inside the back of the stall. "Quickly. Father needs me upfront," she said.

They left their Chokunese weapons behind and were soon munching on street food, looking for a stall selling the knit hats the stallkeeper had mentioned. They had seen a few men and even a woman wearing them. The woman's hat had a fuzzy ball on the end. Masumi groaned, but they bought a couple each when they found a vendor.

Quint took two gray and a black striped caps. Narisu gravitated to blue and tan, while Masumi grabbed a red and white cap and a dark red and black one.

"I suggest you select a darker cap," Masumi said to Narisu, who growled but changed one of his selections.

They didn't wear their caps to the inn but would don them on the road. All three inspected their weapons.

"At least as good as the Chokunese blades," Masumi said. "I'd prefer to take my Slinnon sword, but it is in a safe place in Tiryo."

"I'll trade," Narisu said to Quint. "I like a heavier blade, and you are taller, so the length of this will suit you better."

After stowing their new purchases in the room, they ate dinner in the common room. There were a few people with the knit caps, but they were still fitting in fine. Quint enjoyed the food that had been advertised as Slinnon.

"Not bad," Masumi said. "Enjoy it while you can. Gamiza fief doesn't share a border with Slinnon."

∽

CHAPTER FIFTEEN
~

GETTING INTO GAMIZA WAS EASIER when someone had a map marked with unguarded routes. Narisu acquired it when in Tiryo, at the weapons shop. The horses didn't like the slippery trail after a late-night rain, but the winding trail through a cluster of hills didn't last long. The weather had turned colder with the moisture, and Quint was glad to have the warmer knit cap.

They avoided the first two villages they encountered on their way to the Gamizan capital. Narisu wanted some distance before they were noticed in the fief. The going was slower than through Chokuno since much of Gamiza was hilly. Narisu's map led them west for half a day before they turned south again and intersected a road heading to the capital.

Most of the adults wore the stocking caps, and the cookware seller was right. That was all it took to fit into the growing stream of people traveling to the political center of Gamiza.

"Everything has been simple and easy so far," Narisu said, "but this will be our most dangerous leg. We stay in the capital for two days and then return to Shimato. Our goal is to assess how thoroughly the Greens have infiltrated Gamiza."

The mission hadn't changed from when they set off days ago, but Quint had gained insight into the fiefs, two of them, anyway, and the rumors pointed to a merger with the Gamizans. That was valuable to him. The state of the Gamizan alliances was the most crucial part of Narisu's trip. He had no idea what Masumi's purpose was other than providing a distraction for anyone looking for Narisu and Quint.

The guards at the gate to Tiryo, the capital, were primarily intent on collecting bribes and inspecting what people brought into the city. No papers were examined. Quint wondered why that was so important for getting into the fief and then the urgency was dropped.

Masumi consulted some papers in her bags and conferred with Narisu about finding the way to a four-story inn. The journey ended mid-afternoon when they rode into a shabby stable and removed their bags before walking into the ramshackle inn. Narisu had the Gamizan money, which included coins from Shimato and Chokuno.

"Three together?" Narisu turned to ask Quint and Masumi.

"That is cheaper," Masumi said. "Maybe we can buy some treats if we do that." She looked hopefully at the woman at the counter.

"Three for a few nights," Masumi said. "What is the cheapest?"

"A room for two and a single," the woman said as she accepted Narisu's money.

"Key for Masumi," Narisu said, handing a simple wooden key to Masumi and a key to Quint.

"Same drill," Narisu said as they walked up to the third floor of the inn. Masumi's room was at the far end of the corridor. "Make sure your possessions are secure. Things are different in the capital than in the villages."

Quint didn't respond since Narisu warned them there could be listening posts in the rooms. Quint assumed there would be. Quint and Narisu's room was small, with barely enough floor space to fit their bags and bedrolls. The inn provided the matted floor and a few thin blankets. Narisu rolled one of his blankets into a pillow and sat on the floor to examine his weapons.

"You better do the same," Narisu said. "You never know what might happen in the capital. Don't leave your crossbow in the room, either."

Quint inspected his sword, knife, and tested the crossbow mechanism. He had done it before but so had Narisu. He ran his folded polishing cloth along the knife first, and then he did the same for his sword. The crossbow bolts had already been culled for defectives on the trail, but there were few for Quint's purposes.

Narisu yawned, stretched, and then stretched more along the edge room. Quint had to move when Chibo's aide inspected his side of the space. Narisu put his hand to his ear and pointed at the wall.

"Shall we lubricate our throats to better swallow the swill they probably serve here?" Narisu asked.

"We should. I assume Masumi will find her way downstairs?"

'If she doesn't beat us," Narisu said.

They entered the common room to see Masumi engaged in flirtatious conversation with a male server.

"Can we join you?" Narisu said to the server, who blushed.

"Not me. I work here."

Narisu raised an eyebrow. "It didn't look like it a minute ago," he said.

Masumi smiled up at the young man. "These are my friends," Masumi said and shrugged.

"I'll be back for your order. The menu is posted over there."

Quint turned to see three items on the board. None looked appealing. He did have the foresight to bring along the seasoning packet. It was in better shape after a few days of rearranging the contents on the road.

"I can use the traveling seasoning pouch?" Quint said. He grinned at Narisu. "That was such a good idea to bring that when we started our southern journey."

The server had lingered within hearing distance and returned. "Are you ready?"

Quint pursed his lips. That server wasn't very smooth about listening. There should be more listeners along the way.

"Is it permissible to use my seasoning pouch? I brought it along tonight," Quint asked.

"You'll not be the first. Are you from Narukun?" the server said.

"He isn't," Narisu said. "but I've traveled all the way to Pinzleport and back. We tried out using one on the road."

Quint chose what he hoped was the most benign meal and after the others had ordered, the server left to fetch a flagon of wine for them to share.

The meal was passable. The meat wasn't fresh, but the vegetables were, and the seasonings helped brighten everything up. Even Masumi complimented Quint on his seasoning artistry.

It was quite apparent that the server listened as much as he could.

"A quick walk," Narisu suggested. They were fully armed, but Quint hoped weapons would not have to be used.

A squad of guards intercepted them when they were halfway around the block from their inn.

"Do you have papers?" the leading officer asked.

"No," Narisu said. "We won't be in the capital for long."

"Then where are you going?"

"We thought we'd head north for the hills bordering Chokuno and do some fishing and hunting," Narisu said.

"And then?"

Masumi stood closer to the officer. "Cook the meat and enjoy what Tova and Tizurek give us."

Half the guards put their hands to their hearts, showing they were believers. The captain scowled at the expressions of piety.

"You need papers in the city. I don't know why the guards were so lax at the gate."

Quint knew, but he didn't respond.

"Come with me. Do you promise you won't draw your weapons?" the officer asked.

"We do," Narisu said.

"Don't try, or we will cut you down without warning."

"Is what you just said a warning?" Masumi said.

"Yes," the officer said, blushing, "and it will be the only warning you get."

They walked through the city streets for twenty minutes before arriving at a guard station. The officer insisted that they give up their weapons at that time. He sat them down to wait.

Masumi whispered something in Narisu's ear, earning a disapproving look from a sergeant sitting behind an elevated desk.

"Don't talk."

"We won't," Narisu said.

Quint fondled a crossbow bolt. He had slipped four in his pocket while handing over his bag of bolts and the handheld crossbow.

"Where is the weapon," the sergeant said.

"I left it behind," Quint asked.

The sergeant grunted and returned to his paperwork until a different officer entered the room. "You three, come with me," the officer said.

They entered an interview room. A guard stood with a sword in hand in each corner. Narisu, Masumi, and Quint sat on one side and the officer on the other.

"You have been to the capital before?" the officer said.

"I haven't," Quint said truthfully.

"We are here to get papers?" Narisu asked. "I didn't need them the last time I was here."

"Times have changed. We need them now. Where are you from?"

Narisu gave the information for all of them. Quint paid attention in case he would have to respond. Narisu continued, "We are heading to Hari's village," he nodded in Quint's direction, "in the northeast mountains to do some camping."

"Two men and a woman?" the officer said.

"Can't a girl dangle her line in the water and catch a fish in this world?"

The officer grunted, visibly irritated with her attempt to charm him. "Why are you in the capital?"

"It's on the way," Narisu said, "and Hari's never been."

"You are armed like fighters. Why?"

"Because we are fighters. Not very good ones, of course, or we would be in the warlord's army."

"You may very well find yourself in the army even if you aren't particularly adept with a sword." The officer narrowed his eyes. "In fact, I don't believe a word any of you have said. The penalty for misleading an officer of the Gamizan forces is impressment, and none of you were persuasive."

"Not even me?" Masumi asked.

The officer cleared his throat and stood. "Consider yourselves drafted into Warlord Akimura's service. There is a wagon in the back that will take you to your inn for your possessions; then, it is a ride into the eastern hills to a training camp. Maybe there will be a fishing stream close by." The officer smirked. "The innkeeper gets your horses for pointing you out."

§

The wagon was a rolling prison cell complete with bars. There were two other unfortunates in the wagon. No one was happy except for Masumi, who hummed as they made their way out of the capital.

Quint followed Narisu's gaze at their new companions. They looked too fit to Quint, and the pair didn't talk to them or each other. He guessed they were already in the Gamizan army, but he couldn't say anything.

"Where are you from?" Narisu asked.

"Here and there," one of them said. "We got caught fighting in a pub."

Quint couldn't see any bruises on their faces or their knuckles. A serious fight between these two would definitely leave the marks of battle. Quint doubted they would probably get helpful information, but the wagon was taking them much closer to the Shimato border.

If they were going to be trained, they could leave with weapons, and if they were on the run, it wouldn't matter if Narisu and Quint used magic to escape. Quint wouldn't call it a blessing from Tova, but they could have been put in a dungeon in the capital, which would have been much worse.

They were treated like prisoners. Their meals were slipped through the bars and they each were given a thin blanket. There wasn't much room to lie down, so Quint and Narisu had to sleep sitting up with their backs to the bars. It rained the second night and Quint was thankful the roof was solid to keep a little of the wet out.

At midday on the third day on the road, the wagon turned down a well-worn dirt road and ended up at a fort. Quint was familiar with forts and stockades from when he was abducted by the Racellian Wizard Corps.

"Out. The woman goes over there, and the rest of you come with me."

A female soldier took Masumi away, and a squad of soldiers took the four men in the opposite direction. They still had their bags, which had obviously been ransacked. At least Narisu had been able to get rid of the map before they entered the capital. A soldier carried a canvas sack with their weapons.

The fort had plenty of men idling about, and there didn't seem to be a lot of discipline. Consistent with Kippunese practices, the buildings were one and two stories high. They were led to a building with wooden bars on the windows. Quint shook his head. Most Kippunese structures could be broken out of easily.

They were taken inside and washed up before they were given clean but well-used uniforms. They wore the boots they had with them, and their civilian clothes were taken away.

"You don't get the clothes you wore on your way here returned."

"I don't want them," one of the pair said. "Three days in those is enough for anyone."

Narisu looked at Quint and nodded. Those two weren't who they portrayed themselves to be.

"Time to see how you fight."

"Have us kill each other and get it over with here and now?" one of the two said.

Quint thought it was an idiotic comment. If they were to be killed, they wouldn't have taken the wagon into the mountains. Any long stretch of woods would do. Quint and Narisu didn't listen to anything else the pair said. Some of their comments sounded like they were enticing Quint and Narisu to say something derogatory.

Three women in female versions of the same worn uniforms showed up. One was Masumi, standing out with her black hair among the hubites. All of them were told to line up and listen.

"I'm Sergeant Reiko. I don't want to know who you are until I see if I should treat you respectfully or like dirt. It's time to see what kind of scum you are," the sergeant said. He had a yellow circle sewn on his sleeve, which Quint assumed was the rank identification. They didn't use circles in Shimato.

"Pair off, Sergeant Reiko said." He assigned Quint to Masumi, the two women to each other and he dragged a passing soldier to fight Narisu. The pair would fight each other. "We didn't drag you here to kill each other, so it's wooden swords. Pick one out of that barrel."

All the swords looked alike. The edges had lots of nicks, with cloth-wrapped grips. Masumi looked the most comfortable with a sword in hand among the women, and the pair who had ridden with them from the capital swung their swords well enough as everyone warmed up. A few spectators showed up as Quint worked out the kinks from their travels.

"You'll have to be gentle," Masumi said with her usual smirk.

"If you will be likewise with me. Remember, I'm still a teenager," Quint said.

Reiko cleared his throat. "No talking again unless I permit you. You don't want to know what happens if you don't get permission." He waited for a moment. "Face each other. On Guard. Go!"

Quint had sparred with Masumi as they had traveled, and he knew how she would fight, so they sparred. She threw a few different looks at him that caught him off guard and smacked him. It certainly hurt more than when Quint had a magical shield up.

"Watch out for the person behind you!" Quint said.

Masumi turned around, and he smacked her bottom with the flat of his sword. A few of the spectators laughed, but she groaned. "To think such an ancient trick got to me," Masumi said. "You won't get that opportunity again. Let's continue."

Quint held up his hand and looked at the pair of men going through the motions. Sergeant Reiko looked casually at them and then turned to Narisu fighting an overmatched soldier.

"You're not bad for an old man," Reiko said.

"And not bad for a young one?" Narisu said as he deflected a swipe at his neck from the soldier. Narisu's opponent's swing took him off balance, and Narisu kicked the soldier in the stomach, sending him to the ground. When the soldier looked up, Narisu had the dull point of his wooden sword at the soldier's neck. "Good enough?" Narisu asked the sergeant.

Reiko nodded. "I've seen what I wanted to see." Everyone stopped. He looked at the two men. "You are ready for the field. Head to the administration shack." Reiko pointed. "Go over there and register with the army."

"What about me?" Narisu asked.

"You need a little more seasoning along with the others," Reiko said.

Quint took that to mean the army wasn't ready to set them free.

Reiko consulted a clipboard. "Masumi Hantisu?"

Masumi stepped forward.

"You will be the leader of your training group. Return to your barracks and wait for your instructor."

Masumi nodded to Narisu and did as she was told.

"You two get your things and return here. On the run there and back," Reiko said, sitting down.

Narisu jogged, and Quint followed. "Splitting us from Masumi complicates everything, obviously," Narisu said. "The sergeant didn't waste any time culling out the army's spies. They will probably return to the capital before we get back to the sergeant."

They returned with their bags, which made the return a little more taxing.

"You will be staying in our secure facility," Reiko said.

"Where we washed up isn't secure, sir?" Narisu asked.

Reiko only gave them a slimy smile. "You'll see."

∽

CHAPTER SIXTEEN

THEY FOLLOWED THE SERGEANT BEHIND THE BUILDINGS lining the large courtyard and saw the only stone-built structure in the fort. The bars weren't wood but iron.

"This looks more like a jail, sir," Quint said.

Reiko gave Quint a self-satisfied smile. "So I've been told," he said. "You'll find out if it is or not by your deportment during training. No one trusts you or your stories," Reiko said, tapping on his clipboard. The officer at the capital must have sent a report along with them.

"What does that say, sir?" Quint asked.

"You can figure it out, I'm sure. Inside."

The rooms were like jail cells, with three rooms on either side of the central corridor with each room set up for three inmates.

"You are in luck," Sergeant Reiko said. "There are two empty rooms. You each get one. You can pick any bed. Get inside. Close the door, and someone will fetch you for your next meal."

Narisu's room was one to the left and on the other side of the corridor. They didn't share a wall, which made communication more difficult. Once Quint closed his door, a guard locked it from the outside. He tried the latch, and it wouldn't budge. The bottom of the lower windowsill was six feet high, with the window extending two feet to the ceiling. He sat down and went through his things. His seasoning pouch was gone, along with his money and his tiny cooking kit.

With nothing else to do, Quint reviewed all the strings he knew. His recall had always been good, and after Tova had messed with him, it was even better. After getting halfway through his strings, the door opened. Narisu stood behind the guard. That would have been a mistake if the pair were ready to break out. Quint must remember to do the same if he was released first.

Two soldiers escorted them to the headquarters building. Their travel companions wore much better uniforms as they left the fort on horses. Neither looked at Narisu or Quint.

"What are you looking at?" a guard said before giving Quint a rough shove up the stairs.

Quint didn't respond, but Narisu stumbled as his guard did the same to him. He rolled over and got up from his hands and knees. Quint could see an opportunity to launch into the guard another time. He smiled at his pattern of thinking. Quint would have to continue to look for weaknesses. It gave him some purpose.

He wouldn't have dared to think that way five years ago. The Racellian army was much more disciplined.

They were seated in a rough-hewn conference room. It looked like fellow soldiers had made the furniture. Masumi was pushed through the door, followed by a young officer who strutted into the room followed by two soldiers and a man about Narisu's age wearing a long black knit hat.

"Stand when I enter!" the officer said.

The three stood as one and bowed to the officer, but Quint looked at the older man. He was the one who had a mantle of competence that the officer didn't.

The pair sat across from Narisu, Masumi, and Quint.

"You may be seated," the officer said. "Now, why are you in Gamiza?"

"We came through the capital on our way to hunt and fish," Narisu said. "Hari's family knows of an excellent lake and stream in these mountains. We were looking for private work on the other side of the capital and made the mistake of spending the night. Hari and Masumi have never been, so we walked around until the army snagged us."

"Is what this man is saying correct?" the officer asked Masumi.

"Why else would we be in the capital other than to see the sights," Masumi said. "I'll withhold comments on the sights."

Quint had been looking at the black-hatted man and wasn't surprised to see him cast a string just before Narisu lied. He sighed. It was probably a lie-detection string of some kind.

"And you?" the officer looked at Quint. "Do you concur with what they said?"

"We fully intended to head east from the capital and head for the mountains," Quint said.

The black-hatted man looked up and looked intently at Quint. He leaned forward. "You must be lying, but I couldn't detect a lie like I did for your friends."

"I didn't lie," Quint said.

"Are you a wizard?"

"No," Quint said.

The wizard frowned. "You must be. Tell me a lie."

"I like it here," Quint said.

The wizard's eyes grew. "No string, and yet."

"Is something wrong, Master Gomio?" Quint asked.

"Master," Narisu said. "Good for you. The least the Gamizan army can do is provide you with a uniform more befitting your station."

"Are you a wizard?" Gomio asked Narisu.

"Of course, we are all wizards."

"Another lie," Gomio said, "but it doesn't tell me anything." He looked at the officer. "Let me talk to them by myself. Perhaps I can get more information out of them."

"We already know they aren't common itinerants," the officer said. "You have my permission to skewer them with fire if necessary." The man rose and left with the two guards.

Master Gomio's eyes followed the uniformed soldiers out the door.

"Are you spies from Chokuno or Shimato?"

"Why couldn't we be spies from Narukun?" Narisu asked.

"They don't care enough about the fiefs," Gomio said. "You know that."

"What if we were Greens?" Masumi asked.

"Then you wouldn't be spies, would you? You'd be Gamiza's allies," Gomio said.

"Do you think we are spies?" Quint asked.

Gomio laughed. "Because all three of you are too smart. The two men who rode with you from the capital claimed you said nothing incriminating.

That was strange to me when the woman and the man were lying. I couldn't detect you doing the same. It's as if you are immune to my string, and that doesn't happen."

"It happens more than you think," Narisu said.

The black-hatted man snorted. "And you would know?"

"I've known enough wizards whose strings don't work the same on everyone. You don't need to be a wizard to know that," Narisu said.

"But it's rare, so you have been around many wizards, or you are one." Gomio grinned. "I think you are one. Maybe not master-level, but competent enough. You do carry yourself more like a soldier than a wizard. I'll give you that, and your proficiency with arms is very good, so I'd say you are embedded in a military command. The woman is a hired sword of some kind, but she is bound by more than money to one of you. If she is a wizard, it is a secondary identity, even more so than you," Gomio said to Narisu. "Am I getting closer?"

"Yes," Narisu said.

"But you, young man, are the enigma. I think you are the Narukun wizard who defeated three Green masters not that long ago. The name?" Gomio rolled his eyes in thought. "Quinto Tiroli or something, the South Fenolan wild master. There are rumors you were in Shimato, but I didn't expect you to show up in Gamiza after you were thrown out at the border, I believe."

"You have excellent sources of information," Quint said as he created a shield. "Are you ready to meet Tova?"

"I prefer Tizurek, but not for years yet, and I think you have a shield up, although it is still different from any other I've ever encountered."

"A different magic," Quint said.

"It would have to be for someone as young as you to defeat the two greatest Green masters in Narukun. I was told neither could be defeated."

"It wasn't easy," Quint said. "I almost didn't make it on the second one."

Gomio nodded. "But you did. Impressive. Give me a moment." Gomio invoked a string that didn't excite Quint's shield. He seemed to go into a trance but came out of it pursing his lips."

"I wanted to see your future for myself." Gomio shrugged. "You are destined for greatness, but how? What? When?" He shook his head. "It is all a jumble, but I've seen enough. How can I be of help?"

Quint blinked. "Help?"

Gomio nodded. "Take me with you wherever you go, either north or east. I can't stomach the Greens. I thought I was touched with arrogance. I am a new-born lamb compared with those people."

"Are there Green masters left?" Narisu asked.

"Not at the level that Quinto faced, but dangerous enough for me, you, and the girl."

"Girl?" Masumi beamed. "Thank you for that."

Gomio smiled. "My pleasure." He sighed. "I've been assigned here for a remark I made about the warlord's alliance with the Greens of Narukun. I asked to go with some of my fellow Gamizans into Chokuno, but they wouldn't let me. The idiot who runs this camp shouldn't have let you out of the secure barracks. With you two and whatever magic the girl," he smiled at Masumi, "possesses would be all for the better."

"What about our weapons?"

Gomio grimaced. "I hope they weren't family heirlooms," he said, "My friend is not that much of an idiot, but he doesn't understand wizards. Most military men don't," Gomio looked at Narisu, "with a possible exception in you. We can be out of here in fifteen minutes."

"Aren't you interested in why we are here?" Narisu asked.

Gomio shrugged. "Information about Gamiza. Information about the Greens? Either of which would be valuable to Chokuno or Shimato. I don't care which if that is where Quinto is going. He is important, and I have already been set aside. Our esteemed warlord wants to hear from the Green wizards, not me. I've given all the warnings I can safely give."

"You were an advisor to the warlord?" Narisu asked.

"Not quite," Gomio said with a chuckle. "I advised another Master with better political skills than I have. He isn't listened to, either, but the warlord still wants him close to keep the army wizards calm before the Greens formally take over."

"Then we are ready now," Narisu said. "Our weapons are Gamizan. They can stay in Gamiza. We have everything we need."

"Especially now that my seasoning pouch was stolen."

"You are from Narukun," Gomio said.

"I got used to a little extra oompf to my meals," Masumi said.

"Stay here until the guards take you back. We will make a break before you are locked up again."

Gomio left them alone in the room.

"What do you think?" Quint asked Narisu.

"I have a lie detection string as well, and it is less obtrusive than his. He wasn't lying and I couldn't see how he could have phrased what he told us to defeat my string. Do you want him to come with you?"

"If he is telling the truth, we can find out more from him than we can listening in pubs for a month," Masumi said.

"If we are betrayed, it will be three to one," Quint said.

"If he betrays us, there will be more than just him on the other side," Narisu said. "But I don't see a good alternative. They don't trust us, so we won't get weapons, and we may never leave this fort alive."

Guards threw the door open. Quint thought they were already betrayed.

"Up!" a soldier who had escorted them to the building said. "Time to return you to your luxurious rooms. This time, the lady gets a cell, and the men get to share."

Close to the cell block, where the view was cut off from the courtyard by other buildings; a figure stepped forward wearing a black hooded cape. The hood was drawn over his head, but Quint had a sense of Gomio's magic, and it matched the level of the wizard they met in the conference room.

Gomio cast a string, and two soldiers dropped. Quint and Narisu took care of the other, so they were the only ones standing.

"There! Now, what do we do?" Gomio said.

"You don't know?" Narisu said in an urgent whisper.

"You and the girl are the military ones."

"Drag the guards into the cells," Quint said. Once that was done, Quint led them further north, creating a hole in the palisade by binding the wood and then cutting out an exit hole. He pushed the hole out and when they had scrambled to freedom, he replaced the wood and rebound it to the wall before leading them northwest into the woods.

When they were out of sight, a patrol strolled past them, making a round of the fort. The soldiers didn't even look at the palisade as they laughed at each other's jokes.

"We have to run," Narisu said. He led in the direction Quint had started and found a stream to cross on their right-hand side. "Take your boots and socks off. We have a lot of traveling to do."

The four of them continued north, heading upstream until Narisu jumped out of the stream onto boulders. They crawled on the rocks and then were back in the forest, now walking on an easterly heading.

"Shimato!" Gomio said.

"You could have found that through skillful questioning," Narisu said.

"I'm not that skillful," Gomio said, "I had to convince the fort's commander to accompany you into the conference building. The commander refused to meet you in the cells. Didn't like the smell."

"Does it matter at this point?" Masumi said. "Lead on Nari-kins."

"Nari-kins?" Narisu said, sounding almost hurt by the nickname.

Masumi shrugged and smiled.

"We have the rest of the western range to cross," Narisu said. "It won't be easy."

Gomio chuckled. "We call it the eastern range." Gomio began to solicit questions about Shimato's strategies, but then he complained about his fief. The Gamizan warlord was ready to sign an alliance with the Greens. The Chokunese were a military disappointment, and Gamiza and the Greens didn't want to depend on them as they launched their conquest of North Fenola.

The wizard gave them more information than they could hope to glean as spies, but was any of it accurate?

∽

CHAPTER SEVENTEEN
~

Quint spotted a berry patch, which they stripped quickly before proceeding.

"Do you have a knife?" Quint asked the Gamizan wizard.

"I do, but it isn't very big."

"Can I use it?" Quint said. "I can teleport a knife wherever I like. Maybe we can scare up some meat. Berries aren't enough for me."

Gomio handed the blade to Quint. It might be something Quint would use at a meal, but it was better than nothing.

There was no close pursuit, but they kept moving even as the sun set. Quint spotted movement in the underbrush, saw a pair of bunny ears, and immediately cast a string, sending the knife into a large rabbit.

Narisu volunteered to skin the animal, and Gomio and Quint provided the low flame to cook the meat without resorting to a large fire. Since Gomio had the knife, he sliced the meat and handed out morsels.

Narisu leaned back against a tree. "Always better than berries," he said.

"Perhaps a berry sauce might make this more palatable," Masumi said. "That is if we had Quint's seasoning pouch and his cooking kit with us."

Quint had learned to ignore tastes he didn't particularly like, and rabbit wasn't at the top of his list; however, the food was warm.

Night began to fall, but they had more energy than they thought, especially as the darkness revealed a few parties with torches wandering around on the same slope.

"They are after us," Narisu said. "Are there other wizards at the fort?"

"A few, but no masters. Perhaps you were found with a predictor string," Gomio said.

"I avoid the things," Quint said. "I didn't know that was possible."

Gomio shrugged. "I threw it out as a possibility."

Quint didn't know how to detect if a string was tracking them or how such a thing would work. Even masters such as himself didn't know all the spells that could be cast.

"I think a more probable reason is they have sent multiple teams to the east, thinking we are spies from Shimato," Masumi said.

Quint felt some relief from Masumi's observation. The simplest explanation was likely the best. He spent a few moments watching the lights move below them.

"They aren't heading straight to us, but we can't stop," Narisu said.

The night seemed to go on forever. Each of them tripped or fell or both multiple times in the darkness. Unfortunately, it was a moonless night, and everyone felt the fatigue of their hasty escape.

They found a rocky overhang to protect them from an evening rain and spent an uncomfortable night far off the track that they followed. Masumi shook Quint awake just before dawn and covered Quint's mouth. "One of the teams is getting close."

Masumi woke the others. They looked at the lights in the false dawn coming up the same trail they had used.

"Was last night's rain enough to cover our tracks?" Gomio asked.

"Do you know some kind of illusion string that might protect us if they move off the path?" Narisu asked Gomio.

Gomio made a sorrowful face. "Don't ask me. I'm not the only master here. I'm a wizard, not a fighter."

"It's too light," Quint said. "I can make it dark, but that only makes dark darker. I can cast a confusion string, but it would be better for them to call off the search on their own."

Masumi and Narisu almost nodded in unison.

"However, getting out of here without being captured may require us to fight. Our pursuers probably have food and weapons," Narisu said. "Killing them for provisions and swords isn't a good reason, but stopping them from doing the same to us is."

"You are willing to fight without weapons. I can cast shields. They will protect you from magic, but they only slow a sword thrust or an arrow," Quint said.

"That is good enough for me. Cut a staff, and I'll do the rest," Masumi said.

"I can use my magic to attack, but I'd rather do it until I can grab a sword," Narisu said.

Quint grunted. He couldn't bring himself to smile. "You need more string practice."

"Ask the war leader," Narisu said.

"I will," Quint said, "if we make it out of here."

"What about me?" Gomio asked.

"Can you cast a shield string on your own?"

"Mine only work against magic."

"Then I can do it for you. Do your best. If you can get close enough for a sleeping spell, do that. We will decide what to do with any slumbering enemy after we've prevailed," Quint said.

"He likes sleeping spells," Narisu said. "He's too soft-hearted."

Gomio smiled. "Perhaps I am, too."

The search party was farther up the trail when dawn brought enough light to find some straight saplings.

Quint used a one-handed string to cut down four saplings with the correct diameters. He brought them to the overhang where the others waited.

"I'll go first," Quint said. He cast shield strings for his companions and created a stronger one for himself. That was how the string worked.

"We should catch them on flat ground if we can. If they are higher than us, they will have a tactical advantage," Narisu said.

Quint knew that, and Masumi probably did, too, but looking at Gomio nodding his head, the concept looked new to him. Gomio looked in possession of himself at the fort, but once they were on the run, he acted like an inexperienced teenager. Quint smiled at the thought that he was getting to be an experienced teenager, but that would only last as long until he turned twenty.

They reached the trail. Quint could tell the rain had protected them. He wondered if they should have just waited for the searchers to fail to find them and returned down the same path. It was too late now.

The ground had dried a bit by the time they reached a meadow. The path was a bare patch threading its way through the grass, but the footprints of the search party were easy to see.

"Seven plus an officer," Narisu said.

Quint looked at the tracks and could see the officer's slimmer sole. The soldiers had hobnailed boots or just big boots. They reached the end of the meadow and walked over a dry streambed. On the other side, He counted two soldiers and the officer.

He stopped and gathered his party around him. "They have split into a group of four soldiers and another with two soldiers and the officer," Quint said. "We will be attacked once we get into the thick part of the forest again."

"I read it the same way," Masumi said. "Good work, Quint!"

"I'll still lead with Gomio behind me and Masumi and Narisu guarding against the four guards in the rear. They could attack as soon as we pass the rear guard," Quint said.

Quint held tightly onto his staff, using it as a walking stick but thinking the staff was a weapon. They walked fifty paces into the woods before being confronted by the search party.

A lance of lightning hit Gomio in the side. The light crackled and spread over a third of Quint's shield. Narisu returned fire, but the wizard was shielded against Narisu's weaker attack. Quint still had Gomio's knife and used his crossbolt string to throw the knife through the shield and into the wizard's chest, who went down immediately.

The three survivors drew swords, and the fight was on. They still concentrated on Gomio, who took a cut to the shoulder. The fighter leaned down to see if Gomio was killed, but the wizard reached up and put the fighter to sleep.

Masumi fought with a swordsman who was good at whittling her staff, but Masumi knocked it against the opponent's neck hard enough to make him drop his sword. She was quicker to the sword and disabled the soldier permanently,

Narisu played with his opponent, expertly deflecting the flat blade of the sword as the soldier attacked. He got in an undefended move to the groin. When the soldier doubled over, Narisu struck the man's chin. He took the dropped sword and finished the attacker off.

The action was over so quickly that the officer and the two soldiers hadn't reached the battle site.

Quint picked up a sword. Gomio was still on the ground, clutching his shoulder, and Narisu and Masumi were waving their new weapons, getting a feel for the weight.

"Kill them!" the officer said.

It wasn't the fort commander, but they were obviously cut from the same cloth. He stood behind the other two, unconvincingly waving his sword. The other two soldiers hadn't drawn their weapons, which meant they were wizards.

"You can stop right there," Quint said. "I'm going to give you a choice. You can leave and take whoever is still alive behind us, or you can fight. We will not return."

"Your master is wounded. He can't use both hands, which means you are defenseless," the officer said from behind his protectors.

"He isn't my master," Quint said.

"Nor mine," Narisu said.

"Nor mine," Masumi repeated.

"You are all that powerful? I don't believe you."

One of the two wizards made a big show of creating a string and cast a fire spear at Quint. The attack spread out and died away on Quint's chest.

"My turn?' Quint asked. He sent a lightning bolt through the wizard and singed the officer's sleeve. "You don't even have shields?"

"W-We do," the other wizard said. He dropped to his knees. "I surrender."

That left the officer gawking directly at Quint.

"And you?" Narisu asked with a grating laugh.

"I can't fail," the officer said.

"He could be killed for failure," Gomio said, "but not if there are multiple search parties out."

Masumi's staff sailed over Quint's shoulder and embedded itself just below the officer's ribs, making him fall back. Quint looked back. "What did you do?" Quint asked.

"I sharpened one end while everyone else was chatting," Masumi said.

Two of the seven were alive. They left the wizard who surrendered and the recovered soldier behind, securing them with the handcuffs the search party had brought with them. If the other soldiers were to be buried, that would be up to the survivors.

They continued up the trail, armed, fed, and not fearing anyone behind them. Narisu thought the Shimato border was a few hours away. That would mean little to a Gamizan pursuit, but they were also hampered by a slowing Gomio, whose shoulder needed better attention than any of them could offer.

§

Mid-afternoon, they could see the trail on the other side of a valley. Toward the top was an outpost. Quint could see a couple of soldiers standing guard. From their point of view, they couldn't tell if it was a Shimato or a Gamizan border crossing.

There were a few other avenues up the hill, but the trail was the easiest.

"Should we fight, or should we evade?" Quint said.

Gomio had already cast a predictor string. He shook his head and balled his fists. "You make predictor strings go crazy," Gomio said.

"I have used predictor strings in the past. Maybe it's time to try again," Quint said. He hadn't cast a predictor string in a long time and now, everything related to him was blurry, other than he thought they would be successful.

He frowned. "I can't see the outcome of whatever we do," Quint said. "Let's make a decision based on what we know and what we see."

"It could be a trap," Masumi said. "Showing a few soldiers and having others lurking around."

"Then we forge our own path," Narisu said. "Which is the third best way?"

Quint looked across the valley. They would be exposed for half of the way along the forest floor. "Why don't we circle the valley under the trees and then go up the best path? If they can't see us coming, they will be less prepared."

"You want to fight?" Gomio asked.

"If they see us coming, they can rush to cut us off no matter what trail we take."

"If that is a viable way," Masumi said, "I agree with Quint."

"That makes three of us," Narisu said. "I concede."

"It wasn't a competition," Quint said.

"Between two men, it's always a competition," Masumi said.

§

Masumi volunteered to slip through the foliage as they approached the outpost and ferret out any lurking soldiers. Narisu kept close to Gomio to make sure he didn't slip on the slope. His injury had made him less steady on his feet. Quint did the leading.

Masumi showed up on the trail within one hundred yards from the top.

"Gamizans. Three to the left and two to the right. They are wearing swords, so I don't think there are wizards."

"Can we take any of them from behind?" Quint asked.

Masumi nodded. "I can't do it on my own," she said.

"I can stay off the trail with Gomio while you take down the three soldiers," Narisu said.

Quint didn't see an alternative. Perhaps it would have been better to take another path. He followed Masumi, staying crouched down to avoid detection from above. They went beyond where the three were and worked their way back toward the trail, hitting the guards from an unexpected direction. Quint put his stronger shields on both of them.

When the soldiers were in sight, there was a call from the outpost. Narisu and Gomio had been spotted. Two guards jumped from the tiny camp and ran toward Narisu and Gomio.

"I'll cut the enemy down in size," Quint said, moving past Masumi.

The three guards left, realized someone was behind them, and turned as one to confront Quint. One of them had a hand-held crossbow and shot. Quint automatically put his sword hand up to ward off the bolt, but it penetrated his shield and hit his right hand squarely in the middle, making him drop his weapon.

His first thought of putting all three to sleep wouldn't work with the painful bolt in his hand. He lost his physical weapon and part of his magical attack. Masumi bounded past him and attacked all three.

Quint hesitated momentarily until he raised his left hand and cast a lightning string at the archer. The man went down, and Quint quickly launched another lightning bolt at another guard. The pain hadn't affected his aim, but he couldn't continue for long, with his hand dripping blood.

Masumi fought an equal battle with her opponent. Quint quickly picked up his sword with his left hand and approached the pair. His presence allowed Masumi to end the fight, but as she did, Masumi sustained a cut to her side.

They stood over the three bodies, catching their breaths.

"Go through their packs for bandages," Masumi said, clutching her side. "Luckily, my shield kept me alive."

They helped each other quickly wrap their wounds, but Quint paused to pick up a pouch of crossbow bolts and the crossbow and led Masumi over the bodies, going as fast as Masumi could to rescue their friends.

By the time they reached the trail, Narisu and Gomio had been captured. Narisu didn't appear to have put up a fight. Masumi pulled Quint back, and they observed the end of the capture.

"Where are your companions? There are four, including the woman warrior," a guard said.

"We ran into one of your search parties. As you can see, there is only us," Narisu said.

"But you must have defeated the scouts," a guard who appeared to be the leader said. Two more guards they didn't count arrived from the top of the ridge. Now, there were four confronting Narisu and Gomio."

"What about the boy?"

"Dead," Gomio said. "He was caught unaware by a wizard. His shield wasn't strong enough. We had stopped fighting, thinking we had taken care of them all. Masumi died killing the last wizard."

"There will be hell to pay," one of the guards said.

Quint didn't know if he referred to Narisu and Gomio or the failure of the scouts.

One of the guards looked around. "Sergeant Hinoto's group should be here by now."

Quint shot a bolt, hitting the leader square in the chest. As the Gamizan fell, Masumi entered the path immediately moving between Narisu and the other guards.

"Stay where you are," Quint said, holding the loaded crossbow. He managed cocking it with one hand.

"We were told you were left along the trail," one of the three remaining guards said.

Narisu shrugged. "So, I lied. What does that change?"

The guards raised their weapons.

A spear of fire hit one of them, brushing past Narisu. Quint cast a string, sending the bolt into another guard, and Masumi and Narisu took care of the last guard.

Quint had to cast a water string to extinguish the fire on Narisu's arm.

"I'm sorry about that," Gomio said.

"Let's get going," Narisu said, picking up his sword.

They stopped at the empty border post to re-bandage their wounds.

Gomio found a small pot of ointment for Narisu's burns, and then it was downhill from there into Shimato.

Quint was relieved they were back. After an uncomfortable night under the stars, they were approaching a crossroads; one of those routes would take them to Morimanu, the capital.

Masumi hugged Narisu and then a surprised Quint. She waved goodbye as she left them, heading back to Chokuno fief.

Gomio watched her go. "Why doesn't she accompany us to the capital?"

Narisu sighed. "She isn't allowed in Shimato. The story is she is wanted for the murder of an over-anxious guard in a border town," Narisu said.

"But she was a help. You just let her go?" Gomio said.

"Don't worry. Masumi will get a reward. She stays in touch with the right people in Chokuno."

Quint hoped Narisu was truthful about the reward. Masumi had proven herself a few times on their journey.

Narisu spent more time with Gomio as they walked into a town, squeezing as much information about the state of Gamizan politics as possible. Quint understood most of it, but his knowledge of fief matters didn't allow him to get some of the nuances.

They hired a carriage and driver at a town, and after a few minutes on the road, all three were snoring away.

∽

CHAPTER EIGHTEEN

GOMIO WENT WITH NARISU, AND QUINT CONTINUED on to his new quarters at the former Three Fork mansion. He stepped through the gate and wearily walked back to his quarters. His weapons had already been shipped to the capital and were laid out on his bed.

"You made it back," Dakuz said, leaning against a doorpost. "I was hoping I'd pick up some new weapons."

Quint chuckled. "You don't like swords and crossbows. I'm not sorry to disappoint you."

"As it happens, I'm not. I'd rather see you here. The soldier that brought those said Narisu and you had headed into Gamiza fief."

"We did. I knew it would be an adventure, and it was. I'll tell everyone what happened at dinner. Is everyone in?"

Dakuz shrugged. "Where else would we be? Thera and I have been building files of the other fiefs. Shira has been visiting us daily, diligently learning a new craft. I'm surprised how well she is doing."

"Todo?"

"He's been managing the Three Forks faction, after all. We are close to getting their endorsement, which will help us attract the Shimato wizard factions."

"We brought a master wizard with us from Gamiza. He knew everything we wanted to know, so I'd grade our foray a success."

"Except for your wrapped hand?" Dakuz said.

"Part of the adventure. The back of my hand was a target. Luckily, I had an active shield, but it wasn't enough for a close crossbow bolt, even if it was a hand-held one."

"Do you need to see a healer?"

"It wouldn't hurt, I suppose," Quint said. Nasiru said he would send someone over.

Thera, Dugo, and Todo arrived.

"We heard you were back," Thera said. She paused for a moment. "We were told Narisu and you were accompanied by an attractive Slinnon woman."

"Masumi. She is a friend of Narisu's. You would be challenged in a sword fight, but she isn't the wizard you are."

"I suppose that is a compliment," Thera said.

"I suppose it is," Quint said, feeling a little testy. "I'm going to rest until dinner. Dakuz can wake me, if he would."

"I will. You might want to wash and change your clothes."

Quint ran a hand through his hair. "I suppose I'm more tired that I thought." He knew it was a weak apology, but it was all he had the energy to give.

Feeling much better after a bath and fresh clothes, Quint was ready for dinner before Dakuz came by.

"I thought I'd have to shake you awake," Dakuz said.

"Being clean helped. I lost my seasoning pouch, and my injury is keeping me awake."

Dakuz smiled. "Someone will be eating better for a while."

Quint wasn't used to eating at the Three Fork mansion. He told everyone about his adventure and the rest of dinner was filled with conjecture on how Gamiza would change if the Greens took over.

"Narisu knows that better than we do, apart from Todo. As an outsider, I don't understand enough of the political intricacies between the fiefs."

"You know more than you think. Gamiza doesn't operate with much nuance," Todo said. "My impression of the Greens is that they are after domination of all North Fenola."

"Your impression is correct. Gomio, the Gamizan wizard, said as much," Quint said. "We need to continue to work on our charter while Chibo, the warlord, and his advisors digest what information we brought back. Everyone discounts Chokuno fief and for good reason. However, even they have use in a battle. Narisu thinks some diplomacy might defuse the alliance, especially after Thera and I were able to help defeat them."

§

Quint held out his hand while the healer that Narisu sent over unwrapped the bandage. His hand didn't look good and the sound the healer made confirmed that it didn't.

"Do you have use of your fingers?" the healer asked.

"I do, but my hand feels a little stiff." Quint looked at the damage. The torn edges of his skin had taking on white edges and was beginning to pucker. The bleeding had stopped, but the soaked bandage told him the wound was probably beginning to fester.

The healer nodded. "The bolt didn't damage your bones, but the wound is infected."

The hand was soaked and gently dried. "I'm going to apply some magic. My herbs and poultices will need some help. This will hurt."

"I've experienced magical healing before," Quint said.

Quint found a comfortable position. His hand was hurting already, and it would soon get a lot worse. The healer laid a bandage over the wound and used both hands to create a healing string and then immediately applied the string to Quint's hand.

The pain was excruciating. Quint had been comatose for most of the healing during his recovery from his fight with the Green wizard, but this was concentrated in a single spot, and Quint knew that the healing was more effective if he was conscious while the string was administered.

He couldn't help taking deep breaths once the string had done its work.

"That hurt you more than I expected," the healer said.

"I was severely injured months ago, but unconscious for a long time," Quint said. "I've never felt a healing string that intensely."

"Let's see how your hand did," the healer said, removing the bandage. "The magic might have irritated your hand. Let's give it a day to clear up. I'll be here tomorrow afternoon."

Quint tried flexing his fingers and the stiffness seemed much better, but his skin was an angry red. The healer cleaned the wound, applied a poultice, and wrapped another bandage around his hand before leaving.

After a lunch served in his quarters, Quint laid down to rest. He didn't know if his tiredness was from his trip or from the healing. His wound pulsated with pain, but he found himself relaxing.

The healer woke him up from a nap the following day.

"How do you feel?"

"Much better," Quint said. "My hand almost feels normal. Is that possible?"

"No," the healer said bluntly. "I think we will have to have four or five sessions just to save your hand."

Quint groaned and held out his hand for bandage removal.

"Flex your fingers," the healer said quietly.

The movement was painless. Quint looked away while the healer cleaned his skin. When Quint was able, he looked down at a normal hand with normal color. An ugly scar, however, was plainly seen on the back of his hand.

"I can try to remove your scar, but that generally causes more pain than healing," the healer said.

"No," Quint said. "I need a reminder that I'm not invincible."

"You look pretty indestructible to me."

Quint sighed. "My hand was infected. If I didn't treat it, I might have lost my hand or worse. Right?"

"Worse case," the healer nodded.

"It is a small price to pay for a lifelong reminder," Quint said.

"Suit yourself. I'm happy to have been an instrument in your healing, although I think you must have been able to add some of your own magic. I can't explain the fast result any other way."

"How much do I owe you?" Quint said.

"The warlord is paying for my services."

Quint took a deep breath. He wouldn't have believed his hand would have healed like that if he hadn't been touched by Tova. The scar was ugly, but it didn't cover the back of his hand, and he stared at the disfigurement, drilling the pain that he had felt into his head. He had to remember the pain as well as the appalling appearance of his hand before the healing.

"You can report that you saved my hand and my life," Quint said. "Thank you."

The healer grinned. "Thank you for letting me witness a miraculous recovery."

Quint wasn't dressed for escorting the healer out of the compound, but he felt the need to take another bath and change into clothes suitable for the street.

Thera was available. Dugo had ridden to the Shira's manor for magic lessons and Dakuz was visiting a wizard faction, introducing the concept of the charter.

"Have you gotten over your lady love?" Thera said.

"Sandy? Yes!" Quint said.

"No, Masumi of Slinnon."

Quint shook his head. I don't understand."

Thera took a deep breath. "I just want to make sure you haven't thrown me out for another."

"Are you serious?"

"I am," Thera said.

"I haven't thrown you out, but we don't have a romantic relationship," Quint said. "I've never given you any indication."

"As long as there isn't anyone else," Thera said, "then we can walk the streets of the capital together without embarrassment."

Quint didn't have any idea what Thera was getting at. He might have to ask Dugo if he could contribute information if something had happened while he was gone. It was a mystery that Quint wanted to ignore, but he knew he couldn't do that, living in the same compound. He tried to ignore the encounter as they stepped through the gate and into the streets of Morimanu.

Each fief had its own flavor, but the architecture was mostly the same. The polennese-style dress dominated. The food was slightly different and that thought gave Quint a purpose for his getting out of the Three Forks mansion.

"I need to replenish my seasoning pouch. It was searched once in Chokuno and the stolen in Gamiza," Quint told Thera.

"I remember you mentioned it. I've had to add to mine, so I know where to pick up most of what you will need."

They spent the rest of the afternoon laying in a supply for all four of the travelers from Narukun. Quint made sure there was enough to make a sample pack for Narisu. Quint didn't know if Chibo's aide was being polite or was honest in his praise of a little more seasoning the Kippunese cuisine.

Quint spotted a person following them when they began their return to the mansion.

"Did you know we were being followed?" Quint asked Thera.

"A man about thirty, wearing a blue tunic over black trousers. Dark red shoes, which is an odd choice for someone not wanting to be noticed."

Quint hadn't seen the red boots, so he turned back and found that Thera was right.

"Shall we let him follow us, or should we see what he is about?" Thera asked.

"Let's be the aggressor," Quint said. He looked down at his new scar. "First a shield for each of us."

"It wasn't so effective on your last trip," Thera said.

"I wondered about that after I've returned," Quint said. "I wonder if the bolt was spelled with a string."

"Do you still have it?"

"I do," Quint said. "Souvenir."

"Something to do this evening," Thera said. "It's time to turn around."

They caught the tail slipping into an alley.

Quint ran faster than Thera, he found, and cornered the man in the dark red shoes in the blind alley.

"You've been following us," Thera said.

The man began to cast a string.

"Stop!" Thera said. "We mean you no harm."

The man mumbled something that Quint couldn't quite hear, but he dropped his hands, letting the threads dissipate in a shower of pale motes.

"What do you want of me?" the man said.

"A simple answer to why are you following us?" Quint said.

"I was sent to meet you," the man said.

"By whom?"

"The Whole String faction. We are strongest in northern Shimato."

"Your people haven't contacted us."

"We didn't come to the Three Forks meeting, and then their leaders were killed."

"Attacking us at night," Thera said.

The man nodded his head. "I heard. I was too afraid to approach you. Even the way you two walk is intimidating. You don't move like wizards."

"But you were bold enough to follow us."

The man sighed. "I'm not good at such things."

"Are you the leader of the Whole Strings?"

"His eldest son," the red-shoed man said.

"Consider us met," Quint said. "How can we help you?"

The man looked relieved. "We heard about the charter and wanted to get a copy."

"I've had my people contacting wizard factions."

"But we don't operate in the capital. It might have been months or years before we heard from you."

Thera put hands to hips. "Today is your lucky day. Consider months and years saved, weeks, even."

"Come with us to the Three Forks mansion. The warlord has given us the mansion to do our work in Shimato." Quint said.

"Can I?"

The three of them crossed the gate threshold and went to the main meeting room. Quint grabbed a copy of the latest charter document and gave it to Akomono. They spent all the time until dinner discussing the ramifications of the charter.

"My father would lose his standing," Akomono said.

"No," Quint said. "His status would change. His options going forward would change. We are proposing this for wizards, not for wizard leaders."

Dugo walked in.

"Have you heard of the Whole Strings faction?" Quint asked Dugo.

"No, but I haven't gotten to the small factions out of the capital."

Thera said. "We have a faction member in this very room. I'd like to introduce Akomono, eldest son of the leader."

Dugo gave the man a bow. "Welcome to our compound. We don't have a name for the charter faction other than calling it The Charter."

Akomono stood and bowed. "We are not an aggressive faction," Akomono said.

"Can you stay for dinner?" Dugo asked.

"I'm in the capital to meet you," Akomono said. "It is part of my duty to the faction and my ancestors. There have been Akomono leaders for generations."

"Good," Quint said, rubbing his hands and noticing his scar when he did.

Dinner intimidated Akomono more than initially meeting Thera and Quint on the street. Narisu brought Gomio, who introduced the wizard as a master from Gamiza fief. Dakuz arrived with Shira, and Todo was known as the current Three Forks leader to Akomono.

"And how goes it in the north?" Narisu asked.

Akomono almost winced when asked. "You should know that better than I, being aide to Shimato's war leader."

Narisu bit his lip. "Why are you so afraid of us? Don't take offense," Narisu said. "The army doesn't fight Shimato's citizens."

"That isn't quite right," Akomono said, wincing this time.

"Is it the army or a guard unit?"

"There is a difference?" Akomono asked.

Narisu nodded. "There is. When you get back, send a note with a detailed description of their uniforms. Lord Bunto isn't the most noble of warlords, but he doesn't want his subjects trampled by arrogant guards. The only arrogant trampler is supposed to be Lord Bunto," Narisu said.

"I'll do that. We feel defenseless sometimes."

"Have you read the charter?" Narisu asked.

"I've had it explained to me," Akomono said.

"Read it and talk about the wizard corps with Quint and Thera. There is an offset to arrogant guards."

"Right!" Dakuz said. "Arrogant wizards."

Quint chuckled. "The charter is not intended to change the power structure, but more importantly, it is intended to give wizards more of a chance in Kippun."

"All of the country?" Akomono asked.

Quint nodded. "We can talk more about it tomorrow. Let's have an enjoyable dinner," Quint said.

§

Akomono sat in the courtyard re-reading the charter when Quint found him.

"Have you been enlightened?" Quint asked.

"Enough," Akomono said. "I will return to my home and discuss everything with my father. Personally, I think this is a great move forward for wizards in Shimato. I can see why you are sponsoring this. I'm surprised the warlord allows you to do this."

"Between you and me, I think he is looking for an edge to keep from being swallowed up by other fiefs."

"Gamiza?"

Quint nodded. "Life is not good in Gamiza."

"That's not what Master Gomio said last night."

"Don't believe him. What do you need from us?"

"A handwritten invitation?" Akomono asked. "I'm not sure my father will believe my bringing the charter as proof."

Quint laughed. "I don't think an invitation will be much better, but it's something I can do. Stay there. I'll be back.

Quint gave the invitation to Akomono and saw him to the gate.

Dugo ran up to Quint an hour after the man had left. "He's gone?" Dugo said, out of breath.

"He is," Quint said.

"The Whole String faction has been defunct for a century, although it was centered in the north."

Quint looked across the courtyard at the closed gate. Akomono was surely gone. "You are sure about that?"

"There were no leaders named Akomono," Dugo said.

"Let's all write a description of him to give to Narisu," Quint said.

Dugo pursed his lips. "What if he was wearing a disguise?"

"We would have detected one," Quint looked at the gate. "What is that wizard up to?"

Dakuz passed by with Shira Yomolo.

"That wizard last night?" Quint said.

"Akomono?" Shira said.

"There is no Akomono who is the leader of the Whole String faction. In fact, there is no Whole String faction," Quint said.

"And?" Dakuz asked.

Quint was confused by Dakuz's response. "Aren't you concerned?"

"About what?' Dakuz said. "You gave him a charter. That's not a secret. What exposure do we have if more people know about the charter? We want to let the world know about it."

"He's right," Dugo said.

"That's not an unusual event," Quint said. "I won't be worried, but I can be curious."

Dakuz gave Quint a half smile. "Even I am curious. Why go to the trouble to make up a story?"

"He said we weren't getting to all the factions," Dugo said.

"Ako-what's-his-name is right about that. My only concern is that we brought him into our courtyard without verifying his identity. If he was a Green wizard, he could have attacked us at any time. No one was wearing a shield by the time we had dinner," Dakuz said.

"Thera and I had shields on when we met him, but then we let them fade after he introduced himself," Quint said. "It should have been a concern, but we made a mistake."

"It wasn't the first time, nor will it be the last time," Dakuz said.

Quint didn't want to be chronically suspicious, but perhaps he was going to have to change his point of view while he was in Kippun.

"I'm more like Quint," Shira said, "but I see I'm going to modify my behavior if I'm going to follow Quint along with the rest."

Quint closed his eyes. Followers, he thought. How many would he accumulate? He had picked up two more in the last few months, and he suspected there were more to come.

Narisu walked into the compound. "Where is Akomono? I wanted to ask him a few questions."

"Gone," Quint said. "Likely never to be seen in the capital again. Dugo discovered there is no Whole String faction. We have written up descriptions of the imposter for you."

"You expected me?"

Dakuz shook his head. "No. We were about to decide when to present the documents to you."

"I'll get them," Dugo said, hurrying out of the courtyard.

"Did you have an inkling about him?" Quint asked Narisu.

"I wish I could claim cleverness and say I wasn't duped, but I was. Akomono did an excellent job of convincing me he was afraid. He was especially brazen to have returned today to discuss the charter."

Quint pursed his lips. "How did you know he returned to our compound this morning? None of us told you."

Narisu smiled. "Someone must have told me."

"No one did," Todo said. "I was at the gate and escorted you here."

Narisu sighed. "I admit it was a setup. Akomono claimed he could convince you to reveal your real motivation for the charter."

"I was honest with him," Quint said.

"So, he told Chibo and me. I about died last night when he was sitting at your dinner table," Narisu said. "I promised Chibo I would tell you later today."

"And we are supposed to believe that?" Dugo asked Narisu.

Narisu held out his hands. "When have I been false with you?"

Dakuz laughed. "You really want to know?"

"All right. The truth is we are trying to verify everything. I bet Chibo that Akomono, his real name, couldn't get into your compound without sneaking in and exposing himself."

"I suppose Chibo succeeded on the first count…"

"And failed on the second. I'm glad you found out he was an imposter before I told you. Technically, Chibo won the bet and when Chibo is happy, I'm happier," Narisu said.

"What happens from here?"

"Akomono is a member of an eastern faction who knows Hari Bitto, so I suppose the warlord is involved in this ruse, as well. Quint converted him from an antagonist into a supporter of the charter. Gomio has played his part in informing Akomono what the Greens are doing in Gamiza," Narisu said. "Akomono was anxious to find out the truth."

"And where does that leave us?" Quint said.

"You've already talked to Akomono's sect on these very grounds, and perhaps they will volunteer to help. Since he is a friend of Bitto's, I'm not sure I can trust him," Narisu said.

"At some point we are going to have to trust someone," Quint said.

"I agree," Dakuz said. "We need better discernment of our possible partners. Will we see Akomono again?"

"It is likely, but I would ignore him for the present and let Akomono's faction come to you. For now, Chibo wants a report tomorrow with any modifications you include in your plan after our visit to Gamiza and your encounter with Akomono. You need to be prepared to take the next step as soon as possible."

"Begin uniting the factions," Quint said.

"That's right. Chiba and Lord Bumoto have agreed to proceed on an accelerated basis. Chiba wants one more meeting at his office tomorrow morning one hour before noon. Please have some kind of plan that outlines what you will do throughout Shimato. The Greens won't wait for more indecision on the part of the warlord."

CHAPTER NINETEEN

~

QUINT WORKED ON A REVISED PLAN MUCH OF THE NIGHT. He spent the morning going over his work with Thera, Dugo, Dakuz, and Todo. He made another copy and arrived at Chibo Hobona's office exactly on time.

"Let's start with your impressions of Chokuno and Gamiza," Chibo said.

Quint had brought Dakuz, and Narisu joined them. "I thought Narisu would have thoroughly gone over our trip."

"I want to get it from you," Chibo said.

Quint tried to give the war leader as much as his viewpoint as he could, but he traveled with Narisu the entire time, so he thought the report was a waste of time. The revised charter was more important and had some key additions and subtractions, but it was ready to implement and the warlord had already said he would support it.

Chibo asked questions about the Gamizan capital and the veracity of Master Gomio. "Do you trust the Gamizan?"

"Halfway," Quint said. "Externally, he appears to be telling us the truth, and he could have exposed us any number of times when we escaped and yet…"

"And yet…?"

"I can make a case for him acting like he has to work his way into the warlord's councils. He could do that to find out what Lord Bumoto is thinking or scouting for opportunities to attack from the west."

"I thought you were the trusting one?" Chibo said.

"I am, but I think you were looking for what Gomio could do to Shimato if he wasn't on our side," Quint said.

"What about your judgement of Akomono?"

"We let him into the compound, something we didn't have to do," Quint said. "But he got more information from Narisu and Gomio at dinner than he did from us." Quint shrugged. "I'm always willing to share information about the charter."

Chibo turned to Narisu. "What did you or Gomio tell Akomono?"

"A few tidbits about our escape, nothing more. The Greens know as much about our escape by now," Narisu said.

"What did you tell him about Masumi?" Chibo asked.

Mention of Masumi's name piqued Quint's interest.

"I didn't mention her, at all."

"Gomio said he was impressed by her," Narisu said.

"No more talk about Masumi," Chibo said. He stood.

"What about my report?" Quint asked.

"Leave it with Narisu. I trust you. Give me a few days and I'll show the warlord the final version, so you can begin to recruit." Chibo smiled and showed all three to the door.

Quint waited to say anything until they were alone in the corridor on the way to the stairs.

"What was that about Masumi?" Quint asked Narisu.

Chibo's aide looked up and down the corridor. "She is the illegitimate daughter of the ruler of Slinnon. Chokuno and Shimato have agreements with him to send her back to Slinnon."

"Under guard?" Dakuz said.

Narisu nodded. "She's more important to Shimato than she is to Slinnon as she keeps company with an underground of Chokunese spies who would rather die than hand her over."

"Until the reward reaches a certain point," Dakuz said.

"That point has been reached in Shimato. Masumi, not her real name, stays out of Shimato."

"Unless she is using the border to get out of Gamiza," Quint said.

"Right," Narisu said. "We haven't expressly forbidden Gomio to talk about her, but the warlord would be embarrassed if Slinnon knew we were using a princess as a spy. Gomio doesn't know about her heritage."

"Why did she let us take her to Gamiza?"

Narisu shrugged. "She likes adventure and living a less structured life. Masumi is illegitimate and part-hubite which presents problems to the royal family."

"She has siblings?"

Narisu nodded. "We won't talk more about her. She is out of your life. I suggest you concentrate on getting the charter going. All it takes are wizards to sign up. Other than a few minor changes, everything is ready to implement, and the warlord is eager to see wizards under his control."

"Wizards under their own control," Quint said.

"Yes. With them being less pesky," Narisu said with a smile.

A few days later, Quint received a summons to a meeting with the warlord. He didn't know what to expect. He had an unexpectedly good relationship with Chibo and his time with Narisu had been a pleasure other than the adventures on their trip through Chokuno and Gamiza.

"I hear you have made progress," Lord Bunto Bumoto, the warlord of Shimato, said to Quint in a private audience room. Quint met alone with the warlord. "I am impressed that you performed so well on your trip to Chokuno and Gamiza, especially Gamiza. War Leader Chibo says you were instrumental in bringing back the Gamizan master wizard."

"There were two others with me. We did it together," Quint said.

"You mean one other. There were two of you who brought Master Gomio out of Gamiza."

Quint closed his eyes for the briefest of moments before responding. "I stand corrected, Lord Bumoto. We are ready to begin implementing the charter."

Bumoto nodded. "War Leader Chibo said you recently convinced one of Hari Bitto's friends to support your work. That was an excellent move. Bitto doesn't always have the best interests of the fief in his heart."

Quint gave the warlord the barest of nods. He didn't understand why the warlord let the wizard remain by his side.

"You don't like Bitto, do you?" the warlord asked.

"It's not a matter of like or dislike. I don't trust your wizard."

Bumoto grunted. "I don't trust him either, but he is so well connected with the wizards in my domain that I am reluctant to let him get his hands dirty out of my sight. Master Gomio doesn't like him either."

"I'm not sure you can trust Gomio either. He seems fine, but he could have engineered his escape."

"Commander Narisu has the same view." the warlord said. "Who do I trust Bitto and Gomio, master wizards or Narisu and you, nearly master wizards."

"I'm as much a master as Gomio is," Quint said, "although I am loathe to boast. I can't see Bitto being a master."

"Stolen honor?" the warlord asked.

"Stolen is probably as good a term as any, sir," Quint said. "I would term him a pesky wizard in the manner that you describe us."

"Are you a pesky wizard?"

Quint smiled. "Pesky wouldn't be the appropriate term. Gomio is simply insufficiently vetted. Bitto has been vetted, in my eyes, and he is found wanting."

"Good! We agree on Bitto, then. As I said I keep him close in front of me so he doesn't stab me in the back."

"He can have some of his friends do the stabbing," Quint said.

"Then what do you suggest I do?"

"Let's get the wizard charter going, and we can put him in some kind of benign position where you can continue to keep an eye on him, but Bitto won't be idle."

"Is that your general strategy? Keep the wizards busy so they don't complain?" the warlord asked.

"No. Keeping a person busy works for any group. Idle hands may have a greater chance of resentment for imagined slights. We give them a different framework to work in and a way to advance in their craft, either as a wizard, as workers in a structured business or military environment."

The warlord nodded. "Just like your charter outlines?"

Quint nodded. "The goal hasn't changed. The way to achieve the goal has moved around a little bit. After traveling through Gamiza, everything is urgent, and I hope we aren't too late to establish a working wizard corps."

"Who do you recommend to run the wizard corps?"

"I'd defer to Narisu's judgment. He knows the military side and understands the wizardry part. Todo, the former Three Fork administrator, can run the charter operations: registration and ranking. We may not have time to flesh everything else out other than get the training started."

"I thought you'd rent out a big room and let everyone choose what they want to be," the warlord said.

"The wizards should choose their paths, as long as they have the aptitude," Quint said.

"That is where the registration and ranking come in?" the warlord asked.

"It is."

"Then make it happen. I'll fund the charter for one year, and you will find a way to fund it after that."

"The Charter needs to pay for the wizard corps?" Quint asked.

"No. Once they are in the military, War Leader Chibo owns them."

"Owns?"

"Metaphorically speaking," the warlord said. Bumoto scribbled instruction on a piece of paper. "My finance advisor is standing outside waiting to talk to you. Sooner the better, Tirolo."

§

"The warlord surprised me," Quint said. "We have enough funds to accelerate our efforts among the wizards."

"He told you we weren't moving fast enough?" Thera asked.

"Essentially, yes. The wizard corps is what Lord Bumoto is after, I think. We can start with that."

"He uses us as a recruitment arm for Chibo's army?" Dakuz said.

"That's what Narisu told me. The information from Gamiza, and I'm sure from what Gomio told him, gives the warlord a new sense of urgency," Quint said.

"How long do we have?" Thera asked.

"Six months to get a core group trained, and that is the beginning. In the meantime, Thera will work with Narisu to set up the organization. Todo, just as we discussed, can use the time to create the wizard infrastructure and work on getting wizard factions in the capital signed up. Dakuz and I will recruit wizards and Dugo will help Todo."

"I can't help you?" Dugo asked.

"If any of us need help, you'll be available. Will that work?"

Dugo pursed his lips, but didn't say anything.

"If I give you the responsibility for the continued training of Shira, would that help?"

Dugo grinned. "It will."

"Shira will want to do something. She has arranged her performances to give her more time for wizard training," Dakuz said.

"Then I leave her duties for you to manage. Dugo is her personal magic trainer, and you are her manager as far as our efforts go. A beautiful face might be useful anywhere," Quint said.

"Isn't that a shallow view?" Thera asked.

"Her beautiful face and beautiful voice have served her quite well," Dakuz said. "She is also a quick learner, so she can help us like Dugo, helping the charter where it needs it."

"I can see that," Thera said.

"Good. It's settled then," Quint said. "You know what to do to get started?"

Thera nodded. "Assemble a roster, interview the wizards, and then slot them into a new organization. Those who are officer material will help establish corps rules."

"With Narisu and Chibo's input?"

Thera nodded. "It's their wizard corps not mine. I will also survey the current strategies…"

"That won't take much time," Todo said. "We had conversations about helping the military before Rimo grew too much and no one could tell him what to do. The basic strategy is stand in a group and throw magic as lethal and as far as you can."

Thera cleared her throat. Quint took that as a signal of distaste. "That has its place in a battle plan, but there are more effective strategies depending on the opponent and the terrain."

"Not to mention the talents of the wizards," Quint said.

"Of course," she said.

"And what will we do?" Dakuz asked.

"A grand tour of Shimato, followed by a grand tour of the fiefs including Chokuno, but excluding Gamiza."

"Maybe we can convince Gomio to come with us," Quint said. "That will get him out of Morimanu. We need to get started tomorrow after I've informed War Leader Chibo of our plans."

§

Narisu dropped by the Three Forks compound and escorted Quint to the common room of the pub where he first met Chibo.

"I understand the warlord is ready to go," Chibo said drinking from a large mug of wine.

"He is. Should I have brought Thera?"

"No. Narisu and I will talk to her tomorrow at your compound. She should have ink and paper ready."

Quint nodded. "She will have more than that ready," Quint said. "She already has ideas on how to reorganize the wizard corps in your forces."

"You have seen these plans?" Narisu asked.

"I have," Quint said. "I think you will like them. They don't rely on superior wizards leading the charge like she and I did on the Chokunese border. But they don't eliminate heroic acts if they are called for."

"You consider your attack on the Chokunese forces as a heroic act?" Chibo asked.

Quint sighed. He didn't expect any resistance. Was it because of the warlord? "It was what it was," Quint said. "It eliminated a stalemate and saved soldiers' lives on both sides. Battles of attrition carve up the soldiers and accomplish little."

"They can and do, but when two forces are intent on enforcing their borders, that kind of action usually evolves."

"Then the warlords need to negotiate out of it," Quint said.

Chibo laughed. "Easier said than done. That's not why I called you here. I don't want my staff listening in. I trust every person in this room," Chibo said.

Quint looked around at the sparse clientele in the common room. They were all male and the inn's people were just turning away a small group of customers.

"Then what needs to be said?"

"Gomio has finally coughed up his biggest piece of information. Hari Bitto is employed by the Green faction in Shimato."

"Not the warlord?"

Chibo nodded his head. "That makes it worse. The faction leader of the wizard you invited into the Three Forks compound ran into Narisu and has the same suspicion. The warlord found out before he talked to you."

"He had already found out before he made the decision to go ahead?" Quint asked.

Chibo worked his mouth for a moment. "Lord Bumoto changed his mind because of it. He always had a soft spot for Bitto. They go back years. The time to finish recruiting all the factions has come. They are looking for a leader."

"Hari Bitto wasn't leading?" Quint said.

Chibo laughed. "At times, I thought he was the war leader's fool. Hari and I were never friends, so my thoughts were biased."

"Were?"

"You won't see Hari Bitto again. Nor will anyone else. Gomio will be traveling with you to the outside fiefs. The warlord wants him out of the capital as much as possible."

Quint wondered how Gomio and Dakuz would get along. He didn't know.

"We will start at the northwest and circle the capital," Quint said. "I'm ready to leave tomorrow."

"Good. I was going to suggest it. Gomio will show up at your gate this afternoon. Tell him of your plans, but Narisu and I don't fully trust him, so that makes all three of us."

"But you believe him about Hari Bitto?" Quint asked.

"We have confirmation from more than one of the faction leaders Hari had thought he controlled." Chibo stood. "You can go now. I have some drinking with friends to do. It clouds my thinking, but sometimes things are clearer when I sober up."

The war leader sat back down as Quint left the common room. The men in the room and those guarding the entrances sat down close to him, and they were laughing before Quint walked out the front door.

Chapter Twenty

Quint, Dakuz, and Gomio left Shira's Manor, heading to northwest Shimato and the Flat Plains faction. They stopped midday at a roadside station for a meal and to rest the horses.

"It's quite okay if you don't fully trust me," Gomio said

"For that I am so glad," Dakuz said sarcastically. "Just don't do anything that will spoil our mission."

"Why would I do that?" Gomio said. "What do I have to do to prove I have left Gamiza behind?"

"Leave him alone," Quint said to Dakuz before turning to Gomio. "What would happen to you if you returned to Gamiza?"

Gomio's face turned solemn. "It would be my death."

"And if you betray the fief that has given you sanctuary?"

Gomio swallowed. "My death?"

"Most likely," Quint said. "Remember that. No betrayal and you get to live a free life."

"I think of it every day," Gomio said.

"I'm sure you do," Dakuz said. "Stay close to us. You are the length of Shimato away from Gamiza." They were a day away from Chokuno and Gomio could find refuge in that fief if he wanted. That was assuming the wizard had any intention of making mischief.

"Enough of that, Dakuz," Quint said. "Let's not incentivize Gomio to kill us in our sleep."

"I'd never—" Gomio stopped his sentence as Quint raised his hand to stop him.

"We could do the same, but we won't," Quint said. "I'm not on this mission to test you, Gomio. I'm here to begin spreading the charter among the Shimato factions, and that is something I intend to do to all Kippun, if I can."

Gomio laughed. "You want to tie the hands of all the warlords? You didn't tell me this when we escaped from my home fief."

"Why do you scoff?" Quint asked Gomio.

"It's impossible," the Gamizan wizard said. "The warlords do not cooperate."

"Maybe it is time they did," Quint said. "They should become a real country. All the fiefs drag everyone down. It costs money to have standing armies. Money that could improve the lives of the people. Narukun for all its faults is more advanced than any Kippunese fief."

"And that brings down all of North Fenola," Dakuz said.

"I suppose it doesn't hurt to try. The worst you can do is fail or die. All I must do is stay out of the way," Gomio said.

"Failing would mean my death, I think," Quint said.

Dakuz chuckled. "Your death would certainly lead to failure."

"Perhaps we should end this discussion," Quint said. "Now that you know what I intend to do, please come along for the ride."

"I don't have a choice," Gomio said. "Narisu said I wasn't welcome back in Morimanu unless I'm with you."

"Good. Then let's craft a triumphant return," Quint said.

Gomio looked at Dakuz. "Is he always this optimistic?"

"It's not optimism. He is determined to succeed. Why? It's all about his longer-term mission to find someone on another continent. Quint has to prepare himself for that." Dakuz said.

"Is the someone a king? How could he need so much preparation?"

"Maybe Quint will tell you, if he finds he can really trust you."

Gomio pondered for a few moments. "I will have to change the comment I made that started this unfortunate conversation. I will do my very best to earn the trust of both of you."

"I would consider that a good start," Quint said.

Quint was armed with a map and a few pages of notes about two of the outside factions, the Flying Golds and the Flat Plains. He didn't know how the names came about, but there must have been a lot of history with the faction names.

First up was the Flat Plains wizard faction. They were concentrated in the small city of Teritoto which sat in the middle of the largest agricultural region in the fief. That would make sense for the plain part, but Quint thought that by definition all plains were flat. They were to contact Master Bifomu. An address in Teritoto was under the name.

"The notes say the faction is mostly apolitical and focused on helping farmers," Quint said.

Dakuz grumbled. "Not true. All the farmers I ever knew had strong political opinions. What gets grown, when, and how are political considerations. That's before you get into arguments on rights of way and water rights."

"Let's talk to Bifomu. He will be speaking with two masters," Quint said. "The wizard part won't be a problem, but I'm no farmer."

"I'm a city boy," Gomio said. "I can give you my uneducated opinion if it comes to agriculture issues, but I'm sure they will be more valuable than your own with my years of living experience."

"I'd appreciate your observations," Quint said. "What about you Dakuz?"

"I have academic experience and lived experience like Master Gomio's," Dakuz said, "but no practical experience." He bowed to Quint. "You have more than I do because you worked that herb plot at Seensist Cloister."

"You were a simple farmer's hand?" Gomio asked Quint.

"I'm the son of a wheelwright and apprenticed with my father. My mother grew vegetables in a plot on our property. I am familiar with local markets, Master Gomio. I was assigned a plot to work when I started at the bottom at Seensist Cloister in Narukun. I know how to get my hands dirty," Quint took a deep breath before he continued, "and I know how to clean them."

"What do you mean by that?"

"My background gives me some ability to empathize with farmers and their suppliers. That might include the Flat Plains faction members. Observations from both of you will be appreciated, but I have valid means to evaluate the situation, too. As for cleaning my hands, I mean that I have the mental tools to understand and solve problems. Our best way to win the Flat Plain faction is to give them a way to solve some of their unique problems through the charter," Quint said.

Gomio wagged his finger at Quint. "You are craftier than I expected, and you even have a strategy, although it is more of an approach than a solution."

"I'm glad you noticed the difference. The three of us need to listen to what is said and what isn't to determine how we and the charter can help," Quint said.

§

Teritoto reminded Quint of the two towns within one day of his father's wheelwright shop in Racellia. The buildings weren't as fancy as those in the cities, especially Morimanu. The roofs were still almost flat with curved up corners and many structures had cheap silk or waxed paper pasted over a stick grid for windows, but the essence of the town exhibited its agricultural roots.

The three travelers ended up on the doorstep of Master Bifomu, if Quint's information was correct. There were three lines almost finger length and width carved into the doorframe. The top was blue, the middle green, and the bottom brown. Quint had everyone cast a shield.

A woman as tall as Narisu opened the door. "I hope you aren't selling me anything."

She looked more closely at them and worked her hands. She was casting a tiny string. "None of you are from Shimato." The woman narrowed her eyes at Gomio. "A Gamizan master," then she turned to Quint and Dakuz. "One as good as a master from Narukun, and you, young man, exceeds the capacity of my string."

"You are Master Bifomu?"

"I am today," the woman said. "My late husband had the title until three months ago. I was his equal in magic, so I assumed the title."

"And the head of the Flat Plains?" Quint asked.

"How did you know that?"

Quint rapped his knuckles on the three lines. "Your faction's sign."

"Indeed. I'm sure it is written on a paper in your bag," the woman said.

"Your name and address are. We are sorry for your loss," Quint said. "We come from Morimanu with the warlord's permission. I have an offer, no fee to be charged, for you and your faction."

The woman folded her arms. "You are the one waving a bloody shirt and proclaiming a new era for wizards?"

"That's me, but there isn't a bloody shirt. Can we enter your house and explain it to you? If you don't like what we are selling for free, we will leave you and Teritoto in the morning," Quint said.

"I'm in the warlord's bad graces enough as it is. Come in and tell me your tale."

The three entered Master Bifomu's house, stepping down into a square area and removing their shoes before rising on a few steps that led into a receiving room. The woman sat at the far end and the three of them took low chairs on facing rows like Shira's and the Three Forks meeting hall.

"We follow Slinnon customs more than others," the woman said, "since you are outsiders."

"Common Gamiza homes are similar," Gomio said.

"This is not a commoner's house," Master Bifomu said frostily.

Gomio turned red.

Dakuz pulled a charter copy from his bag. "We are here to present a concept that can improve the lot of wizards in Shimato."

"The Flat Plains faction isn't as needy as other factions. We don't require help from the capital."

"You are on the warlord's bad side," Quint said. "Perhaps there is an opportunity to improve that."

"You would have to be more than a master wizard to do that," the woman said. "Are you?"

Quint nodded. "I am. I wished I knew how I was more, but I have been touched by Tova. Ever since my powers have been different. Enhanced, but I'm not sure to what extent."

"Tova touched?" the woman said, putting her hand to her heart. "I've never heard of such a thing, but I am an adherent. You have heard of Tova's chapel in Narukun? Is that where you were touched?"

"It was," Quint said. "She has blessed the chapel with apparitions that she has personally sent, at least she did when I served the Feltoff Cloister in Tova's Falls."

"Perhaps that is why my string didn't work on you," the master said. "My name is Huma. You, boy, can call me that. The others must address me as Master Bifomu."

"I am Dakuz," Dakuz said. "This is Master Gomio from Gamiza and the Tova-touched one is from Racellia in South Fenola."

"You escaped the unpleasantness there?" Huma asked Quint.

"I did," Quint said.

"Now, back to how you were Tova-touched. I am vitally interested."

Quint gave her a watered-down version. Tova was behind a mist in his new version. "I don't know if it was a vision or a real thing, but I was almost killed in a duel with a Green master wizard, when I recovered, I found my magic had changed."

"You fought the wizard at the Narukun stronghold where the king was kidnapped?"

Quint nodded. "There were three masters. The last was the strongest. I was lucky, but with my enhanced magic, I was barely able to prevail. You seem to be very familiar about Narukun matters," Quint said.

"My son left Teritoto to seek his fortune outside of Kippun and entered the Narukun wizard corps. He writes me from time to time about what goes on in the world. Otherwise, my late husband and I wouldn't be able to lead the faction as well."

"Is that why you are on the warlord's bad side?"

"Part of it," Huma said. "The other is my constant fight with the local farmer's guild about wizard remuneration."

"One of my people was in the Narukun wizard corps in Baxel. Perhaps she knows your son."

Huma smiled. "The world can't possibly be that small."

"It is when there are mutual connection points," Dakuz said. "Perhaps it might be useful for you to read the charter." He stepped forward and presented the charter.

Huma read the first page and cast a dubious look at Quint. "You aren't serious about this, are you?"

"I am," Quint said. "Two organizations. One overall organization for wizards that provides services to all wizards and the other a wizard corps organization that is incorporated into the warlord's army. My wizard corps associate is currently hammering out the details with War Leader Chibo and his aide."

"What is his aide's name?" Huma asked.

"Commander Narisu," Gomio blurted out.

She nodded.

"There are more details. Factions will change, but they will continue to exist in their areas of focus."

"Long ago, the factions were created to do just the opposite."

"Make them weaker?" Dakuz asked.

"It worked," Huma said, "until recently. Gamiza has their eyes on Chokuno and Shimato and has sought outside allies."

"I left Gamiza because I didn't like the outside allies," Gomio said.

"They have begun to infiltrate the factions," Huma said. "Including the Flat Plains. My husband was too curious and I suspect…" She sighed.

"I have been attacked by the Greens," Quint said, "in Kippun and in Narukun. I had Green enemies that meant me harm in Racellia."

"Fedor Danko? He was notorious for his work overseas until he was killed…" She looked at Quint with alarm. "You killed him in the fortress!"

"I had something to do with it," Quint said.

"You two were with him?"

Dakuz raised his hand to ear level. "I was. Gomio is a more recent recruit."

"I'm not a recruit," Gomio said.

"Not yet," Dakuz said.

Huma returned to her reading and took her time. When she had finished, she looked back at portions of what she had read. "This changes the balance of power in Shimato."

"But the warlord still commands the fief," Quint said. "He is concerned about the Greens taking over Gamiza."

"He and the Flat Plains are united in that," Huma said. "I need to talk to my leaders. They are all in Teritoto at present and have been after my husband's demise. Come back tomorrow at sunset. We will eat and talk about this." Huma waved the charter documents as she stood up.

§

Huma recommended an inn not far from her house, and the three assembled in a dining room for dinner. There was a different common room for drinking.

Quint had a seasoning pouch that wasn't as good as the one he brought with him, but the food was different enough that he didn't need as much seasonings to brighten up the food.

"I see you augmented your dinner," the server, an older woman, said.

"I got used to more flavor when I cooked trail food," Quint said. "I don't need as much with what you serve here."

The woman chuckled. "That's because what you are eating is fresh and cooked more like a Slinnon chef would. It's a happy combination, don't you think?"

"I do," Gomio said. "Most of what we eat in Gamiza is aged."

"Aging improves some cooking and doesn't for other preparations," the server said.

"Are you offended by my friend's seasoning pouch?" Gomio asked.

"Not at all. We want our customers to enjoy their food."

"You are the owner?" Quint asked.

"I am and if I stand here talking to you, my customers won't enjoy waiting around. Stay after you've finished if you have questions."

The wait was long, but they were served free desserts, a fruit concoction that was very good.

"I have a few minutes. I provided you with something on the house while I took longer than I expected," the server said.

"I do own this inn," she said. "I was also told by Huma Bifomu you were guests."

"Are you a faction member?" Dakuz asked.

"I am, although my talents are unremarkable. The faction is the only place that is willing to give an older lady instructions."

"Can you answer some questions about your customers?"

She nodded.

"Do you have Greens come through here?" Quint asked.

"I refuse to serve them. Any that come to Teritoto stay at the Lord Mayor's mansion."

"I'm sorry to hear that," Quint said.

"He won't hear anything about you," the owner said. "I know how to keep my lips tight."

"Huma knows about this?"

The owner nodded. "She does."

Quint didn't need to expose the server any more than he had to. "Do you know of anything we can do until dinnertime tomorrow?"

"Three men of various ages seeking a good time?" the server said with a smile.

"There is a lake to the north. If you wish, I can have the kitchen prepare suitable picnic supplies and you can spend a pleasant day. The water is clear and swimmable, if you don't go too far. It is what is called a sinkhole, but there is water from a spring deep in the lake, that makes the little lake's water crystal clear, if a bit cold. It is the source for a modest river that provides water all around Teritoto."

In the morning, after breakfast, a young man who served them, presented them with three baskets.

"Your lunch. Please return the baskets and things."

They decided to hire a wagon and give their horses some additional rest at the lake. They followed Quint's map to the lake. Evidently the plain was filled with similar waterholes that made the area a renowned food source for Shimato.

There were a few fisherman lining the lake and one boat floating on the other side of the small body of water.

They found a suitable place to stop and took in the view.

"For being so flat, I never thought I'd find a scene of this quality," Gomio said. "I wish I could swim. It certainly is going to be warm enough."

"I will give it a try," Quint said.

Dakuz stared out at the water. "I think I will, too."

They ate their lunch which was unexpectedly good and the three took naps on the blankets provided in one of the baskets.

Quint blinked his eyes at the sun when he woke up and stretched. He saw a few other swimmers a few hundred paces away. Evidently people stripped down to their underwear.

They had enough time to dry everything, Quint thought looking at the sun. He dipped his foot in the water. It was clear, for sure, but it was also cold.

"You'll get used to it," Dakuz said as he jumped from the bank and began swimming toward the center of the lake.

Quint hadn't done much swimming since his days working for his father, but after a few strokes, it all came back. He headed for Dakuz, who was treading water.

"I thought we could talk here, away from Gomio, who is still napping, after eating half of our food. What do you think?"

"About Huma?"

"And the Flat Plains and the Greens."

"We are going to have to be careful," Quint said. "If Greens are cozy with the mayor of the city, then our job will be harder."

"Or easier, Quint. We will have to help them eradicate the Green influence in the city."

"The three of us?"

"Nobody said there was a Green army in the vicinity. The Greens are traveling in small groups at this point," Dakuz said. "Let's swim for a bit. I'm getting a little cold."

Dakuz proved to be a faster swimmer than Quint, despite his age. They found a shallower area which had warmer water and were able to stand, but they kept their heads above water and nothing else.

"Why don't we offer our help?" Quint said. "We can't do anything without a lot more knowledge of what is going on in the city."

Dakuz nodded. "If the Flat Plains are willing to help rid themselves of the Greens, then they will be more inclined to sign the charter."

Gomio was now sitting and rummaging through the food basket.

"Time to get back," Quint said.

Dakuz beat him back to their picnic site. Quint thought he might have to learn how to swim better.

"You have a good time?" Gomio said, finishing off a chicken leg.

"Swimming is great exercise," Dakuz said.

"I'm surprised you like it. It looks too cold," Gomio faked shivering. "What did you talk about?"

"Huma and the Greens," Quint said. "Do you think they will tell us about them?"

"Oh no," Gomio said. "I'm sure they are too afraid to tell strangers. Even the innkeeper didn't want anyone to overhear us."

∽

CHAPTER TWENTY-ONE

Q UINT DIDN'T GET THE IMPRESSION THEY WERE WELCOMED into Huma's house with open arms. They were ushered into a different room with small tables littered on the open floor. They were in lines like the chairs in the meeting room, but the dining room was larger. The house seemed to have been built like a headquarters, and this would be the main meeting room for many wizards.

"Sit close to me," Huma said.

Quint had his own table, and Gomio and Dakuz shared. The other tables were almost filled with about twenty-five faction members.

Huma stood.

"We have gathered as the faction leaders to discuss an interesting proposition proposed by the warlord and presented by Quinto Tirolo, a very young master wizard with a pedigree of achievements."

"How is he going to fix my practice?" one of the wizards said.

The rest broke out with more demands. Quint wondered if the Flat Plains was even a united faction.

Huma raised her hands. "All questions will be answered in due time. That's why we are here this evening." He turned to Quint. "Would you give us a summary of the charter and then answer questions? Our faction would like direct answers rather than pretty words and lofty ideas."

"I'd be happy to do just that, Quint said. He presented the latest version of the charter and then began answering.

Most of the wizards were employed in specialized tasks, sharpening blades and going from farmer to farmer to use their strings to improve the productivity of their agricultural clients. The universal problem was taxes and fees. The local authorities taxed wizard's earnings and charged fees to practice magic.

"Does the warlord know about your situation?" Quint asked.

Nobody knew. Huma and her husband, the former leader of the faction only dealt with the mayor of the city and no one higher.

"The charter charges membership fees, but that is all. I will have to find out what the fief-wide policy is," Quint said. He was frustrated that he didn't think far enough ahead to have included advisors to the warlord to answer questions like this.

"Are we returning to the capital?" Dakuz asked.

"I don't see how we can avoid it. We can't go from city to town to village and not know for sure what is local and what is fief-wide," Quint said to Huma. Quint stood and addressed the group. "I will return in four days. I will bring a person knowledgeable in fief laws for other questions, but I will get what has been asked answered as well as I can."

Quint wasn't happy about the murmuring after his declaration to withdraw back to the capital.

"You are doing the right thing," Huma said. "You won't get the support you seek if you make up solutions that have no chance of being implemented."

"We have to ride back?" Gomio asked. "I may not return with you."

"That is a chance I'll have to take," Quint said. He would rather not have Gomio accompany them.

They rode faster back than the way they came and were soon trotting on Morimanu's streets. He let Gomio return to his quarters while Dakuz and he headed directly to Chibo's building.

"Give up already?" Narisu asked, sitting at a desk in front of the war leader's office.

Quint quickly told him what happened. "I will turn around and return to Teritoto as soon as I can get someone who can help me answer legal questions."

"Hari Bitto is available, but I suppose you don't want him any more than Gomio," Narisu said with a grin.

"I'm trying to get the charter approved," Quint said, "and you are right about both. They are hindrances not helpers."

"Sit here. This time it's better for me to privately talk to the war leader."

Narisu went into Chibo's office. He wasn't gone for long when both of them came out of the office.

"I know the right person," Chibo said. "If you leave immediately, Gomio can be left behind." He nodded to Narisu who left them.

"In my office, both of you."

They sat down. "How was Gomio?"

"He didn't expose himself as a Green, but he was a pain in the behind," Dakuz said. "Some masters are idiots despite their training."

"Narisu is arranging for an assistant minister to join you. His name is Dasoka. He is a contact of Narisu's in the Fief Ministry. He knows more than anyone else how the fief works. Unfortunately, that doesn't always work to our benefit. I suggest that Dasoka remain in the background and not talk to the wizards. He has no power and detests them."

Quint sighed. "And you expect me to get along with him?"

The war leader smiled. "He is twenty-four and a young prodigy like you. You two should get along. If you don't, you should be able to understand each other's plight."

"He will be better than Gomio?" Dakuz asked.

"At least you can be assured he knows what he is talking about, and Dasoka will love getting out of the capital."

Dakuz grunted. "And the warlord is fine with this?"

Chibo sighed. "As long as he doesn't find out, you'll be fine."

Narisu accompanied Dakuz and Quint to the north gate where they met Dasoka.

"You are the South Fenola wizard?" the young man said. "Narisu said you are a master."

"I am," Quint said. "I'm not here to show off my magic and my strings but set up a charter."

"I've read the charter. I have criticisms to argue about on our ride to Teritoto. The Gamizan wizard isn't coming with us?"

"I let him return to his quarters and didn't tell him we are leaving as soon as we arrived."

"Good! I don't trust Gamizans."

"I don't know if I do or not, and neither does Dakuz, one of my followers," Quint said.

"And a person with your age and experience trusts Quinto Tirolo?" Dasoka asked Dakuz. The young man's use of Quint's formal name meant Dasoka had done some research prior to this encounter.

"I do. We have been through enough adventures." Quint said.

"Then on to adventure. You can begin by telling me exactly what happened on your way to Teritoto and your meeting with the Flat Plains faction."

Quint didn't hold anything back, even though part of it was Quint's realization that he had bitten off more than he could chew.

"I'll think about our position as we go, but I'm interested in your story. I'm not usually curious about the doings about wizards and wizardry in Shimato, but you have stirred things up since you first crossed the border."

"I'll be honest with you, if you are honest and forthright with me," Quint said.

Dasoka asked for Quint to tell him about life as far back as becoming an apprentice wheelwright with his father.

As they travelled, Dasoka asked so many questions and clarified lots of things, that Quint felt like Dasoka was researching a book on him. He finally asked what Dasoka was going to do with all the information.

"I suppose you don't want me to broadcast your encounters with Tova, if that's what they were," Dasoka said.

"I would greatly appreciate it," Quint said. "I would also rather you not reveal that I received a different kind of magic after I recovered from my efforts to retrieve the king of Narukun."

Dasoka smiled and shook his head. "I can think the goddess is putting you through quite a training program."

"Is that what you think?" Dakuz asked. "I've wondered the same thing, not that I am a devout religionist."

"Neither am I, but Quint is proof there is something out there, especially when he's been able to banish people from North Fenola to somewhere else," Dasoka said. "I honestly thought you would be a charlatan. Many wizards who seek to advance quickly in the fief are, you know."

"Hari Bitto," Quint said.

"Currently in the descendant, if you are into astrology," Dasoka said.

"I know enough about it," Dakuz said. "What is your opinion of the Greens?"

Dasoka laughed. "I was ambivalent until I heard your story and it matched with all the negatives I've learned. They are a disease."

"Narisu said you were difficult," Dakuz said.

"I am, especially when confronted with people who want to convince me through a veil of falsehoods. As I said, I thought that was what you were doing." Dasoka grinned. "I think we can get along."

Quint took that as an approval.

"Now let's talk about the charter. I have the latest version memorized…"

CHAPTER TWENTY-TWO
~

BY THE TIME THE TRIO RETURNED TO TERITOTO, Quint was hopeful that Dasoka was on his side and could add fief knowledge to Quint's charter.

Huma Bifomu was out when they arrived at her house. They were about to find an inn and return the following day, when a servant ran out to fetch them.

"Please come back. Something terrible has happened," the woman said. "I am Huma's housekeeper, and she has gone missing. The faction doesn't know what to do and neither do I."

"Does Huma have a family?" Dakuz asked.

"His wife and two children are inside. We need your help."

Dakuz looked at Quint. No servant would make that kind of mistake describing Huma as a man.

"Has the leader been abducted?" Dasoka asked.

"If you come with me, you will find out," the servant said, and ran back and entered the house.

"Very well," Dakuz said. "I think we should put our shields on, Quint."

"I'm no wizard," Dasoka said.

"But I am," Quint said as he cast a string on Dasoka and himself.

Dasoka lifted his arms and looked down at his body. "I don't feel any differently," he said.

"Don't worry about it," Quint said. "It is a defensive measure. There is something strange at work, here."

"Strange doesn't describe it," Dakuz said.

They entered the house. The servant had left the sliding door ajar and wasn't waiting for them.

A spear of flame lashed out from the side, bathing Dasoka, who was the last to enter. The fire washed him, and he stood, shocked, looking at his hands. "The shield," he said.

"Stay here. I'll chase the attacker," Quint said, immediately running toward the flames' source. A bolt of lightning hit him. He could barely feel the effects, but he stopped to assess. The bolt was particularly weak. Would the Flat Plains be after them? Why did they attack Dasoka first? He wanted, needed, to find out, but the attacking wizards retreated.

The thought didn't last long as bolts and spears were cast at Quint. He continued to chase after their assailants. He caught up to them. One was a woman and the other was Gomio. The wizard hadn't gone to his quarters in the capital but must have quickly headed back to Teritoto.

Quint cast a lightning bolt that hit Gomio's heel, sending him careening into a wall. The other assailant, the servant who had stopped them, turned around and sprayed Quint with fire. When he saw the wizard master, Gomio was clutching his foot, and was out of the attack. He cast another fire string, hitting the wall in front of Quint, lighting a fire in Huma's house.

Quint cast a water string and doused the wall, permitting Dakuz and him to proceed. He quickly knelt by Gomio and put him to sleep.

The woman cast a lightning spell, but Dakuz was ready with a wind string that blew the woman back, pushing her halfway through the thin wall.

"What is this?" Dasoka asked. "Gomio attacked me? We talked a few times in the capital."

"He's on the other side, you fool," Dakuz said.

Quint rushed past them and put the woman to sleep and looked up at Dakuz and said, "You need to search the house to see if Huma Bifomu is still alive. I don't know if she has family but see whoever else is here."

Quint dragged Master Gomio to where the woman was, still embedded into the wall. He pulled her out and tore the hem of her dress, twisting the cloth for strength and binding their hands.

He heard Dakuz call for him. Quint sighed when he saw Huma and two women and a young man, dressed as a servants, dead in the kitchen.

"We need to get out of here," Dasoka said.

Quint shook his head. "Not today. There were people on the street who saw us follow the servant into Huma's house."

They heard heavy steps in the house and went to meet five guards in the process of untying Gomio's hands.

"Don't do that," Quint said.

"Who are you to tell me what to do?" a guard said. "We heard that three men murdered Huma Bifomu."

"How did you find out?" Dakuz asked.

The guard pulled out a note. "This was delivered to our station not more than a few minutes ago. We came as fast as we could. It looks like an open and shut case."

"Not really," Dasoka said. He pulled out a token and showed it to the guard.

"That doesn't mean anything if you murdered these two."

"They aren't dead," Quint said. "Come with me."

Two guards were left behind to guard the front door as Quint led the men to the kitchen and the site of the murders.

"We came to Teritoto on business with Huma Bifomu. I brought Dasoka since I don't know much about Shimato fief law. We were led inside and attacked by the man and the woman. The man is a master wizard from Gamiza who goes by the name of Gomio. I 've never seen the woman before."

"You expect me to believe that?"

Quint showed the guard a copy of the charter. "I'm here on behalf of the warlord to convince wizard factions that they need to organize to help defend Shimato against Gamiza and their new Green allies. Gomio was 'rescued' by Chibo Hobona's aide and me in Gamiza. He was waiting for a chance to kill me."

The guard looked quickly through the charter. "This almost looks official."

"It isn't official since I haven't been to all the factions, yet."

"Why didn't they hurt any of you if it was a wizardly ambush?"

"Take out your sword and run the edge across my arm," Quint said.

The guard looked suspiciously at Quint. His sword didn't penetrate Quint's shield.

"I could have run or fought you when you arrived, but I didn't," Quint said.

"You put the two in the hallway to sleep rather than kill them?"

Quint nodded. "I was in a wizard corps, but I prefer not to kill. Besides, I want to question Master Gomio and his accomplice. These poor people were not killed by me."

A uniformed woman walked into the kitchen. "Those are the bodies?"

"We haven't searched the entire house, ma'am," the guard said.

"And this is one of the killers?"

"He claims he was drawn into the house by the servant woman who is asleep."

"Did you push the woman through the wall?" the woman asked.

"No," Quint said, "but I quenched the fire she started just up the corridor."

She looked at Quint and then the guard. "That took a powerful string to generate that much water," she said.

"I'm a master," Quint said, "I'm on assignment for the warlord and was to meet with Huma Bifomu."

"The wizard charter?"

Quint nodded.

"Search the rest of the house. I know who this is. He wouldn't have any kind of a motive to kill Bifomu," she said.

"Did you know her?" Quint asked.

"Our paths crossed enough. I'm a lapsed member of the Flat Plains faction. I had to leave that behind when I joined the city guard. I keep up on what's happening. There are going to be a lot of angry wizards when they find out about this."

"I can understand. I'm not very happy myself," Quint said.

She kneeled and turned some of the bodies over. They were all killed with lightning strokes and were still in their nightclothes except for a woman dressed as a servant."

"Did Huma have a family?"

"They didn't live in this house and were somewhat estranged from their mother," the woman said. "When did you arrive in Teritoto?"

"An hour ago," Quint said. "We came straight here."

"Do you have any way to prove that?"

Quint shrugged. "We left our inn this morning at 8:30, but we could have traveled faster than we did."

"Don't worry about being arrested," the woman said. "That is good enough for me. Time for you to wake up the suspects."

They walked back to where Dakuz and Dasoka were held, close to Gomio and the servant accomplice.

Quint squatted down to check the wrappings.

"I'll have one of my guards change their bindings." She pulled four contraptions from her bag and tossed them to the guards. "Make sure these are secure. Didn't I hear you say the man is a master?"

"The woman was just as powerful," Quint said.

The uniformed woman walked to the hole in the wall. "Who did this?"

"I did," Dakuz said. "I'm good with wind strings."

"Obviously. I wouldn't have thought to disable a fleeing wizard that way."

The woman flicked a quick string at Dakuz and saw the tendril of lightning splatter and fizzle on his chest. "That's a serviceable shield."

Dakuz grimaced more than smiled. "Thank you."

She walked back up the corridor. "You doused the flames by yourself?"

Quint had already said he did. "You both are masters?"

"Never wanted to be tested," Dakuz said.

"And you?" the woman stepped toward Dasoka.

"I'm the extra baggage," Dasoka said, handing her his position token.

"A big wig for Teritoto," the woman said, "if this is genuine."

"It is," Dasoka said with a confident smile.

She nodded and returned to napping wizards. "I'll let my guards leave and cast a shield."

"I can protect them," Quint said.

"I'd like to see that," she said.

Quint covered them including the officer. "Everyone is protected."

She tested one of her men just as she had tested Dakuz. "You are a master," she said to Quint. "Wake them up, please."

Quint woke the woman first.

"She's all yours," Quint said.

The woman opened her eyes and moaned. "I'm injured." She lifted the contraption that splayed her hands. "He's the one you should be arresting," the woman said glaring at Quint.

"He says you lured him into the house and then you attacked them."

"No. Not me. I'm a servant here," she said.

"Shall I have some of my friends in the Flat Plain society tell me that you've served here?"

"I'm new," she said. She made a face at Quint. "Very new."

"And your claim that Huma's family was inside?" Quint asked.

"Who said that? Me? The Flat Plains master is away on business. He took his sons with him."

"Daughters," the officer said.

"Daughters? I said I was new."

"Who burned the wall?" the officer asked, turning to look at the mess down the corridor.

"He did," the female servant said, pointing at Quint.

"Then did you quench the flames?" the officer asked.

"Of course, I did," she said.

"Then do it," the female officer said, removing the woman's hand bindings.

"My power is a little light right now."

"Try," the officer said. "It is very important."

She cast a string at the officer and the lightning fizzled on the shield that Quint cast for her. The officer's eyes grew as the woman servant

ran past while the officer who was still surprised. Quint disabled her, like he had Gomio. She fell to the floor in a heap.

"Get her," the officer said to a guard.

By the time the guard reached the woman, she was convulsing.

"Poison, I think," the officer said. "Do you have an antidote string?"

"I can put her back to sleep, but she will likely die anyway."

The officer sighed. "Let's hope the Gamizan will sing. She still didn't understand that Huma was a woman." She brushed off her uniform. "That was a great shield."

Dakuz played like his feelings were hurt, but he came closer to Gomio.

"This is the dangerous person."

"I have something for him that I had intended to use on the woman."

"A truth string?"

The officer nodded. "I was about to use it on the female accomplice, but…"

"Put it on Gomio before he wakes up," Dakuz suggested.

"It works through a shield?" Quint asked.

"Usually. You were able to stop him with a lightning bolt."

Quint didn't want to brag about being able to defeat shields, so he just smiled. "Let's give it a try."

The officer cast her string and then Quint cancelled his sleeping string. Gomio started when he woke. "You haven't killed me!"

"Guilty of something?" the officer said.

Gomio looked down the corridor at the body of his accomplice.

"What did she say?" Gomio asked.

"That you killed Huma and the others in the kitchen," Quint said.

"I didn't kill anyone," Gomio said.

"You aimed a fire spear at Dasoka," Dakuz said. "I saw it come from your hands."

"He was shielded, wasn't he?" Gomio said.

"And if he wasn't you'd be a liar," the officer said.

Gomio sat up straighter but winced when he moved his injured foot. "But I didn't kill him, did I?" he said truculently

"Why did you aim at him rather than Dakuz or me?" Quint asked.

"I'll do the questioning," the woman said.

"Because he's from the fief headquarters. I couldn't have him poking around. Bitto told me to turn around and head back to Teritoto and maim Dasoka. I didn't even have time to get fresh clothes."

"You fear him more than you do two powerful wizards?"

Gomio pursed his lips. "I don't like to attack people I know very well," he said not very convincingly.

"Then the woman killed Huma and her staff?"

Gomio nodded. "In their sleep, except for the servant who was preparing breakfast. She just arrived from elsewhere in Shimato. I arrived after she had done the job and moved them into the kitchen under her orders. We didn't have time to talk before I arrived."

"How were you going to take care of Dakuz and myself?" Quint asked.

"There are others in the city," Gomio said.

"A Green master?" Dakuz asked.

Gomio seemed to be struggling with himself. "No! Don't ask me! I don't want to kill myself!"

Quint stepped forward and put him to sleep. "If he hasn't reached the poison in his mouth, I think you've found out enough. I don't know why the Gamiza would send a Green master to Teritoto."

"I would ask that question when you find a Green master. Are they that powerful?" the officer asked.

Quint shrugged. "Some are extremely powerful and others, I can handle. Gomio is likely the source of all the information you need."

"And they don't want you setting up your charter, so they killed your contact."

Quint nodded. "We have to find Gomio's wizard," Quint said.

"Are they powerful enough to punch through your shield?" the officer asked.

"I hope not, but I've met three who likely could," Quint said. "We should leave you to do whatever you have to do. I will walk around the town and draw the wizard out."

"I didn't sign up to do that," Dasoka said.

Quint turned to Gomio and back to Dasoka. "Gomio said he only wanted to maim you. If there is a Green wizard in this town, that is the person who wants to kill me."

"I know a place where he should be safe," the woman officer said. "You can leave at any time, so I won't have to make a fortress out of this house to protect you."

Quint and Dakuz left after Quint reinforced Dasoka's shield and Dakuz's. They could be hit from anywhere.

They were halfway down the street when one of the Flat Plain wizards stopped them.

"What's going on at headquarters?" the wizard asked.

"There has been some trouble," Dakuz said. "The city guard is taking care of it. We were told to leave."

"Is Huma all right?" the wizard asked.

Quint shook his head. "You should ask the police,"

"I will," the wizard said and walked briskly past them toward Huma's house.

"Should we have told him?" Quint asked.

"It's better to stay out of the way. Who knows what that woman wants us to do? It's better to have him find out from those in the house," Dakuz said.

They stepped into a square. There were more people about. A lightning bolt slammed into Dakuz, knocking him to the ground. Quint turned and saw a short man with an evil look on his face casting something. The sheet of flame went wide and into a group of older women chattering away as they were struck.

Quint quickly doused them with water and fired back at the wizard. His shot splattered against the wizard's shield, but the distance was too far to get through the wizard's defense.

He ran forward thinking the wizard would flee, but the man stood his ground. Quint's shield colored from a sheet of flame launched too far away to do any damage, but there were innocent bystanders all around.

Quint couldn't be responsible for the injuries, but he had to get the bystanders out of harm's way. He gathered his magic and cast a sleeping spell on those in his sight as he turned around. People dropped where they were.

Three people were left standing including the short, angry man. Quint pulled three crossbow bolts from his bag and shot at each of the wizards. Two went down, but the short man didn't. He must be the Green master, thought Quint.

When Quint focused on the remaining wizard, he ran towards him and used his one-hand strings to cover his approach with streams of fire, which had a better chance of disturbing the wizard's aim.

Quint caught up to the wizard. The man turned around and fired a lightning bolt at close range. It penetrated Quint's shield enough to make his chest tingle, but he ignored the sensation. He wasn't going to let pain that was less than what he experienced at the Narukun keep stop him.

He reached inside the wizard's shield with his hand and felt a shock move up his arm before he applied a sleep string inside the man's protection. The wizard went down as if he didn't have a bone in his body.

The tingling got worse, but the Green wizard was down. He wondered how that was when he fainted, falling on top of the Green wizard.

∽

CHAPTER TWENTY-THREE
~

Q UINT CAME TO WHILE HE STILL WAS ON TOP OF THE WIZARD. He checked to make sure his opponent was asleep before shaking his head and letting hands help him up.

"I thought you killed each other," Dakuz said, owner of the helping hands.

"Some of the wizard's string made it past the shield, but right after I reached inside his shield and put him to sleep. He might have a poison pill in his mouth like the woman at the Flat Plain headquarters," Quint said.

His head buzzed and his heart was pounding irregularly. While they waited for city guards to reach them, Quint's heart settled down and his head was clearing, but some of the buzz remained. Suddenly, the buzzing increased, and Quint barely registered falling into Dakuz's arms again.

Quint blinked a few times and found himself in Tova's room, again. "I thought you were through with me," Quint said to the goddess.

"We need each other for some time yet, Quinto Tirolo," Tova said. "I was monitoring you and realized your injury might make it easier to initiate a conversation."

"What do you want?"

Tova smiled and took a drink of something multicolored in a goblet by her lounge. "I didn't want you to forget me."

"I haven't done that," Quint said. "I don't know I could.

You've given me magic power that doesn't exist in the world."

"Except for Simo Tapmann," Tova said. "His power and yours are much alike, especially in his condition at present. You'll be able to recognize his magic."

"I figured I would. Is he still on Votann?"

"I don't think so. I'll try to get current. It isn't easy to do that with Simo Tapmann," Tova said. "It would be impossible with Tizurek."

"Will I have to be struck be lightning in order to talk to you?"

Tova laughed, almost a giggle, and shook her head. "You'll have a new string in your head when you wake up. That's it for now. Don't be a stranger!"

Quint sneezed and when he opened his eyes, he looked up at Dakuz.

"We should stop meeting like this," Quint said. "I had a slight relapse, but I think I'm over the worst of it." He couldn't mention Tova since the guards were arriving.

"More carnage?" a city guard who Quint recognized from the Flat Plains headquarters.

"The second part of the Green's agenda," Quint said. "I think this is the most powerful wizard of them all." Quint looked down at the slumbering man. "If he is the most powerful, perhaps he knows the most."

The city guard took over the scene. The female investigator finally arrived. "Your wizard, Gomio, died. I woke him, and I suppose I asked him too many questions before he poisoned himself. He did get his orders from another wizard. Perhaps this one?"

Quint shrugged while he rubbed his forehead. The headache was still there. "If we can keep him alive, perhaps we'll find out."

"His contact in Morimanu was Hari Bitto. I've met Bitto before." The woman shivered. "Slimy."

Dasoka stepped up and handed a sealed note to the woman. "This needs to go to Commander Narisu in Morimanu by special messenger," Dasoka said. "He needs to know about Bitto."

Quint looked down at the Green wizard through narrowed eyes. "Can you keep him secure? He might have enough power to do anything."

"Don't worry about that. The Flat Plains wizards are assembling at the house. I suggest you move your meeting elsewhere. We are going to lock up the house so we can do a proper investigation tomorrow. You and your friends are to stay in Teritoto the next few nights."

"We can do that," Dakuz said. "Quint's mind is a little hazy. He got too close to a lightning bolt. I'll take him to Huma's house and then to an inn, like you suggested."

Dakuz let Quint take it slow, but he was better with every step. City guards were holding back about ten wizards. Dasoka was trying to help the guards calm the faction members.

"Is there a place close by, an inn perhaps, where we could meet?" Dakuz asked. "Quint is still suffering from an injury fighting the other group of assassins."

They walked over a block and then right to a merchant's inn. Dakuz stabled the horses while Dasoka rented rooms. The Flat Plains wizards hired a private room.

Quint needed something to drink and was given watered wine. Dakuz and Dasoka returned. Dakuz called the meeting to order.

"What happened to Master Huma?" a wizard asked.

"She was killed by an attack of the Greens and Gamizans," Quint said. "We found her and those in the household killed. The bodies were moved to the kitchen so they could lay in wait for Dasoka, Dakuz, and me. We were well-shielded, but they were powerful wizards. Gomio, who you met before, returned before us and joined up with the Greens. Hari Bitto wanted to settle a score and tasked Gomio with maiming or killing Dasoka. Luckily, my shields held." He went through everything else except his impromptu audience with Tova.

"Huma was killed because of you nosing about," one of the wizards said.

"Didn't you listen to Quint? How could you say that?" Dakuz said.

"If you hadn't ridden into town, she'd still be alive."

"For now," Dakuz said. "The Greens didn't follow Quint here."

"How do you know that?"

Dakuz raised a finger, but Dasoka grabbed and lowered it before he spoke. "Gamizans and Greens are entering Shimato all the time. I'm in a position where the information of such things come through me," Dasoka said.

Quint didn't think that answered the wizard's question, but the man seemed mollified. He wasn't going to insist on accuracy. Quint needed wizards on his side.

"We need to be united as wizards," Quint said. "I'm not here to lead you, but to guide your transformation into an association of wizards and the charter is the best way I can see how to do it other than have the warlord send non-wizards to supervise you."

"There would be a rebellion if Lord Bumoto did that," another wizard said.

"So, we get together, set up an organization that unites you and is a contract with the warlord regarding wizards in the army."

"What's in it for you?" the first wizard asked.

"I'm a wizard and I want wizardry to thrive in the world, but I can also see it growing in the wrong direction if the charter isn't properly structured," Quint said. "The warlord is leery of wizards and has less respect for you since everyone has their own demands and that irritates him. A charter can fix most of that."

"Most?" another wizard said.

"There is nothing perfect in this world," Quint said, and as he spoke, Quint thought how true that was.

"I'll sign if we don't yet have a new leader," the first and most vocal wizard said.

Dakuz pulled Dasoka and Quint out of the room. "Let them do it without your interference. We have to reconstruct a little trust, if there was any to begin with."

The voting didn't take long before they were asked to re-enter.

The vocal wizard stood as the others sat.

"I'll be the charter's local representative," the wizard said. "We are still in shock about Huma's murder, but nothing can wait at this point. We have ourselves, our families and our fief at stake."

Quint guessed the man was testing Quint through the questioning. "Then tell me if there are any changes to the charter."

"How will the administrators in Morimanu be chosen?" the new leader asked.

Quint looked at Dasoka, who shrugged. He wouldn't let him get away without helping him through the legal aspects since that was what he brought him along for.

"What is legally required to have the charter represent wizards?" Quint asked Dasoka.

"The charter is adequate for now. The association picks its representatives who hire the wizards."

"And if we all want fair hiring?" Quint asked.

"It could be administered through the faction council," Dasoka. "It's in your charter."

Quint quickly turned to the section on the council, and he realized the charter could be interpreted to have addressed the hiring as well as the appointment of the administrators who would run the registrar part of the charter. Quint should have known better since he used to analyze documents as part of his work in Racellia.

He explained the interpretation to the group, and they agreed that would help.

"We will tie up the loose ends of the charter when half the factions have signed. That shouldn't end recruitment," Quint said. He turned to the new leader. "Will your council sign? The Flat Plain faction stays intact."

The meeting turned into an exchange of questions about the legal aspects of setting up a charter organization in Teritoto. After a few hours, everyone had run out of things to say.

"I'll sign. Huma Bifomu was our best leader, and we need something to bind us, anyway," the leader said, signing the bottom of the charter and stepping aside for the others.

Quint nodded. "We will contact you about timing, but delaying anything could be disastrous." He pushed a purse into the leader's hands. "For Huma's children and the families of the others who were murdered."

"This is from the warlord?" a wizard asked.

Quint shook his head. "It's from me."

∽

CHAPTER TWENTY-FOUR

THEY RODE EAST and found that the Greens were actively disparaging the charter to the local wizards, but that actually helped Quint's activities. They arrived at their last destination, the small city where lived Akomono, the wizard who had approached them in the capital under false pretenses.

Dasoka didn't know the wizard, but he knew his faction. They might be hard to sell since they were supposedly under Hari Bitto's influence and that might mean they were solid Greens. The faction leader of the Blue Song faction greeted the three of them at the gate to the Blue Song faction headquarters, but didn't let them in.

"I know why you are here. Akomono told me when he presented a copy of your charter to me," the leader said.

"It's really your charter," Quint said. "I'm just facilitating it. Shimato may soon be in a crisis, and I'd rather your fief survive."

"You are anti-Green?"

"It's no secret," Quint said.

"Our faction allows Green wizards to join."

"Like Akomono?" Dakuz asked.

"Akomono is a friend of Bitto's, but as far as I know he isn't a Green. He said he was convinced you were sincere. No one believes that Hari Bitto is sincere with his airs of being a master. I've never seen a documented test confirming that."

"Can we come in and talk?" Quint asked.

The faction leader sighed and opened the gate wider, letting them lead their horses into the courtyard. A few boys ran up to take care of the horses.

"The Blue Song is more like a Narukun cloister. I'll get our members together to talk."

When the three were shown to a small reception room, a wizard delivered a message from the capital to Dasoka.

"Hari Bitto has fled to Gamiza," Dasoka said as he continued to read. "Your local friends have signed all the factions in the capital. We are to return as soon as we finish here. The warlord needs you in Chokuno to convince them to join with Shimato."

Akomono showed up but wasn't introduced as one of the Blue Song leaders. Nevertheless, he supported the charter and told his fellow wizards about the recent duplicity of Hari Bitto after Dasoka announced that Bitto had fled.

The charter was approved that day and Dakuz, Quint, and Dasoka were heading west to Morimanu before the sun set. The charter was approved by every faction from the northwest to the east of Morimanu. Quint hoped it was enough to get the charter started.

§

Thera greeted them in the stables of the Three Forks mansion as Dakuz and Quint took care of their horses. Dasoka had left them halfway through the capital.

"I can report success and concerns about that success," Thera said as Dakuz and Quint left the stable. "The charter has been activated by Bumoto, but now we are in the midst of a crisis."

"Gomio and Hari Bitto?" Quint asked.

Thera nodded. "Todo is supervising some quick food preparation so you can eat, and we can talk."

They took their bags to the dining hall and sat down on little tables pushed closer together. Todo and Dugo led servants into the room carrying trays and set them on each of their tables. Todo kept a tray for himself as did Dugo.

Quint's followers were seated. He turned to Dugo. "How did the recruitment go? Dasoka received a note that all the Morimanu factions signed the charter."

Dugo looked at Todo and sighed. "We were making good progress, but when Hari Bitto fled, and word made it back to us that Gomio was killed in the act of murdering the leader of the Flat Plains. Everyone knew there would be pressure to sign, so they accepted the charter before they were forced."

"What about the Green-affiliated factions?" Dakuz asked.

"Bitto took sorcerers with him, somewhere between ten and twenty," Todo said. "The warlord lost some of his advisors, but that number has been kept secret."

"So, Shimato is in crisis," Quint said.

Thera nodded. "Well and truly. You are to report to Chibo at an hour after sunrise. I am to accompany you."

"No one else?" Quint asked, looking at Dakuz as he said it.

"You are to get the charter work started so you can devote most of your time to the Shimato Wizard Corps."

"Has it been formalized?" Dakuz asked.

"Narisu is the leader, reporting to Chibo. The line of command remains unbroken," Thera said. "We have most of the basic organization mapped out, but it all needs to be accelerated."

"What do you need me for?" Quint asked.

"A master. Narisu thinks neither of us carries the respect as a wizard that you do."

Quint snorted. "Narisu is always minimizing his capabilities, but he isn't a master. When Narisu and I traveled to Gamiza, I always thought I'd end up fighting more Green wizards. I don't know how they collected so many powerful wizards, though."

"Does it matter?" Dakuz asked.

"It will matter until the threat is taken care of."

§

The next morning, Narisu wore a different uniform. This one was black, like the Wizard Corps in Racellia, but cut in the Kippunese style.

"I see you are admiring my new livery," Narisu said. "Thera and yours are currently being tailored along with one thousand of a simpler cut and cheaper cloth for the worker bees of the corps."

"Now that we have that important issue put to bed, what is on your mind?"

"You have one more trip," Narisu said. "I need Thera, but your new friend Dasoka and you are traveling to Chokuno to convince them that they need to ally themselves with Shimato."

"When do I go to Slinnon?" Quint asked facetiously.

"They are strong enough to provide their own defense," Narisu said.

"Really?"

"That's all you need to know, Quint."

"Am I waiting for my uniform?"

Narisu nodded. "You are, but we need to have a discussion with Chibo before you go. The warlord has issues enough after the defection of his advisors."

Chibo was his usual ebullient self. "You will contact Masumi in Tiryo, the Chokuno capital. Get whatever intelligence she can give you. The situation in Chokuno is very fluid. Don't introduce Dasoka to her until you meet. Her status remains confidential."

Quint nodded. "Narisu has the contact instructions?"

"He does. You and your people have done more than anyone has ever accomplished in corralling the wizard factions in my lifetime. Consider that a commendation. Your uniform will carry commander tokens, but you aren't to wear it on Chokuno territory until Masumi says you can.

"Does anyone know everything for this operation?" Quint asked.

"You will, once you contact Masumi. The warlord wants the Chokuno warlord to sign your charter. You are unique enough to be our only hope of cutting through the political clutter. Chokuno's wizards are not effective, as you witnessed on the border."

Quint didn't remind Chibo that his wizards weren't any better.

"I'll do what I can. Can I take my followers with me?" Quint asked.

Chibo pursed his lips. "No. Only Dasoka, Masumi and you. Now that the charter is in effect, I need your people to recruit wizards for the corps and Thera and Narisu will train them. The warlord is concerned that we can do nothing to stop Gamizan wizards until it is too late."

Quint was sent home to prepare for the trip, and Thera stayed to work with Narisu. When he returned home, he shook his head. Did he have to risk his life in a last gasp attempt to convince someone who had already been swayed by the Greens and Gamiza to go to war against Shimato? He could take his followers and head west toward Slinnon, but then, wasn't this the kind of experience Tova expected he learn to grow into someone who could possibly convince a god to return to whatever heaven Tova lived in?

The instructions from Narisu were brief. An address, a notification that the name of an alternate contact whose address was in the possession of Dasoka. There wasn't mention of the mission or any specifics.

It was clear that Quint would have to make everything up as he proceeded along the path to an alliance.

Quint felt his path lay through Chokuno, back to Morimanu in Shimato, then it was on to Slinnon and away from North Fenola.

∾

CHAPTER TWENTY-FIVE

THE COUNTRYSIDE WAS BUSY HARVESTING whatever food was ready for the season. The possibility of an invasion by Gamiza was not a well-kept secret.

Narisu had hired a four-horse carriage to take them to Tiryo in Chokuno. The roads varied from rough to rougher along the way and would continue until they were closer to Tiryo, if Quint remembered correctly.

Dasoka spent most of his time sipping from a silver flask and napping in a semi-drunken stupor. He was already in that condition when Quint picked him up at his flat. Quint had been tempted to leave Dasoka at his home, but good sense prevailed, as Quint realized that the bureaucrat might have other information that Quint needed for his mission.

Narisu had given the driver an itinerary complete with roadside stops and inns to spend the night, and within four days, they spotted the skyline of Tiryo, capital of Chokuno.

Dasoka had stopped drinking the night before and seemed mostly lucid when Quint had breakfast with the bureaucrat half a day from Tiryo.

"I half expected you to toss me out of the carriage and leave me for dead on the side of the road," Dasoka said.

"Why have you been drinking ever since we left Morimanu?"

Dasoka sighed and pulled out the silver flask. He unstoppered it. A single drop plummeted from the flask to the floor of the carriage. "My mentor fled with his family to Gamiza, leaving me behind."

"I didn't think you were a Green."

"I'm not," Dasoka said. "My mentor isn't either, but I'm afraid he must have taken bribes from the Gamizans on the side, a capital offense in Shimato."

"Can you carry out your duties?"

Dasoka sighed. "I must. The warlord is holding my family hostage. He told me that my life and my family's life depended on our success. If we succeed, I see them again. If we fail, I'll either be killed by the Gamizans or by the warlord's guard." The man ran his hand through his hair. "What did he use on you?"

Quint felt very foolish. "They didn't need to persuade me. I don't know if I should feel like I've been taken or if I'm a willing pawn," he said. "I have my mission to ultimately find Simo Tapmann. To do so, I need to grow."

"You call this mission, growth?" Dasoka asked, astounded.

"It is. I've persuaded others to join me in my travels, in fact, they have volunteered. This time will be infinitely more difficult since I think the Chokunese warlord will be kicking and screaming against the idea of aligning with Lord Bunto Bumoto," Quint said.

"You won't know until you try. The warlord has given us a week to get the alliance signed. It is already drafted and tucked away in my baggage."

Now Quint knew why he needed Dasoka. The warlord wanted everything in writing. Quint wasn't very experienced in negotiating the finer points of anything, but he was sure that Dasoka was.

"I'll do what I can to keep your family alive, Dasoka."

The bureaucrat looked into Quint's eyes. "I appreciate that. The warlord insisted you would support me. I admit I am still doubtful of our success given the facts of our situation."

Quint didn't know if that were good or bad, but the new knowledge gave him a deadline he didn't have before.

"We will find Masumi and then decide what we can do about Gamiza," Quint said.

When they reached the guards, Dasoka found a token and showed it to them. They recognized the thing and waved them through.

"We are ambassadors from the warlord. They won't touch us unless they are already Gamizan vessels," Dasoka said.

Quint gave Masumi's address to the driver and sat back, not knowing where that address was in the city. The driver apparently did since he finally stopped in front of a furniture shop.

"The person you seek is inside this building?" the driver asked.

"Then I think he's in trouble," Dasoka said.

Quint looked out the window and at the upper floor. The top floor of the building had been burned and still smoked. He pulled Dasoka out of the carriage.

"Stay here," Quint said to the driver.

"We have to see what happened," Quint said. He threw the door open and waved the smell of smoke away as he examined the first floor. A stairway was to his right and he carefully walked up to the next level.

"Hello?" Quint called.

He didn't receive an answer. The fire had stopped midway down the walls. The furniture showed scorch marks, but someone had kept the conflagration at bay. Masumi could do that if she had the power and the strings.

After testing the floors as he walked through the wreckage. Parts of the ceiling had fallen in, but it was clear someone had extinguished the flames.

No one was upstairs, and whoever lived here, or a looter ,had removed some of the possessions as shown by empty bookshelves and an open wardrobe devoid of clothing.

Dasoka stood inside the uninhabited furniture shop. "Did you find anything?"

"I didn't find a body, if that's what you mean," Quint said. "You have another address?"

"I was going to question the one you gave the driver, but not when I saw this. I have information in a sealed envelope given to me by Chibo."

Quint opened the door to the carriage, seeing a dark form swaddled in black sitting in the seat. He immediately cast a shield on Dasoka and himself.

"Who are you?" Quint asked.

"You have such a short memory," Masumi said, pulling back a hood.

"I hoped you were alive," Quint said as he climbed in followed by Dasoka.

"Barely," Masumi said. "I woke to creaking timbers on the roof and was able to quench the fire, after fighting it for more than an hour two nights ago, right after I received a message from Narisu. There is a traitor among those you met the last time you were here." She looked almost accusingly at Dasoka.

"Who is she?" Dasoka asked.

"Meet Masumi. She is an old friend of Narisu's."

"Not too old," Masumi said.

"She helped us extract Gomio from Gamiza."

Dasoka's eyes flashed. "I know who you are!"

"Masumi," she said. "I'm a Chokunese spy."

Dasoka took a deep breath. "I'm willing to go along," he said.

"So am I," Quint said. "She knows the situation as well as anyone." He tapped the roof and called out the inn's address to the driver.

Masumi snuggled next to Quint. "You are my new husband," she said.

"I am?" Quint asked, perplexed. "Oh, I am," he said once he thought for a moment. "You marry young."

"Not too young," Masumi said. She tapped a large valise next to her. "My luggage."

Quint sat back. "Can I show her the name and address that Narisu gave you?"

Dasoka shrugged. "I suppose it is permissible now." He handed a sealed envelope to Masumi, who opened it and frowned.

"'Return to Morimanu,' the note inside says," Masumi said, handing it to Quint.

He gave it to Dasoka.

"A note to retreat if I can't be found. How touching," Masumi said. She ripped the note and put the pieces in her mouth. Both men gave her a moment to swallow. "What is your mission?"

"You don't know?" Quint asked.

"I know what Narisu sent me, however the night after it arrived, someone thought I might need roasting," Masumi said.

"Obtain an alliance with the warlord or Chokuno," Quint said.

"That seems easy enough and matched my note, but someone must know that it is Lord Bumoto's intent to get me out of the way."

"How many people knew you lived above the shop?" Dasoka asked.

"Few," Masumi said. "The note was addressed to the weapons shop." She looked at Dasoka and shrugged.

"So, someone followed whoever brought the message," Quint said.

"We are on our own," Masumi said. "We don't have time to find out who the traitor is."

"I'll be the judge of that," Dasoka said.

"I happen to agree with Masumi," Quint said. "That makes it two to one. We aren't in Shimato."

Dasoka pursed his lips. "As long as we work for the same goal."

"We do as long as it is to forge an alliance with the Chokunese warlord," Quint said. He needed both to complete the mission. He was merely magical muscle on this mission, he realized. "How should we proceed?" He asked Masumi.

"I have my own contacts, but we have to be careful," she said. "We will be exposed every step of the way, once I am recognized."

"Then let's make you unrecognizable," Quint said. "Pick a false name. I'll cast a mask."

"Amoki Tirolo," she said with a seductive smile, "dear."

Quint thought of a face that would be close, but distinctively different from her real one. He cast the strings three times to get the right effect.

"Amazing!" Dasoka said. "I'd never recognize you, Amoki."

She made a feminine wave. "You are too kind, Dasoka Hana."

Dasoka raised his eyebrows. "You know who I am?"

"I do. I know enough about you, that my doubts have been reduced by knowing you are here. Quint is a wonderful wizard, but he has his limitations in addition to his tender age," Masumi said.

"Hey!" Quint said.

Masumi patted Quint's wrist. "Don't worry. I won't let it influence the feelings for my husband."

"I will write notes to be delivered in the morning." She looked at Dasoka. "You can edit them, if you wish."

"I do. Then let's get to the inn." Dasoka said.

§

Quint and his "new wife," Amoki, shared a room with one big bed and no couch or easy chair to sleep on. With a real bed in the room, the characteristic straw mats weren't in the room.

"Don't worry. You can sleep on top of the covers," Amoki said with a grin.

She sat down at the table and wrote messages. Quint didn't recognize the names, but he gathered the letters and delivered them to Dasoka, who said he'd have them reviewed by the time they went to dinner in the inn.

At dinner, Masumi clung to Quint like a girlfriend would. He'd never had a girlfriend. His relationship with Sandy at Seensist Cloister had never progressed to a point where he could consider them "together."

"Here are the letters. It is fine to read them, but we should exchange any comments in a more private venue," Dasoka said.

Masumi read the first one and then passed it to Quint. He didn't see anything wrong with the letter, but there were a few grammatical mistakes that Dasoka corrected. She looked at Quint and snorted, looking away from the table, showing she didn't think much of the edits.

The other letters had some suggestions penned in the margins and two had words circled that might lead someone to think Shimato wanted to take over Chokuno.

"I'll fix all but the grammatical mistakes. If I send perfect letters where I didn't before, it might arouse suspicion," Masumi said.

"I grant you that. You understood my comments?"

Masumi nodded. "There were some good catches." She snuggled up to Quint. "Now, we can have some fun, can't we, Honey?"

"Honey," muttered Quint. He wondered how old Masumi really was. Her new face made her look younger than Thera, in Quint's perspective, but he didn't know the real difference.

"What are you thinking about?' Dasoka asked Quint.

Quint raised his eyebrows and quickly tried to lower them. He felt he was caught doing something capricious. "I was thinking about our time in Tiryo." He didn't lie, but his answer wasn't as accurate as it might be. It made him embarrassed.

"Are you getting cold feet?" Masumi asked and kissed the air between them.

"No," Quint said. "This is different from my first trip to Tiryo."

Masumi put her mouth close to Quint's ear and whispered. "You are sweating. Don't you like me?"

"Husbands love their wives," Quint said quietly.

"That's how it should be," Dasoka said. "I love my wife."

Quint saw an escape from attention. "You have a family?"

"I do. I don't often get to enjoy the boys. We live above the pastry shop my wife owns."

Masumi gave Dasoka and encouraging smile. "I pictured you living in a mansion in the best part of Morimanu."

"I do live in the best part of the capital above my wife's shop."

"How old are your boys?" Quint asked.

"My oldest is ten, the middle one is seven and the end of the line is five.

The older two attend a live-in academy, but my youngest follows my wife around all the time."

"What does the live-in academy teach? Does it have a specialization?" Masumi asked.

Quint fed more questions to Dasoka and Masumi contributed her own. Quint learned more about normal life in Shimato, although it was clear Dasoka enjoyed an elevated lifestyle, being a senior civil servant.

Masumi yawned. "I have some work to do," she said. She nudged Quint in the ribs with her elbow. "Don't we?"

Quint rose. He had been embarrassed enough for the day. "Yes. Good idea."

They left Dasoka savoring a goblet of expensive wine that Masumi suggested.

"Time for work, and then we can play," Masumi said.

Quint was still uncomfortable with the teasing. "I'd rather not play," he said.

Masumi frowned, but it was still a tease. She laid the letters on the table. "What do you really think?"

"Some of it is a matter of taste," Quint said. "He doesn't like some of your phrasing and wants the letters to be perfectly written, but I agree with you. They need to reflect you, not a government document."

"I'm not perfect?" Masumi asked in a little girl voice.

"None of us are," Quint said.

"You are close to perfect," she said.

Quint laughed. "I have some strong points, but perfection?" He shook his head. "You tease me, and I'm embarrassed. If I was perfect, I would have some clever words at the tip of my tongue to stop you."

Masumi pursed her lips and looked at Quint appraisingly. "You changed an uncomfortable subject and kept Dasoka talking during dinner."

"He went along with it," Quint said.

"But he and I could sense your discomfort."

"See? My discomfort is an expression of my imperfections. Besides, you both were probably laughing at me behind my back."

"Sensitive?"

"Another imperfection," Quint said.

"I wouldn't call it laughing behind your back, but you were behaving pretty much what I'd expect an inexperienced young man to act when seduced by a slightly older woman," Masumi said.

"I'm not being seduced," Quint said.

"And how would you know?" Masumi said with her eyes half-closed.

Her expression unnerved Quint. It reminded him of how Tova treated him, like toying with a little kitten.

"I would be more than stirred," Quint said, taking a deep breath.

"You are stirred?" Masumi said.

"A little. I am a male, aren't I? Males are affected by the attention of an attractive female," Quint said. Was that why Sandy never really stirred him? She didn't pay him the right kind of attention. He shivered, and Masumi noticed. "I caught a draft."

She laughed. "An uncalled-for memory?"

"No," Quint said. He told himself it was a consciously surfaced memory.

Masumi sighed. "Then let's get this work done so we can go for a walk."

Quint re-read the letters and they discussed what changes needed to be put into the new versions. Masumi made the revisions, Quint made copies for her and slid new versions into the envelopes.

"It's time to cool you off," Masumi said, winking at Quint.

Dasoka wasn't in the lobby or the dining area. They walked outside into the cool night. Masumi rubbed her arms and Quint took his cloak off and wrapped it around her shoulders.

"Isn't this what a thoughtful husband should do?" he asked.

"Of course," Masumi said with a satisfied smile. "We should walk to our right."

"We are hoping to meet someone?"

Masumi nodded her head. "Our messenger's messenger," she said. "It will be someone I know and has seen you."

"At the weapon's shop?"

She smiled and nodded before clutching his arm and putting her head on his shoulder. The monthly market wasn't that night, so they walked past the pools of magic lights and lanterns on the street. Quint recalled that the warlord drafted wizards for his army if caught in Tiryo. Quint knew that wouldn't be a good thing because Masumi was a wizardess, and he wasn't the one with the exemption token, Dasoka was.

Quint recognized the lane of weapon's shops, but Masumi didn't lead him that way, the real reason she held onto his arm, he thought. As they walked across a street to the next block, two men walked out of an alley ahead. Quint put shields around Masumi and himself.

Masumi tugged on Quint to stop as the men approached. She pulled out the letters.

One of the men squinted in the dim light of the street. "Masumi? I recognize your partner."

She laughed. "That's me. Give these to Isano to distribute. I used code names for your people. I'll be in disguise until I'm not, and I don't know when that will be. If I need you, I'll be in touch."

The two men nodded and passed them with the speaker putting the letters in his coat pocket.

"We can go back to the inn, now, if you wish," Masumi said.

"I don't mind walking for a bit more." Quint could put off the awkwardness of sharing a bed until it was time to sleep, or pretend to.

She clutched him tighter and kissed his cheek. "I was hoping you'd ask to continue. For some reason, I feel stronger when I touch you."

"It's no string I'm casting," Quint said, although he made sure of the shields after he said that.

After half an hour of roaming around the shopping district, they headed back to the inn. Walking through a darker section of their route, people began following them. They noticed more people coming out of an alley on the other side of the street ahead of them and walked their side looking over at them.

"Do you have bolts in your pocket?" Masumi asked.

Quint nodded. "Let's hope we don't need them. In an empty street, I can cast a sleeping spell."

"Whoever has set these thugs on us, will know you are a wizard," Masumi said. "If you use bolts, they might think otherwise."

"Do you carry a weapon other than wizardry?" Quint asked quietly.

"Always," Masumi said. "You have shielded us?"

Quint nodded. "It's best against magic, but although it won't turn a blade it will slow it down, so stay active when we are attacked."

Three uniformed men walked around the corner of a dark intersection and stood, waiting for them to come to them.

"Uniforms," Masumi said. "If they didn't wear them, I would drag you across the street, but those are officers. We will have to talk to them. Be ready with your sleeping spell, although you may have to flee with me on your shoulders. I'll forgive you for any bruises if you have to." She gave him a squeeze and then held him back making the officers walk toward them.

"Good evening," Quint said. "Did you know we are being followed by thugs?"

"My soldiers are not thugs," one of the officers said.

"We haven't done anything wrong," Quint said. Masumi stayed silent.

"You have entered Chokuno under false pretenses," another officer said.

"Really? When did I do that? I'm here with Lord Dasoka to see the warlord. This is my wife, Amoki. We didn't expect a confrontation."

Dasoka walked around the corner at that point and stood with the officers.

Quint shrugged. "Are you a traitor like Hari Bitto?"

"I haven't decided yet."

"Is our mission to the warlord over?"

"Your contribution is," Dasoka said., turning to Masumi. "Where are the letters? They weren't in your room." He held out his hand. "The Chokunese would like to see them."

"I ate them," Masumi said. "They are all gone. If you copied them, all the names were fakes, so they won't help. I can't say I ever trusted you."

"Search them," Dasoka said. "Then you can do whatever you wish with them. There are those on the warlord's staff that would prefer the boy be killed."

"You say that knowing that I am a wizard?" Quint said. While he cast a sleeping string, his shield fended off all kinds of attacks from those following him. He put all his will behind the spell and everyone in the street fell to the ground.

One of the wizards still stood behind him. Quint turned around as a lightning spell of some kind obliterated his vision as it splashed against his protection, penetrating his shield before Quint could reinforce it. He felt his insides shake and he tried to calm down, but his mind was slipping.

His last, hazy thought was to throw himself on Masumi to protect her, but before he blanked out, he realized that did no good when he was unconscious in the midst of their enemies, sleeping or not.

CHAPTER TWENTY-SIX

QUINT OPENED HIS EYES AND GROANED. Whatever that lightning spell was, made his bones ache when penetrating his shield, but he didn't get burned. He was glad to be alive. The room was dark, and Masumi was slumbering at his side.

He lifted his bound hands behind his back and found his fingers wrapped together as well. He sighed when Masumi was bound in the same way. He stood on his unbound legs and stretched as well as he could. That helped with his aching body. He looked around at the room. It wasn't a cell, but a large bedroom. The rooms were curtained, but Quint could see light leaking around the edges. It was daytime.

He used his teeth to pull the curtains open. They were next to a park in or out of the city.

"You woke before me?" Masumi said sitting up and shaking her head.

"Barely. Stand up and let me see if I can untie your bonds with my teeth."

The woman struggled to stand, and Quint got on his knees and worked on her bonds. They were leather thongs, but Quint was able to loosen one thong and then it was a matter of grabbing the loose end with his teeth and pulling before doing the same thing over and over again.

They heard a key unlocking the door and Quint helped Masumi lay down before he rolled over her to his side, but didn't lay down.

The door opened. The captor's eyes went to the curtain. "You've been up and about, I see."

"I wanted to see how long I've been out'"

"About a half day. It's lunch time. You are invited. Is your wife awake?"

His wife? Quint thought. He looked at Masumi. Was Dasoka playing a game?

"Yes. She was still a little groggy."

"I still am," Masumi said. Struggling more than she needed to sit up. "Where are we?"

"In a safe place, if you both behave. We know your wife is a wizard. One of our masters detected a shield."

"That I cast," Quint said.

"You can explain that. Will you agree to listen and observe?"

"Can we talk?" Masumi asked.

"If you are civil."

"I can be civil," Quint said. "So can Amoki, I think."

The man untied their bonds. "I see you've been at work on these. I suppose that is a good sign that you've recovered your wits."

Quint rubbed his wrists as did Masumi.

"I didn't expect I'd need a towel to wipe away your saliva, husband," Masumi said, wiping her wrists on a sheet once they were unbound.

"Follow me," the man said.

They walked down to the main level and into a dining room. Six men and two women sat at the table. Their captor took a seat. All were well dressed.

"I don't recognize any of you from last night," Quint said.

One of the men shrugged. "We weren't there. Our force noted that you used a powerful sleeping string. A few of our own succumbed to the spell. We followed the officers through the capital and had to fight the two masters who defeated the great Quinto Tirolo, but we did. Their strings sapped them of their strength giving us the opportunity to eradicate two more Green wizards. More Greens showed up and were able to retrieve Dasoka."

"So, you aren't Gamizans, yet?"

"Quite the opposite. The best dressed man said. "I am Goryo Tatatomi. If you were Chokunese, you would recognize me."

Quint looked at Masumi who solemnly said two words. "The warlord."

Quint shot a look at Tatatomi. "Your lordship. Is that the honorific you use? I don't know."

"Warlord or Lord works," Tatatomi said. "Your companion, Dasoka, was compromised by the Greens, however, he exposed three of my military officers as traitors and a brigade's worth of magicians. The two Green masters were with the Gamizan delegation lobbying for an alliance with Chokuno."

"So Dasoka was one of them?" Quint asked.

One of the women shrugged. "He is playing a dangerous game, but we don't believe he was acting on his own."

Quint wondered if Dasoka had been subjected to a persuasion string. His mission partner resisted well enough to hide Masumi's identity.

"Are you really married?" one of the women said. "We don't have any record of that happening while you were in Shimato fief."

"No," Masumi said. "I am a Slinnonese occasionally visiting Shimato and Chokuno. I have an influential friend…"

"Commander Narisu," the warlord said. "We can end the charade. I know who you are, but the situation is critical enough to let that slide. You are Tirolo's wife until we've finished with the Gamizans. For that, I'm sure we are on the same side."

"We are," Masumi said.

"Good. Do you want to rescue your friend, or shall we discuss why you came to Chokuno."

"I'll be blunt. Dasoka and I are here to create an alliance against the Gamizans. As you found out, the Greens are not to be trusted. Any agreement you make or have made with them will be broken as soon as it suits them."

"And that won't happen with Bunto Bumoto?"

"I can't answer that," Quint said. "My impression of Chibo Hobona and the warlord is that they will abide by an alliance. If you ally yourselves against the Gamizans and the Greens, I believe Shimato will truly be your ally until the Gamizans have been pacified. If you don't trust them past that, then write that as an end date to your agreement."

"I can consider that," Tatatomi said. "He has been hit with betrayals as much as I have. If we let the Gamizans attack us separately, we will fall faster than if we are united."

"And that is Shimato's position. I think we need to rescue Dasoka since he has the power to work an agreement out and I'm just a hired wizard."

Masumi snorted. "Just a hired wizard?"

The Chokunese all laughed.

"I need to devise something against a one-two punch," Quint said.

"They were killed, and you survived," one of the men said.

"And I thank you for that," Quint said, nodding to them.

The warlord sighed. "Then rescue Dasoka, it is. We know where he is, but we believe there are two more Green masters with them."

"Where do they come from?" Quint said.

"They are trained on Amea. There is a great wizard, Simo Tapmann, who is responsible. Tapmann came from somewhere else, but he runs Honnen and has an academy or something in a regional capital. Some say he surreptitiously rules Amea and Votann."

"I know where Honnen is," Quint said. "But I've not heard of Simo Tapmann." He couldn't reveal what he knew of Tizurek, who was Simo Tapmann, but wasn't Tapmann on Votann? Quint wasn't ready to confront an entire school of Green master wizards.

"You look surprised?" the warlord asked.

"An entire school graduating all those monsters…" Quint said.

One of the other men shook his head. "It puts the fear of Tizurek in you."

"And Tova, it truly does," Quint says. "We have to concentrate on Dasoka and the alliance."

"There is a wizard charter?" the warlord asked.

Quint ran a hand through his hair. "There is." He gave them a two-minute explanation. "It is something you should consider. I'd like the charter approved for wizards throughout North Fenola," Quint said.

"You want to run all the magic?"

Quint shook his head. "Not me. Your wizards can decide that, but it would bring order to Kippun," he said. "I think you need the fiefs united."

"That is a tall order," a man said. "Every warlord has a different vision."

"I don't doubt that," Quint said, "but everyone puts up with factions."

The warlord looked at his staff. "I suppose we do. I hadn't thought of it that way, but it won't be so easy."

"Neither are the factions. The charter will eliminate the power of the wizard factions and it's up to good leadership and good citizenship to do the rest," Quint said.

The warlord laughed. "You are more than a hired wizard, Tirolo. We'll talk more after we save your friend and find out what Bumoto has on his mind."

§

Quint, now dressed in black along with Masumi at his side, looked across the street at the Gamizan Embassy in the twilight. Twenty Chokunese wizards and warriors bided their time in alleys close to the embassy. Quint fingered the whistle that would bring reinforcements.

According to the warlord, there were fourteen people in the embassy, but Masumi told Quint that there were more Gamizans in Tiryo. Most of the attackers from the previous night were Chokunese traitors, not Gamizans. She guessed that Gamizan reinforcements would arrive in moments if there was a frontal attack on the embassy.

Although Tatatomi had already put some measures in motion, the defection of the three officers and the Chokunese wizards required some adjustments. What orders had the officers quashed? Tatatomi had to find out.

Quint agreed with the Chokunese warlord's approach. He felt that Tatatomi was a better people leader than Bumoto, but the Shimato warlord was the better defender. He shook his head since he didn't think he could trust either one. Quint had other things to think about.

Masumi stepped out of the shadows and bumped into a couple strolling on the street. She returned with a small, rolled strip of paper. After reading it, she burned it with a candle-lighting string.

"I have the signal. We have a hundred partisans ready to help."

Quint took a deep breath. "Won't Tatatomi be angry if rebels get in on the action?"

Masumi smiled slyly. "They aren't what I would consider rebels," she said. "Partisans for a free Chokuno. They aren't necessarily out to assassinate the warlord. If they did, Tatatomi would have been long dead."

Quint shook his head. Uniting Kippun might be much more complex that putting a wizard charter together.

"Upper window," Masumi said. "Dasoka."

The light had gone on as the sky darkened and Dasoka stood looking out the window. His face was purpled with bruises. The bureaucrat moved well enough when he left the window.

"If I could only fly that high," Quint said. "I can float, like jumping off a building and landing so I don't kill myself."

"You could have killed him with a bolt from here, couldn't you?"

Quint nodded. "I don't want to kill him, but my sleeping string doesn't have that kind of range."

It was time. Masumi led Quint across the darkest part of the street and through the yard of the next mansion, the Pokogon embassy building.

"Would you do this if it was the Slinnon embassy?" Quint asked.

"No! Why did you say that?" She whispered and put a finger to her lips. "You still remember the layout?"

"Committed to memory," Quint said.

She climbed over a fence and waited for Quint, restraining him when he landed. "Someone is putting out the garbage."

Quint could smell it from where they stood. They slipped closer to the garbage cart until Masumi stopped him. "Here."

They threw heavy blankets over the fence. Masumi cast an air string and floated slowly up to the top of the fence. Her string didn't quite get her all the way, but Quint's did, and he had to take her hand. They sat uncomfortably on the blankets protecting them from shards of thick glass and sharpened metal.

Quint's string was strong enough to get them both on the ground close to a stair leading them below ground level to the cellar. After Quint disabled the doorlatch, they walked into a dark hallway.

"There will be traps," Masumi said.

They lit tiny magic lights and slowly defeated the traps set for magicians and for common intruders. A back stairway wasn't in the plans that the warlord had of the embassy. There were more traps to defeat, and their ascent ended on the floor where Dasoka was kept.

A door opened and a woman carrying a tray screamed when she spotted the two black-clad figures. A green-shirted man jumped into the corridor and began to create a string. Quint had a bolt ready and put an end to that threat. He couldn't use the sleeping string because he couldn't carry both Masumi and Dasoka.

Dasoka was sitting on his bed. The open window was now covered with a rolling blind.

"You!" Dasoka pointed his finger at Quint, who could see a mental struggle.

Quint cast a string to eliminate the persuasion string. He quickly replaced it with a shield while Masumi bound the door to the corridor to the frame. Quint rolled up the blind and slid the window open. She jumped, floating over the small garden in front of the embassy and landed in the courtyard. Quint had to carry a groggy Dasoka and did the same. He propped Dasoka against a wall as he quickly used a powerful fire string to cut through the padlock on the gate and then they were out. He felt a bolt zoom past his head and blew on his whistle. A cart recently pushed in front of the embassy gate blew up after a lighting string came from across the road.

Fighters streamed out of alleys and the doors of houses. The Gamizans wore bright green armbands, and the battle was instantly turning in to a chaotic melee.

Dasoka leaned against an alley wall while Masumi called out instructions to her people.

"They aren't mine to command, but they can fight with a common purpose for now." Masumi said.

Dasoka shook his head. "That wasn't me," he said rubbing his head.

"Who?" Quint said. "The person loyal to Lord Bumoto or an ally of the Gamizans?"

"I'm with Bumoto, of course," Dasoka said. "They wrapped a magical string around me and drained out most of my will."

"But you didn't expose little me," Masumi said.

Dasoka managed a grin. "No, I didn't. Calling you Quint's wife was my little victory."

"The Gamizans know all about the alliance?" Quint asked

Dasoka sighed. "Of course. Hari Bitto and his defectors knew it was inevitable."

"Then what do you do?" Masumi asked.

Dasoka took a deep breath and stood a little straighter. "The inevitable, of course. We still need a conduit to the warlord."

"Done," Quint said. "Stay out of fight and don't get recaptured."

The Green wizards, three of them, stormed out the house and one of them generated a brilliant blue globe of light about ten feet in diameter. It was an illusion, Quint knew, so he sent a string that would dispel the light. It popped as Quint's counterspell hit it. Now all the attention was on the wizards.

Quint reinforced his shield and ran behind a low wall and shot a reinforced lightning string at one of the wizards. That one had forgotten to set up an effective shield and he fell back with his chest smoking.

The warriors in the battle dropped to the ground as the fight became one of fire spears and lightning bolts from wizards on both sides. The two remaining Green masters were impervious to it all as they waded into the street and began to make their strings count.

Quint countered with a magically enhanced crossbow bolt striking one of the wizards in the neck. She toppled over, laying still. That left one more. Quint gambled that Tatatomi's wizards from the previous night were ready to pounce.

He stepped out into the street after reinforcing his shield another time. The lightning bolt from the last wizard standing knocked Quint off his feet, pushing him back on his rear end, but he was gratified to see the wizard bathed in magic from Chokunese wizards which the wizard's weakened magic state couldn't overcome.

Rising painfully, Quint observed the fight. Without wizards the little battle had turned bloody.

He thought powerful strings were awesome, but when shields were weakened by casting the massive strings, the wizards weakened, and it was an obvious weakness of Simo Tapmann's wizards. Quint sighed. It was his weakness, too, and the enemy had to know it.

Quint hadn't lost his magic, and he quickly emptied his bag of crossbow bolts. The fight was ending and six people walked out of the embassy with their hands on top of their heads. Gamiza had lost the Chokunese as potential partners.

Dasoka and Masumi walked up to him.

"Are you injured, dear?" Masumi said, smiling.

"Only where it hurts," Quint said, rubbing his rear end which had borne the brunt of the wizard's lightning bolt.

∽

CHAPTER TWENTY-SEVEN

~

"WE HAVE TWO AGREEMENTS TO SIGN," Goryo Tatatomi said at a large conference table in his castle.

Dasoka smiled. "First, the alliance, as negotiated."

"Good," Tatatomi said, writing his name and stamping a seal on top of his signature on four sets of documents. Dasoka had already signed and used the surface of the token as a stamp to indicate the will of the Shimato warlord. "You will return to Morimanu as quickly as possible?"

"Those are my instructions," Dasoka said.

"The charter," one of Masumi's friends said. Quint was surprised when he showed up representing most of the factions in Chokuno. Masumi did not attend.

The charter was signed. There were four copies of that document, too. Tatatomi, Dasoka, and as Tatatomi insisted, Quint's signature was also required by the Chokunese warlord. Since Quint didn't have a seal, he had to use his thumb.

Quint would be returning to help organize the charter organization as soon as he could, but he had already spent time with Masumi and her wizard friends and outlined what measures Thera and Todo were implementing in Shimato.

He was hopeful the charter would be honored by Tatatomi, but the signatures meant a lot to an alliance strong enough to push back the Gamizan aggression. Despite the performance of Tatatomi's wizard corps on the battlefield, the Chokunese had proven that their cluster strategy against the

Green wizards was effective. Quint and the Chokunese wizards had killed five since he had arrived in Tiryo.

Masumi rode with Dasoka and Quint out of the Chokunese capital, but they stopped a few hours later at a roadside stop. Masumi, Quint, the driver and Dasoka took a table.

"As much as you made me younger, I'd rather face myself in a mirror for a while," Masumi said.

"I'll teach you the mask string. You should be able to handle it."

Masumi removed Quint's mask on the second try, and it took a few trials to get the hang of creating a new face. Dasoka laughed when she used Quint's face as her model.

"It's time for me to leave," she said before turning to Quint. "My Chokunese friends are your friends. Let's walk by ourselves for a few minutes before our divorce," Masumi said and then turned to Dasoka. "You can stay and admire the scenery and Chokuno's superior food."

Quint wasn't so sure about the food claim, but he followed Masumi into the little woods surrounded by farmland.

She pulled out the fourth copy of the alliance agreement. "Unless Dasoka tries to switch things. It is for Narisu."

"Do you have any endearing words for him?"

Masumi laughed. "None. We haven't known each other that long and there was no real relationship. It was all fun."

"You, on the other hand." She cast a string, and a younger version of Masumi appeared. "This is the real me. I was 'stringing' you along about the mask casting. "I'm a year older than you. I hope that makes a difference," she said. "You know all about age and respect. I had to flee Slinnon when I was young. When you return to Tiryo, ask for Amoki at the weapons shop, I will find you. By the way, I burned the flat above the shop. I wanted a little sympathy when you arrived, and it was time to move, anyway."

She stepped closer and put her arms around his neck and pulled him down for a long kiss. "There is more where that came from," she said pushing him away and looking at Quint with emotion in her real face. "One more thing…" she pulled back her sleeve revealing a tiny pink butterfly tattoo on the inside of her wrist, "if you ever need proof of who I am, this is it."

Masumi took a deep breath. "My mother had that done to me before I left Slinnon." She gave him a quick kiss on the cheek. "We have to get back."

By the time they returned, Amoki, as Quint had seen Masumi for a week, had returned.

She stayed behind and waved as the carriage continued its trip to Shimato's capital.

§

Quint winced as they entered Morimanu. He wondered what Thera would think about competition. Where Thera hadn't ignited the spark Quint expected in a relationship, Masumi was quite a different problem. He had to tell him that the younger face was the mask, and the kiss was a tease like all the other times they had posed as husband and wife. He had dreamed about Masumi with different faces twice on their way back to the capital.

The warlord's castle appeared, and they were ushered into the warlord's presence without taking the bags back to the Three Forks mansion or washing up. Quint had a copy of the Chokunese charter and his surreptitious copy of the alliance in the only bag he was allowed to bring to the meeting.

By the time they were ushered into a large room Quint had never been in, the warlord had assembled a group of ministers. Quint guessed there would have been more except for the defections of Hari Bitto's followers.

They waited for some time before Bunto Bumoto arrived with Chibo Hobona and Narisu in tow.

"Sit, all of you. I don't care where," the warlord said.

"I received a message in the middle of the night that your trip was successful. I admit I didn't expect it." Bumoto looked at Dasoka for an answer.

Dasoka described their activities in the briefest of terms, but emphasized the defecting officers and the fight at the Gamizan embassy were all caused by Quint. Masumi wasn't mentioned.

The warlord looked at Quint. "Proving your presence in my delegation. Good job." The warlord ignored the story Dasoka told. "We had Tova and Tizurek with us when we assigned the right wizard to accompany Dasoka," Bumoto said.

Narisu and Quint exchanged glances with Narisu giving Quint a nod. Dasoka merely gave Quint a dark look.

"It's time to get to work," the warlord said. He excused Narisu, Quint, and a couple of his ministers. Dasoka and Chibo stayed behind.

"How did Dasoka and you get along?" Narisu asked on the way out of the castle. "It was obvious he was lying about your contribution."

Quint sighed. "I wouldn't call us friends, but I had thought were able to work together."

They stepped outside. Quint saw the carriage that had taken them to and from Tiryo. The driver had gone, but Quint's things were still in the carriage. He noticed that someone had taken Dasoka's bags.

"Did the driver take Dasoka's things?" Quint asked Narisu.

"Probably. The driver is one of Dasoka's aides."

"A spy? For me?" Quint said. "Let's find a place to eat, first."

When they had settled into a small restaurant, Quint repeated his question about the driver being a spy.

"To counteract anything Masumi might do, most likely," Narisu said.

"Does Dasoka live above a shop with his wife and children?"

"Children?" Narisu asked. "Dasoka isn't married. Do you mean he has a mistress?"

"No, he was clear in his story. He lied to me, and if the driver is a bodyguard, how did Dasoka get captured and not him? I would have thought the driver would run to us for help. He disappeared when we weren't in the carriage like drivers usually do."

Quint pulled out the copy of the alliance. A note was tucked between the second and third page. He handed it to Narisu.

"Dasoka and his driver met with the Greens while we were strolling through the city. There was no persuasion string observed, and the driver and the Green representative seemed to know each other. Warn the warlord and Chibo." Narisu crushed the note in his hand. "I'm going to have to be careful about this. If Bumoto knows this came from Masumi, he is likely to disregard it."

Quint asked for the document and read. He had an excellent reading memory and didn't see any changes from what was discussed with Tatatomi.

"This hasn't been changed by Masumi or her group," Quint said.

Narisu ran a hand through his hair. "It doesn't end, does it?" he said. "Return to your mansion. Thera will be there. Tell her what happened. I trust her more than my own people. Pay for my meal," Narisu said with a smile as he left Quint in front of his unfinished meal.

Quint needed the food. He had wanted to talk to Narisu about Masumi. Was she as devious as Dasoka? In a way, the answer was yes. Had she played the same game Dasoka played in a different fief? The answers would have to wait.

When he was done, he grabbed his bags and walked to the Three Fork mansion.

"I need to see Thera," Quint said to Todo as he walked to his rooms.

Quint hadn't had time to do much more than make a mess of his bed with his travelling clothes.

"How did your trip go?"

"I thought it was a success until I just met with Narisu."

Thera only interrupted him twice as he described the trip. Both times it was related to Masumi. Quint had two aggressive ladies on his hands, and he was sure jealousy might result. He couldn't think more about that at present.

"How is the training going?" Quint asked.

"Surprisingly well," Thera said.

"You'll have to apply the string to see if any are persuaded by the Greens. Dasoka did a brilliant job of faking it. He had me fooled."

Thera smiled, "Not entirely, I'll bet."

"The suspicions were there. They always are in Kippun. Sometimes I have to have my nose rubbed in reality."

"Masumi?"

Quint shrugged. "I don't know what her reality is."

"What do we do now?"

"Let's get everyone together. I can only wait here until Narisu visits. We need to play out some scenarios." Quint said. "I trust Warlord Tatatomi more than I do Lord Bumoto, but the Chokunese warlord doesn't have a good reputation either, unfortunately."

Shira was touring the fief, entertaining, and took Dugo with her. That left Dakuz, Thera, Todo and Quint.

After a description of the situation, Todo looked concerned. "Are you going to leave me here?"

"I don't plan on going anywhere until the situation is resolved."

Dakuz snorted. "Which situation? Dasoka, Shira and Dugo, Gamiza, or Chokuno?"

"You missed Chibo and Narisu and Bunto Bumoto," Thera said.

"I amend my list."

"I have another concern," Quint said.

"There is another betrayer?"

Quint nodded. "Green wizards are trained on Amea."

"That is far away from here," Dakuz said.

"The trainer runs the continent, and his name is Simo Tapmann," Quint said, solemnly.

"Tapmann is one of the enemy?" Thera asked.

Quint sighed. "He might even be the source."

"You've verified this?" Dakuz said.

"How can I do that other than get on a ship sailing west?"

Todo looked at the others. "Who is Simo Tapmann?"

"You don't want to know," Thera said, "except he is probably the most powerful wizard in the world."

"And he is your enemy?" Todo asked.

"Unfortunately, it makes sense if he is the source of Green wizards. They are all so powerful that someone with extraordinary powers must be training them. It makes sense."

"Does one problem at a time seem like a good strategy?" Thera asked.

"No," Dakuz said, "but I think we can group them."

Quint had similar thoughts. "How?"

"Morimanu, first. Get the alliance signed, which is done. Solidify the charter, deal with Dasoka, and get an idea of where we stand with Chibo," Dakuz said. "Chokuno can be lumped with Gamiza, then we head through Slinnon to Port Okinono for a ship to Amea. That would be the best passage."

"In Amea, we will have to gather information before we do anything else. There are four countries on the continent," Thera said.

"Then that's what we will do. I will suggest one more thing. We keep travel bags packed in case everything collapses. We have horses." Quint looked at Todo. "We have to keep them ready, too."

"Can I come with you?" Todo asked.

"Situationally, maybe," Quint said. "It depends on where we are with the charter. We must do what we can to leave that intact. Someone might have to stay behind to make sure it happens."

Todo sighed. "I'm the best one for that," he said.

"You are," Thera said, putting a hand on Todo's shoulder. "We might have to leave Dugo and Shira behind, too."

Todo nodded. "I understand." Another sigh.

Quint felt bad for the man, but the crises were jumping on top of each other. He could, of course, leave immediately, but Quint would let himself down if he did that. He had more to do before he left Kippun.

"There is little we can do until Narisu shows up," Quint said. "Let's get our emergency bags done. That includes you, too, Todo. You oversee the horses and camping supplies. Keep it as light as possible. Everything we will need for traveling cross country except for what would rot or spoil."

Quint looked at the mess on his bed and he put what he needed back in his bag and hoped they had time to wash clothes so he could do some replacing in his bags. He would leave the wizard corps uniform he had never worn behind.

Exhausted he laid down on his bed now that he could and closed his eyes. He sat up in an entirely different place…Tova's place.

"What now?" Quint said, still tired.

"Is that a way to treat your goddess?" Tova said.

"I thought you weren't going to bother me so soon after the last time."

Tova bit her lower lip. "I hadn't thought you would find Simo Tapmann so soon."

"Tizurek is being a naughty boy," Quint said. "Participating in world domination isn't a godlike activity."

"It's worse and you should know about it."

"He is the source of the Greens, isn't he?"

Tova sighed. "He trains the wizards and is now the emperor of Votann and Amea. Tizurek is in the country of Honnen on Amea."

Quint was hit by an insight. "And Fedor Danko left South Fenola for more instructions, right?"

"It would seem so," Tova said. "I still need you to bring Tizurek to me so I can turn him back."

"He probably doesn't get magically tired like the Green wizards do, so invulnerable would be the operative description," Quint said.

"Not exactly. You will need to go to Slinnon to see a retired wizard. He may hold the key to righting my godly counterpart," Tova said.

"Any help I can get," Quint said.

"I see you met a girl," the goddess said out of the blue.

Quint snorted. "I thought you didn't keep up on the details of human lives."

Tova twisted her head a little and turned it into a shrug. "You are special. Everyone knows that."

"Even you," Quint said sarcastically.

"Even me. I would encourage your little fling with Masumi."

"Or whatever her real name is."

"We both know whom I'm talking about. She may be the key to getting the retired wizard to help."

"Masumi is a key to a key. Can I have something else?"

"Perhaps," Tova said airily. "Here is a token. You can give it to the wizard." She held up a little figurine.

"Tizurek or the wizard?"

"You'll need more than a token for Simo Tapmann," Tova said. "Few wizards can feel the power in that, and you are one of them. You might find another trinket along the way, if you are a good boy. Good luck!"

The goddess waved, and Quint opened his eyes in his bed chamber. Something was in his back pocket. Quint was hoping he had a normal dream, but he pulled out a little jade figurine of a polennese man. The worn statue looked ancient.

He could feel Tova's power in the figurine. Quint hoped that the power could only be detected by someone touched by Tova. Would that mean the old wizard in Slinnon had met the goddess, too? He shook his head. He now had to scour Slinnon for the old man, but didn't she say Masumi was a key to finding him? She was a key to something regarding the wizard.

He sat up, his sleepiness had vanished.

Quint rummaged around the main building's library for a map of Slinnon. All he could find was an old document that had some inaccurate proportions of the coastline that he knew.

He found Dakuz helping Todo with the horses.

"Do we have any good maps of Slinnon?" Quint asked.

"I have a good set of North Fenola. The last time I looked, Slinnon was on it," Dakuz said.

"Bring them, please," Quint said. He would also take the old map. Perhaps there would be some detail that would add to whatever Dakuz had.

Dusk had settled in the mansion when Narisu entered.

"You tipped over a beehive," Narisu said as he sat in Quint's private quarters, "and it was a good thing. Dasoka had manipulated the inside pages of the alliance. No one would have noticed if I hadn't showed up. The warlord wasn't affected. His shield had held. I applied the shield remover and two of the remaining ministers had been made captive, again. Dasoka's act wasn't as convincing, and he is being interrogated. It won't be pleasant for him."

"Who cast the persuasion strings?"

"Hari Bitto sneaked back to the capital and left again. Dasoka must be leading the rebellion in Morimanu. Wasn't it possible he gave the information that brought Gomio and that female wizard to Teritoto?"

"He could have," Quint said. "He was injured in the fight, so it proves I'm incompetent to be taken by a faked injury."

"Don't give me that. We both know it wasn't faked, but it was intentional," Narisu said. "You can be disappointed, but no one can live thinking every person he meets is going to betray."

Quint sighed. "I suppose not. When this is done, we are heading to Slinnon to find a retired wizard. I don't know his name or where he lives, but I get to prove I'm not incompetent by finding the wizard." Quint thought for a moment. "Do you have a replacement for Thera?"

Narisu gave Quint a half smile. "You plan on taking her with you?"

"I do."

"Of course. I have three of the best in the wizard corps. They aren't as creative as Thera, but they will be close. I can't rely on you sticking around Shimato for the rest of your life. Do you have a candidate for the head of the charter?" Narisu asked.

"No. Unfortunately, I was quite taken by Huma Bifomu, but she is unavailable."

"I have some candidates, but I want you to talk to them. They will be available tomorrow. I won't give you their backgrounds, so you aren't biased when you meet them," Narisu said.

"I'd appreciate the help. I'm afraid everything is going to crash all at once."

"It would have if Dasoka hadn't been exposed. I've taught the anti-persuasion spell to a few of my wizards including those who have been working with Thera. It will have to be used often in this fight."

Quint nodded.

"Now," Narisu leaned forward. "How did Masumi do?"

Quint gave Narisu the unadulterated story of Masumi's involvement in the affairs in Tiryo. He even included her farewell kiss in his story.

"She has a soft spot for you, boy," Narisu said.

"I thought you two had something going," Quint said.

"An act, although I enjoyed every minute of it. Masumi is something else. I was sure there'd be some real fire between you. As it was, she entertained herself with some major teasing," Narisu said. "Are you going back to Chokuno?"

Quint shrugged. "It depends on where the warlord needs me."

"The lord has already sent a messenger with my copy of the alliance with his signature to Tatatomi," Narisu said. "There is always your trip out of Shimato. Going through Chokuno is almost mandatory."

"I'm not going to think about that," Quint said. "What can we do to help?"

"The warlord and Chibo are probably talking about that right now. Shimato will be on a war footing as of tomorrow at dawn. War among the fiefs is a perilous time since any of our bordering neighbors may invade if all our attention is on the other side of the fief."

"So a citizen's army?" Quint asked.

"Led by regular army officers," Narisu said. "We train for this all the time, since there are always border incursions. This will be a little different, but our neighbors to the east and north have not been overtaken by the Greens. Narukun isn't going to invade us from the south, so that leaves the west, Gamiza, and Chokuno to the northwest. The alliance, if it holds, will give us a united front against Gamiza."

"Dasoka shouldn't have permitted the street battle. The Greens were defeated twice in Tiryo. Whoever led the Greens was overzealous."

"And that was to our benefit. I think you were what drove the Green attacks," Narisu said.

"Then the Greens are driven by hatred."

"Or fear of what you might do or become in the future," Narisu said. "I have to go. I won't be getting much sleep tonight." He threw a few coins on the table by Quint. "For my meal." He grinned and whistled tunelessly as he walked out of Quint's quarters.

"I agree with Narisu," Thera said, walking from behind a partition.

"You were listening in?"

She nodded. "I'm good at sneaking," she said. "You have a thing for this Masumi woman?"

"Didn't you hear? She is too old for me," Quint said.

"And I'm not?" Thera said, raising her eyebrows.

"You haven't met her," Quint said. "You look much younger."

Thera let out a breath. "That's good to hear. I don't want the competition."

"There is no competition," Quint said a little untruthfully. "Did you know Narisu was training your replacement?"

"It was my suggestion," Thera said. "Narisu even knows who I think is best out of his three officers."

Dakuz knocked on the open door with a leather tube of maps. "Can I join you?" He looked at Thera with a look of disapproval. "You listened uninvited?"

Thera lifted her chin. "I did. I think we have another night before everything breaks loose."

"Narisu exposed Dasoka. Two other ministers were 'persuaded' by Hari Bitto during his quick visit to the capital. The signed alliance is on its way to Chokuno. I can only hope it arrives intact."

"We have orders from the warlord?" Dakuz said.

"Not yet. I have something to show you." Quint stepped into his bedchamber and returned with the figurine. "A gift from Tova."

Dakuz's eyes went wide. "She visited you here? Now?"

Quint nodded. "I took a nap and she talked to me in my sleep. I thought it was a dream, but this was in my back pocket." Quint handed it to Dakuz.

"Centuries old polennese figurine. This type of jade is rarely seen in hubite lands," Dakuz said, as he returned the figurine to Quint. "What does this mean? Is Simo Tapmann in Slinnon or Pogokon? You told us he was in Votann."

"Tova said Tapmann was the emperor of Votann and Amea. But I need something from a retired wizard in Slinnon. This will help me find him."

"Would Masumi know?" Thera said. Quint cringed with the coldness of her voice.

"Maybe. Tova said she might be the key to finding him."

"Figures," Thera said. She walked out of Quint's rooms.

Dakuz looked at her leave. "Touchy?"

"Narisu talked about Masumi when she was listening. She thought the field was clear. It still is, but how can I convince her of that?" Quint said.

"By being honest," Dakuz said, "with her and with yourself."

Quint didn't have a reply and didn't try to justify himself with the strong possibility of Thera still listening in.

"We have to be prepared for anything. Chibo might want us to join his army when it invades Gamiza. How can the chartered wizards help?"

Thera walked back in and cleared her throat. "We drafted our first wizard corps recruits after you were gone. With the charter, there were more recruits than we could handle."

Dakuz agreed. "The wizard factions are sending trainers to accompany their recruits to get some emergency training as a home guard that will patrol the borders with non-belligerent fiefs. Everyone recognizes what might happen if all united against Shimato."

"What do they need me for?" Quint asked.

"The faction leaders will be here tomorrow," Dakuz said. "Narisu warned me on his way out. Had he forgot to tell you? They want to choose a leader and even though there is a movement for that person to be you..."

"That can't happen," Quint said, holding up the figurine. "My long-term focus is Simo Tapmann, except he's not so long term, not anymore."

"What is the plan now?" Thera said.

"Fight for Shimato and Chokuno. I feel responsible for the war."

Dakuz shook his head. "You aren't the cause, you are the excuse," he said.

"Whatever doesn't change the fact I feel that we have to see this and the charter to the end. If it works in Kippun, the charter should work anywhere," Quint said.

"I don't dispute that," Dakuz said. "You should send a copy of the charter to King Boviz and one to Pol Grizak at Feltoff Cloister. If something happens to us, they might be able to keep your idea alive."

"I should probably let them know where we are and what we are doing," Quint said. "I'll also tell them how Chokuno dealt with the Green wizards. The more that is spread around, the better."

"Keep it brief. You don't have much time," Dakuz said. "I brought the maps of North Fenola. We might as well go over them after dinner."

"Dinner!" Quint said, suddenly noticing a hollow feeling in his stomach.

CHAPTER TWENTY-EIGHT

TWENTY FACTION LEADERS AND THEIR ATTENDANTS SHOWED UP mid-morning. Quint remembered Narisu said he'd have an opportunity to talk to some leaders, but he didn't expect they would all show up at the Three Forks compound.

Quint recognized a few faces and nodded to them as they helped him set up chairs in the meeting hall. Narisu slipped in and sat in the back once Quint called the meeting to order.

"I'm not sure what Narisu wanted us to talk about," Quint said, "but we can discuss the implementation of the charter. Have all of you signed?"

A few hadn't, but since the fief was going to war, those faction leaders said they would join. Thera rose and gave them a report on the Shimato Wizard Corps. With a new mission and new operating orders, the faction leaders asked quite a few questions about the corps and what was demanded for the home defense.

"I thought you would make the best leader," the new faction leader of the Flat Plains said.

There were murmurs of agreement.

"I can help like I have been helping," Quint said. "I may be called into the fight, for one, and my journey through North Fenola continues. One of my steps is to meet a wizard in Slinnon. I can't delay that for very long."

Quint sighed as he looked into the disappointed faces. "But I'm not from Shimato, and the leader should be from here. Are there any nominations for leadership? We should have a leader and two assistants as specified in the charter."

Hands went up, and nominations and volunteers were identified. Narisu rose.

"Quint will interview those of you who have volunteered and have been volunteered. He has the power to reject, but whoever survives his searing questions will be voted on. I've seen enough and will take Thera with me. War has been declared. Gamiza beat us to announcing the conflict. Chokuno, Shimato, and Gamiza share a point where the borders meet called Three Corners. There will be a meeting of the parties within days to talk of surrender or the rules of engagement."

"It's going to happen," one of the faction leaders said.

"Maybe a miracle will happen, but I don't see one coming. Be vigilant. I wouldn't be surprised to see a preemptory strike from Gamiza." Narisu nodded to them all and left with Thera.

"So I don't waste any more of your time, I'll answer any questions you have, and then those not to be interviewed can return to your factions and manage your wizards," Quint said.

"Are you sure we can't talk you into staying?" the Flat Plains leader asked.

Quint thought of the jade figurine. "No. I really can't. But let's make my time here count."

"Whatever you decide is fine by us. Right?" the Flat Plains leader looked at his fellow leaders. They all nodded in agreement, which surprised Quint.

He spent almost an hour talking about the charter organization after the war was over, assuming Shimato would prevail. It was unthinkable to contemplate what would happen to Shimato if Gamiza won, even to Quint.

In the end, Quint dismissed three of the seven candidates. The other four were clearly the best after getting Dakuz's opinion. The candidates had different strengths. Three were masters, and the Flat Plains leader was the most pragmatic. The Flat Plains leader would be the charter head, Quint decided. One of the masters had served for a few years in the Shimato wizard corps and would act as a liaison with Narisu and his wizard corps leader. The other two, including the lone woman, would assist the charter head in whatever capacity the new head would decide.

Quint personally told the rejected candidates they were still faction leaders and sent them on their way. The four Quint selected helped put chairs away and sat in the rearranged meeting hall. Quint told them of the results together.

"I can do the administrative duties," one of the masters said. "I've got a good system for my faction, which will make a quick start."

The new head agreed and asked the remaining master, the female, to be the assistant head.

"That was as painless as I could hope for. Why did it go so smoothly?" Quint asked. "I thought there would be days of infighting."

"Most of that is behind us," the new head said. "Narisu said our lives depended on making this charter work."

"He threatened you with death?" Quint asked in disbelief.

"No," the former Flat Plains leader shook his head. "We know he would make our lives difficult."

"He's already done that with me, although not as I would have imagined," Quint said. "I want you to return to your factions and get your succession taken care of and then return here if my people are still here. Most of the barebones decisions have been made, but there is a difference between a plan and what the charter does."

The new leaders left, and Quint returned to his rooms for a snack and drafted a formal document of his decision on charter leadership to give to Narisu.

Narisu returned with Thera after dinner. Both had eaten, as had Dakuz and Quint. Quint invited everyone to the meeting hall.

"The charter leadership has been chosen." Quint looked at Narisu. "Thanks to Narisu, the discussions were, at all times, constructive." He stated his reasoning and handed his write-up to Narisu. "My decision. Dakuz helped me with some perspective."

Narisu nodded as he quickly read through Quint's report.

"I would have chosen a master, but I see your point regarding a more detached charter head. I like the idea of a liaison with the wizard corps. I envisioned it being the charter head, but I think this is better," Narisu said.

"It makes the charter wizards seem more independent. That is my hope when I thought of it."

"No, no, no. You made the right decision." Narisu and Thera discussed wizard deployment, but it was clear whatever was done could be undone by an unexpected move by the Gamizans.

"You need to train them to converge on Green wizards once they let loose with one of their massive strings," Quint said.

"Thera has already put that into engagement plans. Chokuno's discovery of that technique will be implemented. It makes the Green wizards seem more vulnerable."

"Don't be fooled. They are all very dangerous, some incredibly so," Quint said.

§

In the afternoon of the next day, Todo and Dakuz were working with the new charter leadership, discussing how to set up the charter after the war, when Chibo and Narisu rode into the courtyard.

"The messenger was killed close to the border, and the alliance agreement was stolen. One of our officers and a detachment of soldiers will soon leave for Tiryo, but I'm going to ask you to take the new copy, which is currently being prepared, to the Chokuno capital."

"Can I take my group?" Quint asked. "Todo can stay here and continue to work with the charter leaders. Thera and Dakuz can accompany me."

"I insist you travel with the officer and his detachment of mounted soldiers," Chibo said.

"This is more important than Thera playing nursemaid to her successors. We've done a lot of work in the last few weeks," Narisu said.

"Is Shira back from her entertaining?" Quint asked.

Todo nodded.

"Then we will pick up Vanitz Dugo and take him with us."

"If Shira permits," Dakuz said.

Quint turned to Dakuz. "Do you know something I don't?"

"Dugo might not be going to Slinnon with us," Dakuz said.

Quint raised his eyebrows. "Shira and Dugo?"

Dakuz smiled and nodded without saying another word.

"Then we will say goodbye to him."

§

All three had taken everything they would need if they left from Chokuno to Slinnon. Quint hoped it wouldn't come to that, but Gamiza was an unknown. In weeks or months, if Gamiza could prevail over both fiefs, the rest of Kippun would fall easily, if Narisu's confidence in the other fiefs was as poor as he said.

They reached Shira's manor, and the entire entourage was allowed to enter. The horses and people filled up Shira's courtyard. It appeared that the soldiers and the officer wanted to see Shira close up.

Shira welcomed them and spoke with Quint, Thera, and Dakuz, along with the officer. Dugo joined them in moments.

"What is happening?" Shira asked.

Quint told her about the impending war. "We are on our way to deliver a treaty between Shimato and Chokuno," he said. "We may head onward after that, depending on the circumstances."

Shira looked shocked and reached out for Dugo's hand. "You want us to go with you?"

"I wanted to say goodbye and see if Dugo is still a follower."

Dugo blushed. "I'm a follower, but not of you anymore," he said. "Shira and I…"

"I'm afraid I will have to renege on my promise to do likewise. Dugo and I want to make a life for ourselves in Shimato. I have entertained in Gamiza before, but not recently, and I don't think whoever is running Shimato will change what I do." She said with her eyes watering. "I am a better wizard. Dugo will agree."

"She is," Dugo said. "She needs more tutoring."

Shira smiled and put her head on Dugo's shoulder. Quint didn't understand what the entertainer saw in Dugo, but he was looking at two people in love.

He smiled. "Then I wish you the best of luck. Make sure the fighting doesn't get close," Quint said.

"I've always had an escape plan if needed," Shira said.

"I won't impose on your hospitality any longer. Your courtyard is filling up with horse droppings," Quint said.

"Oh!" Shira said. "I don't care. My mind is at ease having told you face to face."

Quint, Dakuz, and Thera gave the couple hugs. The officer tried to do the same with Shira, and she gracefully treated him like the others.

As they reached the main road, Quint sighed. It seemed like another chapter in his life had just ended. The war was merely an epilogue after his experiences in Shimato.

He tried to shake the feeling because there was still much to do to save Shimato.

"We need to ride for Tiryo!" Quint said to the officer.

The column formed up with the three of them in the middle as they headed for Tiryo. There would be no inns. Meals would be at roadside stops, and they would sleep for a few hours every night.

∽

CHAPTER TWENTY-NINE

THE ENTOURAGE WAS WELCOMED INTO GORYO TATATOMI'S CASTLE after an uneventful ride to Chokuno. Quint presented the signed treaty to the warlord and was instructed to stay at an inn at the warlord's expense while a suitable reply was made.

Quint had his freshened seasoning packets and was enjoying his dining experience when he was interrupted. A messenger summoned them in the middle of the much-anticipated dinner.

A minister led Quint to a familiar planning room. He recognized most of the attendees.

"We have added some advice that Bunto should have," Tatatomi said. "The soldiers you brought will take this. I'm afraid I'm insisting that you remain here."

"As a hostage?" Quint asked, a little disconcerted about being ordered around.

Tatatomi laughed. "No! Not at all. I need you to help with our defenses. You have been to Gamiza, and I need someone on my staff who can advise. We think the Gamizans will attack Shimato first and then wheel around and attack us."

"How do you know that?" Quint asked.

"Don't ask," Tatatomi asked.

"Can I look at the alliance?" Quint asked.

"Surely. I have a copy here."

Quint read the document. The advice included the method that the

Chokunese used to fight the wizards. He wondered why the warlord thought that would be important.

"Dasoka was always a traitor," Quint said when he finished. "He had a wizard place a persuasion string on him so I would defeat it and think Dasoka was forced to be a traitor."

"I couldn't bring myself to fully trust him," Tatatomi said. "I'm not surprised."

"You need to keep neutralizing," Quint said. "I can teach you a shield that can resist a persuasion string now that you are allied with Shimato."

"I can learn that," one of the ministers said. "I'm the warlord's wizard advisor."

Quint nodded.

"If you come with me, I'll learn the string and we can deliver you back to your inn," the wizard said.

Quint left the room, receiving thanks from Tatatomi's staff. The wizard took him to a nearby room. Quint hadn't met the man before, so he cast a shield to protect himself.

"You have cast a string?" the wizard said.

"Just a precaution. I've been attacked numerous times since I entered Kippun."

The wizard frowned. "You shouldn't have done that," he said ominously before reaching out and casting a string from his hands within inches. The attack made Quint's insides vibrate. At first, he thought this was a new kind of attack, but he wondered if it was like the strings that shook his internals from one of his fights in Tiryo and fighting a Green master on Teritoto's streets. The shield held back the brunt of the string, but it was too much cast so close. Before Quint was incapacitated, he took a bolt from his pocket, sent it through the wizard's shield, and killed him. The worst of the spell died with the wizard.

Quint sat down, still shaking inside, and tried to calm down. What could he do? Would Tatatomi believe the warlord's wizard attacked him? He suspected the spell was ordered by the warlord. That meant the soldiers might never make it to Shimato.

The shaking was subsiding enough for Quint to rise, lock the door with the wood-joining string, and open the window. The sky was almost dark. It was three stories down, but there was a stretch of grass beneath him, but he couldn't tell if there were any impediments in the way.

His intestinal system was complaining, and Quint panicked. He jumped out the window and cast a string to drop him gently to the grass, grateful that it was clear. Quint frantically sought out a secluded place behind shrubbery to relieve himself. What an ugly string, he thought. If he hadn't thought to cast the shield, Quint shuddered to think that he would be dead at the wizard's feet.

He spied a postern gate and crawled to it, letting the shrubbery hide him from view. His system was calming down enough to allow him to unlock the thick wooden door and slip outside, descending the steep incline to level ground.

A pair of guards turned around as he reached the bottom of the castle hill. He put them both to sleep before creeping in the twilight across a broad expanse of pavement and into the city.

He went to the inn and looked through the dining room windows. The soldiers were gone, and so were his friends. He climbed up the side of the building to the second floor and looked in Thera's window. She was lying on the floor, unconscious. He opened the window and slipped in.

The string that counteracted a sleeping string worked, and she woke.

"Something's wrong," Thera said.

"Obviously," Quint said. "The warlord's wizard attacked me. I don't know whose side the warlord is on, but I suspect the alliance is over. A warlord who contracts with brigands to rob his own citizens can't be trusted at all. We must get out. Where is Dakuz?"

"I fell asleep at the end of dinner," Thera said. "Why didn't they capture us before?"

"I'll tell you later. We need to grab Dakuz. His room is two down from yours. I'll climb along the ledge outside. Grab your things while I retrieve him."

Quint left Thera to get ready to flee. Dakuz had been tossed on his bed. Quint repeated his string and woke his friend.

"You are in danger!" Dakuz said.

"As are we all," Quint said. "Gather your things. I have my purse, my bag of bolts, and the figurine. I'm not going back to my room."

"How will we survive?" Dakuz said.

"Masumi. I hope her friends haven't been turned yet," Quint said.

Quint helped Dakuz slip along the ledge to Thera's room. She was waiting. They climbed down to the ground. Dakuz and Thera had all their possessions, and it looked like Quint would get a new wardrobe like he'd done before.

They walked as calmly as they could. Twilight was an asset as the city's lights hadn't yet been lit.

Quint finally found out where he was and took them to the weapon shop. It was closed, but Quint had no alternative. He knocked, and a familiar face opened the door. The man had stopped them on the street on Quint's last visit to Tiryo. Masumi had given him letters.

"Is Amoki available?" Quint asked.

The man smiled. "Masumi said only you would ask for her with that name. Quickly, come in. The city is stirring."

They were taken to a basement room.

"Are you hungry? Thirsty?" a woman said, coming down the stairs.

"Not me!" Quint said, his system still not quite settled.

"I could use something to drink," Dakuz said.

"Me, too," Thera said.

The wine was served from a sealed bottle. Quint thought the enemy wouldn't serve drugged wine to one of them and not to another.

"You don't trust us?" the man said.

"I had an unfortunate experience with a new string cast by the warlord's wizard."

"And you lived to tell the tale?"

"You've heard of it?" Quint asked.

"It's awful. Was it the one that stirs your guts until you die? I've never heard of anyone surviving. It's a new weapon introduced for the upcoming war."

"I used a shield. My guts were stirred, but not so bad that I died."

Thera laughed. "It's probably worse on a full stomach?" she asked their host.

"Worse, much worse." He shivered and then looked at Quint. "A regular shield?"

"It needs to be strong," Quint said. "I don't recommend experimenting."

Another man opened the door at the top of the stairs. "She has been fetched. "I'm going to lock you in," the new man said. "There are now patrols on the streets."

Quint leaned back in his chair. "Is this happening in Morimanu?" their host asked.

"Maybe," Dakuz said. "If Hari Bitto could infiltrate the castle and cast persuasion strings, anything could happen."

They waited for over an hour before the door opened. Quint made sure everyone in the room wore a shield that he had made before the lights were extinguished.

Masumi stuck her head through the door. She wore an older version of the Amoki face she used on Quint's last visit.

"Quint?"

"I'm here."

"Good. There is a sweep heading our way. We need to leave the shop. Everyone is evacuating. We will be heading south," she said.

"We can get out of the city?" Thera asked.

"You must be Thera," Masumi said. "Yes. We have been dreading this day for months. Our efforts have been for naught."

They grabbed their bags and were about to go up the stairs.

"No," Amoki said. "We leave through the basement."

She tossed a string against storage shelves and pulled them open, revealing a dark passageway.

"Through here. Cast the dimmest light you can," Amoki said.

Their host, two more men, and the woman who served wine brought their own bags down the stairs. The last man locked the door behind him.

The shelving had handles on the back. One of the men pulled the shelves tight against the wall before Masumi cast another string. The man tried to move the shelves with the handles but couldn't budge the cabinet.

"I brought more bolts and a good sword for you," their host said, handing Quint a lumpy pouch and a sword complete with sheath and belt.

Masumi looked at everyone and examined Quint. "You travel light. Tell me along the way."

Walking down the passageway, they heard muffled noises coming from the shelf.

"Not a moment too soon," the wine-serving woman said.

§

The tunnel was narrow, and at times, other basement walls were on both sides. They passed three doors until they came to an alcove with a ladder.

"This is a stable," their former host and fellow evacuee said as he scampered up the ladder and slowly raised a trap door. Dirt and debris rained down, but the man disappeared.

"We go together," Masumi said to Quint, Dakuz, and Thera. "The others will scatter. We know where we are going, but no one knows exactly where. It's safer that way."

"Truth strings," Thera said, nodding.

"Take your pick of horses after you have changed your clothes. We are dressed too well not to be stopped," Masumi said.

There was a stall that provided modesty for the women, and within moments, the weapons shop people rode out of the stable, leaving Quint's group and Masumi.

"The fiefs will be assembling where the three fiefs share a boundary."

"Hasn't Gamiza won?" Thera asked.

Masumi grimly smiled. "Not at all. There is no alliance, and each fief will fight the other until there is one left standing. The Greens are stirring the pot but can't overcome centuries of fief mentality. I hoped it would be different this time, but Gamiza was an expert at jumbling things up." She kicked dirt and sighed before looking up. "Time to leave. There are lapses in the wall on the city's east side."

They left the stable and trotted away from the city center. Masumi was right about the lapses in the wall. They entered a newer part of the city where the wall had been torn down to permit expansion, and departing Tiryo was uneventful.

What was not uneventful were the stories of a chaotic city as they joined other evacuees on the road.

"This is the worst it's been in my lifetime, one man said, driving a wagon filled with his family and their prized possessions. I have a farm close to the Slinnon border in hill country. My tenant won't be happy I'll be displacing him, but I've read the horror stories about enemy fiefs sacking cities."

Quint's mind turned to the destruction of the hubite sector in southeast Racellia. He could understand why the family would pick up and leave.

It was a story repeated as they rode, but soon, they passed the evacuees and rode into the hill country that the man talked about.

"These hills join up with the little mountain range that we crossed to get into Gamiza," Masumi said. "We will camp in these hills tonight and figure out what to do."

Masumi knew of a campsite. No one else had beat them to the site. Dakuz and Thera had a portion of their camping supplies, along with a pack of dried food and cooking implements, stored in the stable where they emerged from the basement tunnel.

Quint didn't even have a blanket, but he had worn a coat to his meeting with Goryo Tatatomi. He put that over his plain clothes to keep warm in the cooling evening.

They sat by a campfire that Quint made up while Masumi and Dakuz huddled together, going over the maps that Dakuz had made sure to grab on his way out of the inn.

Quint and Thera looked over their shoulders. Quint could see Three Corners on the map where all three fiefs met. One of Masumi's people said it was a large meadow in the hills. Quint's real interest was finding the best way out of Kippun.

At first, time spent in the fiefs wasn't different from the squabbles in South Fenola, but then Gamiza flipped everything over, and the country became as crazy as everyone had warned.

"Why should we head into trouble?" Thera said. "I vote to head to Slinnon."

"Deserting Narisu so easily?" Dakuz asked.

"His superiors have deserted us by sending us to Tiryo," Thera sighed and bent over to look at the map closer. She pointed to a tiny gap showing in the map. "Is this map accurate?"

Masumi nodded. "Looking for an escape route?"

"There it is, leading all the way to Slinnon. We can stay in Chokuno all the way," Thera said.

"And that means we have to move close to the battle site before we head west," Dakuz said, nodding. "You have given us the option to fight or flee."

"Fight for a while. We have enough power between us to kill our share of Green wizards," Masumi said. "Then we can leave it to the fiefs to determine who wins."

"I'm all for that," Quint said. "There can't be legions of them. Tapmann can only train so many."

"Including however many are festering in Pinzleport and the rest of

Narukun," Thera said. "We have our mission, then?"

Quint nodded. "If Masumi, our guide, agrees."

She looked up and grinned at Quint and then back at the map. Quint saw Thera frown for a moment before smoothing her face. The competition hadn't been cast aside despite Masumi's appearance.

"The resistance will be along this road," Masumi said, running her finger a more northerly approach to the three corners. I know the area well enough."

"What will we need to get into Slinnon? Do we have to go through checkpoints?"

Masumi sighed. "We will have to leave our horses behind. Slinnon is a difficult place for me to be, much like Shimato fief."

"You have your disguise," Thera said. "It is a disguise?"

Masumi smiled. "It is, and you have just illustrated my dilemma. Any good magician will be able to tell, and there are a lot of good magicians in Slinnon. It is a unified country, and they have their own version of Quint's charter in place."

"Quint is looking for a retired wizard in Slinnon," Dakuz said.

"You didn't tell me," Masumi said.

"I found out when I returned to Morimanu," Quint said. He retrieved the figurine and handed it to Masumi. "My only clue to where he is."

"This isn't the wizard," Masumi said. "Where did you get this? It is worth a lot of money."

"Tova gave it to me," Quint said.

"Tova." Masumi paused to run her fingers over the jade. "This is so valuable, I can almost believe it. There is a tower near Port Okinono, the main port of Slinnon. The attraction isn't the tower but a statue one hundred feet tall. It is said Tizurek created it." She held out the figurine. "It looks just like this."

Masumi raised her eyebrows and clutched the figurine tightly. "This has power."

"Tova's power. She told me few wizards in the world could sense it."

Masumi grinned. "To think I am one of the few."

Thera held out her hand. Masumi gave her the token. "I don't feel a thing," Thera said.

"So what?" Quint said. "I didn't expect anyone else to sense it. It doesn't matter. I'm hoping the retired wizard can."

"We must make it through our next battle," Masumi said. "Okinono is at the far end of Slinnon."

∽

CHAPTER THIRTY

MASUMI'S WIZARDS GRADUALLY RE-JOINED THEM as they moved closer to Three Corners. There were finally twelve in the party, and the weapon shop host declared that was all they could expect.

According to the newest arrival, Chokuno was on a war footing now, with the warlord's forces heading south. The Greens had not taken over Tiryo, with Chokuno's warlord formally declaring war on Gamiza and Shimato. The latest word confirmed that Bunto Bumoto was taking his army to Three Corners. Gamiza had to be doing the same.

The fight could start as soon as the following day.

"Has anyone been to the battlefield?" Quint asked the group as they camped for the last time before reaching the battle area.

A few hands went up, and Masumi nodded.

"Let's make a map in the dirt so we can approach the battle with some kind of strategy," Quint said.

"Brilliant idea," Thera said.

Quint let Masumi and her two friends create the model while everyone else watched and munched on dried meat and dried grain. Quint used water strings to fill everyone's water bottle, provided by one of Masumi's associates.

"Done!" Masumi said.

Quint walked around the model. "And north is where?"

One of the men picked up a twig and placed it pointing to the north. "It is oriented in the right direction."

Quint and Dakuz walked to the west side, approximately where they might enter the fray.

"Where are the fief boundaries?" Dakuz said. "We've got to have those."

Masumi sketched in lines leading to the center. "The exact boundaries are vague in this meadow, but what I've laid out is close enough."

"We will be fighting with the Chokunese?" Thera asked.

Most of Masumi's rebels nodded. "That's where we choose."

"But if we are to fight Green wizards as a group, shouldn't we be close to the boundary between Chokuno and Gamiza?" Quint asked.

"Probably," Masumi said, "since they must know Chokuno has a way to defeat the Green wizards."

"So we enter along the northern edge of Chokuno's boundary with Gamiza." Quint took his sword and pointed the way without disturbing the dirt. "The fight will have to be opportunistic unless the Gamizans cluster their wizards. If they do, we might have to withdraw. Our shields might not last long under a barrage."

"And if they don't?" Dakuz asked.

Thera had her hand to her chin. "If Tova is with us, the Gamizans will deploy their wizards in three places."

"Left, right, and center," one of Masumi's people said.

Thera nodded. "No one can concentrate their force since the other two can flank whoever directly attacks another fief."

"Can anyone cast predictor strings?" Quint asked.

Masumi raised her hand. "I'm not very good, but I can look into the future dimly."

Quint groaned. "Then I will do it. I restrain myself from casting them, but our lives depend on it this time." He looked at the map. "Where is the highest ground on the west side?"

One of the men pointed.

"If this spot is vacant, that is where we will observe the fighting. We will move across the battlefield to the east side. I don't think we can get that far unscathed, but it gives us a strategy," Quint said.

"How long do we have to endure on the battlefield? It will be us against thousands," one of the women said.

"That is a good question," Quint admitted. "I think that is a group decision."

They talked about what constituted success and expecting to eliminate the Green wizards was agreed to be a futile goal. They decided their primary goal was to eliminate them on the western side and then the center if they were still able.

"We could be attacked by soldiers on both sides," Dakuz said.

"I don't see Tatatomi aggressively going after us if we are killing Gamizan wizards," Masumi said.

Quint sighed. "I don't know if we will receive forgiveness in the heat of battle. Once we have achieved our objective, we must withdraw to the west. We can't get more specific than that," the weapons shop owner said. "Is it settled?"

"This isn't a suicide mission, but it will be perilous," Quint said. "We fight together, but if we get separated, you are on your own to return to this campsite."

"Let's get dinner over," Dakuz said.

Thera and Dakuz emptied their seasoning packets, and the flavors surprised Masumi's people. Quint looked at this as a last dinner. Some of his fellow warriors wouldn't last through tomorrow, and everyone knew it.

Dawn was still an unrealized thought when the little army rose and cleaned up the camp. The remains of the fire remained, but the dirt map was obliterated before they mounted and headed west.

Masumi led the group. Quint rode in the rear with Thera along a small track winding through the woods.

"She looks older," Thera said after an hour's ride, "but what is underneath the mask?"

"How would I know?" Quint said.

Thera smiled. "You may be accomplished at many things, but lying isn't one of them."

"You can always tell when I'm lying? Even when I'm telling the truth?" Quint said.

Thera pursed her lips. "Is there something going on between you? I've seen her lingering looks. I recognize them because I do the same thing," she said. "You are mine."

Quint sighed. "You aren't mine, and Masumi isn't mine," Quint said. "That is the truth. She can be provocative, and I can't say I am entirely unaffected. On our trip from Tiryo to Gamiza she was doing more flirting with Narisu than she ever did with me."

"But she did flirt with you," Thera said.

Quint sighed again. "Yes, on my second trip to Tiryo. She left us a few hours on the way back to Shimato." Quint took a deep breath. "Look. We are headed into battle, and I don't think it does us any good to dwell on this. If you want to talk more about it after, feel free."

"You don't like me," Thera said.

"When did I say I ever liked you in a special way?" Quint said.

She pursed her lips. "You've had your mind on our mission."

"As I always have," Quint said. "Sandy burned that kind of thing out of me."

Thera smiled at him and reached over and patted his hand. "I'll rekindle the flame…after the battle. Give me a chance."

"I can do no less," Quint said.

"And I believe you." She nudged her horse with her heels, rode forward, and joined Masumi at the front of the line.

Dakuz drifted back to Quint.

"Girl trouble? I caught a word or two. It's something I didn't want to hear," Dakuz said.

"Trouble, and it may get worse," Quint said, looking toward the front of the column. He couldn't see Thera and Masumi, but he feared the worse.

The two women kept talking until Masumi stopped the column.

"Quint, go forward," Dakuz said.

Masumi and Thera had dismounted, and the rest did the same.

"We are close enough to need a predictor string," Masumi said. "Are you up to it?"

"That is not the problem," Quint said. "I don't want to see too far into the future. I want to be in command of what I do, not some notion of fate."

"That is an issue?"

Quint frowned. "It is for me."

Thera put her hand on Quint's shoulder. "I'm here to support you."

"I know," Quint said, knowing he had no choice.

He stood away from them and cast his predictor string. It felt different from the last time he used it in South Fenola.

His vision darkened as he focused on the upcoming battle and let the scene unfold. Quint saw the primary battle unfold as Masumi had described.

It was each fief for themselves. The Shimato wizards fought with more order than when Quint observed them in the border clash with Chokuno until the Green wizards deployed into two groups. There was no center group in his vision.

The fighting continued, but he couldn't see his group enter the fray.

Both fiefs fought the Green wizards using the cluster strategy of attacking after massive strings were cast. It was more effective than Quint imagined, and as the Green wizards died, even more of the fief wizard corps on both sides were decimated until it was a melee of conventional arms.

The battle became a sea of confusion until all three fiefs withdrew.

Quint snapped out of the vision. "I could see what happened because we weren't there," he told Thera and Masumi. "The Green wizards were neutralized at tremendous cost."

"Where were we in the battle?" Thera asked.

"I'll have to look again," Quint said.

He cast the string. His vision darkened again and then his vision was a riot of images. There was no flow in what he saw. Quint could even catch glimpses of Narisu and Hari Bitto in the mix. It was as if he was thrown out of the vision, and he opened his eyes.

"It was like I had expected the first time," Quint said, shaking his head.

"Did you see anything?"

Quint rubbed his forehead. "A jumble of scenes. They weren't in chronological order. I saw Narisu and Hari Bitto, but we were fighting for our lives in this one."

"Did anyone die?" Thera asked.

"There were bodies, but everything was so chaotic, I couldn't tell what happened or when," Quint said. He took a deep breath and tried to find a constant thread, and after a few moments, he found it. "We didn't make it to the battlefield, but I had the impression we ran into a detachment of Green wizards."

"Do we need shields?"

"My shields," Quint said. "They are the strongest amongst us."

Quint cast shields on all the wizards. They cast their own to reinforce what Quint did. Quint counted his bolts and sharpened his sword. All he could see about himself was that he was in the middle of it all.

They set out toward the battleground. Masumi led, and Dakuz brought up the rear, being the oldest among them. Masumi stopped about a mile from the battle.

Quint couldn't hear any noises at first, but then he heard rustling to their right.

"Off the track and stay silent!" he said. "Be ready for anything."

Everyone drew their weapons or readied themselves for string-casting as they lined up ten paces off the track. Voices were heard, and a column of ten riders guarded by a squad of soldiers wearing Gamizan uniforms emerged onto the track. They didn't look like they were after Quint, but this had to be the group in his prediction.

"Could Tirolo be coming this way?" Hari Bitto asked Dasoka.

"I was told the predictor string was too vague," Dasoka said, "but this is the most likely path for him to follow from Tiryo."

"I still don't believe the boy will come. He is probably drinking himself silly in Slinnon," an unknown person said, but he wore the same livery worn by Green wizards in Narukun.

"The predictor strings forecast he would show up," Dasoka said. "Tirolo was never seen in the main battle. I've looked at the maps. He will be coming up this trail."

"Which way?" Hari said.

The wizard looked east and then west. "West would be my guess."

The soldiers approached them and then rode past. They hadn't gone fifty yards before Quint heard the voices get louder.

"They saw our tracks!" one of the men said, riding up.

"Get ready. Disable the soldiers first since your shields won't fully protect you from a sword's edge." Dakuz said. "Quint and I will start on the Green wizards."

"I get Dasoka," Masumi said between clenched teeth.

The enemy riders turned and walked their horses more slowly. Quint felt exposed since the tracks would reveal their locations. "Engage before they reach us," he said.

There wasn't time for a sophisticated strategy. Everyone would concentrate on the wizards once the soldiers were down.

"Hari?" Dakuz asked Quint.

Quint dismounted and tied his horse to a branch. "Magic is better done on foot."

Dakuz and Quint quickly walked away from their horses and hid behind a bush beside the track. In a moment, they saw Hari and Dasoka behind the officer leading the force.

"Now!" Quint whispered.

A bright purple lightning bolt struck Dasoka, knocking him off his horse. He lay still on the ground. Masumi waved and proceeded to kill a soldier before the Gamizans jumped off their horses and ran into the foliage on the other side of the track.

Quint and Dakuz attacked Hari, but their lightning bolts were too far away and splashed on Hari's shield. The force knocked him down, but he continued into the woods.

The fight began. Wizards against wizards. At first, the Green wizards lost a few of their number to concentrated fire and lightning bolts, but then the track was empty except for the inert bodies of soldiers, two wizards, and Dasoka amidst standing horses.

Quint sent a smoke string into the track that covered Dakuz, Masumi, and himself while they waited for the first onslaught of wild lightning bolts piercing the smoke.

Soon, the track was filled with smoke on both sides, and the fighting became tougher.

A wizard cast a wind string that cleared the track, but everyone was disbursed, friend and foe on both sides of the trail.

Masumi led them away from the track, and then she turned back. "Spread out. It is too dangerous to cluster."

Quint wondered where Thera was in the conflict until she joined them. Her body was covered in dirt.

"It's a new look," Thera said to Masumi, who nodded.

They advanced and stopped when they spotted Hari and another wizard crouched down, looking around. One of the Quint's group stepped on a twig, and the cracking sound made the pair turn around. The other wizard shot a powerful lightning bolt and was covered with bolts from the four. He went down smoking. When they could concentrate on Hari, he had taken cover.

Sounds of fighting echoed through the wood. Quint had no idea where Hari had gone, but they confronted two more wizards and killed them as their backs were turned, tossing lightning bolts across the trail.

"Has anyone been counting?" Dakuz whispered to the group.

"At least half the wizards, all the soldiers. I don't know Dasoka's condition. He had to have been wearing a shield," Thera said. "That makes four wizards left."

There was a scream from the other side. No one knew if it was a Green wizard or one of Masumi's rebels.

After spreading out again, they found another wizard. This one was the strongest Quint had confronted. Dakuz was thrown against a tree and had a burned side. He was still conscious but out of the fight. Quint was ready with a crossbow bolt after the Dakuz went down and took care of the wizard.

He wished he had known about the weakness when he fought Green wizards before.

There wasn't anyone left on their side. Quint didn't know if Hari Bitto had run off or crossed the track to the other side.

"I'll cast a smoke screen," Thera said.

They waited again for lightning bolts and saw only one pierce the smoke. There were no more strings as the wind cleared the track while they hunkered down. They ran across the road and left Dakuz behind. He was in as safe a place as any.

They spotted Hari Bitto standing over the woman who had served them wine. She was holding onto her arm and unable to fight back with a string.

"Chokunese swine!" Hari said quietly through his clenched teeth. "Did you think you had a chance against the might of the Greens?"

"Not Gamiza?" the woman managed to say.

"The warlord has already pledged his fealty to the empire and our leader."

Quint reinforced his shield and stepped forward. "Simo Tapmann is your leader?" Quint said.

"How did you know?" Hari said. He bathed Quint with a torrent of fire.

Quint could feel the pressure of the flames. The forest would surely burn down if no one quenched the fire, but that would have to wait.

"It is common knowledge in Chokuno," Quint said.

It wasn't, but how could Hari know?

"He is on my list," Quint said.

"You don't even know where he is."

"His empire is in Amea and Votann. His imperial city is in Honnen. I suppose it is still under construction."

"I don't know. I haven't yet been to his school, The Strings of Empire, to learn under Tapmann."

"And you won't." Quint launched a crossbow bolt with Tova's magic, which threw Hari over his intended victim, and his head slammed into a nearby boulder.

Quint was finished with the fiefs at that point. He didn't care what happened at Three Corners. He worked through some of his anger putting out the fire his duel with Hari caused.

"I'm going after Dakuz," he said. "Keep at it and see who is alive and who isn't."

A figure was crouched over Dakuz, talking in low tones. Quint drew another bolt and aimed just as the figure stood up. He quickly put his arm down.

"Narisu! What are you doing here?"

Narisu stepped toward Quint, who drew his sword. Narisu was a superior swordsman, but perhaps they could come to terms, and the sword would be better than a bolt.

"Put that down before you cut yourself," Dakuz said.

"What?" Quint said.

"He's coming with us. Bumoto and Chibo are dead, and it's a free-for-all at the battleground. Narisu talked to Dasoka this morning before the battle. Dasoka shared with Narisu his suspicions about where you'd be."

"You came to help?" Quint asked.

"Chibo tried to reason with Bumoto about returning to Morimanu, retreating from the battle, and the warlord stabbed him in the back after Chibo turned toward the battlefield to point out how the predictor strings showed no one winning the battle. I'm afraid my emotions got the better of me, and in my anger and my grief that Bumoto murdered my best friend, I dispatched Shimato's warlord," Narisu said. "Will you take me?"

"He will, if no one else will," Masumi said with a smirk, approaching with Thera.

Quint thought of Thera and was glad to hear her call to them as she approached.

"Help me up," Dakuz said.

"What happened across the trail?" Quint asked.

"We prevailed, but at a cost. All the wizards are dead. Two by the sword because their shields were too strong," Thera said. "We lost two men. The woman you saved will survive, and there are burns on the others. We saw Hari Bitto's remains. Good shooting. Are we going east or west?"

"West," Quint said. "I don't know if anyone will follow us, so we should get going. Let's drag the bodies to the side of the track and check the horses for supplies."

"We will be quick about it."

Narisu and Quint helped Dakuz to the site of the seven fallen wizards, eight including Hari Bitto. The last body was Dasoka. Quint grabbed it by the ankles, and he could feel the leg muscles tense when he began to move him.

"You're alive," Quint said.

"Playing dead isn't going to work?" Dasoka asked, cracking open his eyes.

"Hardly. The Green wizards are dead, but most of the fief wizards are, too," Narisu said. "Due in no small measure to your betrayal."

"We can't stand up to the force of the empire growing in Amea," Dasoka said.

"Tapmann's empire," Quint said.

Dasoka sat up. He was injured and winced. "You have no chance against him. He wields the power of a god," Dasoka said.

"Not quite," Quint said.

"How would you know?"

"Tova told me," Quint said.

Dasoka scoffed. "That again? You are delusional."

Narisu drew his sword and ran it through Dasoka. "And you, sir, are dead. No better state for a traitor."

"He got to die twice today. I don't think it's in him to do it a third time," Dakuz said.

Quint barely smiled. An empire full of deadly, god-given strings in the hands of his enemies, he thought. He felt very inadequate to fight Tizurek, but his path was set.

They finished piling Dasoka on top of the other bodies along with Hari Bitto. They buried the rebels who didn't make it. Burials were much quicker to manage with wizards around.

They looked at the pile of booty, tossed the Gamizan coins into the woods, and took the food. A few nice cloaks were taken, and they had plenty of horses to choose from.

Quint took the officer's horse, but he replaced the Gamizan military saddle and tack on the horse with Chokunese versions.

In less than an hour, they were trotting through the forest to the west, and then they'd head north to the Slinnon border.

∽

CHAPTER THIRTY-ONE

TWO HOURS LATER, MID-AFTERNOON, NARISU JOINED QUINT at the head of the column.

"I spotted riders at the crest of the hill behind us. I think there were a few green wizard cloaks," Narisu said.

"The Greens are reluctant to let us go," Quint said. "How did they know we were here?"

"The same way Hari Bitto did. You took the most logical route. What is the trail like ahead?"

Quint stopped the column and told them about the pursuit.

"We can split into groups when we reach the road in an hour, but they will be close."

"I'm not going to Slinnon," one of Masumi's people said.

The other survivors agreed. They volunteered to leave as a group, returning toward Tiryo.

Masumi hugged each one. "Good luck. Don't return to the capital until everything settles down."

Everyone took another look at Dakuz's map before they resumed their escape. There was no time to talk as Quint and his group increased their pace.

The pursuit didn't appear on the hills behind them, and Quint took that as a bad sign. The Green wizards had to be catching up. He cast shields on everyone and their horses, moving from rider to rider.

The trail emptied out on the road, and the Chokunese headed right while Quint, Thera, Dakuz, Masumi, and Narisu headed left.

Quint took the time to cast a wind spell to obliterate both groups' hoofprints before they took off again, but he decided he would gift them with a sea of mud. It only took a moment of magic for Quint to turn the trail's entrance into the road into a pond of mud.

Quint spurred his mount and galloped and stopped just as the road turned, not quite obstructing the view of the trail's entrance. Riders burst into the road just as Quint lost them to view. The horses slipped in the mud, and the pursuit was a tangle of wizards and horses.

"I captured a little time. They are right behind us," Quint yelled to the others from behind.

They continued to ride into twilight, and the pursuers were occasionally spotted behind them.

"They split up back at the trail," Narisu said while riding behind Quint.

"Fewer to fight," Quint said.

Narisu looked back. "We are still outnumbered."

The sky began to darken, and Dakuz drifted back. "I can't go on. I hurt too much. Leave me behind, and I'll delay them."

"There are too many," Quint said.

Narisu nodded in agreement. "I will stay with him."

"We will make a stand up ahead," Quint said.

Thera spotted an outcropping of rock a hundred paces ahead, and they stopped at a tiny clearing barely past the formation.

"Lead the horses to the back of the rocks and stay there," Quint said to Dakuz. "You are not without your magic as a weapon, but let's hope the fighting never reaches you."

Everyone found places in the rocks for protection. Fighting Green wizards in the open could wear down their shields Quint told them. Thera worked on Dakuz's wound for a moment and then joined the defenders.

The pursuers stopped when they spotted the rocks. They were close enough to hear.

"They have to be in the boulders," one of the Green wizards said.

Under a darkening sky, Quint could barely see, but he had never met any of the Gamizans.

"If you can see better than me, describe what damage this does," Quint said to Thera.

"I'll look, too," Masumi said, still wearing her Amoki mask.

Quint grabbed a crossbow bolt and shot it at a wizard not wearing a green cloak. The man fell backward.

"Did I kill him?"

"I think you… No, he is getting up and rubbing his chest."

"Damned crossbows!" Quint could hear the man saying.

The moon was rising, but it wasn't casting much light. One of the wizards cast a string for a globe of light and moved it.

"Don't look at the light!" Narisu said. "You'll lose your night sight."

Quint could hear Dakuz curse behind him. The light moved closer to them and stopped, illuminating the rocks and the clearing.

Two could play that game, Quint thought. He spelled three lights and sent them directly at the wizards. His intent wasn't illumination but spoiling their vision. The lights didn't stop until the globe bounced against the men in front. The lights were destroyed after some commotion and cursing more livid than Dakuz.

Masumi used a string to extinguish the globe above them. It took her two tries, but the battleground was back in darkness.

"What's next?" Masumi asked.

"An attack, but I doubt if it will be frontal. Now they know we are wizards, too," Narisu said.

Thera and Masumi can enter the woods on our side of the road. I'll go on the other side. Narisu stays with Dakuz to keep any frontal attack at bay," Quint said. "If there is an extraordinarily gifted wizard, we need to focus on him or her with all our lightning strings right after that person's attack."

"Sounds good to me," Narisu said. "I need the protection more than you."

Quint slipped across the road. A fire spear erupted on the Green side, but Quint was too fast, and the caster was too slow. He entered the woods and lit a dim magic light as he approached the wizards.

He heard sounds in the woods. It was a wild animal or a Green animal, he thought, extinguishing his light, relying on his ears and other senses.

The moon continued to rise, dappling the forest floor with moonlight through the trees. Quint searched for pattern changes and found two wizards approaching his direction. He hid behind a tree, retrieved two bolts from his pouch, and stood still, watching the rippling shadows come closer.

When the patterns could be discerned as humans, Quint shot one bolt at close range and then another. Both wizards dropped to the ground. Quint drew his sword and examined his work. Both men appeared dead, but remembering Dasoka's trick, he slit both their throats, wiping his blade on a green cloak. He was ashamed it gave him some satisfaction.

A thin thread of lightning lit up the woods. Quint kept his eyes averted, but the afterimage of the first glance revealed where the following wizard was. Quint ducked down and sent a lightning bolt of his own toward the wizard.

He heard the wizard cry out, but then he could hear shuffling. The figure was too far away to ensure his attack succeeded, and Quint was too excited to wait for shadow patterns.

He crept toward the road and saw lightning bolts and fire spears exchanged, and then the fight emerged onto the road.

Quint was about to go to the women's aid, but the injured wizard was on his side and could help the Greens attack Thera and Masumi.

He stayed in the trees and crept and crawled toward the fight. The injured wizard didn't look too impaired as he stepped into the road facing the women.

Quint shot a bolt and hit the wizard's shoulder through the shimmering of a shield. The attack string died as the wizard's arm dropped to his side. The man was out of the fight, but he joined the other two wizards on the road.

A powerful lightning bolt emerged from the cupped hands aimed at Thera. She was thrown back despite her shield shining with magic energy.

"All magic on the wizard!" Quint yelled. Masumi dropped to one knee as lightning bolts emerged from Masumi's side of the road, going over her head and splashing against the Green wizard. Quint's bolt was more potent and thicker, and the wizard's shield began to radiate energy. The wizard Quint injured, succumbed to the high energy swirling over the shield until Masumi's lightning finally punched a hole through the wizard's weakening defense, spearing the wizard in the chest. There would be no faking that death.

Quint shot a crossbow bolt at the remaining wizard standing and dropped him. Six wizards were dead, and there was one more to find.

Masumi and Quint ran to Thera, who was moaning. Narisu ran past Quint and made sure the wizards had gone to Tova.

"She might make it," Masumi said, wrapping a bandage around her midsection. "Let's take her off the road and to the rocks."

Quint picked Thera off the ground. She looked up at him with half-closed eyes. Thera put one arm around his neck and touched his cheek with the other hand. She struggled to lift her head and kissed Quint on the cheek.

"Mission accomplished," she said. Quint looked into her eyes and noticed them widen with alarm.

She wrapped both arms around his neck and hugged him as a lightning bolt emerged from the trees. Quint saw the final wizard, but the string was cast, and it barely stopped as it passed through Thera's shoulder and slammed into Quint's shield. Just as the powerful Green wizard's shield became a weapon to anyone who touched the flood of energy, Thera's back arched, and then she went limp.

Quint dropped her to the ground and ran after the wizard. The enemy was already bathed in lightning from Dakuz, Narisu, and Masumi. Quint didn't add to the attack. It was easy to see the wizard was struggling with lightning bolts.

He walked up a pace from the wizard, who was cupping his hands to create a string. Quint took his time extracting a crossbow bolt and shot at point blank.

The wizard clutched his throat, and as he dropped to his knees, Quint sent him to Tova's special place. "I'm sorry, Tova. He didn't deserve to die in this world."

The threat was eliminated. Thera was gone. Masumi's friends had left them. Narisu had been in the fight more than Quint thought, but his shields had done their job.

They buried Thera in the moonlight, just behind the rocks. The wizards were piled a few paces inside the tree line to feed the local fauna, as Narisu put it.

§

Now, with a string of horses, they pushed ahead. Masumi said there was a roadside stop at a crossroads an hour away.

Narisu woke up the proprietor, who complained but admitted that being roused out of bed was part of his business. They sat at an outside table in the moonlight. None were in the mood for much else. Masumi and Narisu dressed Dakuz's wound. Neither could match Thera or Dugo for talent as a healer.

Quint's mind had been numb for the last hour as they rode through the dark. It looked like it was the same for the other three.

"She was a good soldier," Narisu said, starting the conversation.

"Loyal to me, anyway," Quint said. "She finally was able to kiss me." He touched his cheek where she had kissed him. Quint didn't know if he felt guilty that she died shielding him from the wizard's attack, but truthfully, she already had a hole in her stomach from that first lightning bolt. She was probably breathing her last when he picked her up. He sighed.

Masumi put her hand on his wrist. "We all feel her loss."

Quint was about to ask how she did because they weren't traveling for long, but fighting together in a battle was a bonding experience.

He looked into her face, and the real Masumi looked back at him. "I hurt for that and because you hurt," she said.

Narisu looked up. "A mask?" he said, astonished.

"No. This face is mine," Masumi said. "I fudged on some of the dates I gave you in the past."

"I guess," Narisu said, but then he smiled. "I knew the real timeline, though, you trickster."

Masumi shook her head. "No more levity."

The proprietor brought them warmed stew and mugs of hot watered wine. "You can sleep on the tables if you wish. At least you'll be under a roof," he said. "I'm going to bed and locking up." He asked for a hefty fee, which was paid with Gamizan coinage. The man looked at it. We are so close to the border I don't have a problem with this."

They ate in silence. Quint decided the ground would be more comfortable and laid down.

Dakuz rolled out some blankets next to his. He put his hand on Quint's shoulder. "We all are heartbroken about today," he said. "Everyone lost someone close."

"I know," Quint said. "I was going to say something to Narisu, but Masumi beat me to it."

"She seems to be a deeper person than I thought she was. Did you notice how strong her lightning bolt was at the end?" Dakuz said.

"I know she has more power than she ever uses. On our trip through Gamiza, she used conventional weapons." Quint sighed. "I'm going to try to get some sleep."

He was uncomfortable singing Masumi's praises while Thera was still cooling in her grave an hour away.

The sun was up but behind trees when the proprietor woke them up, clearing up the dishes from the night before. Quint didn't feel wonderful, but he guessed he was over the worst of the immediate shock of Thera's death.

Dakuz moved slowly, but he was showing signs of improvement. They ate a warm breakfast and headed west. Another two hours and they would intersect with the road leading north and then northwest into Slinnon.

∽

CHAPTER THIRTY-TWO

"We have a problem," Narisu said, riding back after scouting ahead.

"I thought we had left all the wizards behind," Dakuz grumbled.

Quint smiled. Dakuz was getting better if he could complain like that. "Another detachment of wizards?"

"One. He's sitting in a tent on the side of the road, interrogating every person heading west or north."

"Those going to Slinnon?" Masumi said.

Narisu nodded. "We can cut through the woods," he said.

"Do you think he hasn't thought of that?" Quint asked.

"Of course he has. We can take a heading and start now."

Masumi pursed her lips. She was Amoki, the slightly younger version, since breakfast. Quint didn't know what to make of her. "How far back would he set traps?" she said.

Narisu shrugged his shoulders. "This far?"

Thera might know, Quint thought. "We can try," he said. He steered his horse toward a gap in the trees and felt a magic tingle. "This far. It disturbed some kind of detection string. Would it be better to forge ahead into the forest, wait here, or ride to confront the wizard?"

"You can make the decision," Dakuz said. "I trust your judgment better than mine."

"Then we confront him head-on. Cast shields, and then I'll cast a stronger one on top of it. We will run before we get close," Quint said. "If the wizard is as strong as the one who first struck Thera, the farther away, the better."

They rode slowly up the road. When they saw the wizard, the man rose and beckoned them. He raised his hand high into the air.

"He can't cast a string holding a hand up," Narisu said.

"He can if he's like Quint."

Quint cleared his throat. "One-handed strings?"

Narisu nodded. "Right, right."

Quint stopped within ten paces of the wizard.

"You are Quinto Tirolo?" the wizard said, looking at Narisu.

"That's me," Quint said.

"The boy?" The wizard smiled. "Of course. I forgot. You are my prisoners."

Gamizan soldiers emerged from the corners of the crossroads.

Quint took a deep breath. "I don't think so," he said as he used his other hand to cast a wide-range sleeping spell.

His shields protected his companions, but soldier and traveler alike fell to the ground. The wizard swayed on his feet, but he could steady himself.

"Perhaps I must amend my comment. I'm asking you to surrender. If you don't, you will be hurt badly."

If the wizard swayed, his shield wasn't particularly strong.

"If you don't let us pass, I'm afraid I will have to resist," Quint said. "We have already cut your Green wizard society down in size by at least fourteen of your friends on the way here. Do you want to join them in Tova's lap?"

The wizard chuckled. "In Tova's lap. I'll have to remember that the next time I clean up my fellow wizards' messes."

Quint didn't want to deal with this arrogant wizard. "Then prepare to meet Tova. She won't be happy, but." Quint shrugged and sent the wizard away.

"Where did he go?" Narisu asked.

Dakuz laughed. "To Tova's lap, of course. Quint wasn't kidding."

"Not exactly her lap," Quint said. "There are probably more troops in the woods if the wizard set traps. We need to get out of here. I won't impose on Tova for a while."

They headed north. They planned to travel on the road for half a day and then take the western route to the southernmost entrance to Slinnon by nightfall.

As they galloped along the road, threading through people traveling in both directions, they heard a shout behind them.

"Stop!" the voice shouted.

Quint looked back to see a Gamizan officer's uniform. He turned around and urged everyone on.

A weak lightning bolt splashed against the shield in the rear of Quint's horse. Quint stopped to identify the wizard and sent a crossbow bolt, hitting the officer at the wizard's side. He sent another bolt at the wizard. The man fell from his horse, but he struggled to his feet, holding a hand to his chest and shaking the other at Quint.

The pursuit never materialized, with the two enemy leaders dead or injured.

Later, when they turned to the road to Slinnon, they had to slow their horses and found a clearing with a stream to rest. Dakuz needed fresh bandaging, but Quint hoped the adventure was over.

Dakuz examined his map of Chokuno and frowned as he sat on a rock, chewing a strip of dried meat. "Over the worst part of the hills."

"There is something wrong?" Narisu asked.

After sighing, Dakuz pursed his lips. "I can't handle any more rough riding. That's just the way it is. I'm too weak and will fall off." He slapped the back of his hand on the map. "Plus, our path to Slinnon is too predictable."

"The crossroads taught us that," Quint said. "We don't know what's ahead at the border. It doesn't take a predictor string to know where we are going."

"Then we have to be less predictable or take a route with more paths to Slinnon. Going overland isn't going to work with Dakuz, and we can't abandon him," Masumi said, taking Dakuz's hand. "You are important to Quint and to the rest of us."

"I don't know about that," Dakuz said. His attention turned back to the map. "The easiest route is to get back on the road to Tiryo." He pointed to a small road that led over a few hills to an area of farmland. "On the other side, the population grows, but there are more avenues of escape into the hills."

"Our major risk is not losing our pursuers," Masumi said.

"No," Quint said. "The risk doesn't diminish until we cross into Slinnon. Tatatomi is no longer a friend; he can send his people to blanket this whole region." He waved his hand over the map from their position almost to Tiryo.

"If I can rest at night, I'll manage wherever you go, but I can't climb the rocky border hills," Dakuz said.

Narisu examined the map. "I've not spent any time on this side of Chokuno, but let's make this village by nightfall. If we must, we can sneak into a barn."

"So, it's northeast," Quint said. He looked down at Dakuz. "We'll try to keep the riding flat."

Dakuz grimaced. "Give me a half-hour to rest."

Quint tossed a blanket onto a grassy patch and helped Dakuz lay down.

§

They reached the village after dark, but there was a village inn. The common room wasn't full, and neither was the inn. There were two rooms. Dakuz and Narisu shared, and the "married couple" shared the other. Quint used the name of Dontiz Hannako, Wanisa Hannoko's son whom he met at Seensist. Masumi became Amoki Hannako.

Narisu registered them with the innkeeper and made up names for Dakuz and himself. They were heading to Tiryo to attend a mutual friend's wedding.

Quint and Narisu found their way to the common room. Masumi was rebandaging Dakuz and doing what little she could with her meager magical healing skills.

"Did you hear about the big battle at Three Corners?" one of the villagers sitting close to them said.

Narisu nodded. "We've run across a few who were there. It was awful. Wizard against wizard fighting in ways we haven't seen before," he said.

"The Shimato warlord was killed by one of his own fighters," the man shook his head. "How could someone be so filled with hatred? Luckily, our Goryo Tatatomi survived and is preparing us to expand into Shimato."

Narisu looked at Quint and sighed. "I'd rather there wasn't any fighting," he said. "It brings out the worst in us."

"I'll agree with that," Quint said.

"I see you two are carrying swords on your way to Tiryo," a villager said.

"Big battles make the roads dangerous," Quint said. "We had to protect ourselves. We already ran into bandits, and one of us was injured."

The villagers took up Quint's observation and began telling stories about brigands on the road to the closest market town. The conversation took on a life of its own and an hour later, Quint and Narisu took meals to their room partners.

Masumi was asleep on top of the double bed in their room. She blinked her way awake when Quint walked in.

"How is Dakuz?" Quint asked.

"His wound is better, but he has difficulty recovering his strength. The poor man isn't young."

Quint frowned. He had lost Thera and now Dakuz wasn't bouncing back from his wound. Dugo must have survived along with Shira at the capital, but Quint didn't know if he could bear leaving Dakuz behind to an unknown fate.

"We need to keep his wound clean and his stomach full," Quint said. "He needs energy and there isn't a string that rejuvenates that doesn't cost strength when the magic wears off."

"Is that something you use?" Masumi asked.

Quint shook his head. "I can generate bursts of internal strength that don't cost me in the long run."

"Is that helped by Tova's touch?" Masumi said.

"I thought you didn't believe in her."

She soberly looked at Quint. "I believe in you, so I believe you have seen her. That figurine didn't come from a shop in Tiryo."

Quint pulled it out of his purse. It had survived so far. He could still feel the power.

"Sometimes, I can feed some power into other wizards," Quint said. "Maybe this can do the same to me."

"Are you going to try it?"

Quint shook his head. "Only if I need to. I want to get to Simo Tapmann on my own."

"Even if you are Tova-touched?" Masumi asked.

"Yes." We need to leave early tomorrow if we are to get to the border tomorrow. Our route…"

"I know our route," Masumi said. "If we have to deviate from the road close to the border, it will be tough on Dakuz."

"Rocky hills. That's been a good barrier for Slinnon all this time," Quint said.

"And barriers work both ways," Masumi said.

Quint pulled a blanket and pillow off the bed and made a bed on the floor. He wished the inn had floors of woven mats like most inns in Shimato, but then Chokuno was more hubite than Shimato. Why it was escaped him; Kippun was a crazy place, and he didn't think he would miss it.

§

They left before breakfast was ready but took a jug of wine and a basket of fried rice cakes, something Quint hadn't experienced before. The air was chilly, and Dakuz was ordered by the other three to wrap himself in a blanket as they rode.

The road to Tiryo, the capital of Chokuno, began having more lanes branch off and after passing a three-road intersection, Dakuz told them to look out for a lane leading west. That would be the first road they were to take to Slinnon. The lane was an out-of-the-way route to a town at the foot of the rocky hills that made up the border.

The lane wasn't used much, but enough that it wasn't overgrown. The road would have made for rough walking, Quint thought, but the horses negotiated it well enough.

"I'll miss Chokuno," Masumi said as they rode, skirting fields of grain and passing the occasional farm compound. "It was easy to keep out of the way."

"And free from Slinnon soldiers?" Narisu asked.

She nodded. "I hope we don't spend much time in my home country," she said. "I have much fonder memories of Chokuno than Slinnon."

"How long have you been in Chokuno?" Dakuz asked.

"Eleven years," she said. "I wasn't yet ten when I had to flee. My father died, and my mother stayed behind, but my nursemaid came with me. The nursemaid returned to her family in the capital after four years when I could fend for myself, but I never knew what happened to my mother."

"Where did you get all your martial arts and wizardry training?" Quint asked.

"There was an underground of Slinnon defectors. I was told emphatically that I couldn't divulge my background, and life in Chokuno meant I'd have to fend for myself. After four years of hard training, I thought I was ready."

"When your nursemaid left?" Narisu asked.

Masumi nodded. "I wasn't, of course. A fourteen-year-old can learn skills, but it isn't enough and for a fighter, I needed to physically grow to wield a sword and wait to see if I could cast strings. I couldn't be too open about any of it."

"Or you get abducted into the Chokuno wizard corps," Quint said. "I know exactly how that is."

"You really don't. The wizard corps is run by non-wizards and is pathetic. You've seen them in action," Masumi said to Quint.

"I have, but they learned to fight from someone."

"That has been a recent development. I don't know who insinuated themself into Tatatomi's inner circle to change the corps, but they went from awful to merely mediocre in the last few years."

"Merely mediocre is also how I'd describe Shimato's wizards," Narisu said. "I stayed away from them as I moved up the ranks. Chibo, may Tova care for his soul, rescued me from exposing myself, and the rest is history. The end was not glorious for Chibo or Bumoto." The former army officer sighed. "I look forward to a future where I can redeem myself."

"I'll do what I can to help you," Quint said.

Narisu gave a painful smile. "I know you will," Narisu said. "We have to get to Slinnon before that can start."

They rode on. Dakuz didn't share much of his background, but he had spent more time in Baxel than Quint thought. He might have run into Thera at Baxel University, but neither of them remembered contact. Eventually, Dakuz ended up at Seensist Cloister living a secluded existence. Dakuz confessed his life had become boring, and he admitted he wasn't suited to running the Cloister.

Quint knew Dakuz's personality wasn't compatible with joining the cloister leaders, although the man could have done an admirable job in most things.

Quint talked about Tova's Falls and Feltoff Cloister. It wasn't a big part chronologically, but his life and outlook had changed, not the least of which was his crazy relationship with Tova and his impossible task of reviving Tizurek's sensibilities.

"I have to wonder if Tova isn't wrong," Quint said. "What if Tizurek knows full well what he is doing? A god taking over a world? Who could defeat Tova's partner? I don't think I have that ability. I've only been lucky fighting Green wizards."

"But you have prevailed, even if you had to send them away from this world," Dakuz said. "I wouldn't call it luck; I'd call it using all your tools, even if you were almost killed saving King Boviz."

"I'm not afraid of death," Quint said, "but I don't seek it."

"Well, that's a good thing to tell your followers," Dakuz said. "I would hope you want to take care of yourself."

"I do. I can't neglect my mission. Tova wouldn't forgive me on the other side."

Narisu shook his head. "I'm glad I'm not you. I'd rather be ignored than have to confront Tova."

Masumi shivered. "I'd rather not think about what happens when I'm gone. As far as I'm concerned, I'm gone."

"Like Thera," Quint said. "I hope Tova treats her well."

"As do I," Masumi said.

CHAPTER THIRTY-THREE

They reached the town of Yokokyo mid-afternoon and rode to an inn on the west side. Quint's group was seven miles from the border; however, the border was at the ridge of the rocky hills to the west.

Quint looked at the people on the street while Narisu and Dakuz went inside to register them for the night. A few riders passed the inn, but one returned and ran inside.

Narisu approached Quint and Masumi. "Don't panic. Walk to your horses and wait for us to mount. We need to get out of Yokokyo as soon as we can. There is a detachment of Chokunese guards heading this way. They will be establishing a curfew while they do a house-to-house search. They are looking for two men, a teenage boy, and a polennese woman."

Quint helped Dakuz onto his horse and laughed as if Dakuz had told a joke. They walked to the end of the street. Quint noticed a commotion at the street's eastern end and urged everyone off the main road.

Dakuz looked pale when they reached a small gate. It was unmanned, and they slipped out of the town. Narisu took a sharp left. Dakuz couldn't control himself and fell off his horse.

Quint looked back. A few people on the road saw Dakuz tumble off his saddle. Quint cast a string to put Dakuz back on his horse, and they continued.

With too many observers, the Chokunese guard would soon be on their tail. Dakuz was swaying in his saddle.

"I'll do my best," Dakuz said, obviously in pain.

Narisu took them north again. They crossed three lanes heading to Yokokyo and rode into a small village. Night was falling, and even if the village had an inn, they couldn't risk it.

They waited for a farmer to tend to his livestock in a barn for the night. Tying their horses in the back, they slipped inside. Dakuz showed them his ankle.

"I can't ride a horse," he said through clenched teeth.

Quint put Dakuz to sleep.

"I don't know how to set an ankle."

"He won't be able to ride a horse or walk," Narisu said, "but I can set the ankle so that he won't damage it more."

"We will leave him here?" Masumi asked.

"No," Quint said. "We will take him with us. He and I can ride double."

"I can do that. I'm lighter," Masumi said.

"And I'm stronger. Dakuz isn't a youth, and I have a good horse."

"You do," Narisu said. "I can do the riding."

"No. He's my friend and my responsibility," Quint said. "Set it, and we will leave before dawn. We all need some sleep, and the horses need the rest more than we do."

They settled down until Masumi woke him up. "Soldiers."

They went to the door and looked through gaps in the timbers.

"Three," Masumi said.

"Then let them in here, and I'll put them to sleep. What time is it?"

"A few hours before dawn," Narisu said, walking up to them.

The soldiers were joined by two more and surrounded the barn.

"Is anyone in there?" one of them called out.

"There are horses tied up in back," another voice called from the other side of the barn.

Five against three. It would be hard in a fight, Quint thought. He put the two in the back to sleep, hoping the shields on the horses were enough to protect them from the string. He thought he could do the same with the three in front, but two were wizards with shields.

"We are truly in trouble," Quint whispered. He grabbed three bolts and nodded to Narisu, who unbarred the door and threw one of them open.

Quint didn't waste any time. He killed the two standing soldiers. The farmer and the other soldier were asleep on the ground

"We didn't mean to bother you," Quint said to the sleeping soldier. It was the only apology he uttered.

They carried Dakuz out the front door and to the back of the barn, where Quint's mount stood by itself, sniffing the slumbering soldiers. The other three horses had run off into the night.

"Put him over the saddle," Narisu said. He tied Dakuz to the saddle as best he could and in moments after a rushed attempt to cover their tracks, they were jogging through the farmer's fields with Quint leading their only horse.

Dakuz groaned and struggled with his bonds, but Quint put him to sleep again. Quint did what he could to camouflage their movements, and when the sun rose, they stopped to rest.

Narisu looked the worst, other than the slumbering Dakuz. Quint looked back but didn't see pursuit.

"What do we do now?" Masumi said.

"Head west," Narisu said. "I don't see an alternative. We will have to manage Dakuz as best we can. The horse will carry him unless we have to do some climbing."

"We can't avoid scrambling over the rock," Masumi said. "Another hour is all we have with the horse. There are no tracks if we head directly to Slinnon."

"We might have to rig a sledge," Quint said.

"What's that?" Masumi asked.

Narisu nodded. "It's a frame where two ends drag on the ground. I've seen them made by hunters carrying their prey."

"I used to make them for my father for carrying wood through the forest. He was a wheelwright, and we lived among our wood supply."

"Then it's time to leave the trail," Narisu said.

Quint found a thick sapling that he could cut down by casting a string, and Narisu and Masumi removed the branches with their swords.

He spotted a tree that also grew in South Fenola. He stripped the bark and quickly twisted the ungainly strands into binding lengths. In less than an hour, they lifted Dakuz onto the sledge and tied it to the horse.

They used the animal as long as possible until the rocks became too large. They put their possessions on the sledge with Dakuz, and two of them pulled the sledge at a time, dragging a slumbering Dakuz over the rocks.

"You do good work," Narisu said.

"And our work isn't done. If the going gets much worse, we must carry Dakuz using the bark ropes as straps," Quint said.

They worked until late midday, inching their way up and down the beginnings of the stony hills until they came upon a track leading west. Narisu looked at the dirt.

"This is used regularly," Narisu said. "There are lots of hoofprints and droppings."

"Bandits?" Quint asked.

"Or smugglers," Masumi said. "We are on the border, after all, and Slinnon goods are prized in Chokuno. It doesn't matter if they are bandits or smugglers, or both. They are criminals, just the same."

"What choice do we have? The going only gets harder," Quint said. "If this track takes us to Slinnon, bandits will be just as bad as Chokuno soldiers, but we are here, and I don't relish finding another way. Dakuz seems to be getting heavier with every step."

"We will have to be vigilant," Narisu said. "They will be mounted."

"Unless we defeat them," Masumi said. "Three magician-warriors against rabble?"

"A blade has its own eyes," Narisu said.

Quint hadn't heard the phrase before, but he knew anyone could get lucky swinging a blade wildly.

He picked up his end of the sledge and slipped the bark rope over his neck. If nothing else, the track was much easier than scrambling over boulders with Dakuz.

§

Quint looked eastward. He stood at the summit of the smuggler's path. One more step, and he supposed he would be in Slinnon. The track's danger didn't diminish but increased since they hadn't run across anyone on the path.

Everyone was exhausted. Quint had kept Dakuz asleep on the trek. When his friend woke, there would be plenty of unexplained bruises on Dakuz's body from all the jostling.

There were some steeper parts heading down to Slinnon, but Masumi stopped them after less than an hour.

"The road forks. One goes north, and the other continues west."

Narisu pulled out Dakuz's maps. "There is nothing to the north. Could it be to the smugglers' hideout?"

Quint heard voices above them. "Let's head north. The trail is narrower here."

Masumi helped Quint as they carried Dakuz and the litter far enough away from the road to be out of sight. They found a little clearing that widened the track considerably and put Dakuz down. Quint shielded everyone, including Dakuz.

"They are coming this way!" Narisu said in a loud whisper.

Quint sighed. They had made the wrong choice at the fork. There was nothing they could do about Dakuz, but Quint stayed with his friend while Narisu and Masumi hid behind rocks on both sides.

There were four smugglers, including one driving a narrow wagon full of goods when the smugglers rode into view. Quint drew his sword. In his left hand, he held a crossbow bolt.

The smugglers stopped at the entrance to the tiny clearing and laughed.

"Why are you standing there defending our house," one of the smugglers said.

Quint looked north along the track. "You live at the end of this?"

"We do, and you are in our way, but we won't let you go easily. The Chokunese are looking for some people, and I imagine you are them. Your friend on the ground doesn't look like he can put up much of a fight." The smuggler gave Quint an evil grin and leaned forward over his saddle in Quint's direction. "So, it looks like we will dull our swords on you, lad."

"I'm allowing you to continue toward your home," Quint said.

"You and who else?" one of the other smugglers said.

"Me, for one," Narisu said, getting to his feet behind a rock close to the smugglers.

"Two against four. Not good for you. I will take care of the boy and then you," the lead smuggler said.

Masumi didn't expose herself, which Quint thought was a good thing.

The wagon driver yanked a crossbow from the wagon and began to straighten the folded steel ends to create a bow. "I don't even need to get off my cart to kill you, boy."

Quint nodded to Narisu. The smugglers followed Quint's nod and began to pull out weapons. Only one had a crossbow, so he was the first casualty. Quint cast his teleportation string and ended that threat with the smuggler falling backward into the wagon bed.

The lead smuggler looked shocked, but he didn't flee. His next expression was one of anger. The man raised his sword and charged. While Quint rummaged around in his pocket for another bolt, the one the barbs stuck in the fabric when he tried to extract it, and he didn't have the time to get another.

Quint put up his sword to fend off the smuggler's blow. Narisu's words about a blade having its own eyes came to mind, and as the smuggler turned his horse around for another strike, Quint used the teleportation string with the sword. It pierced the chest of the smuggler but not deeply enough.

"It takes more than a bush wizard to kill me," the smuggler said as he tossed Quint's sword at Dakuz. The magic shield was enough to deflect the blade.

Quint, now unarmed, leaped for the bolt on the ground and rolled away from the hoofs of the advancing brigand. The horse was almost on him. Quint groaned. He had no shot at the smuggler. He grimaced and shot his bolt through the horse, upwards.

The horse reared up and fell on the other side from Quint. The smuggler was underneath the horse, struggling to get out. The man's sword was out of the smuggler's reach as Quint ran and reached the sword before the smuggler could stretch for it. He made sure the smuggler would never fight another battle.

He stood up to see Masumi finishing up her opponent, who had dismounted. Narisu was pinned against a boulder, clutching his shoulder. His opponent was reaching back for a big swing. Quint had an easier time with his next bolt and shot the last smuggler. The man fell off his horse, and Narisu slid down to sit on the ground.

"Secure the horses," Quint said to Masumi.

"Please? You shouldn't order your wife around so harshly," she said.

"Please," Quint said.

He checked the smugglers and dragged each one into the rocks while Masumi tied up the horses and saw to Narisu's wound.

"We need to get him to a healer," Masumi said.

"I'm still here," Narisu said. "I need to get to a healer. We have mounts, now."

"Can you ride?"

"I'll have to. What will you do with Dakuz?"

"In the back of the cart. I'll ride or drive, whatever works the best for Narisu."

"I'll ride," Narisu said.

They had to toss a few bags of booty to make a proper bed for Dakuz. Quint tied the sledge to the wagon and then they were headed back to the track that led down the hills into Slinnon.

∽

CHAPTER THIRTY-FOUR
~

THE LITTLE ROAD WAS A CHALLENGE FOR QUINT, but as night descended, they were out of the worst of the hills. A forest covered the slopes, giving them some cover in case anyone was looking from above at the crest of the mountains behind them.

They found a small meadow and found a secluded corner, giving them cover from the track. There wasn't water, but Quint handled that. One of the sacks was filled with supplies. They ate a cold dinner but were able to fill up. Quint finally woke Dakuz up.

"I am still alive?" Dakuz asked as he opened his eyes. He tried to sit up, but bark ropes were all over him. "What is this?" he said as he tried to free himself.

"Patience, patient," Masumi said as she removed the ropes with Quint and helped Dakuz to a sitting position. "How is your wound? It has closed despite our journey."

"It still hurts, and my ankle hurts, too," Dakuz said, "but other than needing a drink and shuffling around, I'd rather feel the pain than the alternative."

Quint uncorked a small bottle of wine. "See how this tastes."

Dakuz winced and spit out the sip he took. "This is vinegar, not wine."

Quint spelled a magic light and read the label. "So, it is. There are more bottles." He found one that said spring wine. He had no idea what that was. "Try this."

Dakuz managed a smile. "Much better. I think I need another sip."

Narisu was sitting against a tree and snoring after eating his fair share of the smuggler's supplies.

"Want a little something to take care of the snoring?" Quint asked.

"I don't snore, regardless of reports that say otherwise," Narisu said.

"I'm one of those who reported," Quint said. He handed the bottle of spring wine to Narisu.

"This is good. I'd almost call it watered wine, but it has too much flavor," Narisu said.

"It is light," Masumi said, helping Dakuz limp in the little glade. "The smugglers came from the Slinnon side, but spring wine is a common concoction sold in pubs in Chokuno, too."

She put her hand on Narisu's forehead and frowned. "You have a fever. As your only available healer, I command you to ride with Dakuz in the wagon. Quint and I will make it comfortable."

They arranged the bags in the wagon bed. It was barely wide enough for both, but Dakuz rode with his head facing the rear, and Narisu was on the driver's end.

"I could almost sleep this way," Narisu said.

"Good, because both of you are bedded down for tonight. Masumi and I will be sleeping close."

"There is no one around. You don't have to pretend to be married," Narisu said.

"Not that kind of close. Close to the wagon," Quint said, yawning.

Masumi and Quint used what they could from the smugglers' bedrolls and slept on either side of the wagon. In the middle of the night, Masumi joined Quint.

"It's too cold. I need a source of warmth. You fit the bill," she said.

Quint grunted and turned, with his back facing her. She still snuggled up against him, giggling a bit, Quint noticed, until she began to snore like Narisu.

§

In the morning, in the false dawn, Quint woke up and jostled Masumi enough that she rose as well. Quint made sure the horses were watered, thanks to his water strings, and fed, thanks to the little clearing's flora.

They hitched the cart up to a horse, tied the other to the back of the cart, and left the glade before the sun kissed the tops of the hills behind them.

Quint put both injured men to sleep as he drove the wagon, and Masumi led the fourth horse behind him. Quint didn't feel like he was free, and Masumi said she was almost afraid to be back in Slinnon.

The "almost" made Quint wonder. She had never revealed she was a princess or a half-princess. She was a member of the royal family who would rather prefer her dead, being half-polennese and half-hubite. She had to keep a low profile, but Quint didn't know what that meant to a young woman as accomplished as she.

Quint didn't know what the future had in store for Masumi, but he still needed her, according to Tova. As soon as he found the retired wizard, he would head for Amea to prepare for the dreaded confrontation with Tizurek in Simo Tapmann's guise, with or without Masumi.

Their track finally exited into the bottom of a small draw that led to a road. None of them knew exactly where they were since the road didn't appear on the map.

"North," Narisu said, sitting up in the wagon as Quint watered the horses in a nearby stream. "There are more towns and villages along the border hills. That would mean more healers. Of course, I'm thinking of Dakuz."

"Thinking of yourself," Dakuz said. "But I agree, thinking of myself. I'd feel better if I were looked at."

Masumi nodded. "Healers are a little different in Slinnon. There is more folk healing that involves needles."

"Needles?" Dakuz asked. He furrowed his brow until he smiled. "Acupuncture, it's called in Narukun, at least in textbooks. The body supposedly has energy lines, and the needles siphon off bad humors. I don't know if the writer knew what they were talking about, but does that sound like it?"

Masumi nodded. "Slinnonese have folk, magic, and what the fiefs call conventional healing."

"I'll take all three," Narisu said.

"North," Masumi said as Quint joined them.

"North?" Quint said.

"To healers of whatever ilk!" Dakuz said. "Let's get moving."

Quint nodded and smiled. The conversation had been interesting, and he didn't add that he wouldn't be comfortable with needles stuck in him.

They passed a Polennese farmer pushing a cart full of tools. "Where is the nearest town? We are lost," Quint said.

"Kippun is over those mountains. Isn't that where you belong?" the farmer said, clearly not a hubite friend.

Masumi sighed. "We were climbing in the mountains, and two suffered falls. They require a healer's attention.

Dakuz and Narisu assumed expressions of pain and agony. Narisu even whimpered.

The farmer rolled his eyes. "Turn west at the next crossroads. You'll reach a town large enough for whatever or whomever you seek." He shook his head and resumed his journey south.

"He was shaking after he left us," Narisu said.

"He wasn't shaking," Masumi said. "He was laughing at your groaning."

Narisu grunted and folded his arms. "I'll not do it again."

"Good!" Quint said.

§

By mid-afternoon, they rolled into a town of decent size. The hills were a purple haze on the horizon and for that, Quint was glad. He'd had enough of Kippun, but he was sad to have left Thera in a grave. He hoped Dugo was happy serving Shira. Dugo was never satisfied as a monk in Seensist or Feltoff cloisters.

They found a healer supposedly proficient in the three medical sciences, so said the sign on her clinic. The waiting room had one person seeking attention, and the attendant helped bring Narisu and Dakuz into the clinic.

The attendant requested payment in advance after quickly assessing the wounds of both patients. Quint almost gasped at the price. He thought they had enough money to get them to Amea, but that might not happen if everything was as expensive as this healer.

The waiting patient was ushered in, and in a few minutes, the healer came out with the patient, who was obviously a friend. Quint had expected a polennese woman, but not one so tall.

"Two serious wounds?" the healer said to the attendant before turning to Dakuz and Narisu. "You've both been in a fight? Are the Slinnon authorities after you?"

Narisu shook his head. "Our wounds came to us in Chokuno fief."

"How did you get all the way here without dying?" the healer said, alarm now showing on her face.

"I know a few healing strings," Masumi said. "Nothing good enough to heal, but enough to keep the wounds from festering."

"You'll need to learn new strings," the healer said, looking at Dakuz's wound. "This has festered, and then this poor man's body encapsulated the rot." She looked down at Dakuz, still sitting on a chair. "You'll be first."

The healer put a hand on Dakuz's forehead. "No fever. In this case that may be a complication, but hopefully, not a fatal one."

The attendant and the healer took Dakuz to the back. The healer returned and pointed to Narisu. "You stay here. It will be an hour or so." She looked at Quint and Masumi. "You two can find an inn. You must stay here a few days before you leave our lovely town."

"I'd rather stay here," Quint said.

"That was a polite command. You will leave now and return no earlier than tomorrow at noon," the attendant said.

"Will you need more money?" Masumi asked.

The attendant looked at them in disbelief. "Tova's bosom, no!" she said. "You've paid enough. Now leave."

Quint looked at Masumi once they left the inn. "Tova's bosom? Really. Is that a Slinnon expression?"

"I think so. It isn't used in Chokuno, but before I left, no one would have used it before me."

Quint went back into the clinic and returned. "There is an inn close by, she said."

Masumi worked her lips. She was uneasy about something.

"We must be husband and wife again since you are so practiced at it," Quint said.

"Amoki returns? Her face has been with you for this entire trip."

"Except for one moment," Quint said.

She ignored Quint's comment. "Husband, you drive the wagon, and I'll manage the horses."

They had to ask directions twice to get to the inn. It seemed that people were more inclined to speak the truth to Quint than Masumi.

Registering for two to three nights at the inn, the innkeeper ignored Masumi and only dealt with Quint. They went up to their room. The room had traditional sleeping mats, so Quint wouldn't have to worry about being placed in an inappropriate sleeping situation.

"Why didn't the innkeeper talk to you?"

"Half-breeds aren't appreciated in Slinnon," Masumi said. "My Amoki mask is part hubite-part polens, just like my real face."

"But you look like you were from Slinnon with either face."

"I wouldn't if you were Slinnonese," Masumi said. "A pure Slinnon face is different. I'll leave it to you to discover the difference."

Quint could tell he had crossed the line and was impolite.

"It doesn't matter to me," he said.

"I know that," Masumi said. "If I were pure Slinnon, we would have never met."

"Probably," Quint said. "You never know what fate will throw at you."

"Fate has done a good job of throwing bad things at you and me," she said. "I suppose I could cast a Slinnon version of my face as a mask, but I don't think I can bring myself to do that."

"Don't," Quint said. "I like you the way you are."

"Amoki or Masumi?"

"Masumi, but that's not your real name, right?"

She smiled. "No, but I don't want you involved in my past. It could be dangerous."

"That's fine. My past is dangerous enough. I'll never be welcome in Kippun again.

Masumi snorted. "Neither will any of us," she said. "Let's get our meager possessions up here and find a restaurant and a market. We need Slinnonese clothes."

"I'm not sure that will help disguise either of us, but I need more necessities and all we have are some Chokuno military cloaks and the clothes that we have worn for days straight," Masumi said.

Quint noted that the Slinnonese swords were thin and worn with shorter or longer knives. There weren't as many men wearing weapons on the street, and no women carried weapons that he could see.

"Do we need Slinnon weapons?"

Masumi nodded. "There is a code of behavior for armed men. They must attend a martial arts school to be granted a token to carry. You can carry a weapon since you are a hubite and a foreigner. For me, it's more problematic since I'm a woman and a half-breed, but I can use my magic until I am caught."

"Caught? Is it illegal for you to use magic?"

"I don't have a token," Masumi said, "and neither do you."

"I'm a hubite, so I get a pass?"

"No, you will get a warning, but we can go to a magic school and take a test."

"Will you change your face?"

"I will have to use my natural face," she said. "Wizards can…"

Quint raised his hand. "I know. We can detect masks if we are looking for them."

"Why, husband, you are so smart," Masumi said facetiously.

CHAPTER THIRTY-FIVE

THEY WALKED INTO A WIZARD CLUB NEAR THE MARKET that could administer magic tests. They would get tested first and then go to the market.

The lobby was empty, but there was a bell on the counter. Masumi grinned and hit it hard.

A polennese not much older than Quint with a scraggly beard walked through a curtain behind the counter.

"We are new to Slinnon and would like to get tokens for magic," Quint said.

"My husband and I are touring Slinnon," Masumi said.

Quint looked at her as she talked and was surprised by Masumi's natural face again. She was much better looking than Amoki. She winked at Quint and squeezed his arm.

"He's even better than I am," Masumi said.

"Fill out your name and address in town and where you live out of the country."

Quint did the writing, putting Feltoff Cloister, Narukun as their address since he had no permanent address and Quint wasn't about to ask his wife for hers.

"Narukun, eh?" the bearded man said. "You've been through Kippun?"

Quint nodded. "They were having a massive war when we came through. We managed to miss the battle." He smiled as if he had made a joke.

"You know we don't allow people to walk around with swords unless licensed," the man said. He looked outside and then leaned a little over the counter. "I can fix you up with a sword token for a little more."

"It isn't a counterfeit token, is it?" Quint asked.

"Not at all," the man said. "You will have to spar with our registered martial artist. We are associates with the martial arts academy next door."

It seemed a bit shady to Quint, but Masumi squeezed his arm and nodded her encouragement.

"I'm better at magic," Quint said, "but sometimes magic wears out."

"Oh, you are experienced fighting with magic?"

"I've had my moments," Quint said. "I have to protect my wife, don't I?"

"Certainly, certainly," the man glanced at Masumi and nodded. "I'll be back in a few moments. You'll have to complete this form, too."

They were alone in the lobby. "Are you sure this is legal?"

Masumi shrugged. "How would I know? I've never been to Slinnon as an adult, and my mother was younger than me when I left." She winked at Quint.

Someone had to be listening. "I'll feel better walking Slinnon's streets with a token. I never felt at ease while we traveled through Kippun," Quint said.

They waited until another person came to retrieve them. "I'm here to test your magic. Could you follow me?" an older woman said.

She walked without energy. Quint thought the woman wasn't happy about something. Maybe working in a dingy wizard school was a downgrade for her.

They ended up in a room lined with brick, with rusty metal sheets on the ceiling. It was set up to endure errant fire and lightning strikes, that was for sure, thought Quint.

"You sit in the corner," the woman said to Quint.

The woman ran Masumi through a series of string tests. Masumi couldn't perform some strings he had seen her use without effort. She was holding back. Quint took that as a warning.

In the end, Masumi performed less than thirty strings, but Quint could tell she was close to master, just as Narisu and Dakuz were.

Quint performed a few more than thirty strings, but the extra ones he demonstrated were the most mundane he knew. Thirty strings meant a sub-master level in Slinnon. Quint's actual level, according to the chart their tester carried would be a supreme master, the highest rating in Slinnon.

"My, you are both powerful. If you need employment, I can recommend employment at a better academy than this one," the woman said.

"Why not work here? If we needed to, of course."

"Just take my word for it." She signed their forms. "You will be tested for martial arts," their tester said to Quint. She looked at the forms. "Amoki can wait in the lobby for you to return there. We will make your tokens quickly, and you can be on your way."

Amoki knew the way out, but the tester led Quint to another room. "The martial arts person will arrive in a few minutes. Don't perform well," she said. "If you do, you will likely be pressed into the royal Slinnon army."

"Do all those with swords on the streets have royal service?"

"No. I say that because I can tell you are much more practiced than you let on. So is your wife. Be careful in Slinnon. Some rules are easily broken, and the penalties for breaking the rules are not easily evaded."

She left Quint to think about the woman's warning. Narukun looked increasingly like the best place to live on North Fenola. Quint wondered where he could end up when a short, even for a polennese, swordsman entered carrying an armful of swords.

"Quinto Tirolo of Feltoff Cloister in Narukun?"

"That's me," Quint said. He rose and loosened the Chokuno sword in the sheath at his hip.

"Take that off. We will use Slinnon swords," the man said. "The token permits Slinnon swords and nothing else. You can keep that out of sight until you leave the country."

"I don't have one of your swords."

"Not to worry. I can sell you one of these," the man said.

Quint caught the undertone. He wouldn't get a token if he didn't buy a sword.

"Pick one," the man said.

Quint drew each one from their scabbards. One was obviously better than the others, but Quint figured that one was probably ten times more expensive than the others, so he picked a mediocre sword. It didn't fit its scabbard very well and needed sharpening.

"How much is this one?" Quint asked.

The swordsman gave a price. Quint thought the price was exorbitant.

"And this one?" Quint picked up the best of the lot.

"Half the price," the swordsman said.

It was still expensive, but Quint could see him using this one. "I'll take the better one, then."

"I thought you would," the swordsman said with a faint smile.

Quint knew he had been taken, but he got the warning from the tester, which had to be worth something.

They faced each other in a circle drawn on the floor. Quint looked up at the circular skylight that lit up the circle. During the day, they didn't need magic lights in the room.

"Address me," the swordsman said.

Quint used a conventional Kippunese stance, and the swordsman grunted an acknowledgment.

"Move at me slowly. I want to see your technique," the swordsman said.

Quint didn't try to be better or worse. All the swordsman wanted were basic moves, and Quint knew them all, but the moves came out a little different with the lighter, longer sword. He imagined he would have to do some work with Masumi or Narisu to improve.

"A few quick sparring sessions. Nothing long and nothing dangerous," the swordsman said.

The first session was humbling. Even trying as hard as he could, Quint was easily beaten by the swordsman. He'd never seen anyone move so fast. It was as if magic was involved.

The second session was less so, but Quint caught when the man cast a subtle string. It didn't speed him up, but it affected Quint's senses, so time changed for Quint, making the swordsman seem to move faster. He would have to move much quicker to compensate consciously.

The third exchange of blows was much better. Quint almost scored, but still, he was beaten.

"That's enough. You picked up my string. I've had few wizards who can see my casting and do anything about it."

"You still thrashed me."

"And that is how I will record it. For another ten silver coins, I'll teach you the string."

Quint shrugged. "I'm always up to learn a quick string," he said.

The swordsman moved away from the skylight.

"The light helps to disguise my casting."

The string was easy enough. It was new to Quint, but he could see uses for the string if he had time to work on it. "I've got it," he said.

"I'll cut my fee in half if you've already got it."

Quint could quickly cast it using both hands and large gestures that he didn't need to use. The swordmaster began to talk so slowly that Quint couldn't get most of what he said.

"You did it. I can tell when you are affected. There is no counter, but the string only lasts for half a minute or so." He held out his hand, and Quint paid on the spot. Quint suspected the string was relatively common, but the token was signed off, and Quint was to take the form to the front counter.

The swordsman bowed. "It was a pleasure, a foreigner." He left by a different door.

Quint found "Amoki" sitting with two tokens in her hands. Quint handed over the swordsman's form.

"I've taken the liberty of creating a token for you already. Thank you for your business today. Don't forget to tell your friends."

§

They left the wizard school and spent the last vestiges of daylight buying clothing for themselves, Dakuz, and Narisu.

A Slinnon outfit was a series of robes over separate top and bottom undergarments. The Kippunese adopted robes but wore more conventional Narukun undergarments, trousers, shirts, and vests. Not everyone wore all the robes in any of the fiefs, but they did in Slinnon.

Quint wore a black hat with a flat brim and rounded top with room for a topknot, which Quint didn't have. Boots were different, with softer soles, something the Kippunese didn't emulate.

Masumi wore a similar outfit, but the colors were lighter, and the fabric's designs were woven into the material. She bought one like Quint's, but it had a white veil. Quint saw a few other women in the market wearing the same hat.

"I'll need this later," Masumi said. She bought a few ornaments for her long dark hair, and they were done when they passed a shop with women's clothes in the window. "One more outfit," she said.

Quint was told to wait outside. Masumi walked outside, and Quint was stunned. How could she not look like any other polennese? Her hair had been put up, wound in an intricate style, with the ornaments holding the arrangement in place, but that wasn't the stunning part.

Quint had never seen Masumi wearing a dress, and the woman came out in her appearance. Her dress was of two contrasting but complementary colors, but everything seemed to flow.

"Silk?"

"Low quality, but I don't care," she said. "It brings back memories I thought I had forgotten. I won't wear it again until we enter the capital."

The dress didn't look low quality to Quint, but he had no idea what the quality levels were and took Masumi's evaluation as the truth. It didn't matter, though. She was stunning.

Quint looked closer and lit a magic light to lighten up her face.

"You are wearing makeup!" Quint had to admit it made her look more beautiful.

"Quiet," Masumi said, putting her finger on his lips. "People are looking, husband."

Quint looked around, and she was right. People were looking at them.

One person passed them and muttered, "half-breed."

Quint extinguished his light. "I can't imagine."

"I can," Masumi said, visibly upset. "I should have known better."

They walked as the twilight deepened and reached the inn. They went to their room where Masumi changed back into the plain outfit she bought and wiped off the makeup.

"Why did you do that?"

"Commoners don't wear makeup. Look around when we go down to eat."

Masumi took the ornaments out of her hair except for a long hair thing that looked like a stone knife.

"Let me see your sword," she said.

"Not bad. What did you pay for it?"

"That is more expensive than the same sword would cost in the weapon shop in Tiryo. Although, it is a good serviceable sword."

He told Masumi the story.

"I haven't heard of a string like that. Can you show me?"

They spent some time with the speed spell, Masumi called it, until Masumi had it mastered.

"Now we both know the spell. That means we only paid half for that, too," Masumi said. "I add that to the cost of the tokens. We needed those to survive in Slinnon."

"What about Narisu and Dakuz?"

"They won't be in any shape to fight for a week or two, and we will be gone from here long before that," Masumi said.

§

"I suppose you did a better job healing them than I thought," the healer said to Masumi. They can leave tomorrow anytime."

Quint and Masumi visited Dakuz first.

"She cleaned out my side, washed it with something with a medication in it." Dakuz made a face. "That didn't feel good at all. After she used little clamps to close the wound, she applied the magic. It made the cleansing seem like heaven. Then the needles came out. Those weren't so bad. The healer spread a cream over where she poked me. I had needles in my feet, in my head, and in my side. Two had little balls of moss, which she burned. That was before she applied more magic healing to my ankle. That was the worst."

"You look much better," Quint said, meaning it.

Masumi kissed Dakuz on his forehead. "We leave tomorrow, so don't get used to this," she said.

Narisu was much the same, except the healer didn't use magic. "The flesh wouldn't accept it, she said." Narisu opened his shirt. "She had to trim the flesh and then sew it up. I got a needle treatment. Did Dakuz?"

"He did," Masumi said. She leaned over and kissed Narisu on the mouth.

It wasn't a lingering kiss, but Quint felt a little odd. Was that jealousy? He thought.

Mid-morning, Quint, and Masumi showed up with the wagon. They had bought cushions and helped both men.

"They are both to take it easy for another week," the healer said. "See another healer if they get feverish or the wounds get red. Dakuz said you were heading to northern Slinnon."

"We have business on another continent," Quint said.

"Oh," the healer said, grinning. "I wish you well. I learned new words and heard tall tales from both while they were here. Suppose I should pay you!"

With that, they left the healer's clinic and traveled out of town. They stopped at a roadside inn and rented a room for a few hours. It included lunch, so Narisu and Dakuz changed into their new Slinnon-style clothes.

"Here are new hats. If you wear these, you won't get sunburned while we travel," Quint said.

"And we won't be so recognizable," Narisu said. "I get it." He looked at the wide-brimmed hat. "I saw these all over the place on our ride out of town."

Dakuz grumbled that his clothes didn't fit well and that he didn't like to wear hats. Quint grinned. His friend was feeling much better.

They finally spread the map out on a low table in their room and looked at the map that Quint and Masumi had purchased in the town.

"There is the road that we entered at the end of the smuggler's trail," Narisu said. "This is a much better map."

"It better be," Masumi said. "We are getting ripped off everywhere in this part of Slinnon."

"You need to bargain harder," Narisu said. "Slinnon is known for having to work a quoted rate down. They saw hubites coming and decided to up the prices." He jerked his thumb up a few times.

Quint had already figured that lesson out, but he didn't want to stick out, following Masumi's advice. Quint shared his slow-motion string. Both Narisu and Dakuz eagerly tried it out. Dakuz mastered it before Narisu. After an arduous escape, Quint thought the two hours spent at the inn were actually fun.

Quint felt they should cross Slinnon to a small port town called Gikoma on the Slinnon west coast. There weren't many ports on the west coast of Slinnon. Dainoto, the capital of Slinnon, was on a paved road from Gikoma, and Quint was told it was the fastest way north to Port Okinono, where ships could take them to Amea.

∽

CHAPTER THIRTY-SIX

IT TOOK THEM NINE DAYS TO TRAVEL TO THE PORT OF GIKOMA with the last few days on a decent road, proving how much larger Slinnon was than Kippun. Quint enquired about passage to Amea and was told by a few captains that it would be faster to travel to Port Okinono on land rather than by sea.

They found an academy willing to test Dakuz and Narisu for magic and martial arts. Neither of them had to buy swords and the prices were more reasonable with Narisu negotiating.

After acquiring their tokens, they were buying swords of equal quality to Quint's in a shop close to the port's city center when Quint spotted an antique Slinnon sword that attracted him for some reason. The little figurine in his pocket warmed. Quint didn't pull it out, but he grabbed the jade object, which warmed up again when he touched the sword.

"This is for sale?" Quint asked.

"I won it gambling. It is ancient, but it won't take an edge. It's not worth repairing the scabbard, either. I can give you a good price," the shopkeeper said.

"It would look good in my office in Feltoff," Quint said.

He let Narisu negotiate for the sword and gave Dakuz the one he bought in the magic school. Dakuz didn't care.

"Why did you buy that old thing?" Dakuz said while he admired his new weapon.

"Tova, I think," Quint said. He told his friends about the sign from the figurine.

"And it is, regardless of your feelings," Dakuz said.

They spent the night in Gikoma. Masumi didn't tire of teasing him about being married. He wished he could brush the teasing off, but it still irritated him for some reason.

While Masumi left the room to wash up before bed, Quint drew his new sword to examine the blade in more detail. He looked closely at the worn etching on the blade and realized it was a thread diagram on one side and a string weave on the other. The figurine led him to a magic sword!

He memorized the thread diagram and then practiced the string weave in his head before he attempted the string with his hands while the sword sat on his lap.

Nothing happened. Quint cocked his head and wondered if this required a one-handed spell. The blade certainly looked old enough to predate the move to two-handed strings.

He held the sword in one hand and cast the string one-handed. Again, nothing happened. He tried again but to no avail. He put the sword in its scabbard and made another try.

The sword lit up the room with a golden glow. The hilt burned his hand, but Quint couldn't let go until the glow faded.

Quint dropped the blade and held his burned hand. He spelled water to cool it off, not caring if the mat got wet. In his palm were two concentric circles. One was red and the other blue. Tova and Tizurek?

He tried to rub the marks off, but they were like tattoos. He picked the sword up by the hilt. The blade and the scabbard were transformed. No longer a tattered sheath, the sword's cover was a deep red leather with a pebbled texture.

The hilt was now covered in a wound strip of the same material. The metal fittings were now dark, almost black, but mirrorlike. Quint drew the sword, and the blade was out of the same metal. The string and thread diagrams weren't worn at all.

He took a page from a notebook Masumi had purchased in the first town and ran an edge over the exposed blade. The paper immediately caught an edge and Quint cut the paper cleanly in two.

After examining the paper for tears, Quint realized the blade was sharper than anything he had ever owned. He picked up the other half and let it drift onto the blade. The edge caught the paper, and the blade had sliced through most of the paper.

Masumi walked in, toweling her long black hair. "Are you playing with your toy blade?" She looked at the sword in Quint's hand.

"You can't see this?"

"What?"

"The sword I bought today."

"I see it," Masumi said. "Did you try sharpening it? The shopkeeper said it didn't keep an edge."

Quint put the sword back in the scabbard and showed her the pieces of cut notepaper. "This sword did this," Quint said.

"It did not," she said. She took the sword, and it immediately took on the same appearance at the weapons shop. Masumi drew the sword, running her thumb down the edge, and showed it to Quint. "See? No edge."

"Hand it back," Quint said, "Please."

Masumi smiled at him. "That's better. We will make you civilized in a decade or two."

"You and who else?" Quint asked.

"We meaning me!" Masumi said playfully, tossing the sword to him.

When Quint caught it, the sword transformed. The red hilt and the black metal returned. "Do you still see the old sword?"

"Why wouldn't I?" Masumi said.

"Then watch." Quint took Masumi's towel and tossed it in the air. When the towel fell over the blade's edge, it separated into two pieces.

Masumi's mouth dropped open. "How did you do that?"

"Try it," Quint said. "Please."

"That's better." She accepted the sword and duplicated Quint's trick, except this time, the towel draped itself over the blade. The old blade was too dull to cut anything.

"Let me try something," Quint said. He took the sword by the hilt with the towel still on the blade. Quint moved the blade, making the towel part, and both pieces fell to the mat.

"Magic." Masumi said.

"Wizardry. Ancient wizardry," Quint said. "Perhaps I will need this to defend myself against Simo Tapmann." He put the sword down, and it returned to its old look.

Quint examined the circles on his palm. He picked up the sword with his left hand and the sword remained old, but when he transferred the sword, so the circles were touching the sheath, the sword transformed.

"I can control the transformation," Quint said. He grabbed the larger half of the towel, wrapped it around his right hand, and picked up the sword. The new sword didn't appear until he removed the towel, and the magic sword returned in all its glory as soon as the circles in his palm touched the sword or the sheath.

"I'm glad you can because it hasn't changed all the time I've been looking at it."

Quint put the sword down and showed Masumi his palm.

"Can you see this?" Quint asked, holding out his palm.

"Do you want me to read your fortune? It probably won't work any better than a predictor string," Masumi said before she looked more closely at his hand. "There is a double circle on your palm. I can barely see them."

"They control the sword," Quint said. "When I covered my hand with the towel, the sword didn't transform."

She giggled. "You have the circles, and I have the butterfly on my wrist. Let's hope we don't have to use them to identify a body." Masumi picked up the towel and examined the edges of the cut towel. "I can't deny this. It is a perfectly sharp cut."

"What kind of magic is in Slinnon?" Quint asked.

Masumi shrugged. "You'll have to ask your retired magician. He might have the answers," Masumi said. "Promise me you won't sleep hugging your new friend. As much as I love you, dear husband, I don't want you bleeding all over the sleeping mat.

THE END OF BOOK THREE

STRINGS OF EMPIRE: CHARACTERS & LOCATIONS

CHARACTERS

THE WIZARD CORPS

Quint Tirolo - Fifteen-year-old boy with magic awakening inside him.
Zeppo Tirolo - Quint's father
Master Geno Pozella - magic trainer
Amaria Baltacco – junior officer in the Wizard Corps
Colonel Sarrefo - commander of Strategic Operations
Field Marshal Chiglio – Army commander
Specialist Gaglio - old friend of Pozella
Pacci Colleto. Master Wizard in the Gussellian army.
General Emilio Baltacco - over the Wizard Corps military arm. Amaria's father.
Zoria Gauto - assistant to Colonel Sarrefo
Marena Categoro - housekeeper of Quint's shared flat
Colonel Julia Gerocie - head of the Military Diplomatic Corps.
General Obellia - Head of Military Foreign Affairs
Henricco Lucheccia - Racellian Foreign Secretary reporting to the council.
Calee Danko - daughter to the Narukun professor.
Fedor Danko - Narukun professor teaching at Racellian University.
Grand Marshal Tracco Guilica - War Minister and Head of Racellian Forces
Horenz Pizent – Purser of Narukun ship
Captain Goresk Olinko – captain of Narukun ship

THE CLOISTER WIZARD

Oscar Viznik - The monk who saved Quint
Sandiza "Sandy" Bartok – cloister guide
Eben – Seensist master gardener
Hintz Dakuz - librarian and teacher
Pol Grizak - Cloister monk

The Wizard Charter

Tizurek - God of the world
Tova - Tizurek's handmaiden
Shinzle Bokwiz - religious leader
Croczi - religious supporter
Kozak - cloister carpenter
Wanisa Hannoko - citizen of Pinzleport
Andreiza "Andy" Hannoko - Wanisa's daughter
Dontiz "Donnie" Hannoko - Wanisa's son
Vintez Dugo - injured monk
Zim Pilka - local lord
Olinz – Lord Pilka's aide
Silla Pilka - local lady
Gallia Pilka - lord's beautiful daughter
Criz Pilka - lord's youngest son.
Finir Boviz - King of Narukun
Phandiz Crider - Aide to the king
Thera Vanitz - military strategist.
Omar Ronzle - Pilka's soldier
Master Jelnitz – Green master wizard

THE WIZARD CHARTER

Hari Bitto (sensei) - Shimato master
Bunto Bumoto - Shimato's warlord
Shira Yomolo - Shimato entertainer
Miro Gorima - head of Three Forks faction
Rimo Gorima - son of Miro
Chibo Hobona - A Shimato war leader
Narisu - Hobona's assistant.
Todo Yinsu - Three Fork mansion gatekeeper
Masumi - female spy - half hubite-half polennese
Huma Bifomu - female leader of the Flat Plain wizard faction
Dasoka – a Shimato functionary
Goryo Tatatomi - Warlord of Chokuno

LOCATIONS

CONTINENTS – COUNTRIES - RACES

Amea – last expanded into by gran race - an offshoot of hubites
Honnen
Progen
Chullen
Lekken

North Fenola - Oldest settled - by hubites and polens (or polennese)
Pogokon – polens
Slinnon – polens
    Gikoma - Slinnon port city
    Dainoto - capital of Slinnon
    Port Okinono - Port on Slinnon Estuary
    Kikuro Town and Temple
Kippun – hubites who have assumed polennese customs.
    Gamiza fief - borders with Narukun
    Shimato fief - borders with Narukun
        Morimanu - capital of Shimato fief
        Teritoto - Agricultural center in Northwest Shimato
    Chokuno fief - northwest of Shimato
        Tiryo - Chokuno capital
Narukun – hubite
    Pinzleport – Southern port
Seensist Cloister
Baziltof – large village to the north of Seensist
Zimton – the principal town in the Pilka domain
Tova's Falls – village at the edge of mountains
Parsun Cloister
Feltoff Cloister
Baxel – Royal capital of Narukun.

South Fenola – Willots pushed most hubites out of continent
Barellia - willots
Gussellia - willots

The Wizard Charter

Nornotta - capital of Gussellia
Vinellia - willots
Racellia - Till's home country home to willots, hubites
Bocarre - Capital of Racellia
Fort Draco - wizard training

Resoda - Most recently settled - first by grans, but the other races followed
Volcann - all four
Akinnonn - gran/hubite
Logedonn - gran - hubite
Wippadann - gran - polens
Loppodunn - willots - polens

Frosso — most recently settled by grans. Willots coalescing in New Balloo
Boxxo - grans
Loppo - grans
New Balloo - Willots

A BIT ABOUT GUY

With a lifelong passion for speculative fiction, Guy Antibes found that he enjoyed writing fantasy, as well as reading it. So, a career was born, and more than fifty books later, Guy continues to add his own flavor of writing to the world. Guy lives in the western part of the United States and is happily married with enough children and grandchildren to meet or exceed the human replacement rate.

You can contact Guy at his website: www.guyantibes.com.

†

Books by Guy Antibes

THE STRINGS OF EMPIRE
The Wizard Corps
The Cloister Wizard

~

JUSTIN SPEDE
An Unexpected Magician
An Unexpected Spell
An Unexpected Alliance
An Unexpected Betrayal
An Unexpected Villian

~

GAGS & PEPPER
Plight of the Phoenix
The Wizard's Chalice
A Tinker's Dame
A Spell Misplaced
Comrades in Magic

~

THE AUGUR'S EYE
The Rise of Whit
The King's Spy
The Queen's Pet
The Knave's Serpent

~

THE ADVENTURES OF DESOLATION BOXSTER
Prince on the Run
Theft of an Ancient Dog
The Blue Tower
The Swordmaster's Secret
A Clash of Magics

~

WIZARD'S HELPER
The Serpent's Orb
The Warded Box
Grishel's Feather
The Battlebone
The Polished Penny
The Hidden Mask
The Buckle's Curse
The Purloined Soul

~

MAGIC MISSING
Book One: A Boy Without Magic
Book Two: An Apprentice Without Magic
Book Three: A Voyager Without Magic
Book Four: A Scholar Without Magic
Book Five: A Snoop Without Magic

~

SONG OF SORCERY
Book One: A Sorcerer Rises
Book Two: A Sorcerer Imprisoned
Book Three: A Sorcerer's Diplomacy
Book Four: A Sorcerer's Rings
Book Five: A Sorcerer's Fist

~

THE DISINHERITED PRINCE
Book One: The Disinherited Prince
Book Two: The Monk's Habit
Book Three: A Sip of Magic
Book Four: The Sleeping God
Demeron: A Horse's Tale - A Disinherited Prince Novella
Book Five: The Emperor's Pet
Book Six: The Misplaced Prince
Book Seven: The Fractured Empire

~

POWER OF POSES
Book One: Magician in Training
Book Two: Magician in Exile
Book Three: Magician in Captivity
Book Four: Magician in Battle

~

THE WARSTONE QUARTET
Book One: Moonstone | Magic That Binds
Book Two: Sunstone | Dishonor's Bane
Book Three: Bloodstone | Power of Youth
Book Four: Darkstone | An Evil Reborn

~

THE WORLD OF THE SWORD OF SPELLS
Warrior Mage
Sword of Spells

~

THE SARA FEATHERWOOD ADVENTURES
Knife & Flame
Sword & Flame
Guns & Flame

~

OTHER NOVELS
Quest of the Wizardess
The Power Bearer
Panix: Magician Spy
Hand of Grethia

~

THE GUY ANTIBES ANTHOLOGIES
The Alien Hand - SCIENCE FICTION
The Purple Flames - STEAMPUNK & PARANORMAL FANTASY
Angel in Bronze - FANTASY

~

Printed in Great Britain
by Amazon